PRAISE FOR THE NOVELS OF SHIRLEY KENNETT

"Shirley Kennett is a polished and poised addition to the ranks of contemporary mystery writers. You're going to enjoy her books."
—*Mystery Scene*

"Will keep you turning the pages till the very end."
—Jean Hager, author of *The Fire Carrier*

"Solid entertainment!
—*Publishers Weekly*

"Kennett's devious creativity and bloodcurdling, realistic descriptive passages result in a terrifying and explosive thriller."
—*Booklist*

"If you're looking for a thrilling suspense novel, look no further than author Shirley Kennett."
—*Iowa City Press-Citizen*

"Not since *Red Dragon* has a more menacing serial killer roamed metropolitan St. Louis. Gripping and unique. A rip-roaring good read."
—John Lutz, author of *Single White Female*

BOOK YOUR PLACE ON OUR WEBSITE AND MAKE THE READING CONNECTION!

We've created a customized website just for our very special readers, where you can get the inside scoop on everything that's going on with Zebra, Pinnacle and Kensington books.

When you come online, you'll have the exciting opportunity to:

- View covers of upcoming books

- Read sample chapters

- Learn about our future publishing schedule (listed by publication month *and author*)

- Find out when your favorite authors will be visiting a city near you

- Search for and order backlist books from our online catalog

- Check out author bios and background information

- Send e-mail to your favorite authors

- Meet the Kensington staff online

- Join us in weekly chats with authors, readers and other guests

- Get writing guidelines

- AND MUCH MORE!

**Visit our website at
http://www.pinnaclebooks.com**

FIRE CRACKER

Shirley Kennett

Pinnacle Books
Kensington Publishing Corp.
http://www.pinnaclebooks.com

PINNACLE BOOKS are published by

Kensington Publishing Corp.
850 Third Avenue
New York, NY 10022

Copyright © 1997 by Shirley Kennett

Pinnacle and the P logo Reg. U.S. Pat. & TM Off.

First Kensington Hardcover Printing: July, 1997
First Pinnacle Printing: May, 1998
10 9 8 7 6 5 4 3 2 1

Printed in the United States of America

To my son Thomas, who always shares the last cookie

CHAPTER

1

Will Carpenter sat up in bed. He knew he was screaming more from the shape of his mouth than from hearing the sound. Then he heard it: that high, childish wail that wavered between terror and anger, issuing from someplace inside him that never made itself known in the daylight.

He was drenched with sweat, and more than sweat. His bladder had emptied, and his palms were slick with blood. His clenched fists had forced his fingernails into the fleshy mounds just below his thumbs.

Will sat up and swung his legs over the edge of the bed. He rubbed his hands together until the heat of the friction dried the blood, then ran his hands up and down his arms, peeling away the shreds of the nightmare that clung to him like leeches. His wet underwear, the only clothing he wore, was clammy against his skin. He stood, steadying himself by leaning the side of one leg against the bed, and stripped it off. Then he pulled the sheets and mattress pad from the bed and jammed them into the small stacked washer/dryer that stood in a corner of his kitchen. He fretted over the fact that he should have dumped the laundry detergent into the tub first and briefly considered pulling the cold mass of bedding out to do so. Then he wrinkled his nose, not at the smell, but at the thought of touching the cold material. It was amazing how hot urine came out but how fast it cooled off. Opening the detergent box, he saw that he had misplaced the scoop. Again. Sighing, he dumped some of the bluish powder on top, closed the lid, and started the water running.

Hot wash, warm rinse.

Mom Elly would be proud of her only stepson, sorting the whites like a pro.

Naked, Will wandered over to the sink and scrubbed his hands. Then he pulled out a coffee mug that looked less used than the others and ran water into it. He put the mug into the microwave to make some instant coffee. The apartment smelled like grilled cheese sandwiches, which he had fixed for dinner. He had noticed before that his place must have poor air circulation, because the smell of one meal lingered until it was overlaid by the next. While waiting for the bing of the microwave, he lifted the oversize terry cloth robe from the hook on the back of the bathroom door and wrapped himself in it. It felt good against his skin, but scratchy because he had run out of fabric softener.

Belting the robe about his thin waist, he simultaneously donned his professional demeanor, leaving behind the messy ineptitude, the misplaced laundry scoops, and the gangly body which had never outgrown teenage awkwardness. He was ready to flex his fingers and astonish the world.

Will "Cracker" Carpenter had gotten his start years ago in highway robbery—the Information Highway, that is. Now he earned more than most mid-level drug dealers by compiling confidential profiles for a price.

Cracker took his mug of instant coffee to the spare bedroom of his two-bedroom ground-floor apartment in

University City, a suburb of St. Louis that housed a lot of Washington University students and staff. Some of the profs lived there, too. Cracker drove by their stolid two- or three-storied, ivy-covered homes on his way to the grocery store or deli. His own place was considerably humbler: a remodeled brick cube with one apartment up and one down. The upstairs apartment had an exterior stairway and entrance. The tenant was a quiet, serious Asian graduate student, a woman whom he hardly ever saw.

Cracker's apartment had none of the charming features of other homes in the area, such as leaded-glass windows, fireplaces, architectural details like columns and arches in the interiors, and fine wood trim. These things were generally prized even in those homes given over to student housing. His building had been gutted by a contractor who sold everything to a salvage warehouse and reshaped the home into two functional apartments, breaking the home's spirit as well as its grand curved staircase.

Cracker owned the building now, and he liked it the way it was.

The bedroom he entered was illuminated only by the portion of moonlight that escaped the grasp of the tree limbs outside the window, but it pulsed with electronic life. Yellow-green and red dots glowed, the power indicators and status lights of computer equipment floating in the darkness like lightning bugs. The glassy stares of half a dozen monitors reflected the pinpoints, tossing them back and forth across the room. Cracker never used screensaver programs that would brighten his idle monitors with playful spirals or kittens cavorting on the screen. It seemed undignified. He preferred to let the screens go black when they timed out from lack of activity.

Soft whirring noises from cooling fans and spinning platters inside hard drives seemed louder now, in the middle of the night, than during the daytime. A clock atop a black metal bookcase read 3:12 in three-inch red numbers that reflected in the smooth surface, distorted and fore-shortened there as though they were shining up through water. In one corner, one of the several modems in the room was in a programmed search mode, trolling through a promising list of phone numbers Cracker had recently purchased. Red, green, and yellow lights flashed as it silently dialed one number after another, marking those which not only responded with a modem on the other end, but which required a password or other security measure to complete the connection. Over the next few days, Cracker would check out the new hits to see if there were any worth adding to his toolbox.

He stood for a moment, thinking that the same lights bouncing among the monitors in the room were also bouncing from the smooth, moist surface of his eyes.

If someone was watching, he thought, *I would seem like another piece of equipment: eyes like tiny monitors, lungs for a cooling fan, brain for logic and memory, a digestive system for a power supply.*

It was a pleasant thought, and it dispelled the last of the nightmare jitters. He walked into the room, automatically steering himself around the rolling chairs, and switched on the desk lamp. The lamp was an industrial model, with a head holding two eighteen-inch fluorescent tubes on the end of an extension arm that flexed in three places. The whole thing was weighted down with a circular black base that could probably have held a patio umbrella in a stiff wind. The starter buzzed loudly when Cracker pressed and held the yellow rocker switch. He released it when both bulbs glowed, and the buzz diminished to a hum just at the edge of his awareness.

There were folding tables set up along three of the walls, and every inch of their mismatched surface space was occupied by keyboards, mice, monitors, external hard drives, printers, speakers, CD-ROM drives, a scanner, and cables and cords tangled like electronic spaghetti. There was a battered metal desk in the center of the room which held, in addition to the formidable lamp, the few business necessities that Cracker committed to paper.

To visitors, were any to be allowed into this room, it would look like techno-chaos. To the young man who earned his nickname by breaking into supposedly secure computer systems, it was comfortingly familiar.

Cracker sat in an armless chair and rolled up to one of the computers. He dialed in to Wood Memorial Hospital and put in a request for callback. The hospital's computer security system intercepted his call and quickly disconnected him. He waited while the system checked the phone number, name, and password on file, and called him back. When the password he entered a second time was verified, he was in.

He immediately exited the front end processor that presented user-friendly menus and got into the underlying operating system. Ordinarily, that was off-limits to dial-in users, but Cracker wasn't the typical dial-in user. Once there, he checked the volume of transactions going on and the number of terminals in use, and decided that his own activity wouldn't look conspicuous. At least, the risk was small, and he was awake and drinking coffee, smelling grilled cheese and thinking about fixing a couple more, and sitting in his clean white bathrobe, ready to work.

Going back to the user menus, he checked the census for nursing station 3-PT. Room 3PT-3302, one of the eight private rooms on the nursing station, still held the object of his interest: Rowena Clark, a seventy-nine-year-old woman with emphysema and congestive heart failure. Cracker had been following Rowena's case since admission. She was on a respirator, and her condition was deteriorating. He had snooped into enough cases similar to hers to know that she would probably be dead soon.

He knew from the nursing notes that Rowena was domineering and unpleasant with her visitors, but she was compliant, almost sweet, with the "angels" who took care of her in the hospital. She wouldn't question a confident resp tech who told her that she was getting better and assured her that it was time to cut back on the oxygen and the positive pressure that was helping her to exhale. Rowena would be told that she would have to start doing some of the work of breathing on her own. She probably wouldn't press the nurse call button afterward, not wanting to be a nuisance as she lay gasping in her private room, struggling with damaged lungs and weakened heart to get enough oxygen to her brain. She would try to reach for the call button at the end, but by then her vision would be going black, just like the resting monitors in the room with Cracker.

Her reach would fall short.

Rowena would die in just a little over eight hours, he estimated, not knowing who had murdered her or why, perhaps not even realizing that she had been murdered.

He dropped back to the operating system level and activated the special program he had devised called the Time Bomb. It would cycle patiently in the computer's background processing, sampling conditions periodically, like a snake using its tongue to sense its surroundings. When the preset time arrived, the program would come to life, creating a respiratory therapy order and then walking through Rowena's on-line record like a malevolent cyberghost, altering lab results, vitals, and observations so that her overall picture would be consistent with the order to wean her from the respirator. If her file did not present a consistent view, the respiratory therapy tech would question the order. In fact, there was still a possibility that the tech, upon actually seeing Rowena, would decide to delay and consult with the physician. The tech might even check the manual hard copy file that was kept at the nursing station. Or someone could check on Rowena in person and discover her condition before she had time to die.

There wasn't much he could do about that; some factors were out of his control. Although he could make computers dance to the tune in his head, he couldn't always do the same with people.

In a few hours, if everything went well and Rowena Clark breathed her last, the Time Bomb would remove all traces of its work, including itself. It would put her on-line file back in order so that it matched the manual medical record, with one exception. Cracker wanted to leave the computerized respiratory therapy order intact, hanging inexplicably at the end of Rowena Clark's file like a maple leaf found growing among the needles of a pine tree.

He sat back in his chair and relished the moment. After years of planning, he was finally doing it. Striking back at Mom Elly. Not killing her the way she had killed Dad, the wet agony of it sharp in his mind, but striking out indirectly, and in his own fashion.

Having made his transition smoothly from hacker-for-hire to murderer, Cracker signed off and quickly slipped into dreamless sleep on a blanket thrown over his bare mattress.

CHAPTER
2

Penelope Jennifer Gray, Ph.D., Clinical Psychology, and head of the Computerized Homicide Investigations Project of the St. Louis Police Department, fidgeted in her metal folding chair. The room was not air-conditioned, and the late-evening sun slanted through the tall windows with unexpected vigor for the middle of September. The high ceilings trapped the unseasonable heat of the day, making it feel like she was in a greenhouse. The other warm bodies in the room added to the discomfort, exhaling hot gases that PJ imagined she could actually see, like the trails of comets.

She had worn a classic blue dress and a gold necklace today specifically to make a good impression at this meeting. Now she looked and felt rumpled. She hadn't noticed until she was introducing herself before the meeting that there was a small stain on the front of her dress, marking the point of her pubic triangle. The low-heeled black pumps that seemed like such a good idea this morning lay askew beneath her chair. Her chestnut hair that was supposed to turn under and gracefully brush her shoulders had flipped up instead, making her look like a fifties housewife except that the top of her hair was frizzy rather than pouffed.

The meeting was nearly over, and, except for asking one question about the building's security, she hadn't made much of a contribution. Illogically, she felt that all eyes were on her, and some feminine equivalent to the family jewels was on the line. Reluctantly, she raised her hand.

"I'll bring the cupcakes for the Halloween party," she said. "How many dozen would that be?"

It was Back to School Night. PJ's twelve-year-old son Thomas was two weeks into seventh grade. Tonight there had been a general discussion for all parents of seventh graders about expectations for the year. The brief introduction had been held in what used to be called the school library and had been rechristened the media center, which thankfully was air-conditioned. Then the group had split, with parents following their child's homeroom teacher to one of the classrooms. Mrs. Cartwright, Thomas's teacher, was a woman who managed to convey warmth and caring along with firmness and poise. PJ realized first that she liked and then that she envied the woman, partly because Mrs. Cartwright looked fresh and perky, and not like a person who had spent her day coping with a roomful of twelve-year-olds. Most likely, *Mister* Cartwright was the type who said, "Go ahead, dear, take a hot bath while I fix dinner. I've already drawn the water. By the way, is gardenia oil still your favorite bath moisturizer?"

Then the discussion got down to the nuts and bolts of who was going to volunteer for what. The organized parents, the ones who were expecting exactly this sort of thing, came prepared to sign up for sending in beans to plant for science projects, a box of disks for the computer lab, or a bag of cotton balls to glue to the world map on top of those countries for which cotton was a main crop. Easy to carry, easy to acquire. As Mrs. Cartwright went relentlessly down her list, the early volunteers sat back smugly. They knew what was coming.

"Six?" PJ said. "Six dozen cupcakes decorated with pumpkins?"

"Seventh-graders are big eaters, Dr. Gray," Mrs. Cartwright intoned as she wrote PJ's name in her notebook. "We avoid the sinister side of Halloween, so no witches, ghosts, black cats, anything associated with the occult. It's more of a fall festival kind of thing." Mrs. Cartwright fixed the audience with a stern eye. "The same goes for costumes, everyone. Nothing gross or offensive from a religious or ethnic viewpoint. It's possible to have fun and show good taste at the same time."

And to think that just a few minutes ago I actually liked this woman, PJ thought. "I don't suppose I'll have a weekend to work on this?" PJ asked, somehow guessing that the answer would be no.

"Halloween is on a Thursday this year. The class party will be Thursday afternoon. Please have the cupcakes here by noon. If you ask in the office, someone might be able to help you unload from your car, but don't count on it. Now, who can bring the napkins and paper cups?"

Three hands shot up as the remaining parents sought to grab this plum assignment. PJ left just as it looked like a scuffle might break out, and Mrs. Cartwright prepared to intervene with defusing skills honed by years in the classroom. On the way home, she berated herself for her poor timing. If she'd just kept her hand out of the air thirty seconds longer, perhaps she could have gotten by with napkins and cups that she could buy the night before and make Thomas carry to school. On the other hand, those three remaining parents looked like tough customers, and there was no guarantee she would have triumphed.

It was 8:00 P.M. and solidly dark by the time PJ pulled her faded blue VW Rabbit convertible into the driveway of her rented home on Magnolia Avenue in South St. Louis and drove around the back. There was no garage, but there was a parking turnaround so that she didn't have to back out onto the street. She was glad to see that Thomas had turned on the rear porch light. Her headlights swept over the annual flower bed she had planted months ago and worked on only sporadically since. Around the edges of the yard, where the headlights didn't penetrate, PJ knew the perennial beds left by the previous occupant of the house were unkempt, tall plants lying prone after a recent storm and weeds poking up through the mulch. Although the nights were cool now, there hadn't been a killing frost yet, and there wouldn't be one for another three weeks or more. There was still plenty of time to make the beds look more presentable. Her sister Mandy, whose casual attitude toward child raising and housekeeping did not extend to gardening, would have gotten those beds whipped into shape and then maintained that condition with daily patrols.

PJ considered inviting her sister to visit for a few days and leaving the hoe, rake, weed digger, and gardening gloves on the back porch. Mandy wouldn't be able to resist.

She unlocked the back door, resting her fingers for just a moment on the glass in the top half of the door. She thought, not for the first time, that if the door had been entirely wood rather than half wood and half glass, she would almost certainly be dead now. On such chance things as the style of the door and curtains parted just enough to show a slice of kitchen to a person on the back porch, on such things as those her life had depended. She believed that there are pivotal events which create new paths to the future, like forks in the road, one after the other. She wondered how many other times her life had been and would be in the balance, some small condition or event serving as a turning point: a decision to go out on a rainy night, a phone call missed, waking up before the alarm one morning, a casual conversation, or words left unspoken.

She glanced down at the scar on her right forearm. It had been several months, but the thin white line with its unnatural depression in the skin showed no sign of fading away. She was certain it would be there as long as she lived, along with the lines that had been sliced into her back, high up on her right shoulder. It still ached, and sometimes her shoulder twitched as if trying to pull away from the knife.

"I'm home, T-man," she said, loudly enough for her voice to carry upstairs. There had been a string of nicknames, adjusted to her son's age and perceived level of coolness. Her favorite, Cuddle Bunny, hadn't been acceptable for years.

"I'm upstairs, Mom," came the answering bellow. "Be down in a minute."

Megabite appeared from some hiding place known only to cats and greeted PJ, rubbing against her ankles and testing the air to determine if PJ had brought home takeout food. PJ sat down in a kitchen chair, and instantly Megabite was in her lap, bumping her head underneath PJ's hand, requesting stroking. As PJ ran her fingers over the sleek fur, she admired the diminutive cat's unique coloration. Megabite was classic gray tiger on her back, tail, and partway down her legs. Then a neat band of orange fur around each of her knees—*what do you call a cat's knees,* PJ wondered—announced that things were different down below. Her paws and belly were white, and there was a white tip on the end of her tail, which was now waving gently, in time with PJ's strokes. Golden eyes, a rose-colored nosepad, and impossibly long white whiskers added to the overall effect of a haughty feline queen. But Megabite's personality—of which there was plenty—belied her looks. She was playful, spirited, and not above stealing a longjohn doughnut from an open bag on Thomas's desk and dragging her prize down the stairs, bumping it on each step.

PJ reached under Megabite and found the patch where the white fur was only a quarter of an inch long. She gently felt the scar on the cat's abdomen from the spaying operation. Amazingly, the vet used a special glue rather than stitches to hold the skin together. PJ had worried for days that Megabite would become unglued, but now the incision had healed, the residue of the purple glue had worn off or been rasped off by Megabite's tongue, and the shaved fur was beginning to grow back.

"Good kitty, Purrface," PJ said, tickling Megabite under the chin. She found it impossible to say "Megabite" in an endearing tone of voice. "You know, you'd look pretty good on top of a cupcake, especially if you fuzz up your tail. I might have to use you as a model. Wait a minute. That's probably a reference to witchcraft."

Megabite, reacting to the word cupcake, eagerly scanned the kitchen countertop from her vantage point on PJ's lap.

Thomas came in and arranged himself in a kitchen chair opposite PJ. She marveled at his flexibility as arms and legs draped here and there. At age forty, she found herself noticing the little things that she used to take for granted but could no longer easily do. One of them was sitting the way Thomas was, with casual disregard for the various angles his limbs formed.

"I had sandwiches for dinner," he said. "I made a couple extra ones for you. They're in the refrigerator. If you don't like them, just leave them in there, and I'll eat them for breakfast."

She was hungry, and appreciated the effort he had gone to, and told him so. But some of his past sandwich creations had been enough to turn her stomach, so she didn't make any promises.

"How was the meeting?" he asked as he clucked his tongue and held his hand out in the petting position to call Megabite. She responded by leaping up onto the table and sniffing his fingers.

"You've been feeding her on the table, haven't you?" PJ said. "I thought we agreed not to do that."

"I haven't, but I'll bet you have," he retorted easily.

"The meeting was fine," she said, pointedly ignoring his comment. "Mrs. Cartwright seems very nice."

"She's OK." PJ took that for high praise.

"I volunteered to make cupcakes for Halloween."

"Way cool, Mom. When's the last time you made cupcakes?"

"Oh, about a century ago. When I was a girl in Home Ec class. The first thing we made was Rice Krispy Treats. When we were ready for the big time, Mrs. Alben turned us loose on cupcakes."

"Home what class?"

"Forget it."

Thomas shrugged. "Dad called a little while ago."

PJ nodded but said nothing. Her ex-husband Steven lived in Denver. She had left him when she discovered that he was involved with another woman. PJ had actually met Carla once, in the reception room of the architectural firm owned by Steven and his longtime partner Al Cobin. Carla was in her early twenties, with a face that was transformed from attractive to beautiful by her engaging smile, and a body that didn't need any transformation to be stunning. She had applied for an assistant's position. She didn't get the job, but she got the boss.

PJ felt angry, hurt, betrayed, scared—sometimes all at once. She moved out, taking Thomas with her. Throughout the divorce, her relationship with Thomas steadily worsened. Her son blamed her for the breakup, saying that she was too wrapped up in her work to pay attention to Steven. Things were getting much better now, but it was painful to her as she watched her son grapple with his feelings about his father. Regardless of her opinion of

Steven, she didn't want to spoil Thomas's opportunity to have an ongoing relationship. She had just gotten to the point herself where she could admit that she hadn't worked on the marriage as hard as she could have—should have.

"He invited me out for a visit. Said he'd pay for the airline ticket."

"That sounds like it would be fun. Do you want to go?"

"I don't know yet." Thomas rearranged himself, ending up even more slouched than before. "He wants me to meet my new half-brother. He and Carla are having a baby, and they already know it's a boy."

PJ sat up in surprise. Without thinking, she whistled softly. "So they're really going to do it," she said.

"Come on, Mom, they've been doing it for months."

"That's not what I meant, you dirty-minded imp." *And this is not the type of news I should be getting from my son,* she thought.

Steven had told her that Carla wanted a family. Two, maybe three kids. One of the things that hurt her most about her breakup with Steven was that she had also wanted a larger family. She was close to her sister Mandy, and she felt that Thomas should have a brother or sister. Steven had put off adding to the family and finally admitted that he didn't want any more kids. Now it was obvious that he simply didn't want any more kids with *her.* The realization stung. She was sure that Thomas could see the pain in her eyes, so she didn't gloss it over.

"Well, isn't that shitty news," she said.

"Yeah. Anyway, I don't know if I want to go or not. Dad gave me a few weeks to decide."

"I'll support you whichever way you decide," PJ said. "Don't be in a hurry to close doors, though." She stood up and went around to his side of the table. She hugged him, then ruffled his hair.

"Cut that out," he said, predictably. He pushed her hands away, but not too vigorously.

Thomas went back upstairs to finish his homework, taking the steps two at a time, another one of those things that seemed to have slipped out of PJ's repertoire of physical activities somewhere between ages thirty-five and forty. PJ went up to her bedroom and changed clothes. She was grateful to strip off her panty hose, and rummaged in her dresser drawer until she found her flannel pajamas. Since it was so late in the evening, she decided to skip the intermediate clothes and go straight for the comfy stuff. It seemed just the right sort of evening for flannel pajamas, the kind with the elbows worn so thin she could see through them. As she buttoned the top, which was missing the bottom button and had been for years, she marveled that something so simple as well-washed flannel against her skin could be so soothing. Back in the kitchen, she got the plate of sandwiches out of the refrigerator, and found to her amazement that they were conventional sliced turkey and Swiss on wheat bread, with no strange embellishments such as chocolate pudding or cold spaghetti. She added a couple of oranges and a big glass of milk and sat down at the table with the daily paper, the St. Louis *Post-Dispatch*. Megabite jumped up on the chair Thomas had been sitting in and put her delicate white paws on the table.

"We've got to stop this," PJ said as she tore off a piece of turkey and tossed it across the table to Megabite. "He's on to us."

An hour later, she was on her way up the stairs to make sure Thomas was getting ready for bed when the phone rang. She took the rest of the stairs two at a time, just to prove to herself that she could still do it, and picked up the phone in her bedroom.

"Hello," she said. She was embarrassed to realize that

she was breathing hard, and her breathing was probably audible over the phone.

"Schultz here." There was a pause. "You got this backward, Doc. If you're going to make a heavy breathing call, you generally dial out rather than waiting for someone to call you."

"I'm just a little out of breath." PJ willed her breathing to return to normal.

"Or maybe you're entertaining a gentleman caller. I could call back in a few minutes. Give him time to get his pants on."

"Really, Schultz, that is ridiculous. I just hurried up the stairs to answer the phone."

"Or maybe . . ."

"Get to the point, if there is one."

"Yeah, there's a point. An old biddy died in the hospital, and you and I just got roped into the investigation."

Schultz paused, evidently expecting some sort of commiseration. When he didn't get it, he went on.

"Lieutenant Wall called about an hour ago. I'm at Wood Memorial Hospital. It's on Morganford, down near Carondelet Park. The deceased is Rowena Clark, seventy-nine-year-old white female. She had emphysema and congestive heart disease, died of respiratory failure this morning about 11:30. Rich woman with a slew of relatives, a real crabass according to her son and daughter. Wall's treating it as a homicide."

"What has this got to do with CHIP?"

The Computerized Homicide Investigations Project, or CHIP, was a pilot program to bring computer analysis into criminal investigations by reenacting the crime using virtual reality—VR. Using a combination of sophisticated hardware and programming, PJ was able to create a believable world that existed only in the computer. She had been hired as the outside expert to head the project because of her special interest and expertise in VR. When she started her job four months ago, she was new to law enforcement. Her previous experience had been as a practicing psychologist and later as a developer of marketing techniques based upon consumer response to virtual reality presentations of commercial products. Her teammate, Leo Schultz, was a longtime member of the department and an experienced detective. In one of his moods when he was all bristle and sharp edges, he had told her that if he ever needed to know which shampoo smells appealed most to customers, he would call on her, but if he needed somebody reliable at his back, he'd have to look for a real law-enforcement professional. She knew she had come up a notch in his estimation during the first case they worked on together. But their relationship was still in the formative stages, and sometimes PJ felt it would be there permanently. She would never truly get to know Leo Schultz, and there would always be a surprise around the corner.

"Practically nothing to do with CHIP, I think," Schultz said. "Wall said she was on a respirator, and it was adjusted this morning as a result of an order in their computerized records which her doctor swears up and down she didn't authorize. Adjusted so she couldn't get enough oxygen. She wasn't in such hot shape to begin with, so I guess it didn't take much to push her over the edge into the Big Ashtray in the Sky. I think Wall heard the word computer and his eyes glazed over. Sort of the way mine did, at first."

He made no effort to disguise what he thought of getting called in on this case, and as PJ listened to his clipped words she found herself in agreement. She sighed and looked down at her comfortable flannels. "How come it's been ten hours, and I'm just now getting called?"

"Because it took that long for the hospital to determine, or rather to admit, that the old lady's records were altered. I think they spent the first few hours grilling the doctor on why she ordered the respirator cut back."

"I thought you said she didn't."

"I said *she* said she didn't. There's quite a difference."

"I can be there in about a half hour. Is the doctor still around?"

"Yeah. Dr. Eleanor Graham. I've already spoken to her. We didn't exactly hit it off."

PJ closed her eyes. This was getting worse by the minute. Now it looked as though she'd have to patch up any damage done by Schultz before she could make headway with the doctor.

"One more thing," she said, letting annoyance show. "Why does Lieutenant Wall always call you first?"

"The old boys' network," he said, and hung up.

Wood Memorial Hospital was a three story building with the blocky shape and exact shade of tan bricks that seemed to be reserved exclusively for institutions. In this case, the bricks were also washed with orange light from the numerous dusk-to-dawn lamps. A few dispirited young trees, each held prisoner by three oversize stakes, made the lawn look like a model railroad set that PJ had seen once: a flat expanse of Astroturf with sticks painted green and brown to represent the trees. There wasn't a blooming plant in sight. PJ reasoned that the Floral Shop in the lobby was afraid that visitors, given the opportunity, would pick their own well-wishing bouquets outside. There was a parking garage with a narrow spiral ramp which, judging by the multicolored scrape marks on the wall, was the bane of local auto insurance companies.

PJ showed her ID at the information desk, and after a short wait was escorted to the nursing station on the third floor of the Payton Tower, or 3-PT, by a gum-snapping security guard who seemed young enough to be working his way through high school.

She heard Schultz before she saw him.

Rounding a corner, image caught up with voice, and

she saw the detective in a confrontational stance, with his gut and his chin competing to see which could be thrust forward the most. His tall frame, which had once been imposingly muscular, now carried an extra forty pounds, and all of his contours were softly rounded except for his long, thin face and prominent nose. He seemed as exasperated as PJ had ever seen him. The source of his exasperation came into PJ's view as she walked up to the nursing station.

PJ looked at the nurse's name tag, which identified her as the head nurse. "Hello, Nurse Boxwood. I'm Doctor Gray. I work with Detective Schultz. What seems to be the problem?"

Helen Boxwood stood behind the chest-high counter as though it were the parapet of a castle. PJ guessed her age at about fifty. She was a large woman, tall and blocky, with solid shoulders and arms and incongruously delicate hands terminated by neatly manicured fingernails painted deep red. The same shade of red liberally covered her full lips, drawing attention away from her otherwise nondescript features and pale blue eyes. Her hair was light brown, almost blond but not quite, and tumbled to her shoulders in a mass of curls disarranged in a style that would have looked better on her twenty years ago, and probably had. She stood at her full height, shoulders squared, her matronly chest pressing against her spotless white uniform.

Even though PJ's question was addressed to the nurse, Schultz answered.

"Ms. Boxwood, here, won't give me the home phone numbers of the nurses who were on duty this morning." He said her name with great disdain, emphasizing *Miz*. "She's obstructing my investigation, and being an asshole while doing it. She won't even come out from behind that counter and talk face-to-face like civilized people. She must be hiding something back there. I think maybe she's got no legs, just floats around on a cushion of hot air. When she farts, she scoots across the room.''

"Thank you for that insight, Detective," PJ said wearily. "I can take it from here."

Dismissed, Schultz retreated to the other end of the counter, crossed his arms, and ignored the two women. He studied the floor with the disapproving glare of a city health and sanitation inspector who expected hordes of cockroaches and rodents to cross his path at any minute.

PJ turned back to the nurse, trying to think of something to say that would excuse Schultz's behavior, but she couldn't come up with anything.

"Please forgive him," she said simply.

"I'm used to it, Doctor," Helen said. "You should hear the things patients say. You'd think they'd been lying underneath the back end of a horse with their mouths open. Hospitals have that effect on some people." Her voice was light and musical, almost girlish, and didn't fit with her physique or her words. "That doesn't make it right, of course," she said, launching a withering glance in Schultz's direction, "to take things out on us medical professionals."

Helen moved out from behind the counter, defiantly demonstrating that she did have legs. They were formidable columns, definitely assets for standing hours at a time, and attached to hips that seemed more than adequate for the job.

"Actually I'm a psychologist, not a medical doctor," PJ answered. "Please, call me PJ."

"You can call me Helen, Doctor," she said. "But I'd be more comfortable using your title."

"I understand completely," PJ said. Some doctors were very fussy about their titles, and discouraged informality with the nurses. "What's this about home phone numbers?"

"Mr. Schultz requested the home phone numbers of

the nurses on the morning shift. I patiently tried to explain to him that I was not authorized to give out that information and that he should simply go to Human Resources. There's someone there twenty-four hours a day, although the full staff won't be in until the day shift.'' Helen kept her eyes locked on PJ's but her words were aimed in a different direction. "Apparently he was not in a mood to listen to a reasonable request.''

"Yes, well, that happens with him. I'm sure that now that he understands the situation, he'll be on his way there shortly.''

PJ heard Schultz mumbling under his breath as he headed off down the hallway. She thought she detected a slight limp. Now that he was on medication for arthritis, the limp wasn't as noticeable, but some days his knees still bothered him early in the morning and late at night.

"Were you on duty when the patient died?'' PJ asked.

"Ordinarily, I would have been, but today and for the past three days I switched with the evening head, Yolanda Weber. She had some out-of-town company and wanted to take them around to see the sights during the day. I just came on two hours ago. I'll be glad to get back to my regular schedule tomorrow. This switching back and forth is murder. Poor choice of words, there.'' Helen slipped back behind the counter, as if she were a fish out of water and could only last a short time outside her customary environment. With Schultz gone, she visibly relaxed, letting her shoulders drop. Without her hackles up, she looked almost grandmotherly. Almost.

PJ thought there were probably a lot of *almosts* about Helen Boxwood.

"I'm sorry about that little episode. Some people just get on my nerves,'' Helen said.

PJ smiled. "I know just what you mean.''

"Would you like some coffee? There's a pot in the lounge down at the end of the hall.''

"No, thanks. I really need to get a handle on this case before I talk to Schultz again, and especially before I talk to Dr. Graham. Sometimes it seems like I'm . . ."

"The last to know? Come on around the counter, Doctor," Helen said with a touch of warmth in her voice, "and I'll tell you what I know about the situation. Oh, and I guess I'd better see some ID first."

PJ showed the photo card that identified her as a civilian employee of the police department, specifically as head of CHIP.

"Computerized Homicide Investigations," Helen read. "No wonder you got called in for this one. Are you one of those—what do you call them—whackers?"

PJ laughed. "It's hackers, and I don't consider myself one."

Helen patted the swivel chair next to her. The chair was well padded but armless, and rolled on six oversize casters, as did Helen's chair. "Sit down, and take a look at this." She began making menu selections on one of the three computers at the nursing station. "This is Mrs. Clark's on-line chart. People in different areas of the hospital input the information, but it's collected and displayed in one piece."

She rolled her chair over to the next work area, which did not have a computer. Pulling open a file drawer, she extracted a thick manila folder with assorted colored stickers on the outside. She rolled back with a practiced shove of her feet and spread the folder open in front of PJ.

"This is Mrs. Clark's medical record file, the one that I guess you would call official. For every entry in the on-line chart, there should be a corresponding hard copy in here. Printed reports of lab results, medication orders signed by the physician, that kind of thing."

"Why keep dual records?" PJ asked.

"Right now, we're required to maintain the paper file, especially the items that need signatures to validate them.

That is, if the hospital wants to keep its accreditation. But there are problems with keeping the records just in this form," she said, tapping the contents of the folder. "Only one area can use this file at a time. It can be dropped, misplaced, or have papers fall out."

"Not to mention coffee spills."

Warming to her subject, Helen nodded at the monitor which displayed Rowena Clark's chart. "The on-line chart can be examined wherever there's a computer, since they're all knitted together."

"Networked."

"Whatever. If you've got the proper signon and password, you can find the information you need instantly, whether you're in the ER, at a nursing station, or in one of the ancillaries. Physicians can examine test results as soon as they're posted, right in their own offices or here at the counter before rounds. Everybody's gotten dependent on the on-line chart. We hardly ever use the paper one. In fact, it's usually a little out-of-date. We've got a clerk who files the slips in the folders, but Annie's only in five hours a day. Things pile up until she gets here."

PJ had been sitting back, taking it all in. She had an idea where all this was leading, but she was content to let Helen get there at her own pace. She inhaled deeply, thinking that she could be plunked down blindfolded and would be able to determine that she was in a hospital just by the smell.

"Some of the nurses—physicians, too—don't want to see more computerization. I wasn't wild about it either, at first. It was a lot to learn, and nobody asked me if I wanted to. Suddenly, it was just part of the job," Helen said. She closed her eyes and rubbed at them with balled up hands, looking like a child who'd been allowed to stay up too late. "But I've been adjusting to changes in nursing practices all my working life."

A nurse came up to the counter, and Helen excused

herself to talk to him. While Helen was busy, PJ examined the on-line chart. The display was arranged in reverse chronological order, with the most recent events first. At the top, right under the patient identification, was a cryptic notice of PLU—Patient Left Unit, with an indication that this was a medical examiner's case. Underneath was the time of death, 11:28 A.M., and a brief description of the circumstances. Rowena Clark's body had been discovered by the phlebotomist who came to draw blood for routine monitoring of blood gases.

There was an order for the Respiratory Therapy department, with the words "VERIFIED AND SIGNED BY PHYSICIAN" next to it.

"I see you're getting the hang of it," Helen said as she sat down heavily on the stool next to PJ.

"Isn't it unusual that no one checked on Mrs. Clark?" PJ asked.

"Actually, there were plenty of things going on," Helen said, pointing to a line on the screen with one shaped red nail. "She was given medications at six in the morning. The nurse, that was Tracy Enright, see the initials TNE in the last column, has already talked to the police. Specifically, to Mr. Schultz."

PJ wondered if she knew how irritating it was to Schultz to have that *Mister* tacked onto his name. He preferred Detective Schultz, or Schultz, or just Detective. He was willing to accept Leo from her every now and then, although it seemed a bit intimate. She hadn't heard anyone else call him Leo.

"Tracy's working a double shift today, so she'll be here another hour," Helen said. "Dr. Graham was in about eight-thirty for rounds and talked to Mrs. Clark. Housekeeping doesn't get to this nursing station until after two o'clock. The nursing staff does a routine vitals check every four hours, which in this case would have been about twelve-thirty. She gets blood drawn every six hours, which was eleven-thirty, the time her body was found. There's chest PT—physical therapy—and suctioning every six hours, which today would have been noon. In between scheduled activities, Mrs. Clark can—could have—pushed her call button, and someone would have been with her right away. Otherwise, we let the patients have their privacy, what little they can get with people in and out of the room all day. After all, patients on this station are paying for private rooms.''

For a moment, Helen looked as though she might actually be considering disapproving of hospital practices which disrupted patients' privacy and sleep, but it was transitory. Her face settled back into professional acceptance.

"This order,'' Helen said, pointing to the respiratory therapy line, "was supposedly placed after rounds. But Dr. Graham would never have done that.''

"Why do you say that?''

"Dr. Graham might be difficult to get along with sometimes, but she's competent. She'd never make a mistake like that. That order killed Mrs. Clark.''

The two sat in silence for a moment, letting the activity of the nursing station flow around them, PJ thinking that Helen was the type of person for whom everything was black or white. She wondered when was the last time Schultz had seen things that way, or if he ever had.

"There's something else that's puzzling,'' Helen said. "The RT tech who adjusted Mrs. Clark's respirator—his name is Joe Argyle, like the socks—says that he looked at her records on the computer before coming up to 3PT. He says that everything in her record indicated substantial improvement. I know Joe. I don't think he's just trying to protect himself.''

"Schultz mentioned to me that Dr. Graham claims that she didn't order the reduction in respirator function,'' PJ said. "She's either covering up her own negligence, which you think is unlikely, or there was tampering."

"Of course there was tampering. Joe's got proof. He told me that when he examined the on-line record this morning, he did some screen prints for reference. All we have to do is press this key here," she said, pointing to a function key, "and we can get a hard copy of everything that's on the screen. He turned them over to the hospital president and to Mr. Schultz." She sniffed as if to say *we all know what good that will do*.

"So her file looked one way this morning and looks entirely different now," PJ said.

"And I know who did it." Helen leaned forward, her too-red lips formed in a smug smile. Evidently, PJ had passed some sort of test, because Helen now seemed ready to share a confidence she wouldn't dream of passing on to Schultz.

Up close, PJ noticed, the eyes which had seemed light blue appeared colorless, like melting ice cubes. Disconcerted, she pulled back slightly. The woman had a strong physical presence which reminded her of Schultz without the belly and with a lot more hair.

"It was Charles Horner, her son-in-law. I don't know how he pulled this off, but I'm certain he's the one. They used to have fights in her room, although we could never hear her side of it. She couldn't talk very well at all with the airway in place, and had to write what she needed. He wanted her dead. He actually said so—several of us heard it when her door was open. He's a greedy bastard."

Helen delivered this with so much vehemence that PJ got the feeling that Charles Horner better not show up on the third floor of the Payton Tower anytime soon. He might find a one-woman lynch mob waiting for him.

CHAPTER
3

On his way out of the Human Resources office, Schultz knew that he had bullied the young woman behind the counter unnecessarily. He was aware that his face and voice could be intimidating. It was something he could put on and take off like a mask.

He had known all along that he could get the contact info he needed from Human Resources. But being essentially ordered to visit Human Resources by his boss had given him the privacy and freedom to ask the HR clerk all about Helen Boxwood. She was, after all, on his suspect list. At least that's what he told himself was the reason for his curiosity.

The Fossil, as Helen was known, had worked at Wood Memorial for thirty years. She had gotten a pin for her years of service with a tiny diamond chip set in equally tiny cupped hands. She wore it on her lapel. She complained about sore feet. She was frequently seen eating barbecue chips and drinking fully leaded Coke, which immediately elevated her in Schultz's estimation. She was stubborn.

Opinionated. Demanding. Also highly professional. Treated both nurses and patients as family. Caring. Would go out of her way to help. Very private about her life outside the hospital, if she even had one. The HR clerk didn't even know if there was a man in Helen's life.

Schultz felt charged. He stopped in a men's room on the way back from Human Resources to recycle some of the Coke he'd had with dinner. He half expected his hair—what there was of it, at least—to be standing on end when he looked at himself in the mirror over the sink. Earlier, when he'd talked with PJ, he had resented this case. It seemed that if there was any action on it at all, it would be in her lap, not his. Now the murder— and he was certain it was murder—presented itself as just the thing he needed to work on, just the thing that needed him to work on it.

He smoothed the hair that ringed his bald spot and hurried back to 3-PT. He got there just as PJ was shep- herding Dr. Graham into a conference room, one of those little cubbies where doctors gave the relatives the bad news. There wasn't really room for him, but he pushed in anyway, closed the door behind himself, and leaned against it. He would have helped himself to one of the two chairs in the room, but PJ and Dr. Graham were ahead of him.

Dr. Graham favored him with a look that could have given a popsicle the shivers. "Well, Lieutenant," she said, "ready for another round?"

Schultz opened his mouth to speak, not certain whether he should correct her about his rank, and even more uncertain that anything civil would pass his lips. PJ beat him to it.

"Detective Schultz will be observing," PJ said. "I'll be asking the questions."

He shrugged. It was good police practice to get another

viewpoint. Suspects who clammed up with one interviewer sometimes spilled their guts with a different approach. He was willing to stand by and watch Amateur Hour.

Schultz studied the two women, who were sitting in upholstered chairs angled together but not directly facing each other. A floor lamp in the corner did its best to cast a warm, supportive glow in the room. Insipid watercolors graced the walls.

His boss looked tired. Wrinkles that were hardly noticeable during the daytime were lengthened and deepened by the slanting light. She was wearing a dark red knit turtleneck that covered her from neck to wrist. It was tucked into gray tailored slacks which were supposed to drape easily over her stomach and hips but hugged them instead, indicating that she had gained weight since the slacks were purchased. She wore no jewelry or cosmetics. The lamplight brought out red highlights in her dark brown hair, which looked like it had been crushed by sleeping on it. There was an area on her right side underneath her arm where the turtleneck was liberally coated with white cat hairs, as though she had tucked a cat under her arm to carry it. Her eyes were gray and measuring, intelligent, missing nothing, and certainly her best feature. Except maybe for her breasts, which still had a youthful, almost playful, upturn. For a moment he considered how they would feel cupped in his hands: warm and satisfyingly heavy, nipples firm against his palms. The thought was not unwelcome, but this certainly wasn't the time to indulge himself. He hadn't yet invited PJ into his sexual fantasies, but figured that he would probably do so when he got tired of Casey, the cooperative, caring, and chesty young woman who could be summoned to life whenever he put his mind to it.

Leo Schultz had a wonderfully rich fantasy life, which provided both escape and sexual satisfaction. Of a sort.

He turned his attention to Eleanor Graham, and immediately the hairs on the back of his neck were up. There was something about her, something in her basic makeup, that whispered of wrongness. He had been around killers and rapists, drug dealers and child molesters, men and women with no morals and no conscience. He had an internal compass that rarely steered him wrong after he had spoken to, touched, and looked into the eyes of a person.

Right now Eleanor Graham was magnetic north.

She was a slightly built woman, five-two or -three, small-boned, like a delicate bird. But there was nothing delicate about her. Her hair was steel gray and short, with tight curls framing her face. It reminded him of steel wool. The hazel eyes which should have given her face warmth and interest were merely unrevealing. Window shades had been drawn behind them. Her nose and lips were spare, as if she did not want to waste flesh unnecessarily. She was dressed in a white hospital coat that showed signs of having been worn for too many hours. The coat had a name tag pinned on the front and a stethoscope lurking in one pocket. A peach-colored blouse showed at the open neck of the coat, and the bottom had fallen open to reveal the hem of a black skirt, slim legs crossed at the ankles, and sensible black shoes of the type he would expect to see on a nurse. She looked trim and physically fit, and probably put in hours at a health club every week. He knew that she valued her professional composure, but underneath it might be a volcano of a temper. She would throw plates or vases or whatever was at hand against the wall when she got mad. He had seen that type before. Hell, he had scraped them off the living room wall after their husbands had blown them away.

He couldn't imagine himself holding her breasts.

"Dr. Graham, I'd like to ask you a few questions about

the circumstances of Rowena Clark's death," PJ began. "I understand that—"

"I've already talked to Bert. The hospital's president. I'm hungry and tired. Is this necessary tonight?"

Schultz watched PJ. He knew she didn't like to be interrupted. She was probably wishing she had a desk in front of her and a pencil she could tap on it. She blinked her eyes once and her face set into a look he recognized. She was in Formal Mode.

"Yes, I'm afraid it is necessary. I won't keep you long. After all, we are discussing murder."

Apparently she had already made up her mind that negligence was out of the picture.

Dr. Graham shrugged her shoulders slightly in resignation. "Then ask away."

"How did Mrs. Clark come to be your patient?"

If PJ was hoping to put her off balance by backing up before the events of the day, it didn't work. Women were proficient at that type of roundabout discussion.

"I met her husband, Ron Clark, at a social function, a fund-raiser. When he found out I was a physician, he started talking about his ailments and trying to get free advice. A lot of people do that. I told him to make an appointment, and to my surprise, he did. That was, oh, ten years ago at least. He's dead now. His wife switched to me because Ron recommended it."

"What is your specialty?"

"I'm an internist."

"Does an internist normally treat patients with Mrs. Clark's condition?"

She shrugged again. "The lines aren't always clear-cut. We did have a pulmonary consult. Several times, in fact."

"What do you think her chances were?"

"Hard to say. She had been hospitalized twice before and managed to pull through. I like to keep an optimistic view. She had quit smoking and was watching her diet, getting exercise appropriate for her condition and age. Plus, she was a tough old biddy."

Schultz recognized that he had used the same term on the phone with PJ, but the way Dr. Graham said it, it seemed like a compliment.

"Was she ready to have her respirator removed?"

"It wasn't actually removed, just adjusted so that Rowena would have to do more work. She obviously wasn't up to it. Maybe in a couple of weeks we could have eased her off it, but not now. It's difficult to get COPD patients off mechanical ventilation. They get to like it. It's easier than breathing on their own."

"COPD?"

"Chronic Obstructive Pulmonary Disease."

"How do you explain the order that was placed and verified with your electronic signature?"

"I can't."

Schultz watched PJ try out her patented shrink stare, hoping to elicit more information. After a minute or so, he sincerely wished his poker face was as good as Dr. Graham's. In his view, anybody who could keep her composure like that while being questioned about a murder had something to hide.

But not necessarily murder.

Schultz had feelings, hunches, that were part of his detecting ability. It was something he never discussed with anyone, especially not PJ, since she'd probably fling him onto a couch and put electrodes in his brain.

He could connect to a killer as if an invisible thread ran between them.

When he worked a case, he imagined himself moving along the thread, pulling himself hand over hand. The thread got stronger, shinier, until it was a golden cord drawing him forward.

He held himself still, blocked out the conversation

going on a few feet away, and turned his thoughts loose. There was a thread, yes, but it was faint, so faint he could easily have missed it. Could he be standing next to the person who was the far terminus of the thread and not know it? Possible. On his first assignment with CHIP, he had been within fifteen feet of the killer and not sensed it, not then, at that point of the investigation. Some things had to click into place first.

". . . would be a signed slip in her medical records folder. There isn't. Her computer file was altered." Dr. Graham said. "It had to have been done sometime after eight-thirty, because that's approximately when I checked Rowena's file and added some notes."

"By the time Joe Argyle reviewed it," PJ said, "he got an entirely different picture. That was about nine-thirty. Where were you between eight-thirty and nine-thirty this morning?"

Schultz watched Dr. Graham closely. There it was, that flicker of uncertainty, guilt, something. He wondered if PJ caught it.

"After rounds, I drove over to a nursing home I own. GeriCare, on Lemay Ferry Road. Wednesday is Doctor Day. That's when I see any residents with specific complaints, review lab tests, and update medication orders. I was there until noon, when Bert paged me with the news about Rowena. I came straight back here."

"How long does it take to get there?"

"Less than fifteen minutes." Dr. Graham hesitated. "But I went into my office first to do some paperwork. The office has a private entrance around back. I doubt if anyone saw me there before nine-thirty."

Schultz saw PJ glance in his direction, and he picked up his cue. Time to inject some variety into the questioning routine. "So that's forty-five minutes unaccounted for," he said, letting an accusatory tone slip into his voice. It wasn't hard; it was always right below the surface anyway. "You could have doubled back and entered the order right here in the hospital."

"But I didn't. I have no reason to kill Rowena. How about that, Lieutenant? Isn't there a little thing called motive?"

"There's always motive where there's money. Her relatives could have paid you off or maybe you had something going yourself. It's strange that a dame like you—big-shot doctor—would risk her juicy career over some dried-up prune who was probably going to die soon anyway. I don't know why you did it yet, but I intend to dig until I find out. When I do, you can kiss your fancy-ass lifestyle good-bye and start keeping an eye out for those prison guards with one hand on their guns and the other on their cocks, like maybe they don't know the difference. Or maybe some butch con with flat tits and muscles like Schwarzenegger will be interested in a fine-boned little cunt like you." Schultz moved closer until he was looming over her. He put both hands on the arms of her chair and leaned into her face. "And on top of that, I don't like you."

"Is the interview over?"

"For now."

Dr. Graham rose from her chair suddenly, evidently expecting Schultz to give way. He didn't budge, and she collided with his chest with a satisfying thump. He stepped back and gave her just enough room to get by him. He didn't bother to suck in his stomach, so she bowed her own midsection backwards and left, pulling her dignity around her tighter than the white coat.

"Nice maneuver," PJ said when the doctor had left the room.

"You like that? I've got a whole repertoire."

"I should point out that Dr. Graham could complain about your behavior. All it takes is a phone call to some high muckety-muck, and you and I will be attending Remedial Political Correctness. Or worse. Next time, if you want to grill something, try a steak."

"No shit, Boss. You mean I have to make nice with the suspects?" Schultz opened his eyes wide in mock horror.

PJ nodded, but he could tell that the warning was just standard Boss crap. It was a good sign that PJ was able to dish it out again. For a while after their first case together, she seemed to be tiptoeing around him, like she didn't know how to act with the guy who had saved her life. Now things were back on an even keel. Besides, he knew where the line was in dealing with people like Dr. Graham. He didn't hesitate to get his toes over the line, or even the balls of his feet, but his heels were rooted in restraint.

Schultz lowered himself into the chair vacated by Dr. Graham, imagining that he could feel an icy touch where her ass had rested. He savored the companionable silence that had fallen between the two of them, and let it build up a bit like snow covering the footprints and blood that were the signs of a violent struggle.

"So what do you think about Dr. Ice Cube?" PJ said, apparently having picked up—and cleaned up—his thoughts of a couple of minutes ago.

"I think neither of us likes her. I think she's guilty of some damned thing or other. Did you notice her reaction when you asked about what she was doing this morning?"

PJ nodded. "I did see something in her face. She might be worried because she spent time in her office at the nursing home. No one saw her, so no one can verify her story. I think maybe someone's trying to frame her—make her look negligent."

"I vote against that. She was probably paid off by one or more of Mrs. Clark's charming family members."

"She's got a lot to lose. I can't see her selling out her career for a few bucks."

"So maybe it was more than a few. Or one of those family creeps has something on her that wouldn't look good in the AMA journal."

"That nurse Helen Boxwood seems to think that Mrs. Clark's son-in-law Charles Horner is the killer," PJ said. "She called him a greedy bastard."

Schultz crossed his legs, then uncrossed them, letting his knees fall apart in that male display that usually made women uncomfortable: *Here are my cock and balls, what do you think of that?* If PJ were a dog, she'd probably come over and give him a good authoritative sniff. PJ didn't react. He wondered if that was a trained shrink response or whether she just had too much feline about her and not enough canine.

"Helen Boxwood," he said. "What do you think of her?" There must have been something in his tone of voice, because PJ looked at him quizzically, her dark brown eyebrows pinched together.

"As a murder suspect?" she said.

"As whatever. As a person." He tried to keep his tone neutral. He watched PJ form and discard a couple of responses before she spoke.

"She seems like a very nice person to me. Dedicated to her job. Where are you going with this? Are you thinking that she put poor old Mrs. Clark out of her misery? Angel of Death kind of thing?"

"No, nothing like that. I took a liking to her. A personal liking, I mean."

"Personal . . . Oh."

This time the silence felt awkward, at least to Schultz. It seemed to him that PJ was enjoying herself. "I was wondering . . ."

"Yes?" PJ said, a little too brightly.

"You could let me finish my sentences, Doc. Interrupting

like that is not a pretty habit," Schultz said, as though he would never do such a thing. "I was wondering if you could find out if she's available."

"Available as in single? As in for dating?" Now he was certain that PJ was having a good laugh inside at his expense, but he surged on.

"Are you dense or something? Of course for dating."

"Why don't you just ask her yourself, Detective?"

"You're a woman. She's a woman. You talk about things like that."

"Actually we talked about medical records."

"Christ, Doc, you know what I mean." He felt heat in his face and hoped that he wasn't getting red. "Are you gonna do it or not?"

There was a long pause. Schultz fidgeted in his chair, then forced himself to stop. He felt like a kid nervously waiting outside the principal's office for the third time in the same day.

"I'll think about it," she said.

Tension relieved, Schultz rose from his chair and clapped her heartily on the shoulder. "Great," he said, as though she had already agreed. "There's one last thing we need to do, then you can go home and get some rest. You look like shit, by the way."

Rowena Clark's hospital room seemed stifling to Schultz. Sometimes being in a room where death had occurred chilled him; sometimes it seemed the air was so thick it was hard to draw a breath; other times it simply made him want to loosen his collar, roll up his sleeves, and get to work. He saw PJ's eyes go to the bed, as though she expected to see blood or the impersonal shape of a body under a sheet or a corpse's shadow somehow detached from its owner and left behind. The room was spacious and well furnished, almost like a room in a good hotel rather than in a hospital. Piped-in music. A large window with flowered drapes. A bathroom with a shower that someone Schultz's size could turn around in. A dresser with a cut-glass lamp, a TV on a large stand, not hanging from the ceiling, with a VCR and a stack of tapes next to it. Insurance didn't cover these surroundings, at least not the kind of insurance that Schultz had.

His last hospital stay had been thirty years ago. He had been off duty, out for a walk with his wife Julia, when he noticed a delivery truck heading straight for the sidewalk where two boys were playing jacks. He found out later that the driver had suffered a heart attack and was dead behind the wheel when the truck jumped the curb. Schultz had thrown the boys clear, but gotten partially pinned between the truck and the brick building it came to rest against. He had been fortunate: broken ribs, a punctured lung, a fracture below the elbow in his left arm, enough bruises for a lifetime. His time in the hospital, at city expense, had been spent in a room with another man who coughed his lungs out twenty-four hours a day. The room was located a floor above the laundry facility, so it got damn hot every afternoon and he could hear the tireless *whump-whump* of the industrial washing machines, which at least provided some relief from the coughing.

He hadn't considered himself a hero for saving the boys. He considered himself a man who happened to be in the right place at the right time and who hurt like hell afterward.

Tugging himself back to the case, he retrieved a bag full of items from the top of the dresser. It was one of those drawstring hospital bags that said "Patient's Personals." He dumped it out on the bed.

"These are the personal items Mrs. Clark had with her. The family, such as it is, wants them back. I told them we'd have to look them over first, see if we wanted to keep any and log them in as evidence. Prints have already been pulled, and everything matches up just with Mrs. Clark, so we don't need to be too careful.''

"I guess she considered her personal items really personal. Didn't let anyone else handle them.''

"Or they were wiped clean and then her prints were added back.''

PJ reached for a black object with buttons and a small LCD display. "I wonder why she needed a PDS in the hospital,'' she said.

Schultz kept his mouth shut. He had thought the black thing was a calculator.

PJ started pushing the buttons. Schultz heard a couple of soft beeps. The display was angled away from him, so he couldn't see what was happening.

"I get it,'' PJ said. Excitement surfaced through her tiredness.

"What? Tell already.''

"It's a voice from the grave.''

"Can the melodrama. What do you have?''

"The last ten things Rowena Clark said. Helen told me that Mrs. Clark couldn't talk with the airway, so she communicated by writing. I assumed she meant with a chalkboard or paper and pencil, but she used her PDS. Look,'' PJ said, turning the display toward him, "this unit is just like the one I used in Denver, except it has more features. It stores ten messages of up to thirty-two characters each. You can back up through them one at a time or go all the way back to the first message and display them in order. I've backed up. Here's the first one.''

Schultz peered at the screen as PJ stepped through the messages.

MSG0: *LATE AGAIN DOCTOR HA HA*
MSG1: *THANK YOU AND COULD YOU TURN*
MSG2: *DOWN THE TEMP IM HOT*

MSG3: NO WAY NOT ANOTHER RED CENT
MSG4: MY DAUGHTER MADE THE BIGGEST
MSG5: MISTAKE OF HER LIFE MARRYING YOU
MSG6: YOU SNAKE SOMEBODY HAS TO STAND
MSG7: UP TO YOU THE ANSWER IS NO
MSG8: GET OUT OF MY SIGHT AND DONT
MSG9: COME BACK

"No wonder somebody wanted this returned ASAP," PJ said. "Preferably before we figured out what it contained."

"Looks like we need to have a talk with Charles the Snake," Schultz said.

"It can wait until tomorrow. While we do that, could you get Anita over here first thing to measure and draw up this room for virtual simulation? Better get her to do the hallway and nursing station, too."

Schultz was surprised that PJ planned to pursue this case using a computer simulation of the crime scene, but he didn't bother to ask about it. She would tell him in her own good time what she was hoping to accomplish. Besides, she was the head of the project, something that had rankled him at first, but he had made his peace with it. If she wanted the junior members of her CHIP team drawing diagrams of a hospital room, or scrubbing toilets, for that matter, he certainly didn't object. Did them good.

"Sure," he said. "I'll get them both over here. Dave could always use a little practice with his observation and recording methods. He could be standing next to a saber-toothed cat and put down in his notebook 'one domestic feline, large.'"

Schultz fussed over PJ walking out to the garage alone late at night, and she relented and let him summon a security guard to escort her. Once she was gone, he used a phone at the nursing station to contact Anita and fill her in, leaving it to her to wake up Dave.

"One more thing," he said to Anita. "What's a PDS?"

"Personal Digital Secretary. It's an electronic gadget that stores phone numbers, your appointments, reminders, anything you want. Get with it, Schultz."

CHAPTER

4

"Good evening, Mr. Worth," the doorman said. "Pleasant weather we're having."

Cracker nodded in response as he walked over to the elevator. After three years he still couldn't remember the doorman's name. Gary, Jerry? Out of the corner of his eye—his so-smooth input device—he noticed the doorman go back to his station and press a button to alert 4A that she had a guest on the way up. If the doorman guessed at Cracker's relationship with the occupant of apartment 4A, he kept the knowledge from his expression. Cracker had given him five hundred dollars for each of the last three Christmases to keep a special watch on his Aunt Karen, and, though it was unspoken, to ensure discretion. With the holiday season not too far away now, the doorman was probably already planning to spend another five hundred on riverboat gambling.

The elevator had a mirror across the back. Cracker practiced tilting his head in short jerky movements, as he imagined an android might when trying to collect information from several different angles. When the elevator reached the fourth floor, he let the doors open and close on his arm a few times, enjoying the pretense that his arm was not actually living tissue at all but a much superior cybernetic replacement that could not be crushed. He lapsed into his long-running internal debate over whether he would prefer to be a completely mechanical android or a cyborg with biological components. Both seemed preferable to the fallible body he now inhabited.

His fallible body was the reason that he was here, or so he told himself. Part of him knew better, knew that he came as much for the stroking and the kind words as for the dangerous lure of orgasm. Dangerous because he was out of control then, had to close off his thoughts and let a few square inches of exquisitely sensitive skin run the whole show. There was always the fear that during those few vulnerable moments something would be set loose other than his sperm, something would rip itself from its deep anchorage in his brain and push rudely into his awareness, never to be contained again, like a popped tube of refrigerator biscuits or the internal organs of the deer he had once seen being gutted, its front legs tied to a tree by the side of the road.

Yet he came, because the lure was strong and, when the danger was over, there was the stroking and comforting.

He walked down the short hallway from the elevator. There were only two doors, one on each side of the hall. Each floor of the building held only two apartments, each with a spacious living room, kitchen with eating area, dining room, two bedrooms, and two baths. Cracker had remodeled the inside of 4A and furnished it to Aunt Karen's liking. She had chosen attractive, solid pieces that were meant to be used rather than admired, a description which, he had to admit, pretty much described Aunt Karen, too.

He had raised his hand to knock on the right-hand door when it was pulled open.

"Come in, Billy. So glad to see you."

Aunt Karen was, as always, radiant in his eyes. Rounded and motherly, she was in her late forties, blond hair turning silver, trim-waisted but reassuringly wide in the hips and chest, cheeks reddened from working in the kitchen and from the warmth of the gas fireplace in the living room, wearing a white blouse with a lace collar and a blue pleated skirt. She closed the hall door and helped him take off his sweater, then hung it up neatly in the guest closet. He took a deep breath, inhaling her freshly scrubbed and powdered scent and the wonderful smell wafting from the kitchen.

"Brownies?" he said.

"I had a feeling you'd be coming tonight," she beamed.

She stepped up close and they embraced. He slipped his hand under her blouse and clasped one of her substantial breasts. She wasn't wearing a bra tonight. It was one of those little surprises she loved to spring on him. He knew there would be nothing under her skirt either, nothing to tangle his fumbling hands. He felt the blood flowing to his groin, imagined it draining from the rest of his body into a hot pool at the base of his abdomen. He lowered his head to her shoulder as his fingers brushed her nipples and her warm breath moved gently against his cheek. She lightly traced the bulge in his pants, which grew hard under her touch.

He managed to get only one button of her blouse undone before she took over and undid the rest of them herself. Then she unfastened his belt and zipper, releasing his erection so that it swayed between them. When her blouse and skirt were on the floor, she knelt on the lush carpet and kissed the head of his penis, then playfully licked it. He rested both of his hands lightly on her hair, then felt her turn her face up to him.

"Dear Billy," she said with her infinitely inviting mouth, "come to Mama."

Cracker complied, as he fervently hoped that this would not be the time that the terror got loose.

He made the same wish a while later as he mounted her on the down comforter she had tossed on the floor to cushion his bony knees.

While she cut the brownies in the kitchen, he pulled on the white silk boxer shorts she had handed him, feeling a little less ridiculous with his angular hips, sloping buttocks, and sparse pubic hair covered. He studied the framed photos on the mantel above the fireplace. There were two of Aunt Karen and himself together, from their vacation to Hawaii. He hadn't wanted to go; she insisted, and he had actually enjoyed himself. The other was a family portrait in an ornate gilded frame. A tall, handsome man stood next to a lovely woman seated in a chair, his hand resting protectively on her shoulder. Cradled in her arms was a baby, contentedly sleeping through the portrait session. Father, Mother, and little Billy. The attractive couple was dead now, and Billy existed only in these rooms.

They sat at the kitchen table together, drinking milk and eating brownies, talking of inconsequential things: museum exhibits, the latest best-sellers, things that Cracker kept up with only to have something to talk to Aunt Karen about. Sometimes he didn't know why he bothered. He could have sat in silence if he wanted to; after all, he was paying for it.

He had found Aunt Karen years ago, during his work on one of the first confidential profiles he did for money. She was the mistress of the target of his search, Hank Trisher, a married man who was a founding partner of a software company ripe for takeover. Cracker was intrigued by her, and so he checked into her background with the same thoroughness he applied to the target. Her name was Rachel Collins, and she made her living as a classic kept woman. She had been with at least half a dozen men before Trisher, one at a time, always provided with a place to live and a generous spending account. She was an expert at giving men what they wanted, and in return, she got the freedom to live her life as she pleased, except for the few hours a week that she was actually earning her keep. When Trisher turned up dead a couple of months later, she moved effortlessly into another relationship, this time with a French businessman who imported lace and fine fabrics into the US. He had a family in Paris and Rachel in New York.

When Cracker finally decided to act upon his needs, which he neither understood nor cared to examine closely, he flew to New York and met her in a restaurant. He would have liked it much better if he could have done the whole thing by computer. He liked to work from a distance, through others or through machines, but this task didn't lend itself to that. He had to be there in person to make an on-the-spot judgment of her suitability.

And suitable she was. He knew it the moment she sat across from him, curious, cautious, open to possibilities. As the appetizer was served, he hesitantly put forth his proposition, ever fearful of rejection.

During the main course, they got down to specifics.

She was a professional, and while Cracker felt incredibly awkward, it didn't seem to trouble Rachel in the least to discuss living arrangements and their mutual concern about sexually transmitted diseases. At her urging, and with downcast eyes, he described what he wanted. She nodded and patted his hand. She wanted security, she said. She was getting old, more than twice Cracker's age already and many times his worldliness. European men valued a woman's maturity and experience but most Americans did not. She wanted to live in the US; it was easier to keep in touch with her elderly mother in Dallas. By the time dessert and coffee arrived, he had agreed to a trust fund, so that even if he died or left her, she would live comfortably for the rest of her life.

From that point things moved fast. Rachel and Cracker each provided the other with a medical report that showed they harbored no diseases, neither mild and annoying nor viral and deadly. Rachel had a frank discussion with her Frenchman, matched him up with another like-minded woman, and parted on affectionate terms. Within a couple of weeks Aunt Karen arrived in St. Louis to hunt for an apartment. She settled into the role he desired gracefully, and asked no questions about what he did outside apartment 4A.

She wasn't the first woman Cracker had been with, but she was the first one who managed to make him feel as if he knew what he was doing. His visits were all that he had hoped for, as he explored the narrow ledge between the twin canyons of terror and sexual release.

With brownies resting comfortably in his stomach, he let Aunt Karen lead him to the bedroom, where she propped herself up amid the numerous pillows on the bed. It was time for the part of the visit with no danger attached. She opened her legs in a V shape, and he crawled in, resting his head against her breasts while she stroked his hair, his face, his back, anything within reach. After a while, relaxed, he began to talk. Most of the time he was quiet, but tonight he wanted to tell her about the nightmares.

Cracker had experienced the same nightmare every two or three months for more than eighteen years. The most recent time was last night, so the images were fresh, although they were never far from his consciousness. He saw a harpylike figure torment a man whose face was always blurred, but whom he knew was the protective father in the family portrait on the mantel, his own father. The man fled through a surreal landscape but was cornered in a blind portion of a maze by the flying harpy. The harpy bent over the prostrate man, tore open his body, and began to eat while the man was still alive.

As Aunt Karen expressed her sympathy and concern, all of it boiling down to "there, there, that's all right," a decision made itself known to Cracker. He had almost certainly made the decision before he talked about the nightmares. That was probably why he felt free to do so.

He had embarked on a plan to ruin Mom Elly's life, one way or another. When he succeeded, he would have to disappear, the same way he had disappeared when he ran away from home at the age of fourteen, just eight short years ago. He felt like some imaginary insect on an eight-year cycle, inventing a new life for himself when the shell of the old one got too confining. He thought for a moment what it would feel like to have an external chitinous skeleton protecting his soft juicy insides, a wall between the tender parts of him and the harsh outside world. He had one now, a wall of sorts, that partitioned his memories into those which were safe to experience and those which were not.

Part of disappearing was removing all traceable connections to his former life. Many people who tried to disappear were unsuccessful because they were unable or unwilling to make the sacrifices required for a total break with the past: friends, relatives, lovers, home, hobbies, habits, bank accounts, credit cards, automobile, personal appearance, occupation. It was so easy to get tripped up by small things. Cracker had tracked such people down himself, and it wasn't even a specialty of his. There was the woman who had skipped out on her husband after converting as much of their assets as she could to liquid, which flowed conveniently into her purse. She left behind her children, but couldn't bear to part with her poodle. The animal was tattooed and listed in a computerized pet registry, a service that helped identify lost pets. The "new owner" who had kept the registration active by paying the fee and sending in a new name and address turned out to be the missing woman. He also remembered a land developer who had conned many people, including one livid soul with the resources to hire Cracker. The con man was an avid skier, and although he had changed his looks and his name and relocated to the desert southwest, he couldn't resist ordering the latest ski equipment from an exclusive mail-order catalog, one with only three hundred names on its mailing list and juicy computerized buying profiles. It was all over when Cracker tapped into the mailing list.

When Cracker had engineered his own disappearance as a teen suicide, it had been necessary to eliminate a friend who had provided him a temporary home. He had met Diver through a computer Special Interest Group, or SIG. Diver had sympathized with Cracker's need to get away from home, and had offered him a place to stay that was at least off the streets if not totally sane and safe.

Cracker had hired a killer. He felt some remorse doing it, but convinced himself that it was just a practical thing, like hiring an accountant to do taxes.

When he wasn't sitting in front of a computer, Diver was a motorcyclist, favoring the fast, glitzy type called crotch rockets. Riding on a country road, winding the rocket up, he suddenly encountered a rental truck where there was none a moment before. A baseball cap worn jauntily backwards did not, predictably, protect the contents of his skull. He lived long enough to expire at the hospital, making his organs ideal transplant material and furthering the reputation of his chosen mode of transportation as a "donorcycle."

The idea that Aunt Karen would have to die bothered him a little, as he lay between her legs and her hands moved rhythmically on his chest, until he realized that she was just part of a fantasy, and people discarded their fantasies and moved on, didn't they?

He nuzzled against her and took one of her nipples in

his mouth, sucking gently. She settled back against the pillows, closed her eyes, and immersed herself in her own fantasies. He knew what she liked, and he felt good about providing it for her. She responded, moving her hand down between her legs. He teased her erect nipples with his tongue and his hands, until she had shuddered against him half a dozen times.

CHAPTER

5

In the morning PJ phoned her boss, Lieutenant Howard Wall, to give him an update. He didn't seem to mind getting calls at home at 7:00 A.M.; it was one of the best times to get hold of him. She could hear a commotion in the background as his kids ricocheted off the walls. PJ wondered about the rumors that Howard was unfaithful to his supposedly frigid wife. Because of the events in her own life—the cheating husband, the divorce—she tended to take the wife's side without even knowing the facts. Besides, Mrs. Wall couldn't be *that* frigid. Wall and his wife had four kids, the oldest about Thomas's age and the youngest not quite two years old. Maybe she'd just gotten a little frosty since the birth of the last baby. Who had time for sex, anyway, with four kids, one still in diapers?

She thought about her sister Mandy and Mandy's husband Vince. They had four children also, yet they were the most serene people she knew. Their marriage had such vitality and freshness that she was certain they found plenty of times and places for sex.

Her own sex life could be described with a four-letter word: none.

She pulled her thoughts back to the phone conversation, anchoring them on Howard's voice. He told her that he had set up a meeting for her at nine with the hospital president, Bert Manning. Howard, in that charming way that he had, let her know that the mayor was hounding the chief's backside about this case, since Rowena Clark had been part of his social circle. The mayor had stopped short of calling her a friend. PJ, who was short on sleep and hadn't had her coffee yet, told him that she resented his implication that she wouldn't do her best on a case unless the mayor's cronies were involved. He backed off, so PJ saved her complaint about the old boys' network for another time. She had an idea she thought might defuse the situation, and she wanted to give it a try before confronting Howard.

It occurred to her that she might be mellowing. In the past she would have jumped down his throat if she even thought he might be going around her because she was a woman.

Talking with Howard was like chewing on a lemon. When she got off the phone, she was determined not to let him sour the rest of her day. She soaked in the wonderful old bathtub with claw feet. The house she was renting, a story-and-a-half with two spacious bedrooms upstairs, had terrific oak floors, a working fireplace, and two baths. She had claimed the upstairs bath even before she and Thomas moved in. Megabite sat beside the tub, swatting at drops of water PJ let fall from her fingertips, which she dangled over the edge of the tub. It was a little game the two of them played. As soon as Megabite heard the bathwater running, she turned into a gray-and-orange streak, dashing in from wherever she was in the house.

PJ reluctantly pulled the old-fashioned rubber plug by its chain to let the water out of the tub and toweled off.

She put on gray trousers and a silk blouse in a pale rose color, lighter than Megabite's nose, then added black leather flats and pearl earrings. She applied lipstick and patted her face with a neutral shade of oil-absorbing powder. Looking in the mirror, she was pleased with the results, and felt ready to handle a dozen Howards. The sexy white lace bra and panties next to her skin and the silk camisole she wore underneath the blouse added to her self-confidence. She wasn't sure if it was the same for all women, but for her, underwear was just as important as outerwear. She wouldn't feel well-dressed if her bra had a safety pin or her panties sagged because the elastic waist was stretched out.

Megabite led the way down the stairs, tail stiff in recognition of her important role as Guide to the Kitchen. The cat's efforts netted her a dish of milk and a couple of leftover cheese cubes that were getting dry around the edges.

"Mom . . ." Thomas said, after washing down a huge mouthful of cereal with apple juice.

"I know, I know. Her dry cat food is one hundred percent nutritionally complete. It says so on the bag about a dozen times. But cats like variety, just like people. Would you like to eat the same stuff for breakfast every day, year after year?" She glanced at the table. Two rounded, yellowish objects floated in his oversize bowl, not quite concealed by a mound of Cheerios.

"Yes," he said, "as long as it's Cheerios."

"What are those things floating in there?" she said.

"Pear halves. I poured the juice from the can in, too."

"I had to ask. Now you've spoiled my appetite."

Before Thomas could come up with any response, the doorbell rang. When PJ looked through the peephole she'd installed in the front door a couple of months ago, she couldn't see anyone. Curious, she opened the door as far as the security chain would reach, and found two large boxes, taped shut in a haphazard fashion. After unlatching the chain, she inspected the boxes. There was a note on top of the larger of the two: *From one of Merlin's friends to another. Enjoy.*

"Open it, Mom," Thomas said. He was standing next to her. They dragged the boxes in the front door and sliced the tape on the first one with a kitchen knife. Inside was a Power Mac 8500 in a tower case. Stuck to the front was another note. This one said: *My name is Neptune.*

Merlin was the screen name of a longtime friend of PJ's. They had met on a computerized bulletin board while PJ was attending college. Over the years, Merlin had become a mentor as PJ struggled to combine her fascination with computer technology and her work as a psychologist. She didn't know if Merlin was male or female, young or old, and she sometimes had doubts whether Merlin was human or a computer program. Whoever he, she, or it was, one thing was certain: there were others who called Merlin friend.

"Merlin must have passed the word that we needed a computer," PJ said. She wondered if Neptune was the screen name of the mysterious benefactor or whether the computer was named Neptune. Some people who were heavily into computers named them and treated them as friends. PJ was very involved with computers but would never consider naming one.

Her old reliable Mac Centris 650 had been smashed by an intruder at the beginning of the summer. Because of the expense of sending Thomas to summer classes at Washington University, there had been no money to spare to replace the computer. She did have a laptop at home, but it was outmoded, and besides, she used it exclusively for work. She didn't let Thomas use it for writing reports, educational software, reference materials, or games. Thomas hadn't complained, at least not much; he knew that his mom was adjusting to single parenthood and the loss of much of the family income. Her position with the St. Louis Police Department paid less than a third of what she had earned in Denver, plus she had only minimal child support from Steven.

"Wow! This looks like the latest and greatest, Mom! Why would anybody give this away?" Thomas was tearing into the second box, which held a keyboard, a mouse, speakers, and a seventeen-inch monitor.

"There are people who buy computers like they're shopping for clothes for each new season," PJ said. "They have a lot of disposable income, and this is how they choose to spend it." She patted the mouse appreciatively. "I suppose this equipment is somebody else's hand-me-downs, but it's going to be wonderful for us. This model sold for over four thousand bucks new. I'll let Merlin know that he should pass along our thanks."

"Can we put it together now? Please?"

"There's really no time, sweetie. But I promise this evening we'll see what this critter can do." She saw the disappointment in his face, but it was quickly replaced by a gleam of anticipation.

"Maybe Winston can come over. He's just gonna die when he sees this!"

PJ laughed. "I hope not. I'd hate to have to tell his father."

"I'll bet it's got a 10X CD-ROM and a one-gigabyte hard drive. Probably sixteen megabytes of RAM!"

She managed to get Thomas calmed down enough to finish breakfast. After dropping him at school, she called Schultz from her cellular phone in the car.

"I have to be at the hospital to talk to Bert Manning, the president," she said. "Do you mind interviewing Charles the Snake by yourself?"

"Hell, I'm looking forward to it. I cut myself shaving this morning, so I'm in a foul mood to start with. I could use some rich toady to chew up and spit out."

"Have you spoken to Wall lately?"

"I know what you mean. Don't mind him, he's just having a bad hair-up-his-ass day. Say, since you're going to be at the hospital anyway, do you think you could talk to Helen?"

"For a price." PJ had made up her mind that she didn't mind being used as a go-between. It might prove interesting.

"Name it, Doc."

"Lunch at Millie's."

"You're on. Meet you there at one."

The flow of morning traffic had been in PJ's favor, and she got to the hospital a half hour before her appointment. She stopped in Information Systems to get a general understanding of the computer system and to hear their side of the story. An impossibly young manager welcomed her, gave her a five-minute tour, then succinctly explained why what happened couldn't have happened. She missed a lot of his earnest narration because she was distracted by her reflection in a window set into the computer room door. She could make out the wrinkles at the corners of her eyes, and although the reflection wasn't colorful enough to show it, she was acutely aware of the gray in her hair. The contrast to the reflection of the man next to her— he couldn't have been more than twenty-eight—made her wonder when those signs of age had happened.

It must have been an ambush.

Inside, she felt no different than she had when she was thirty. Those extra ten years seemed to have gone by incredibly fast. By the time she was sixty, would the days and years be speeding by marked only by the most dramatic events, like a strobe light catching and stilling the wings of a hummingbird?

She planned to check the manager's facts herself by

digging into the computerized audit logs and backups, but for now she accepted his statements.

When she arrived at Bert Manning's office, the secretary told her that he had been pulled into an unscheduled conference and would be back in about fifteen minutes. The office smelled of alcohol: rubbing alcohol, not the drinking kind. When the secretary offered her a cup of coffee, PJ took it, just to bury her nose in the hot scent. Sipping her coffee, she used the waiting time to try to gauge the man.

The office was extraordinarily neat. PJ couldn't imagine herself working in such surroundings. The books on the shelves were arranged by size and free of dust, even though some probably hadn't been opened in years. Gleaming frames held diplomas and awards. Instead of rich woods and cushy upholstered chairs, the president of Wood Memorial furnished his office with plastic chairs, the cup-shaped kind that were supposed to fit your behind, and a metal desk with a wood-grain laminated top. The desktop held a telephone, a plastic lamp, and an old-fashioned intercom, whose mate probably rested on the secretary's desk in the outer office area. Next to the intercom was a photo of Manning and his wife standing at the rim of the Grand Canyon. He looked about fifty-five, thickset but not soft, his face intelligent but tense even on vacation. His wife was a good match, and could have passed for a twin sister. Perhaps she was his sister. There was nothing in the office indicative of marriage and family other than the photo. A computer, turned off and outfitted with a custom dust cover, sat on a credenza behind the desk. There was a twenty-four-hour clock on the wall behind her, obviously for the use of the person who sat at the desk. She would have to twist her neck to read the time.

When Manning came into the room, she rose from her chair and offered her hand. He hurried behind the desk without extending his, so she was left greeting thin air.

Seated at the desk, he pulled a small white packet from the pocket inside his suit coat. He tore it open and used the alcohol swab inside to wipe the handle of the top right desk drawer. Then he opened the drawer and withdrew a pen and pad of paper. The pen got a quick once-over before he tossed the swab into the wastebasket.

"Now, Dr. Gray, how may I help you?" He was poised over the pad of paper as if to record her every word.

PJ knew that he was displaying obsessive-compulsive behavior about germs, and that was the explanation for the alcohol, the lack of clutter, the refusal to shake hands, and the plastic surfaces that minimized bacterial contamination. She wondered what drove such a person to work in a hospital, which was surely awash in bacteria.

They discussed Rowena Clark's death, with Manning adamantly supporting Dr. Graham. He said that she was an asset to the hospital, had no motive for murder, and that he believed her story. When PJ pressed him, he offered up the respiratory therapy tech Joe Argyle as a sacrifice, strongly implying that Rowena's family members had paid off Joe. Neither situation—Dr. Graham's involvement or a technician's—was good for the hospital's image, so Manning had opted for the less influential of the two.

She was surprised that he didn't blame the death on a non-employee. Then she figured that it would look even worse for the hospital if strangers were wandering in off the street and fiddling with the patients' life-support equipment.

"It's unthinkable that Dr. Graham would be involved in such a thing," he said. "If I were you, I'd take a hard look at Mrs. Clark's family. She treated them all like dirt under her fingernails."

PJ wondered if obsessive-compulsive Mr. Manning realized that he had just made a revealing slip. Instead of saying dirt under her *feet*, which would have been the common expression, he had made an analogy close to his heart.

"Have you considered the possibility that the tampering was done from outside the hospital?" she said. "By dial-in access, for instance?"

"Of course. Considered and discarded. The InfoSys manager assures me that the hospital's patient files are secure."

"Secure against casual access by curious staff isn't the same thing as secure against a hacker with a lot of experience. I would suggest that you cut off all dial-in lines until your security software can be reviewed."

"Out of the question. We have physicians who call in daily to get test results or do research. I'm not going to lock them out without excellent cause."

"A death isn't cause enough?"

"Really, Dr. Gray, let's not panic." He looked at his watch. "I must be going now. It's been a pleasure talking with you. I'm sure your department will have this incident solved in no time."

Class was over, and PJ was dismissed.

She located a house phone in the hall and called Helen Boxwood. She arranged to meet her during Helen's break, then headed back to the Information Systems department for a more in-depth examination of the computer records. She left the department a couple of hours later, with two conclusions firmly in mind: that the falsification of the records was done in such a clever way that it seemed well beyond the abilities of the relatives, and probably beyond Dr. Graham; and that she hadn't the slightest idea what she was going to say to Helen Boxwood.

CHAPTER

6

Schultz had taken a seat at the end of the counter in Millie's Diner, where the counter curved sharply back toward the kitchen. He had a good view of the door, so he could watch for PJ. One o'clock came and went with no sign of her, so at quarter after he ordered his lunch, exchanging a round of insults with Millie, the owner of the diner, as an appetizer. He wondered how many years he had been filling his belly here. The diner certainly hadn't changed. The stools at the counter still had chrome legs and black leatherette tops; the floor was still black-and-white checkerboard linoleum. The food he always ordered was hot and greasy, even the coffee. The third stool from the end had uneven legs, so the regulars avoided it. He still left a quarter as a tip, no matter how big his bill was. When Millie slid his thick white plate in front of him, there was a mound of french fries, a generous serving of lettuce and tomato slices, and two burger patties on a bun about five inches across that gleamed with grease and was adorned with a little flag on a toothpick, Millie's trademark. He tried to remember how many stars had been on the flag when he first started coming to the diner.

Naturally, as soon as he had taken his first huge bite of burger, PJ walked in. He waved her over. She started to sit on the stool next to him, then she remembered it was the wobbly one and moved down one. Millie glided over.

"You sure you want to sit next to this old coot, dearie?" Millie said, tilting her head in Schultz's direction. "I gotta . . ."

"Wipe the stool with disinfectant after he leaves. The floor, too," PJ said, reciting Millie's standard greeting. "I'll take my chances. What's your special today?"

"Clam chowder, real thick, with lots of oyster crackers."

"Red or white?"

Millie screwed up her face. "White. A classy girl like you should know better than to ask."

"OK, I'll have a bowl, and some of that orange spice tea."

Millie jotted down something indecipherable on her order pad and went to the kitchen pass-through. Schultz always suspected that the order pad was only there to make average customers feel as though Millie was listening to them. As if any of Millie's customers could be considered average citizens.

"It's only thick because it's been boiling for about three days back there in the kitchen," Schultz said. "You're the first one to order it."

"I heard that," Millie said, her back still turned. "Scumbag."

"You watch too much TV, Millie. You're starting to sound like *True Cops*."

"Yeah, well, that makes one of us, don't it? Be right back with your tea, dearie."

Schultz picked up a bottle of hot sauce on the counter. "You want any fries before I heat 'em up a bit?" PJ shook her head, so Schultz shook red drops over his fries, popped one in his mouth, and savored it.

"What's your take, Detective?"

"First, there's something I need to know. What's this electronic signature business I keep hearing about?"

"I talked with Ted about that. Ted Elwing, the manager of their Information Systems department. Wood Memorial uses bedside entry. That means a nurse carries a handheld, specialized computer, identifies a patient by scanning in the bar code on the patient's wrist band, and enters information such as vitals and notes while standing at the patient's bedside. Physicians also use the handheld units on their rounds, recording orders directly. To authorize procedures and medications, they have to enter an electronic signature. At the moment, that's simply a password unique to each doctor and different from the signon password."

Millie brought a cup, a teabag, and a small metal pitcher of boiling water. Schultz watched while PJ brewed her tea. She sniffed it appreciatively, then extracted an ice cube from his Coke with her spoon, without asking, and stirred it into the tea to cool it. It touched him that she acted so familiarly. Schultz felt loyalty and an old-fashioned protectiveness toward PJ, quite a bit different from the open hostility he had displayed when they first met. He was uncertain how she felt about him. Professional relationships were something he could handle, but the personal type made him break out in a sweat. He wasn't looking for any romantic involvement with her, because he had seen bad things happen to cops who got involved with each other. No woman was immune from joining his fantasy harem, though.

Stirring the tea, she continued.

"The hospital added a signature pad on the units where the doctor could actually scrawl one of those illegible signatures. It would be verified against a half dozen samples on file. Since people don't sign their signatures exactly the same way every time, each physician entered six base signatures on six different days. There's an algorithm that's supposed to come up with an 'average' signature. Each physician would have to reenter the base signatures every year, since signatures change over time depending upon a lot of things: eyesight, age, medications, physical conditions such as arthritis or surgery on the hand or arm. The signature recognition routine in the program is supposed to achieve 99 percent accuracy. Wood Memorial's only manages to make a correct match about one in three times. That isn't good enough, so the signature pads aren't being used."

"How come they can't get it fixed?"

"The software vendor would very much like to know that. They're stumped. The same programs running at other hospitals meet the validation criteria."

"So the signature recognition may have been sabotaged, too, forcing the hospital to rely on passwords instead."

"Yup."

PJ's chowder arrived, along with about ten individual packs of oyster crackers. It smelled good, kind of clean and comfortable, like Mom's kitchen on the farm where he grew up. He looked down at his half-eaten burger and hot-sauced fries, thinking that perhaps he should try some other items from the diner's menu, for variety if not for health reasons. Then he shrugged. He was what he was.

PJ used three packs of crackers, and stacked the rest into a tower. He wanted to ask her about Helen, but a sudden sharp and uncharacteristic shyness kept him from mentioning it. He would have to wait until she got around to it.

"Did you get a chance to talk to Charles Horner?" she said.

"The Snake? Yeah. I must admit old Rowena had him pegged. He's forty, married to Patricia Clark, Rowena's youngest daughter, a real spring chicken at forty-nine. Her third marriage, his first. He fancies himself a tough businessman, but everything he tries turns to shit. When it does, he goes to his wife with a hard-luck story, and she bankrolls him in something else. Eventually, Mama convinced her daughter that he should stand on his own two feet.''

A memory of Schultz's own son flared in his mind, so intense that he closed his eyes for a moment. Rick was twenty-five, a shiftless slob who had turned to drug dealing so he wouldn't have to get a real job. The two of them had a confrontation that had gotten physical when Schultz refused to use his influence to get the drug charges dropped. Schultz felt that the only way Rick would ever shape up was to be held accountable for his actions. Rick was serving twelve months in prison, and Schultz worried constantly that he had made the wrong decision. He was keeping tabs on his son through contacts at the prison. After three months inside, it seemed that Rick was an *unrepentant* shiftless slob.

"That's when Charles started selling family heirlooms—the Clarks', not his—to pay off debts," Schultz said.

"So he probably thought that without Mama in the picture, he could continue to manipulate his wife."

"I've got to admit he came off as smug during our little talk. Looked like a fox with a decent alibi, but the chicken feathers are right there hanging out of his mouth. He's definitely up to something, probably humping the maid and thinks his wife doesn't know. Murder? Motive's there. Smarts are not. It isn't any big surprise that his business efforts failed. We're talking one step above a lump of clay."

"Which fits in nicely with your theory that somebody hired Dr. Graham, on whom suspicion now lies like an oil slick in a parking lot."

"Hey, I like that. Sounds like something I'd say, only it's missing the cuss words."

PJ paused for a moment, and he knew that she was trying to figure out which cuss words would have been appropriate in what she said, and coming up blank.

Limited imagination, that's her problem, Schultz thought. *One of them.*

"The problem is," PJ continued, "I don't think she would have been able to do the computer tampering either. So that means a third party, and the bad guys would be tripping over each other." She sipped her tea. "I wonder what Patricia Clark sees in Charles."

"Maybe he's got a horse dick. Shit, who knows? Rich broads have their own rules. Maybe she's in cahoots with him, couldn't care less about hubby's business failures but wants to bump off Mama for her own reasons. Wouldn't be the first daughter to have that thought cross her mind."

Schultz was polishing off the last of his burger when he saw PJ reach toward an opaque blue contraption fastened to her waist. She pulled it off and pressed a button. Now that he could see it clearly, he realized it was a pager.

"I just got paged," she said, looking at the readout. "It's Howard's number." She waved Millie over to get change for the telephone.

"How did you get a pager?" Schultz asked. "I didn't get one." He hadn't heard the annoying beeping, so she must have had the gadget set on vibration mode.

"I requisitioned one for each of us weeks ago. I'm beginning to think Howard buries paperwork on his desk on purpose. I finally got tired of waiting and bought one myself. Today, in fact, on the way over here. I signed up for the monthly service and called Howard to leave him the pager number. I didn't think it would get used so quickly."

"You mean the department's not paying for that?" Schultz was amazed that she actually spent her own money on something job-related.

"Don't look so astonished, Detective. At least I got to

choose the color. Besides, this means Howard doesn't have any excuse for not calling me first."

She walked over to the pay phone near the bathrooms. While she was gone, he counted out money to pay both of their bills to the penny, then added his customary quarter tip. He debated briefly whether two quarters were necessary since there were technically two bills, then decided Millie could take it or leave it. When PJ came back, he could tell by the look on her face that the news wasn't good.

"Howard says there was another tampering incident at the hospital. A patient of Dr. Graham's who is diabetic was given too much insulin by a temp nurse. There was a medication order for the wrong dosage, electronically signed by Dr. Graham and confirmed by the pharmacist, who had to override a built-in fail-safe in the ordering system."

"Dead?"

"No, thank God. An alert nursing supervisor caught the situation before the insulin shock became fatal."

"Come on, let's get over to the hospital."

"Yeah, I'll drive. You going to eat those?" Schultz nodded at the packs of oyster crackers. She shook her head, and Schultz scooped them into his back pants pocket.

"I got a can of chili at home. No sense wasting them."

Schultz and PJ were greeted by an agitated hospital president in his outer office. The greetings were verbal only, no handshakes. Schultz had seen the type before, the ones who thought every germ in the world was out to get them personally.

In his opinion, this guy was pretty far gone.

Seeing Bert Manning's office confirmed Schultz's opinion. He sat down heavily on one of the vinyl chairs. There was a loud crunching noise as his posterior hit the hard

plastic seat. He glanced at PJ and was pleased to see that
her face was professionally composed, for which he gave
her a great deal of credit.

Schultz let PJ take the lead. She had already met the
man, and seemed to have a good handle on Manning. He
made himself as unobtrusive as possible, but he was a tall,
thick man who managed to look disheveled straight out
of the shower in the morning. He knew there were circumstances under which he could blend in and not be noticeable, but these clinical surroundings just weren't the ticket.
He crossed his arms over his belly, aware that what was
once hard and muscular no longer was, and that he was
missing the first button that showed above his belt. At least
he had done the laundry yesterday, so his undershirt was
clean.

At least he had put on an undershirt.

As the president calmed down somewhat, Schultz found
out that the diabetic patient, a man named Jerry Rogers,
was twenty-three years old, unmarried, and not wealthy.
The only thing he had in common with Rowena Clark was
his choice of physician.

Manning seemed scared, and that made him a little
more cooperative.

"Of course we'll cut off dial-in access immediately, as
you suggested earlier, Dr. Gray. I'm not convinced that's
the problem, but we should take precautions anyway. We
certainly don't want to place any more of our patients in
danger."

"Actually, I have something else to propose," PJ said.
"I want you to keep the lines up. We might be able to trap
whoever's doing this."

Schultz perked up. She hadn't mentioned this to him,
which annoyed him. He didn't like being blindsided—
although he wasn't above doing it himself—and she had
already aced him out today with that pager business.

"Tell us both about it, Doc," he said, letting the annoyance slip in. She didn't react.

"Let's go with the assumption that someone is targeting Dr. Graham's patients. That means that risk for the hospital's other patients is minimal, but I don't want to take chances. The entire hospital should go back to manual procedures—you must have them in place in case of catastrophic computer failure—except for Dr. Graham's patients. The killer may be checking on her patients, so it's important to keep entering orders into the computer as usual to show changes in their records, but make sure the staff is using the backup procedures. Double-check everything against the manual records for safety. That's the first part of the plan. The second part is to set up a fake patient in the computer, a high-profile one with lots of tempting meds and procedures, and see if the killer goes for it. We can program a trap in the fake patient's records, like a land mine. If anyone trips it by altering the records, the trap will automatically record the source of the tampering."

Schultz was skeptical, but it didn't seem like any of the real patients would be in danger if the staff stopped relying on the computerized records, so he didn't voice any doubts. Besides, he believed that the department should present a united front when dealing with the public. He would ream PJ later for not briefing him about her plans.

He let his eyelids slide down and tried to get in touch with whatever it was inside him that helped him in his investigations. He visualized the golden thread that would eventually connect him to the killer and let it cast about, the far end groping into the unknown. It seemed stronger, seemed to glimmer more than the last time he tried it.

PJ was on the right track.

When they stood up to leave, he lingered a moment and emptied his back pocket, putting the crushed packages of oyster crackers in Manning's wastebasket.

CHAPTER

7

Billy Carpenter sits up in bed. He hugs his knees and thinks hard about his throbbing toe. It helps to block out the voices, the mad, bad voices that are having a fight down the hall. Dad and Mom Elly are yelling at each other, something about 'puters and money and cheating and lying. Billy knows about cheating and lying. He knows it isn't right.

Dad says so. Dad always knows.

He had stubbed his toe on his wooden toy chest as he hurried to bed to pull the covers up, cover up his ears, not let in the bad voices. His toe hurts really bad, but he knows no one will come to rub it just now. Not Dad. Certainly not Mom Elly. So he squeezes the tears out of his eyes and crawls under the blankets. He tries to make himself as small as possible, tries to quiet his ragged breathing. If he is perfect, a perfect boy having a perfect bedtime in a perfect family, then the fighting will stop.

Maybe they are fighting about him. He thinks back over what he had done that day at Kiddy Care. He had done some things wrong, little things mostly, the kind that only he knows about. If he doesn't tell anyone, those things don't count. But one thing isn't so little. Jeffy had brought in a robot with eyes that flashed for show-and-tell. It was the most wonderful toy Billy had ever seen. He wanted it. He should have it. When Jeffy wouldn't let go, Billy had smacked him in the mouth hard enough to make his lip bleed. Miss Pamela hadn't seen. Everything would have been OK if Jeffy had just made up a story, said he fell and cut his lip on a building block. But no, he had to point at Billy with his finger all bloody from checking out his lip. When Miss Pamela asked him if he had done it, Billy could have lied. But Dad said lying was bad. So Billy had to stand in the corner and got a note sent home. Stupid Jeffy, whose lip puffed up even though he got to use the owie bag from the freezer, teased him all afternoon with the robot.

Now Dad and Mom Elly are having the worst fight ever. They have to be fighting about him. One of the few words he makes out is "liar." He shivers as the bad voices come flying down the hallway, through his closed bedroom door, and right at him under the covers, in the darkness where he smells his own toothpaste breath. His toe hurts, and now his tummy hurts, too. Suddenly he realizes he isn't under the blankets anymore, although he can't remember tossing them off. He is sitting up in bed, knees pressing against his chest, prickly feelings dancing down his arms and legs, tears warm on his cheeks. Some part of him wonders if his toe is bleeding. Maybe he should turn on the light and see.

Then he hears the crash, and the silence afterward.

Something about the silence scares him a lot more than the fighting. He smells the piss smell and realizes that his jammies are wet. On top of everything else, he has to pee in his pants.

He will never be a perfect boy.

Have Dad and Mom Elly stopped yelling at each other

so that they could come and yell at him? Dad doesn't usually do that kind of stuff, but Mom Elly does, when Dad isn't around. Is it quiet because she's creeping down the hall toward his room? What will she do to him? Eat him, like the evil old witch tried to eat Hansel and Gretel? Mom Elly isn't that old, but he is pretty sure she is a witch, and he knows with all the fervor of his four-year-old heart that witches are evil.

Silence.

His heart thuds loudly as the silence beats upon him with its dark wings.

He slips his legs over the edge of the bed, thinking that he could hide in the closet if Mr. Gotcha didn't already live in there. He moves carefully across his room in the darkness, missing the toy chest this time. He goes to the dresser for clean jammies, finding the right drawer with his hands. If he can just clean up, maybe no one will know.

Silence, thick and black.

He sleeps without a lamp or night-light because he wants to show Dad how grown up he is after getting four candles on his cake. Most nights he misses his old Pooh Bear lamp, but now he is glad there is no light. If something awful comes to his room, then it won't be able to see him, and he won't have to see it. He strains to hear, thinks that he might hear low voices, then decides it was just angels talking into his ears, like Dad says.

Dad always knows.

He fumbles with his wet clothes. They seem glued to his skin. Finally he gets them off and puts on the dry ones. Once that's done, his fear bursts on him again, and he stands shivering, like the time he saw the Headless Horseman on TV throw the pumpkin at Ichabod Crane. His feet touch the cold, wet pile of clothing. If he is going to pretend he hadn't peed in his pants, he will have to get the wet jammies out of his room and into the hamper in the bathroom. He can shove them down, put a wet towel on top of them, and maybe no one will know. He gathers up the wet things in his arms and moves toward the door. He is frightened, but he wants those clothes out of his room.

He puts his hand on the doorknob and stops. What if something is right outside the door? Something worse than the evil witch, something so big and terrible he will be swallowed up before he can cross his fingers and toes and eyes to protect himself? He listens carefully for the grinding of sharp teeth or the slow heavy breathing of a giant.

Silence.

There are no monsters. Dad says so.

Holding his breath, he twists the doorknob.

CHAPTER

8

PJ spent the morning in her office at the downtown St. Louis Police Department headquarters. Although it had a lived-in feeling now, her office used to be a utility room. The floor still had rusty circles from the bottoms of buckets, but the walls were clean, freshly painted with three coats of Pearl Lustre White. PJ and her son had come in one weekend soon after she was hired. They had to scrub the walls, starting at the top and working down, with an industrial cleaner obtained from the newly christened utility closet down the hall. Layers of dirt and cigarette smoke dissolved and streaked down toward the baseboard. It took all of Saturday to clean the walls and put on the first coat of paint. Sunday was coat two, lunch, coat three, home, baths, bed. PJ had brought personal items to the office: wildlife prints on the walls, pictures of Thomas, her Mickey Mouse clock, a desk lamp to minimize use of the buzzing overhead fluorescents, and a fan. The fan was in use this morning, creating enough air circulation in the small room so that she could have the door closed to block out the noise from the men's bathroom across the hall.

She had a scarred wooden desk and a green vinyl swivel chair that protested if she tried to lean back in it. On the wall across from her was a blackboard with a few items taped to it: photos of Rowena Clark, before and after her hospital stay; an article about Dr. Graham, with a photo of her at a fund-raiser rubbing elbows with the city's VIPs; and a school-year calendar with a big red C for cupcakes on the Wednesday before Halloween. A square wooden table with flaking green paint and a gray metal file cabinet occupied one corner of the office, and the rest of the floor space was taken up by two metal folding chairs for visitors. There were no windows.

Most of the work surfaces in the office were occupied by computer equipment. Her Silicon Graphics workstation had been purchased using money from a special grant, and then the department had set about hiring someone to use it. PJ was a civilian employee of the department, meaning she hadn't attended police training, yet she was in charge of trained law-enforcement officers. She had been leery of that role from the beginning, and was still struggling with the us/them attitude. She was trying to prove herself in so many arenas: as a computer professional, psychologist and criminal profiler, project head, investigator, woman, and single parent. Sometimes she felt as though she would fly apart from the stress, but on other days she managed to integrate all of her roles smoothly, and those days were becoming more numerous.

Today she picked up the reins and set off at a gallop.

Her first task was installing the modem she had purchased the evening before. She had put in a requisition for a sophisticated dial-back modem for her workstation which would offer some security. When she called from home, her call would be intercepted and the modem would dial her back, allowing only the phone connections it had been programmed to accept. But her requisition sat for weeks on Lieutenant Wall's desk, along with her request for a pager. She had decided to take matters into her own hands, and had purchased a pager and an inexpensive modem with her own carefully monitored cash.

It had finally dawned on her, as she suspected Schultz had known all along, that her requisitions wouldn't be approved. CHIP was, except for its initial grant funding, a low-budget project.

She tested the modem by connecting to a bulletin board dedicated to VR enthusiasts. She was a paid subscriber. The board had about five hundred members, whose dues paid for a computer which sat in somebody's basement, connected to a phone system that would do a mail-order company proud. After logging on, she posted a cryptic message in one of the folders. The message was meaningless, but contained key words that would be picked up by Merlin's background monitoring program. She entered one of the private chat rooms and waited. Soon words appeared on her monitor.

Merlin here. What's the buzz, Keypunch?

PJ's screen name was Keypunch. The name referred to her reputation during college as a fast and accurate keypuncher. At that time, programs and data were entered into mainframe computers via keypunched cards, which were rectangles of flexible cardboard with holes punched in them in patterns. The decks of cards were placed in a cardreader and fed in to the computer, which interpreted the patterns of holes as instructions or data. Although it had been many years since PJ last sat at a keypunch machine, the nickname was still with her.

She quickly typed her response and sent it.

I'm all aglow with gratitude. Thomas and I both really appreciate the computer. Please pass that along to Neptune. Thomas invited his friend Winston over, and the boys were up until the wee hours trying it out. I'm sure they're both dead on their feet at school today.

Say what?

Don't play shy, you old codger. Thanks for putting out the word that I needed a new computer.

I'm usually right on top of things when there's credit to be claimed, especially from glowing women, but I'm in the dark on this, Keypunch. Better start at the beginning.

Really. You are exasperating at times. Yesterday morning there were two big boxes at my front door containing a few thousand dollars' worth of computer equipment. There was a note that said something like 'From a friend of Merlin's, signed Neptune.' I assumed you mentioned to other people you talk to that my computer had been smashed and I didn't have enough money for another one.

I do talk to others who are not nearly as financially challenged as you are, and now that you mention it, it would have been a good deed to prod one of them into parting with some excess hardware. But I can't take the credit. Also, the name Neptune means nothing to me.

Are you sure you didn't mention anything casually?

I may be an old codger, but my memory's excellent.

PJ wondered if anything could be read into that statement. But if Merlin was a complicated computer program, he had unparalleled routines for humor and sensitivity. Before she could think of anything else to say, another message came back from Merlin.

I'm a little uneasy with this, Keypunch.

I'm getting there myself after what you told me. Maybe I should try to give the equipment back. I wouldn't know how, though. The boxes didn't have return addresses.

Hmm . . . Neptune. I'll ask around, shake the tree a little, and see if any fruit falls off. Or nuts, in the case of most of my friends. In the meantime, you think about who would have known about your computerless state. The answer to this little mystery might be right under our cybernoses.

So you think it's OK to keep it? I feel like Bob Cratchit getting the Christmas goose from Anonymous.

Might as well make the most of it. Secrets do spice things up. Which leads me to today's list:

1. *If you find anything that's free, doesn't have a lot of calories, and doesn't ask for respect in the morning, keep it a secret.*
2. *The secret trapdoor is always in the ceiling, where you least expect it.*
3. *I know a great secret getaway vacation spot, and you don't.*
4. *The word for the day is secret. Secrets can be good or bad. Secret treasure and secret love are always good.*

You're just a romantic fool, Merlin, PJ typed.

Fool, maybe. Speaking of romance, how's it going with Michael?

Merlin was in his matchmaker mode again, poking into how PJ was getting along with Dr. Michael Wolf, a biomedical engineer from Washington University. Merlin had arranged for Michael to lend PJ a piece of computer equipment called an HMD—head-mounted display—to use in her VR simulations. PJ was interested in the man, who was warm, intelligent, and raising two daughters on his own. She just wasn't sure *how* she was interested in him.

The first time Mike invited her to his home for dinner, she primed herself for a sexual encounter and showed up in a sexy black dress with condoms tucked away in her purse. Their expectations for the evening didn't match, and she ended up leaving early when Mike had to go pick up his daughter from a date turned sour. Embarrassed by her presumptuous behavior, she avoided him afterward, especially since he was so gracious about the whole thing. He wasn't willing to let things drop, so finally she accepted the friendship he offered. She enjoyed his company, although his sadness and regret about his former wife frequently intruded. He didn't want to talk about her yet, and PJ was willing to wait until he was ready.

Mike was content with friendship, but PJ wanted something more intimate. He didn't seem to be the type who only valued appearance, but she was just insecure enough sexually to think that perhaps her body turned him off. She was much more confident about her independence and single parenthood now than she had been right after her divorce from Steven. She knew now that she didn't *need* a man in her life, but she *wanted* one. She felt that Mike could be that man, but if the spark wasn't there on his side, she'd just have to find someone who could welcome a forty-year-old woman with twenty extra pounds and a twelve-year-old son into his heart.

She considered her response to Merlin carefully, because she thought it would probably get back to Mike.

He's a really nice guy, but we seem to be stuck in a brother-sister thing. I'd like to move our relationship to man-woman, but sometimes I think he's intimidated by me. Because I'm a shrink.

I doubt it. I can't see Mike being intimidated by anything short of a supernova. How about tweaking him a little? See if you can make him jealous.

I'm a bit beyond teenage love games.

Oh, really? Then I suppose tempting him with a slinky dress and no bra is too mature for you.

Mike told you that?

Merlin sees all, knows all, tells only a small portion.

Sounds to me like Merlin lives vicariously and needs to get a life of his own. I just had a thought: Mike could be the one who sent me the computer equipment. He knows the whole story of my dead computer.

If so, he probably hopes you'll figure it out.

There was a knock at PJ's office door, followed immediately by Schultz's entrance. He looked as though he had slept in the clothes he was wearing, and the fan carried over an odor that caused her nose to wrinkle. The office

suddenly felt too hot and cramped. She upped the fan
from slow to medium. Schultz didn't seem perturbed by
the fact that she was busy at the computer. He inflicted
his bulk on one of the folding chairs and waited, eyes
unfocused but somehow attentive, like a frog waiting for
the movement of a fly to trigger a lightning response.

*I'll drop some hints and see how Mike reacts. Gotta go now.
Take care, Keypunch.*

"Come in and make yourself at home, Detective," PJ
said. The eyes slid up and met hers. The challenge that
she saw in those eyes had unnerved her a little at first, but
now she found it appropriate. It came with the package.

"Don't mind if I do."

"I wanted to discuss something that happened yesterday.
I talked with Dr. Graham again, this time in her office. I
was trying to get a feel for how knowledgeable she is about
computers, and specifically about the hospital's computer
system."

"And?"

"I would rate her as average. She's comfortable with the
user end of the system, the part that she has to deal with
to do her job. I can't see her doing anything nearly as
sophisticated as the tampering that killed Rowena Clark
and almost killed Jerry Rogers."

"So she's not on your suspect list."

"No. In fact, I think she's a victim. Somebody's trying
hard to make her look incompetent."

Schultz scowled. "I'm not ready to let her off the hook.
My gut—or maybe it's my nose—tells me she smells bad.
She's got a scent of wrongdoing about her."

"How poetic. I don't like the woman either. When I was
in her office, I noticed that her composure slipped. For
just a moment, her face showed surprise, or fear, I'm not
sure what. She was glancing at her monitor at the time.
From where I was sitting I saw something flash on the
screen but couldn't make it out. She quickly erased the

screen and tried to cover up her reaction by saying that a staff member had sent her an obscene message, apparently as a joke.''

Schultz was sitting forward in the chair. "You thinking blackmail?''

"Would Charles the Snake be up to it?''

"He hasn't got the balls for it. That wouldn't be his style. Sneaky, that's what Charles is.''

"So where does that leave us?''

"In the usual spot, Doc,'' Schultz said. "Up shit creek without a canoe.''

"Isn't that without a paddle?''

Schultz shrugged.

PJ turned back to the computer, frowning. "Anita got almost all of the information entered in last night for the simulation. I'm not sure why CHIP was assigned to this case. I don't think examining Rowena Clark's death in VR is going to give us any new information.''

The frown deepened as PJ realized that she was bothered by this case for exactly that reason: her skills didn't seem to be necessary. Schultz had done a one-eighty, going from disinterest to apparent fascination. Was she missing something that he had picked up?

"Keep that up and your face will freeze that way,'' Schultz said. "Didn't your mama ever use that one on you?''

His humor pushed the frown from her face. "Yes, and I've passed on the tradition to Thomas,'' she said. Her practiced fingers called up the simulation, and she angled the screen toward Schultz.

"No helmet? No gloves?'' he said.

"Not for a first run-through. You can immerse later, if you think it would be worthwhile.''

The software PJ had developed allowed her to create a spatial environment within a computer's memory and disk storage, an environment as simple as a maze for a child's game or as complex as an operating room in a hospital. Events happened in real time, so if it took three seconds to walk across a room, it took three seconds to "cross" that same room in a VR simulation. There were two ways to experience it. A user could simply watch the world on the computer screen, which is known as "looking through the window." Everything was simulated on a scale of twenty-four to one, so a six-foot person appeared to be three inches tall on the screen. Objects looked 3-D, but only by clever shading and use of perspective. Three-dimensional movies carried the illusion one step further, by projecting two images slightly offset from each other. The special glasses worn by the audience melded the images together and achieved a better-than-flat effect.

A better way to experience VR was to "immerse," placing yourself directly in the simulation using a head-mounted display worn like a helmet. Inside were two small computer screens which project images to each of your eyes separately so that the mind interpreted three-dimensional vision. The helmet blocked other visual input, so a user saw only the virtual world. More powerful systems also incorporated a data glove, handheld input device, or body-suit which contained sensors that detect finger, hand, or body movement. Software translated those movements into movements within the virtual world, so a user could walk through the environment and even handle virtual objects, which were reactive to touch. There was complete freedom to move, turn, or look in any direction.

Some people couldn't take it. Their eyes said *Wow! We're really getting somewhere!* while their inner ears said *Nope. Standing still.* Result: nausea, dizziness, headaches.

Immersion allows an architect to walk through a building before laying the first brick or an automobile designer to sit inside a new model long before it hits the assembly line. Or an investigator to witness a crime that's already happened. When PJ first tried entering a murder scene from the killer's viewpoint, she found it eerie, terrifying, and sickening. Her psychologist's objectivity was scant protection against experiencing the darkness of a human soul, not just by hearing about it but by living it.

Immersing didn't seem to faze Schultz, either physically or emotionally, so she generally left it to him.

Displayed on the screen was a 3-D view of the nursing station outside Rowena Clark's hospital room. A perfectly scaled female figure stood behind the counter, dressed in a nurse's uniform. The figure was still.

"That doesn't look like Helen," Schultz commented. "Not wide enough or mean enough. Looks like she's missing her warts and witch's hat, too."

"Funny man. One of these days I'll put you in a simulation and you'll find out how the rest of the world actually sees you."

"An exhilarating experience, no doubt. Be sure to try it on yourself first."

PJ ignored him and pointed to the figure on the screen. "You're forgetting that Helen wasn't on duty when the victim died. That's a Genfem, a generic female character. If I have a chance, I scan in a photo of a person and replace the Genfem or Genman or Genkid. It's a lot more important when you immerse, because then all the characters look life-sized instead of three inches tall, so you can see their faces better. The computer animates the facial features and general body shape from the scanned photo. I call it scanimating, from scan and animate. I can get the lips to move in sync with the words—more or less—and there are gross facial expressions, but subtle ones are lost. Most of the time it looks pretty good. For now, you'll have to use your bountiful imagination."

"You have no idea how bountiful my imagination is, Doc."

PJ's software departed from the norm because it used artificial intelligence, or AI, to extrapolate situations to a logical conclusion. She could manually try out different sequences and perspectives, forcing the action in the direction she wanted to go. Or she could set up an initial condition and let the computer take it from there, showing her some possible scenarios. She was working on enhancing the AI with fuzzy logic, which meant giving the computer the ability to take into account more than concrete factors when making a decision. If a person had an appointment two miles away in fifteen minutes and could only walk three miles an hour, a computer would decide that it was logical to take a faster mode of transportation. But a person, using the fuzzy logic that was the delight of the human race, might choose to walk anyway, to savor a beautiful spring day, to purposely annoy the person waiting, or to put off an unpleasant encounter. PJ was very interested in fuzzy logic, because, as a psychologist, she ran into it all the time. She was still a long way from incorporating anything resembling human decision-making into her models.

"I started at 6:00 A.M., when Rowena was given routine medications," she said. "Here, let me put a clock on the screen that will show the playback time." She fingered a few keys and a digital clock appeared in the upper right corner of the screen, counting off the seconds so fast the numbers were a blur. The Genfem dashed jerkily back and forth behind the counter. "I don't want to sit here for five and a half hours, which is the elapsed time of the whole simulation, so I've sped up parts where there is no interaction with Rowena."

Schultz leaned his elbows on the desk and cradled his large head in his hands. The light from her desk lamp reflected from the bald spot on his crown. She watched him watching. His gaze was intent, his eyes unreadable, lips slightly apart. His strong initial resistance to computers had given way to a reluctant acceptance that there might be some contribution to his work, but he would never rely upon them exclusively. PJ had learned to value his skepticism. It forced her to examine an issue from many vantage points instead of just the computer's.

Abruptly the simulation dropped into real time, and a figure that was a twin to the one behind the counter entered the scene, pushing a cart with rows of something too small to be made out as anything but circles.

"What are those things on the cart?"

"Individual doses of meds are put in plastic cups with patient ID labels on the outside. It's called the unit dose system. The lower shelves contain preloaded syringes and bags of drug solutions which are piggybacked onto IVs. Wood Memorial uses an RN to deliver all the meds, so the nurse can administer by IV or syringe. Some hospitals send the oral meds separately via nurse's aide. Since a respirator tube had taken up residence in Rowena's throat, she had to take all her meds by some other route."

The twins on the monitor talked briefly.

"Can we actually hear what they're saying?" Schultz asked.

PJ leaned over and turned up the volume on both of the detached speakers.

"When I have transcripts or statements," she said, "then the characters actually say meaningful things. Otherwise, the computer invents conversation based on a mood parameter: angry, curious, concerned, neutral small talk. I even have a value for whispering sweet nothings, but I haven't had a chance to use it yet."

"Doesn't surprise me in the least. You need to get out more, Doc."

The cart was rolled away from the nursing station. The 3-D surroundings changed to show a hallway, then the entrance to Rowena Clark's room, then a woman lying in a bed. The head of the bed was elevated, so the woman was bent at the waist, her upper body at a slant. The woman was recognizable as Rowena, if PJ squinted just right. It was one of her scanimated creations. Schultz actually winced as Rowena got an injection.

The simulation sped up. There was no relevant activity for another couple of hours. At about eight-thirty, a Gen-fem nurse came to record Rowena's vitals: blood pressure, temperature, pulse. On her heels, a diminutive Dr. Graham entered the room. Schultz raised his eyebrows.

"I found her picture in a hospital newsletter," PJ said.

The nurse recorded the measurement into a handheld computer while Dr. Graham conducted a brief exam and got some questions answered with nods or shakes of Rowe-na's head. Dr. Graham then used the same handheld computer to enter her observations, and left the room.

"Christ, there goes a seventy-five-buck charge on the old lady's bill," Schultz said, "for maybe three minutes of the good doctor's time."

At five minutes after nine, a Genman entered Rowena's room and began a discussion. Rowena used her PDS to type in messages to the man: what he read obviously made him mad. He began gesturing, ending up by giving her the finger.

"Anita put that part in," PJ said. "That's supposed to be Charles, of course."

"Nice touch."

Rowena pointed to the door, and Charles left in a huff. A three-inch-high huff, but one that got the point across.

At nine-forty-five, respiratory therapy tech Joe Argyle came into the room.

"Got him from personnel files," PJ said. "He's grown a mustache since his badge photo was taken. I tried to add one in, but it doesn't look very good."

"That's OK. I don't think we have a case of Murder by Mustache."

PJ glanced sharply at him, but his face was enveloped in an aura of innocence she wouldn't have thought possible.

Joe fiddled with the equipment next to Rowena's bed

while talking to her. His words were clear, not patter inserted by the computer. After a few moments, she seemed a little distressed and pointed to her throat. Joe reassured her that getting off the respirator was sometimes hard work, but that he and Dr. Graham had confidence that she could do it. He patted her hand, plumped the pillow behind her head, and left the room, saying that he would be back to check on her in a couple of hours.

The simulation sped up as soon as Joe left the room. PJ pulled her eyes from the screen, knowing what she would see next, and watched Schultz instead. His gaze didn't waver. The clock in the upper right corner of the screen impassively counted down the last minutes of Rowena's life. By ten o'clock, she was agitated, reaching hesitantly toward the nurse call button but pulling her hand away; by ten-thirty she was thrashing about, scrambling the tucked-in sheet and blanket; by eleven, she was lying still in the bed, the nurse call button loosely held in her right hand. At eleven-fifteen, a Genfem phlebotomist came into the room for a routine blood draw. She bent over Rowena, then pressed a button on the wall behind the bed. The room filled with nurses and doctors responding to the code. There was a flurry of activity, and then people began leaving the room. The simulation ended at twenty-eight minutes after eleven, Rowena's official time of death.

Schultz sat back, the chair creaking under him. "Shit. She had the button in her hand. Why didn't she call for help earlier?"

PJ sighed. "She may have been a terror with her family, but according to the nursing notes, she was cooperative, almost meek, with the medical staff. She probably felt they knew what was best for her and didn't want to be a bother, and then it was too late."

They sat for a minute or two while PJ tapped her pencil on the desk. "One thing that I doubt you've been considering is why the orders were left on file."

"Huh?"

"As far as we know, both patients had their computerized records tampered with and then restored to their original condition. Except for one thing. The final orders were left in place. Whoever left them there did it for one of two reasons: to implicate Dr. Graham, or to taunt the police. It's like saying, *'Look what I can do, and you can't stop me.'*"

"Arrogant. Sick."

"Or obsessed with Dr. Graham. Or all of those things. Why don't you spend some time digging around in Dr. Graham's life, see what could inspire that kind of obsession. You're good at that stuff."

"That *stuff* is pure old-fashioned detective work. The mainstay of this or any other investigation."

"Don't get your hackles up, Leo. It was meant to be a compliment."

"Oh. In that case, it'll be my pleasure. Let's see what the lady doctor has got in her closets. Bet it isn't just power suits, workout clothes, and scruffy old bunny slippers."

"That's the spirit." The frown surfaced on PJ's face again. "No results so far on my idea about simulating a high profile patient of Dr. Graham's with a vulnerable-looking chart. I got the fake patient put into the system, but the program trap hasn't caught any activity against it."

"Maybe the killer found out it wasn't a real patient by calling that room number on the phone."

"Nice try. The president arranged for any calls to the room phone to be forwarded to Anita, who can wheeze really well. Anita said that my test call was the only one she's received."

PJ paused long enough that Schultz pushed himself up from the chair. She noticed that he rose rather smoothly for a man of his bulk. His arthritis medicine must be doing him some good. Every now and then, though, he would have a day of limping and gritting his teeth.

"There's something else I'd like to talk about, if you've got a few minutes," she said.

"Doc," Schultz said as he lowered himself back down, "you sometimes forget that you're the boss. You got something to say, you don't need my permission."

"Helen."

She wondered what it was that attracted Schultz to Helen. It probably wasn't her face or figure, and the side of her personality Helen had shown to Schultz so far wasn't endearing. She and Helen had gotten to know each other fairly well, as two women will do when left together for a couple of hours. PJ had a sense of Helen's immense strength of character, and the sensitivity and depth of caring she brought to her work but carefully shielded herself from in her personal life. Schultz had interacted with the woman for only a few minutes. How could he see through Helen's complex layers of protection?

Looking at it objectively, it was too soon after his separation from his wife. Any relationship he could develop now would have "rebound" written all over it.

PJ had found Helen easy to talk to, and had gotten into discussing the pain and anger surrounding her own divorce. It was the first time she had talked to another adult about it—except Merlin, and she wasn't quite sure what category he fit into in her life.

Schultz kept his face neutral with effort. Hearing Helen's name sent a jolt through him that played havoc with his insides, then settled as a nice tingle at the base of his spine. He wondered if that was what it felt like to be in love. He didn't remember that particular tingle from the time he courted his wife Julia back in the Ice Age, but it had been so long ago that maybe he had forgotten. Or was that something the body remembers, that first buzz of love, like riding a bike?

He and Julia had been many things together: lovers, parents, friends, companions, then for a long time just roommates, then not even that. Julia now lived with her sister in Chicago. Their son Rick was surely a factor in the breakup. Rick the screwup, Rick the drug pusher, Rick the convict. Schultz had been only a shadowy presence in the boy's life. He had his job and Julia had hers, and hers was the boy. Rick was their only child. After he was born, Julia's plumbing went wrong, some mysterious female thing, then an operation, then she couldn't have babies anymore.

When Rick first started going bad, skipping school and hanging out with the wrong crowd, he could have been nudged back into line. Later on, when he smashed mailboxes and got high on weekends and then on school nights, he could still have been shoved back. It just would have taken a bigger push. The older Rick got and the further he deviated from being a good cop's kid, the more caring, concern, and tough love it would have taken for the salvage operation. When Schultz opened his eyes, blinked, and took a look around the old homestead, he discovered that Julia was indulging a serious delinquent. He fought with her about it, but even then he let things slip. Finally the situation was dumped in his lap when Julia walked out. Schultz was determined that his son should pay for his drug-pushing by serving his sentence. Then Rick would get a fresh start, whether he wanted to or not.

There would have to be a fresh start for himself, too.

"Yeah," he said as casually as he could manage, "I was wondering if you'd had a chance to talk with her. I mean, I already paid for it."

"Thanks for the lunch at Millie's. You'll be glad to know I did earn it. The way we left it, Helen was supposed to call me if she'd changed her mind. She hasn't called, so I guess it's time to talk about it."

"Christ, you're making it sound so serious, like she's got a terminal disease or something." His knee started bouncing nervously, and with an effort, he stilled it. "Does she?"

"No, nothing like that. She . . ."

"She doesn't like men, that's it. Got the hots for young broads, probably lives with one. Two, even."

"Shut up, Detective, and let me talk. Did it ever occur to you that she just might not like you?"

Chastened, Schultz slouched down as well as the rickety folding chair would permit. "Yeah, it occurred to me. I'm no prize. But I've got my good points, and hell, she's no beauty contest winner either."

"Appearance isn't the issue. Did I say anything about appearance? Why do men think that's the only basis for a relationship?"

"Take it easy, Doc." He spread his hands out in front of him. "I've been known to keep my dick in my pants while actually standing within grabbing range of a woman. I have a shitload of social graces. Give me a little credit here."

He saw her settle back in her chair. The small red circles of anger that had formed beneath her cheekbones faded. The devil's fingerprints, his mother used to say. "Sorry. That really had nothing to do with you."

"OK, so give."

"Helen doesn't have any diseases and she isn't gay. She has grown children, twin girls, both doing family-practice residencies, one in California, one in New Mexico. She doesn't like you, said you were a pushy slob."

Schultz rubbed his hands together. "Seems like there's something there I could work on. Sometimes I don't exactly make a good first impression."

"She's also married."

Schultz felt his cheeks sag and his mouth fall open.

"Her husband Jack is in prison. He's a violent man, used to beat Helen when he was drunk, which was most of the time. Never touched the girls, though—Helen would probably have killed him on the spot. He beat a man to death outside a bar.''

''Christ.''

''She could divorce him, but she hasn't. Doesn't feel the need, since she's not planning to get involved with any other man. Says she's had enough of men to last her three lifetimes.''

''I'm not like that. I'd never lay a hand on her.''

''That's not the point,'' PJ said, her voice going soft, like a hand stroking his. ''It took her years to rebuild her life, to make it on her own. She's not the same person now as the woman Jack used as a punching bag. She's got her daughters, her job, and her self-respect. She's not looking for a man around the house,'' PJ said.

''Then we don't have to stay around the house. We could go out.''

''I'm genuinely sorry, Leo. But I think you should drop it. Some things just don't work out, no matter how much you want them.''

He stood up abruptly and headed for the door. ''What I said about appearances? I lied. Wouldn't be seen with that witch. She probably celebrates Halloween twelve months a year.''

Somehow the office door slammed a lot harder than he intended.

CHAPTER

9

The shades were pulled on the windows, so there was no light in Cracker's spare room except for the humming fluorescent on the desk. It was midday. There were remnants of lunch on the cluttered tabletop: a banana peel and a bowl with a chip in the rim which had held chicken noodle soup with enough crumbled saltines to sop up all the broth. The banana left an aftertaste in Cracker's mouth. He had found it under a newspaper on the kitchen counter, forgotten and overripe. He ate it anyway, and now it felt like it was fermenting in his stomach. He put the slight discomfort out of mind. Food, unless it was the emotionally laden fare prepared by Aunt Karen, held no attraction for him. Anything even remotely edible that was at hand would do. He felt tethered to his physical self by the messy processes of eating and elimination. Part of the appeal of his mechanical man fantasy was the severing of the tether.

The meal forgotten, Cracker went about some paying work. He was doing a profile on the mistress of a wealthy real-estate developer. His client was fifty-five, handsome, healthy, a millionaire many times over from his own efforts and from family money. The mistress was thirty years younger, a schoolteacher whom the client had met when she was trying to raise money for baseball diamonds for underprivileged kids. She had badgered him into donating a useless (to him) bit of floodplain that was under a foot of water nearly every March but dried out in time to get a late start on spring training. His client fell in love with the schoolteacher, and she professed to love him also. His client was ready to divorce his current wife, which was going to cost him plenty. Having a strong practical streak, the man wanted to learn a lot more about his young love before approaching his wife with divorce papers in hand. The profile detailed her consumer spending habits, financial situation, medical records, family background, criminal record (a couple of parking tickets), college transcript, employment record, hobbies, the results of two specialized surveys Cracker had paid a marketing company to conduct, phone company records, community and church involvement, charities, and even several poems the teacher had published in a college journal. Cracker was putting the finishing touches on his report. He never stated any conclusions about his findings. It was up to the clients to draw their own.

In this case, it was clear that the teacher was the real thing. There were wedding bells in his client's future, but Cracker didn't care one way or the other, except for the possibility of extra money. Clients who got the news they wanted to hear sometimes gave Cracker a bonus beyond the contracted amount. Those unhappy with the revelations given them never did. Cracker insisted on payment in advance, and with good reason.

A laser printer across the room perked up and began to deposit his report in its output tray.

"Another day, another fifteen thousand bucks," he said,

breaking a silence that had lasted since his visit to Aunt Karen. Sometimes Cracker went quite a while without seeing or speaking to anyone.

The printer was still shooting out pages as Cracker dialed up Wood Memorial Hospital. He checked the level of activity in the computer system, found that it was the same as yesterday—way down. That meant the hospital had gone to manual procedures, back to paper for everything. Except, that is, for one very interesting pattern. Orders were accumulating as thickly as flies on a cowpie in the files for Mom Elly's patients, including a newly admitted one. He supposed that a monitoring mechanism had been set up.

About time.

He bounced over the network to Mom Elly's computer and found it hooked up but inactive. She wasn't logged on. That was a shame. Yesterday he had gotten a kick out of sending her a message: a scanned-in old photo of himself as a child, with a caption that said *Hi, Mom Elly, I'm back!* He had signed it *Little Billy*. He would have loved to see her face when it popped up on her screen. As far as she knew, Little Billy committed suicide eight years ago. He even sent her a note at the time. He made sure some acquaintances of his heard him talking about putting an end to things, and then arranged for them to see him walking into the ocean. The body was never recovered, but Will Harvey Carpenter went into the California statistics as another teen suicide.

It bothered him about the fake patient and the attempt to trap him. It wasn't subtle enough to stand a chance against him—like throwing a snowball against the Great Wall of China—but it was irritating. He closed his eyes and thought about it for a while. After Rowena Clark died, he had checked Mom Elly's appointment schedule to see who was interviewing her. All of the staff at the hospital used the same schedule program to keep track of meetings.

Some time management consultant had sold the president on it last year. It had an automatic search, so that a secretary could enter the names of the meeting attendees and the length of the meeting. The program would examine all of their schedules and determine a time when all were available. It saved having a round-robin of telephone calls.

It also allowed Cracker to snoop into Mom Elly's comings and goings. And find the posting the day of the killing: *Det Schultz & Dr Gray, SLPD.*

Detective Schultz he had dismissed out of hand as a lowlife cop. No threat there. Dr. Gray was more intriguing. He had called the central information number for the St. Louis Police Department, asked to talk to Dr. Gray. He was put through to voice mail, from which he learned that Penelope Gray was away from her desk and would be happy to return his call. As if that was his mission in life, to make her happy. Then he had phoned the Human Resources Department, pretending to be an officer at a bank where Penelope Gray had applied for a loan. Human Resources, as he expected, was not forthcoming with a lot of information. Name, rank, serial number. He got a confirmation that she was employed by the SLPD and that her job title was Director, Computerized Homicide Investigations Project.

Bingo.

Now, just days after he found out about her, someone had tried to close him out of the hospital's records. He knew it had to be Lucky Penny. He considered finding the monitoring program and disabling the trap. It might be fun, and it would serve Penny right. He had already taken some action about her, the kind of defensive action that had kept him out of trouble in the past. Covering all his bases. Maybe he should do something more overt, shake her up a little.

No. Stay focused. Mom Elly is the target.

He got up and wandered from the room. In the kitchen,

he opened the refrigerator door, still a little hungry. Grazing. He saw a piece of pizza on a lower shelf and couldn't remember how long it had been there. He picked it up, inspected it, and found no fuzzy growths, so he heated it in the microwave. Halfway through the two minutes he had punched in, he got impatient. The slice was still cold on the inside, but down it went. It had a calming effect on the banana.

Cracker roamed the apartment restlessly. It was a habit he had: short periods of intense brainwork followed by coasting. He coasted into his bedroom and went to his dresser to close a couple of drawers he had left open that morning. As he shoved a tangle of socks back into one drawer, the framed photos on the dresser captured his attention. He gathered them up and sat down on the bed with them, the drawer forgotten.

One of the few things he had taken with him when he ran away from home was the collection of photos displayed on the desk in his father's den. Mom Elly had left the den alone, left it just as it was when his dad was alive. Cracker used to go in and sit in his father's desk chair, taking in the smells that evoked the man's presence: furniture polish, pipe tobacco, leather. He could hear himself giggling as Daddy bounced him on his knee, letting him ride the horsy to town.

Cracker picked up his favorite photograph, the one with Mom and Dad and himself as a baby. It was the same photo that was on the mantel in Aunt Karen's place. He had gotten several duplicates made. Mom was, of course, beautiful. She sat in a chair with the poise and grace of a resting cat, long-limbed, blond hair piled atop her head, a few strands curling down suggestively next to her delicate ears. She wore a flowery summer dress that bared her arms and enough of her legs to show that they were well formed. White sandals, showing a tip of red—her painted nails peeped through the open toes. In her lap, a baby in a tiny

sailor's outfit, asleep and enjoying it. Her gaze was directed
at the baby. She seemed oblivious to the photographer,
enraptured with the child, unable to pull her eyes away.
Standing just behind and to her right, Dad was tall and
handsome, trim with just a touch of thickening at his waist.
He wore khaki pants and a striped jersey. His hand rested
on her shoulder, drawing him into the bond between
mother and baby, but not showing resentment or jealousy.
Also lacking was that smug pride Cracker had seen on the
faces of other new fathers: *I really put it to my wife, and now
everybody can see what a man I am.*

Cracker had no memory of his mother. When he was
barely a year old, his mother was killed in an auto accident
when she lost control of her car on an icy highway. Dad
remarried a year later, and Mom Elly came into Cracker's
life.

Two years after that, when Cracker was four, his father
died. Although he was told that his father's death was due
to natural causes, he knew different.

Mom Elly murdered Dad.

He saw her do it.

He felt powerless to do anything about it then, and
concealed his knowledge both from his stepmother and
from himself by relegating the experience to a gruesome
recurring nightmare. Scenes of the nightmare flitted
through his head as he sat on the bed with his eyes closed.

A man running, unable to escape the harpy hovering
over him. The harpy dips frequently, raking at the man
with deadly claws. Then the maze—*no, no don't go in there's
no way out can't you see that don't you know what will happen*—
and the man is caught, trapped against a wall he cannot
scale. The harpy beats him down to the ground with blasts
of air from her wings. When he is prostrate, she lands and
bends over him, rips open his soft belly, and begins to
devour his organs while he watches. His hands hover tenta-
tively over the harpy's head, too late, too late, to pull her

from her grisly feast. The man turns his head and looks directly at the dreamer: mouth open and twisted, tendons standing in his neck, eyes hot, eyebrows shoved rudely together, creating fissures between them, convolutions like the picture of a brain Billy had seen in a book lying open on Mom Elly's desk.

The nightmare protected Billy for years, allowing him to function, to get along first at home and then at school. He withdrew into sullen behavior which masked his fear, and kept to himself. Mom Elly actually got counseling for him, but gradually both of them accepted the way he acted. Mom Elly seemed relieved that she was able to minimize her contact with him. At school, he did well academically but avoided social interaction. His young mind knew that delving into the events underneath the nightmare was too much for him to handle. It would be like turning over a rock and finding your own face, putrescent and wriggling with maggots.

One Saturday morning when Will was twelve, he was playing in his backyard with his dog Wart, tossing a ball and getting it back with a generous coating of slobber. Wart was a happy mutt who looked as though he had been assembled from spare parts lying around the dog factory. A rival dog barked out front, and Wart stiffened and got territorial. He took off at a dead run, Will a few yards behind. The other dog was across the street barking, its tail an erect challenge. Wart ran to meet the challenge, met instead the left front tire of a pickup truck. The truck kept going, tumbling Wart a short distance before leaving him in a bloody heap. Will, who had stopped at the curb, both hands pressed to his ears to block out the sounds, opened his mouth and wailed. The noise brought Mom Elly from inside the house. Assessing the situation immediately, she told Will in a firm voice to go into the house. He did so, numbly, mechanically, but he went to the front window and watched through the drapes.

Mom Elly went into the street, waving aside the few cars. Traffic was light in their residential area, but one truck had been too much for Wart. She knelt down and bent close to the dog, then sat back on her heels and shook her head. She went into the garage and returned with a black plastic garbage bag, eased the remains into it, and left the bag on the porch.

At the moment when she bent over the bloody carcass, something gave way in Will's mind. Walls hastily constructed when he was four years old shuddered and shattered in a web of tiny cracks, and memories seeped through.

He had seen her doing something like that before, bending over, leaning close, savoring death, bringing death to whatever she had trapped beneath her.

The night his father died.

Mom Elly, bending over him in the moonlight.

The white cloth pulled up over his father's face, the body hidden from sight but not from a little boy's imagination.

As his memories engulfed him, Will knew they had come back because now he was ready to face them. A twelve-year-old wasn't quite so helpless, a twelve-year-old could make plans. . . .

Stomach churning, blood racing with the intensity of the revelation, face hot and flushed, Will turned from the window and fled to his room. Mom Elly talked to him through the locked door, but he didn't answer, and she went away. He cried first for Wart, sobbing and wetting his pillow with tears. The dog had been a friend to a boy who had no others. After the first wave of anguish came another, more powerful, for his father. He buried his face in the damp pillow and let years of bottled-up grief wash over him.

When he finally slept that night, he welcomed the nightmare. The harpy now wore Mom Elly's face, and the torn man had his father's features. She had killed his father, and it was up to him to make her pay for it.

Make her pay for it.

Cracker opened his eyes, found himself sitting on the bed clutching the framed picture to his chest. He let wordless rage possess him, anger at Mom Elly for cheating him of the life he would have had with his father. He wouldn't have run away from home at fourteen, wouldn't have been so alone. He would be a big success now, maybe own his own software company, his picture on the front of *Newsweek*, women chasing him.

Dad said he was a superstar, and Dad always knew.

He bit his lip, tasted blood along with the injustice.

Things weren't moving along as well as he'd hoped. By this time, Mom Elly should have been under arrest or turned away from the hospital in disgrace.

Cracker never hesitated to switch plans when results eluded him. He made it a point never to invest too much of himself in one approach. That made it easy to walk away. He thought about his next move.

There was something else on the back burner, as there almost always was with Cracker. Snooping through the pharmacy orders and administrations at Wood Memorial, learning his way around the system way back when the Time Bomb was still a gleam in his eye, he had detected a pattern. He wasn't absolutely sure he had it right, but bluffing had worked in the past. Fifty percent of the adults in this country would turn as white as the thighs of his sixth-grade teacher, Miss Hillman, whom he had seen in shorts at a school picnic, if he sidled up beside them, and whispered, "I know what you did."

So he sidled, electronically, up to a nurse named Patricia Mulligan. He sent her an e-mail message.

Pitty-Pat: I know about the morphine and I know what you did with it. It's illegal, you know. I'm wondering who I should tell about it.

He thought she would ignore the first message, and she did. A couple of days later, he tweaked her with another message.

Pitty-Pat: Does this list seem familiar somehow?

He attached a list of drug reorders that all had her ID as the nurse doing the administration. Doses were marked "wasted," meaning they had been spilled, dropped, chewed and spit out by the patient, or for any of dozens of other reasons had become unusable. Replacements were requested and received. All of the orders were for a sustained-release preparation of morphine, taken orally and used for relief of severe chronic pain, most commonly in terminal patients.

The next day, he put the cards on the table, but didn't turn them face up.

Pitty-Pat: You killed Pearl Greeley. Your secret is safe IF you do something for me. I can cover your tracks better than you ever could. If you don't play, I'll go to the police. Think about it, and call me at 555-9893 tomorrow at 10 P.M.

The next night, when the phone rang outside the bathrooms at Hardee's at precisely ten, Cracker was there, takeout sack clutched in his right hand. He answered the phone, smiling. He liked it when people were as easy to manipulate as program code. He hoped it wouldn't take long, so that he could get home before the food got stone cold. All he had to do was enter the parameters and punch *EXECUTE.*

CHAPTER

10

At lunchtime on Friday, PJ walked over to a Chinese restaurant a couple of blocks away from her office, to get away from the building and out under the sun. The place was tiny, just a counter and four tables. She arrived right when it opened. She bought a newspaper from a dispenser outside, ordered at the counter, and plunked herself down at one of the Formica tables. The metal chair was undersized but well padded. Her Kung Pao chicken was fresh, steamy, and seasoned hot enough to bite back. She inhaled her jasmine tea, then sipped it while watching the pedestrians through the sparkling clean window.

The other tables were quickly occupied, and the place got hectic with the lunchtime crowd. PJ ate slowly and paged through the *Post-Dispatch*, letting the rush flow around her and trying not to feel guilty for taking up one-fourth of the seating capacity. By the time she opened her fortune cookie—*A wise person makes time for play*—the tide of customers had ebbed. On the walk back, she savored the outdoors, although the wind had shifted and the air was lightly scented with the products of the Anheuser-Busch brewery.

PJ wasn't eager to go back into her windowless office.

She used the afternoon to catch up on paperwork. CHIP's work on the Rowena Clark homicide was going nowhere. Without a break in the case, it looked as though the crime would go unsolved. Schultz was still checking into Charles the Snake's activities and digging up information on Dr. Eleanor Graham's background. He was tenacious, so something could still turn up. They weren't shaping up as likely suspects, though. Her direct involvement—analyzing the computer tampering, simulating the murder in VR, and setting up a phony patient to lure the killer—had yielded nothing but frustration.

The hospital president, Bert Manning, called her to say that they were going to continue on manual procedures through the weekend. Some hastily purchased additional security software was going to be installed Sunday night, and Monday morning the hospital would be back to full use of their computer system, including dial-up capabilities.

She pictured him on the other end of the phone, holding the disinfected handset slightly away from his ear, an alcohol wipe freshly deposited in the trash can next to the desk. His obsession was apparent to anyone who met him, but it didn't seem to be hindering him from doing his job. He had reached some sort of compromise. She, on the other hand, had an obsession that wasn't readily apparent. She didn't like to leave a task unfinished. If CHIP didn't resolve Rowena's murder, it would be PJ's first personal experience with the fact that sometimes the killer gets away with it.

In her practice as a psychologist, there were plenty of times when no closure was possible. A patient moved away or discontinued treatment against her advice. Sometimes only a limited solution was possible for a patient, a workaround for a deeper problem that the patient wasn't ready to face. When a patient left her, she could always hope for a better life for the person later on, perhaps with another therapist. She accepted these situations because she maintained some detachment. She cared deeply about her patients, but didn't submerge herself in their murky, troubled lives. She had to stay onshore and fling out the life preserver rather than swim out and get pulled under.

In her work with CHIP, she hadn't acquired enough professional detachment, and probably never would. Her life intersected that of a victim too late to add anything to the victim's life except justice. The people whose pictures got taped to her blackboard had been, with one painful exception so far, total strangers, but she felt a tremendous responsibility to them and to those who had been dear to them. All that was left for the homicide victims that came her way was the dignity of the grave—sometimes not even that—and her group, which was part of the larger criminal justice system.

She couldn't stay comfortable and dry anymore on the shore. She was committed, out there in the ocean. The water was cold and unthinkably deep, and the current was treacherous.

She wondered if Schultz ever explored these issues, and if she could talk with him about it. She knew he was a complex person who projected a simple image. She could imagine what he would say if she came out and asked him how he dealt emotionally with an unsolved case. Her ears would probably burn for a week.

By 4 P.M., PJ was anxious to get out of the office. Schultz was out somewhere, no doubt pinning innocent people to the wall and getting confessions from them. Dave and Anita were supposedly doing some paperwork assigned to them by Schultz. She walked down to the large room where their desks were wedged in with about twenty others. Anita was hunched over a textbook. She was taking night courses in criminal justice. Dave was sailing paper airplanes across the room at another young officer who seemed to be gritting his teeth.

CHIP's morale was plummeting on this case, so PJ decided to take the message in her fortune cookie seriously. Thinking herself very wise, and certainly ready to play, she called Mike Wolf to invite him for dinner and a few games of gin rummy. She caught him at his desk. He claimed to be suffering from "fall fever," and offered to leave work right away to have time to stop at the grocery store before showing up at her place.

At six o'clock, a freshly bathed PJ, hair still damp underneath where it brushed her shoulders, opened the door and helped Mike carry in a couple of bags. It was going to be a cold, clear night, and the air was already much cooler now that the sun was getting low. She hurried to close the door. She had already taken Thomas over to his friend Winston's house, where he would be spending the evening. Mike brought fixings for beef Stroganoff. In her small kitchen, they chatted lightly about their jobs while preparing the meal. Mike stirred the strips of beef as they sizzled and browned, while she sliced the mushrooms for the sauce and put the water on to boil to cook the noodles. She dumped the salads he had picked up at the grocery store's salad bar into large bowls and added some freshly ground pepper, then slipped the half-baked rolls from the store's bakery into the oven. Mike put the red wine into the refrigerator to chill it slightly. They worked so well together that it was already a comfortable joke between them. It seemed only minutes until they were facing each other across the kitchen table, the room filled with the aromas of rolls, the sour cream–and-mushroom sauce on the beef strips, and pepper on the salads. Mike poured them each a glass of wine, having picked out stubby old-fashioneds from her limited glassware assortment.

They ate companionably, like family, talking about their

kids. After the meal, Mike sliced apple pie while PJ put on a pot of coffee.

"I have a wonderful pie recipe," Mike said. "There are some orchards around here where you pick your own apples. I usually go at the end of September and get enough for five or six pies. I spend a whole day making and freezing them. The girls help, too. In the middle of winter we can just grab one from the freezer and in no time the house smells great."

"Is this one of your pies?"

"Oh, no. This one is store-bought. We used ours up months ago."

"Maybe we can get the kids together and all go to an orchard next weekend. You can give me your recipe. If you're willing to share it, that is."

Mike washed the dishes as PJ dried them and put them away. They went into the small living room, carrying glasses of wine. PJ brought the bottle, which had a little more than one glassful left in it.

"I've been waiting for this all summer," PJ said as she walked over to the marble hearth. Earlier, she had piled some kindling and a couple of small logs on top of crumpled newspaper. "I haven't had a chance to try out this fireplace. Tonight's the big night."

She used the long matches on the mantel to light the newspaper. The fireplace drew excellently, and in no time cheery flames snapped at the dry logs. Mike went out to the backyard and brought in an armful of wood from the half cord that PJ had gotten delivered.

"Before we get settled," PJ said, "I'd like to show you something new."

She led him into the study, where the Power Mac tower case sat on the floor next to the desk. The large monitor took up a lot of the small surface area. She watched his face closely, but his expression was neutral.

"This sweet little system popped up on our doorstep a

few days ago. There was a note saying that it was from a friend of Merlin's.''

"No kidding? That's great."

"It sure pays to be a friend of Merlin's," she hinted.

"I'll say it does. After all, I probably wouldn't have met you if it hadn't been for Merlin." He patted her arm affectionately.

So much for the subtle approach.

"I knew it was you all along," she said. "Thomas and I want to thank you."

Mike seemed genuinely perplexed. "But I didn't . . . Well, I wish I had, but I'm not the one who gave this system to you."

"You're not Neptune?"

"Scout's honor," Mike said, raising his hand.

She searched his face. Either he was a great actor, or he was telling the truth.

"I guess it's still a mystery, then," she said. "Why don't we go back in and enjoy the fire?"

PJ was hoping that Mike would sit on the couch so that they could be close enough to snuggle, but he plopped into an upholstered rocking chair. She took the couch, putting the glasses of wine on a small table between them. For a time there was no sound but the crackling fire. Megabite came in, sniffing in Mike's direction. She seemed miffed that PJ wasn't in her usual chair, but hopped up on the couch to make the best of things. The cat curled in PJ's lap.

"Steven—my ex-husband—was allergic to cats," PJ said. "I really enjoy having this one around. I didn't realize how much I missed having a cat." Megabite gently licked the hairs on PJ's forearm, no doubt wondering how the human kept warm with so little fur.

"My wife used to say that she was allergic to everything that made life fun," Mike said. "I think it was just psychological, though."

"How long were you married?" PJ asked, hoping to get Mike talking about his divorce. Sometimes she felt as though his ex-wife was in the same room with them.

"Almost eighteen years. It's been two years since the divorce." Mike lowered his gaze to his lap.

PJ let the silence stretch out. She was there, ready to listen. The good meal, the wine, the fire . . . What more could he ask for to finally open up?

"We had a good marriage. Great kids. Sally was depressed sometimes, but she always managed to snap out of it. Until the last time. That time she turned to drugs. She used to buy cocaine with the grocery money, and there'd be nothing in the house for the girls to eat until I went to the store."

He raised his eyes and looked at PJ. She nodded encouragingly, trying not to put on her professional face.

"I tried to get help for her. Medical help for her depression, counseling for her drug use. Nothing worked. She wouldn't admit she had a problem. She would go along with the treatment for a couple of visits, and then binge on cocaine. She lost weekends, sometimes an entire week. She couldn't function at work, and losing her job made her even more depressed."

"How were you and the girls getting along?"

"The girls couldn't help either, and that bothered them a lot. Their mom was falling to pieces in front of their eyes."

"That's rough."

Mike nodded. "Somewhere along the line I stopped being supportive and started feeling resentful. I filed for divorce, thinking that would shake her up."

PJ kept her face neutral. She thought she knew where this was heading.

"Finally, a group of us who were concerned about her got together to hold an intervention. That's when you force her to see the problems, tell her the effect she's having on others. Tell her you care, and you want her to get better. There were six of us, plus a counselor from a treatment center. The idea was to have an intense confrontation and persuade her to enter a residential program right then and there, leaving with the counselor.''

"How did it go?''

Mike squirmed in his chair. PJ could tell that he was uncomfortable, but he seemed to want to continue.

"We thought it went great. Sally broke down and cried, and agreed to enter the program. She left with the counselor. On the way there, she jumped out of his car at a stoplight and took off. All of us were worried sick. We didn't hear from her for three days. Then a hospital notified me that she had tried to commit suicide.''

Mike's voice was low. The walls of the room absorbed the sound and softened it further. PJ felt as though she was in a museum where everyone spoke in hushed, reverent tones.

"She shot herself in the head. There was a lot of brain damage. She's in a wheelchair now, functioning about on the three-year-old level. She's finally in a residential facility, but not the way we intended it to be.''

"I'm sorry to hear that, Mike,'' PJ said. She got up and poked the fire, sending sparks up the chimney. She added a new log, purposely busying herself while Mike swiped away tears.

"I was mad at her for the way she ruined our lives, and her own. She might still be OK if she'd just taken pills instead. Isn't that the way women usually try suicide? Where did she get a gun, anyway? We never had one in the house.'' Mike picked up his glass and downed the remaining wine in one big swallow. "The girls needed counseling. They still go once a month just to talk things over with the therapist. I went ahead with the divorce. Sally's parents really get along well with the girls, so I worked out joint custody with them.''

They were silent for a moment, Mike lost in his thoughts, PJ wondering how she could help Mike get on with his life. Or if she was even the person to do so.

"You can't take it all on yourself," she said. "Ultimately people are responsible for their own actions. You didn't pull the trigger. Sally did."

"I divorced her. Instead of sticking by her, after . . ."

"Yes, you divorced her. You made a life-affirming decision for yourself and your daughters."

"God help me, sometimes I wish she had died that day," he said, his voice floating across to her over a gulf wider than their physical separation, "or I had."

The pain in his voice levered PJ to her feet. She went over to the chair, put her hand under his chin, and gently tilted his face up. Tears were streaming down his cheeks now, but he didn't turn away.

"It's OK, Mike. It's OK to still love her," PJ said softly. She bent and kissed his cheek. Her lips tingled with the salty taste, the basic seawater taste of life.

Mike left soon afterward, swimming his way to the door through the current of emotion in the room. When she closed the door behind him, PJ didn't have the slightest idea where their relationship was going. Mike was a jumble of barbed emotions: sadness, guilt, anger, love. He wasn't ready for romantic involvement, and maybe he never would be. Should she settle for friendship? Did she want—need—more?

Was he just looking for someone to help carry the load? If so, she wasn't going to volunteer. She had a simpler relationship in mind: man, woman, sweaty bodies, maybe someone to take her son to a Cardinals game next summer.

PJ fixed herself a mug of hot chocolate with a generous handful of miniature marshmallows, gave her emotions free rein, and watched the fire die.

CHAPTER

11

Late Friday afternoon, Schultz was sitting at the bar in Hattie's Saloon, a drinking place at Laclede's Landing for the earnest young men and women who worked downtown. It wasn't five yet, so the place wasn't crowded. There was one large table with half a dozen men and a couple of women who were all apparently left over from lunch. They were drinking steadily, laughing loudly and a little desperately, and seemed to be celebrating the good fortune of one of their number. Perhaps a promotion. The reason for the celebration had gradually generalized as the bar bill mounted. When Schultz had last tilted an ear in their direction, the conversation concerned dolphin-safe tuna.

Hattie's didn't pour cheap drinks. On weekends, the place filled up with tourists. Tonight was the transition time, and there would be a mix of local office workers and out-of-towners. Schultz wouldn't have chosen Hattie's as a meeting place, but he didn't do the choosing. He was meeting someone here, a man he hadn't had occasion to talk to in several years. Schultz nursed his Coke and shifted his rear on the unpadded wooden barstool, thinking that it was made for young, trim asses of either sex, but definitely not for his. Julia had once joked with him that he had enough room in his pants for three buttocks. Of course, that was back in the days when what was in his pants mattered in their relationship.

The afternoon's mail delivery at his desk had brought a hand-addressed envelope with the printed return address of the sheriff's department in Fallsburg, Tennessee. Holding the envelope in his hand, he remembered the place vividly. A previous investigation into a killer's past had led him to Fallsburg. He had gone there to interview the former sheriff, Al Youngman, who had known the suspect Schultz was pursuing. Inside was another sealed envelope, a smaller one, and folded around it was a note from Rita Wellston, the personable deputy he had met in the sheriff's office.

Detective Schultz, the note had said in her no-nonsense script, *I'm sorry to inform you that former sheriff Al Youngman committed suicide on September 30th. Among his possessions was a letter addressed to you, which I have enclosed.*

Schultz had stuffed the inner envelope into his pocket, unopened. He pulled it out in the bar and examined the front, not for the first time. It was addressed to *Det. Leo Schultz, St. Louis Police Department, Homicide Division.* Down in the right-hand corner was a line that said *Rita, pls see this gets to Leo.* The handwriting was smooth and classical in form. Youngman's teachers must have been pleased with his penmanship.

Blood spatters arced across one corner of the envelope. They had dried to a reddish-brown, and he scraped at them with his thumbnail. As the laughter reached him from the table of happy drunks, he tore open the envelope and took out the single folded sheet of paper inside. After stalling a minute or two, he unfolded it and read.

> Leo,
> *If you're reading this, it means I finally scraped up the courage to eat this gun I've been staring at for weeks. I read in the papers, of course, what the kid had done since I booted him out of the county. The Lord will judge what was in my heart that day. If only I had sweated the hate out of him somehow, or made him see that all people weren't like his Ma and Pa, or blown a hole in him and wiped that motherfucking grin off his face. I can't go back and change that now, any more than I can bring his victims back to life. But I can tell you this as one lawman to another: If the day comes when you face a decision like that, I hope to God you aren't blinded as I was. You have my heartfelt thanks.*
> *May God have mercy on his soul and mine.*
> *Al*

Schultz put the note back and stuck the envelope into his pocket. He thought of Al on his front porch, sipping lemonade while sitting in a wicker chair, reminiscing about his wife. He thought of him waking in the dead of night to images of torture and death, with the certain knowledge that he could have prevented it all. It was a nightmare that Schultz faced, too. He already had instances in his past, times when people's lives had been in danger or lost because of his actions. Or inactions. He had his own personal litany of failures, which he dragged out from time to time and used to whip himself. No matter how he berated himself, though, he couldn't imagine lifting a gun to his mouth and pulling the trigger. If he did that, he would never have the chance to make up for the failures, to come to the end of his life with the scales in balance.

If he was a drinking man, he would have lifted a glass

or three for Al. When he was in his twenties, he had a thirst for alcohol. But he had sworn it off, and hadn't had a drink in thirty years, not even a glass of champagne with Julia on New Year's Eve.

In between one sip of Coke and the next, Edward Jennings appeared at his elbow, having taken the stool next to Schultz. Schultz put away his melancholy just as he had put away the bloodstained envelope, and turned to appraise Edward, as the man was doing in return. He knew that Edward Jennings was in his mid-thirties, although he could pass for a sincere twenty-six in his dark blue suit with a cream silk shirt open at the collar. In jeans and a T-shirt, he would look like a college student. He was in good shape, with a slim waist and well-defined chest and arms. His skin was light and untanned—obviously the body didn't come from outdoor exercise—and his hair was such a light blond that it could have been nudged over into white by a little exposure to the sun.

"Christ, Edward, that buzz cut gets any shorter and people will think you're a skinhead."

"Still buying those jelly doughnuts, aren't you?" Edward poked at Schultz's belly, causing Schultz to recoil and nearly fall off the stool.

"Shit! I almost dropped my Coke. Keep your fucking hands to yourself."

"Touchy, touchy. You going to buy me a drink, or do I have to go join that bunch? That woman in green has the hots for me." He nodded in the direction of the noisy group at the table. As though it were operating on remote control, Schultz's head swiveled to take in the woman in green. He saw the frank heat in her eyes, but it wasn't aimed in his direction. Edward blew her a kiss, and she turned, laughing, to the other woman at the table. Schultz waved the bartender over, bought Edward a Chivas, straight.

"You remembered."

"Ain't I sweet. Mind if we get down to business now?"

"Lighten up, Schultz. Business comes around in its own good time. How're Julia and the delinquent?"

"Julia walked out on me. The delinquent is in jail, where he belongs."

"No shit. And you're drinking Coke?"

"I happen to like Coke, not that it's any of your concern."

Edward raised both hands, palm out, in a warding gesture. "OK, strictly business. What do you have for me?"

"I've got a rotten piece of meat I'd like to toss to the alligators. Name's Charles Horner. Little shit fancies himself a big-time businessman, apparently couldn't run a lemonade stand on his lonesome."

"Horner Fine Properties. Bright Futures Investment Services. Right Away Sanitation. Sunset Muffler and Brake. Horner Mergers and Acquisitions. Did I miss any?"

"Beanie Burrito's Lunch Express. 'You Can't Pass Our Food.' Remember that one?"

"That was his?"

"Yeah, and somehow people didn't take that motto the way he meant it."

"He's kind of a joke in financial circles. Don't tell me Charlie's gone and done something sinister?"

Schultz told him about Rowena Clark and the argument she had with Horner shortly before her death.

"Sounds too slick for Charlie. He would have needed heavy-duty help."

"That's what I'd like you to look into," Schultz said. "Did Horner get mixed up in something he couldn't handle?"

"You mean did he owe money to somebody with a really nasty late charge?"

"I don't give a shit if he owes money to the Godfather himself. I just want to know if he hired somebody to kill the old lady."

"You already think so, or you wouldn't have called me. You may be at the bottom of my sliding scale, but it's still going to cost you if you're wrong."

Schultz nodded. Edward Jennings was one of the weirdest informants Schultz had ever known. He worked exclusively with white-collar crime, preferably big-business doings. If the things he turned up resulted in bad guys getting caught, he wouldn't accept any payment other than the drink Schultz had already bought. If he was sent on a wild-goose chase, he expected a thousand bucks for his lost time. In the half a dozen times Schultz had brought Edward in on a case, he had paid out exactly once. He was hoping this wouldn't make number two.

"Done." It was a dismissal; Edward had other things on his mind now. Schultz finished his Coke and went to use the men's room. When he came out, he made a phone call. He needed an address, and he got it from a phone company contact. As he was leaving Hattie's Saloon, he noticed that Edward had gone over to the group at the table, and was deftly cutting the woman in green from the herd.

Schultz decided to drive the department's vehicle to Chicago rather than rent a car. He didn't think his own car, an asthmatic Vega, was up to the trip. He knew that the orange Pacer was assigned to him for police work only. So he figured he just wouldn't charge the gasoline to the department. Nobody would notice a few more miles on the old heap, and if anyone did, he would simply say he was following up on a lead in the case.

He drove straight through, and at nine-thirty Friday night found himself in the parking lot of the apartment complex where Julia was living. Having already tried her doorbell without success, he sat in the car munching a bag of chips from a 7-Eleven a couple of blocks away. The phone number she had given him belonged to James Glassup, and that was the name on the mailbox. James and Julia. Had a nice ring to it. Classy. He wondered what he would do if she showed up on the arm of her new boyfriend.

Her domestic partner.

He tried out the phrase in the car and was certain he couldn't say it with a straight face. As far as he was concerned, a domestic partner was something like a vacuum cleaner.

She was there, pulling into the parking lot. He saw her familiar profile under the dusk-to-dawn lights as she locked the door of the Dart. Something ripped a little inside him, and a chill that had nothing to do with the outdoor temperature made bumps rise, travel across his skin from one arm to the shoulders and down the other arm, as he looked at her.

He could still leave. He could drive away, and Julia would never know he had come.

The Pacer's door squeaked when he opened it, and she looked his way. A little worried, a woman looking at a stranger in a parking lot in Chicago at night.

"Julia," he said. The wind carried the name away. He said it louder, and she cocked her head in his direction.

"Leo? Is that you? What on earth are you doing here?"

"I'm not sure, but I'll know soon," he said.

There were no harsh words or recriminations. Both of them knew what this evening meant. They went to a small Italian restaurant about a mile away. It was an unpretentious place inside and out, but Julia said it had great food. Schultz hadn't eaten, so he ordered a full dinner. Julia had a glass of wine. When the food came there was a mound of spaghetti that filled his entire dinner plate, a separate bowl of meatballs and sauce, a dish of freshly grated Parmesan, and a basket piled high with chunks of hot, crusty bread. He persuaded Julia to share the bread. He knew it was just the kind she enjoyed.

Julia chatted about the classes she was taking and her

part-time job as a receptionist in a busy law office. Some-time during the second glass of wine, she started to talk about James, whom she had met when they were both late for the same class. He was out of town, attending a convention in Phoenix, and would be back Saturday morning. James was a CPA with his own company, which he was expanding from six employees to ten this year.

Her eyes shone when she said James's name. Sadness pulled at Schultz. Bits of their marriage tugged loose from anchoring places in his flesh and coursed through his bloodstream like miniature life rafts. The bones of his life creaked and bent and reshaped themselves, like the Wolfman transforming under the demanding gaze of the full moon. He concentrated on his dinner. Tears pooled in the corners of his eyes, and he dabbed at them with his napkin, being careful also to dab at his lips so she wouldn't know.

She did know, because nothing was hidden between the two of them, and he could see her hopes and dreams swirling about her like leaves driven by a gust of wind.

She asked him about his work, and he talked about CHIP, about how he felt doing fieldwork again. When he talked about their son Rick, she grew still, then told him he was doing the right thing.

On the drive back to the apartment, she reached across the Pacer's narrow front seat and held his hand. As he walked her to the door, his hand tingled with memories. He kissed her on the lips, then turned and left quickly.

He was halfway back to St. Louis, pushing the Pacer to eighty and leaning on the steering wheel to keep the car from crabbing sideways onto the shoulder, before he knew that he was all right.

CHAPTER

12

Billy Carpenter's bedroom door opens inward. He keeps his right hand on the doorknob as the door swings, soundlessly letting the knob swivel back into place under his fingers. His left hand clutches the bundle of wet jammies, which he holds out away from his body.

The night-light in the hallway is burned out. He had told Mom Elly about it days ago, and she said she would replace it as soon as she remembered to buy more of the little bulbs at the store. The hallway yawns ahead of him in the dark, like the throat of a big dinosaur, the kind that tears red dripping pieces from other dinosaurs who throw back their heads and scream. Billy stands swaying in the doorway, one foot out in the hall and one in his bedroom as imaginary screams rush at him from the hall, buffeting him.

He can't see down to the end of the hallway, but he feels the awful length of it.

A drop of cold piss falls from the jammies onto his foot, startling him, raising gooseflesh on his arms. He stares down the hall, and with his dark-adjusted eyes he can make out a pale patch of light on the floor. The bathroom has a window, and Mr. Moon is shining through it, spreading a gentle rectangle on the carpet, like butter on toast.

There are no monsters in the hall, just like Dad says.

Dad always knows.

Billy hears his heart pounding and his own rapid breathing, but nothing else. There is no sound coming from the room where Dad and Mom Elly sleep. There had been a big fight, then a crash like the time he had dropped Mom Elly's bowl when he held it up to the sunlight to make rainbows on the wall. Then silence.

Billy walks into the hall, heading for the patch of light. The blackness is the cottony one that brushes against his face, not the wet muddy kind that clogs his mouth and nose so he can't breathe. He makes it to the bathroom door, ducks inside, and turns his face up to see Mr. Moon through the window. Mr. Moon is winking at him tonight, so part of his face is gone. There isn't as much light as when Mr. Moon gives him a big smile, but he makes out the hamper in the corner. He lifts the lid. The smells of clothing that had been worn drift up at him, but he doesn't stop to sift through all the different odors. Usually he sorts out the heady aroma of Dad's socks and undershirts, Mom Elly's slips that smell like wilted flowers, his own played-in clothes with the usual spilled food odors and the more exotic outdoor smells clinging to them: grass, soil, bird's nest. He is in a hurry this time. He pulls aside the top layer of laundry and drops in his wet jammies. Then he mashes the bath towel and washcloth he had used earlier on top of them. They are still wet from his bath. He puts back the top layer so that, to his eye at least, the contents of the hamper appear undisturbed.

Maybe this isn't so bad after all. The fighting has stopped, and his wet-pants incident is taken care of. He can still be a perfect boy, and there will be no more fights and Mom Elly won't be a witch after all, and she would become his real mom.

Or maybe pretending to be perfect isn't the same as the real thing. A picture comes into his mind of Jeffy at Kiddy Care lying on the floor, eyes wide and mouth beginning to bleed, after Billy knocked him down. No, he will never be a perfect boy, not if everything counts against him, even things that happen when Mom Elly and Dad aren't around.

It is too much of a puzzle for the middle of the night. Billy yawns; he is ready to get back into bed. He goes to the door of the bathroom. Mr. Moon's soft white light on his back is a gentle pressure, pushing him back to his room.

He is out in the hall, one hand lightly tracing along the wall, like the blind man he had seen walking on the sidewalk, checking ahead with his cane with one hand and running the other along the walls of the buildings. Mom Elly had quietly explained that the man's eyes didn't work, so he saw darkness wherever he looked. That was something Billy could understand, and it had been a physical jolt that some people lived that way all the time. In the hallway, Billy senses the doorway ahead of him. The shades are pulled down on the windows in his room, so Mr. Moon isn't much help.

When he first hears the sounds, he thinks they might be the air filling the balloons in his chest, or the food rumbling in his tummy, or even those funny, smelly bursts that came out of his bottom sometimes. But the sounds are coming from outside his body, even outside his self, the clear shell that he wears which is a few inches larger than his skin in all directions. He had tried to explain his self to Dad a couple of times, but lacked the words for it.

Dad doesn't seem to know about selves, or had forgotten about them when he grew up to be an old man.

The sounds are coming from down the hall, behind him, no doubt about it.

Groans, low and hideous. The kind of sounds that he imagines those poor dinosaurs make right before the big mean dinosaurs bite off their heads, when they are already bleeding from a dozen spots, oozing the glistening mysteries of their insides onto the ground.

First the fight, words flying like arrows, then the crash, then silence. Now groans. Something's terribly wrong. A monster, they are fighting a monster in their room, and they are losing, and now the monster is eating them. No, there would be crunching sounds, bones snapping in the monster's dripping mouth.

Billy listens carefully, out in the hallway with his back to the rectangle of moonlight on the floor. There is no crunching.

A tornado, then, like the one in *The Wizard of Oz* that carried off Dorothy and Toto: black, twisting clouds that weren't just clouds but sky monsters with arms to yank people up. No, there would be thumping sounds as the tornado slams Dad and Mom Elly into the walls of their room and tosses the lamps and books around.

The witch, then. It has to be the witch. Mom Elly is doing something to Dad, something Billy's wildly expanding fears shy away from like a skittish horse avoiding a snake. She is making Dad take off his skin, that's it. Dad had once said something about being scared out of his skin. Dad had laughed about it, but sometimes Dad laughs when he's afraid.

Billy turns and starts back down the hallway. It's all up to him. He has to save Dad from the witch, from whatever horrible thing Mom Elly is doing. He wonders if he's brave enough. He wonders if he can put Dad's skin back on him. Should he start at the head or at the feet, putting the skin back on his toes like pulling on a pair of socks? The low sounds, which at first he could barely hear, now stab at his ears. The second time he reaches the patch of moonlight in the hallway, it no longer cheers him. As his feet pass through the light, he feels a sudden chill, as if he has stumbled into cold water. When he looks down in surprise, it seems as though a dangerous fog swirls up around him, and that his bare feet are somehow too far away to see.

CHAPTER

13

By Monday afternoon, PJ was certain all her biorhythmic cycles were at rock-bottom. She was tired and felt mentally sluggish and simultaneously on edge, a discordant sensation. Concerned about the lack of progress on the Clark murder, she felt pressured to show some results, and her newly developed commitment to bringing criminals to justice was stymied. On top of that, she felt the slight ache in her throat and muscles that usually preceded a cold.

She studied the members of the CHIP team seated in her small office. Dave Whitmore had pushed in a rolling chair from down the hall and was now sprawled in it, legs loosely crossed, with the ankle of one resting on the knee of the other. Aside from his height—he was six feet four inches—there was nothing about his appearance that would warrant a second glance. His face had the unfocused look of a two-week-old kitten gazing at the world through eyes just opened. The look had earned him the unfair nickname of Witless, a play on his last name. He was sharp enough to hold his own on the team, and more detail-oriented than any of them, a kind of solid anchor when the rest of them went off the deep end with speculation. He had an endearing way of turning green when presented with graphic representations of society's ills. Until she saw it with her own eyes, PJ didn't think the green part was actually true. He was able to step out of his job when he went home, and go out and enjoy life. Just shuck it like a snake shedding its skin. Schultz told her that wasn't right, that a detective was never really off duty and always carried the job around in his mind. PJ told Schultz that he was an old sourpuss, but her own way of thinking was much closer to Schultz's than to Dave's.

Anita Collings sat forward in her folding chair, elbows resting on PJ's desk. PJ knew Anita had the nervous energy of a racehorse in the starting gate, and kept it in check for the most part, but it leaked out when she was tired or frustrated. It showed in a tossing of the head, a tongue tip making a quick circuit of her lips, a fingertip darting to touch the small scar at the outside corner of her right eye, or the one higher up on her forehead under her wispy bangs. Anita never said how she got the scars, but they looked old enough to have originated in childhood. PJ pictured Anita taking major risks on the jungle gym and not taking any grief from the school bullies. What she couldn't picture was Anita in a dress. Any dress, even a wedding gown.

Anita had a small notepad on the desk in front of her, and a newly sharpened pencil with, PJ noticed, a pristine eraser free of tooth marks. Her own pencils had shortened or missing erasers because PJ nibbled at them while she talked on the phone. She discreetly slid the two telltale pencils that were on her desk into the top drawer and replaced them with the basic black Paper Mate pens the department used. Anita's gaze didn't waver from the bulletin board behind PJ's desk, although she probably saw the desktop maneuver and understood its significance.

If you catch the boss picking her nose or tugging her underwear out of the crack of her ass, it's a good idea to pretend that you were looking elsewhere. Not that Anita would let such an occurrence slip by if it was Dave or Schultz doing the picking or the tugging. PJ was well aware of the chasm that existed between herself and the others. Even though she had been with the department for months, she was still an outsider, a civilian employee who had not undergone law enforcement training, walked a beat, driven a patrol car, and advanced through the ranks. With Anita, that chasm seemed to be bottomless; with Dave, the sides were steep but the bottom was in sight. With Schultz, the chasm was more like a shallow arroyo: she could walk down one side and up the other, and join him on the rim.

Schultz arrived a few minutes late for the meeting and didn't offer any excuse. Closing the door behind him, he shut out the noise of the hallway and the toilets flushing in the men's room across the way.

"You can always tell when Henderson's back on that high fiber shit again," he said by way of greeting.

Schultz got a cup of coffee and sat down heavily in a folding chair, his face as blank and professionally composed as a poker player's. It was a demeanor that had taken PJ years to develop in her practice as a psychologist. *Schultz was probably born with it,* she mused.

"OK, group, let's get caught up," PJ said. "My news is that the hospital's back to its normal routine of using the on-line charts. Dial-in access has been restored. My phony patient was a flop. There wasn't any suspicious ordering activity. Either the killer saw through the setup or has moved on for some other reason."

"Maybe he's just waiting for everybody to relax," Dave said.

"That's possible," PJ said. "I think we're dealing with a person who's methodical and attuned to details. A person who's not killing passionately, really getting in and wallowing in it. This is colder, remote. Machinelike. Consider the way he gets machines, and through them, other people, to do his work for him. And that lack of passion suggests . . ."

"Ice-cold revenge," Schultz finished for her.

"Exactly what I was thinking about. Consider Charles Horner and his emotional fights with his mother-in-law. Does he seem like the cold, calculated type? And if she was the target, how does Jerry Rogers fit in?"

"To throw us off track," Dave replied.

PJ saw a sudden animation in Schultz's face. For a moment his eyes were lit with secret knowledge. She made a note to talk to him later about it.

"Jerry Rogers has been at home for more than two weeks," Anita said. "He didn't mind the round-the-clock police guards at first. After all, somebody tried to kill him in the hospital, and he was pretty shaken up. Now he's getting restless. I think his fiancée's ragging on him about it. Probably doesn't like getting it on with an audience."

"I'll tell Lieutenant Wall to discontinue the surveillance. We should stop keeping an eye on the poor guy and let him get on with his life. I don't think he was a specific target. Besides, Wall said that he could only fund the surveillance for a couple more days, then it's coming out of my salary."

"Well, we certainly wouldn't want that to happen," Schultz said. "Might bring you down somewhere near our level. Say, Doc, next time you invite us all in here, how about springing for some refreshments? Doughnuts are the standard thing at meetings."

PJ wondered what was eating him. The conversation stopped as Anita and Dave found something interesting to study in their laps. PJ and Schultz locked gazes. Schultz blinked first.

"In case you were interested, that is. About the doughnuts," he continued gamely. "Seeing as how you're always bitching about not being treated like one of the guys."

"I'll remember that next time, Detective," PJ said. She found herself pushing a smile off her face. A few months ago, she would have been insecure enough to pounce on Schultz. Now she was more resilient at work; she could let the boundaries blur sometimes.

In her personal life, though, things were still sharp-edged and treacherous. An image popped into her mind of Steven's new wife Carla bringing their soon-to-be-born baby home. They were living in the same house where she and Steven had heard Thomas speak his first word, watched him take his first wobbly steps, proudly brought home his big-boy bed and put it up in his room as Thomas tried out the mattress on the floor by jumping on it.

The light switch in Thomas's room still had a Mickey Mouse plate, worn and stained from years of contact with grubby fingers. She could feel the way it moved under her thumb, caught at the halfway point, then continued up and turned on the lamp on his dresser.

It seemed as though she was caught at the halfway point, too. She had to let go of Steven, get past the point where her emotions got hung up.

They were looking at her expectantly, and she realized she must have been daydreaming. She indulged herself a moment more, summoning up the gentle pressure of five-year-old Thomas's breath against her hair, followed by the brush of his lips against her ear. *I love you, Mommy. Always.*

Dave cleared his throat. "I've been looking into Dr. Graham's background." He took a big swig of coffee and swished it around between his front teeth before swallowing it, an annoying habit that brought PJ abruptly back to the work at hand.

"Did you know your nose twitches when you do that," Schultz offered, "like Bugs Bunny?"

That did it. PJ burst out laughing, followed by Anita and

Schultz. Dave just rolled his eyes. PJ felt her mood lift, as though she had parted a curtain and let the sun shine in just a little. *Quite a feat,* she thought, *in this windowless closet of an office.*

"What about Dr. Graham?" PJ said, pulling the meeting back to order. Dave shuffled through his notes.

"Born Eleanor Louise Lindsey in Louisville, Kentucky, 1942, only child of poor but hardworking parents. Mom died in 1950 of cancer. Might have influenced little E.L. to become a doctor. Married her high school sweetheart, who worked as a mechanic while E.L. attended med school. Hubby got stung by the patriotism bug and enlisted in the army. He got killed on his fourth day of duty in Vietnam. Poor guy barely had time to get his boots muddy."

"Any kids?" Schultz said.

"Nope. Maybe E.L. was too busy doing the doctor thing, or else she didn't care much for kids. She stayed in Louisville for a few years, building her practice, until her father died in 1974. Then she moved to St. Louis. Met Dr. Harvey Carpenter in August 1975 at a medical conference. Carpenter's wife had died a few months earlier in a car accident, and he had a son, Will Carpenter, only a year old at the time. They got married less than a year later, and E.L. became a stepmom."

"I guess she didn't have any better luck with husband number two," PJ said. "He seems to be out of the picture now."

"Way out," Dave said. "He died three years after they got married. Aortic aneurysm blew out, according to his death certificate."

"So Dr. Graham became a single mother," PJ said. "Let's see, Will would be about twenty-two now?"

"A psychologist, a computer expert, and now a mathematician," Schultz injected. "What's next? The tooth fairy?"

PJ scowled at Schultz. He seemed to be working hard to

distract her, perhaps because of that unguarded moment when the topic was Charles Horner. His efforts just reinforced her determination to get him alone and pin him down on Charles the Snake.

"He would be twenty-two, but he's out of the picture, too. Ran away at fourteen, suicide at fifteen. Sent E.L. a good-bye note and walked into the Pacific. His body was never found, but friends saw him go into the water."

"Was he wearing a swimming suit?" Schultz asked, apparently out of the blue.

Puzzled, Dave checked his notes. "Yes. A blue-and-white boxer style. What's that got to do with anything?"

"Drowning suicides go one of two ways. They jump off cliffs or bridges fully clothed. Or they walk calmly into the water after taking off all their clothes and putting them in a neat pile, putting their eyeglasses in a case, and tucking their wallet out of sight, as though they'll be needing their personal things in a few minutes. What they don't do is put on a swimming suit and go to the beach with friends."

"There was a note," Anita said.

"Note, schmote," Schultz answered. "Give me a tablet of paper and a typewriter, and I'll give you a couple dozen authentic-looking suicide notes by dinnertime. Speaking of which . . ."

"Are you saying that you think Will Carpenter's disappearance is suspicious?" PJ said. "That he was murdered?"

"Jumpy, aren't you, Doc? Could have been a simple accidental drowning."

"His friends claimed he was an excellent swimmer," Dave said.

"Yeah, and the Pacific Ocean ain't no swimming pool."

"True. But wasn't there a local investigation?" PJ said.

"Of course. But a runaway teen committing suicide just doesn't stir things up too much," Dave said. "I talked to E.L. about it. She was very matter-of-fact, showed me the note, said she wished they had recovered the body for burial. Didn't seem too broken up, but it has been eight years.''

"Maybe she wasn't broken up because she had something to do with it. The woman was widowed twice," Schultz said. "Could be something there. Either of the dearly departeds wealthy?"

"Hubby number one certainly had modest means," Dave said. "He always wanted to scrape together enough money to open his own auto repair shop. Number two was a successful physician, but by that time so was E.L. In fact, she owns a nursing home out on Lemay Ferry. Her husband had a hundred grand life insurance, but that's not excessive for someone of his earning power. In fact, it's kind of low. He must not have had a very aggressive insurance agent. She does come from a poor background though. Money might be a significant thing to her."

"Money equals security, or money equals power," PJ said, "and either way, she can't get enough of it."

"Take that nursing home, for instance." Schultz said. "Aren't some of those things cover-ups for scams?"

"You mean not reporting a patient's death and then continuing to collect assigned social security benefits?" PJ said.

"Yeah, that kind of stuff. I tell you, my gut says that dame's got dirty feet. Somewhere along the line, she's stepped in shit."

The others mulled that over. Schultz slurped his coffee noisily, even though it was cool enough.

"Besides, I thought you were convinced that Dr. Graham was being set up by somebody," Schultz said. "Christ, now you're back to the start."

"I know. I guess I'm just desperate for a lead." Again that little gleam in Schultz's eye. "You've all had a chance to try out the computer simulations. The playbacks just aren't telling us anything useful," PJ said, letting her frustration out by picking up a pen and tapping it on the table.

"Why don't we get a fresh start tomorrow?" Dave said. "I don't know about the rest of you, but my brain's circling like a dog looking for a place to crap."

The meeting broke up, but PJ asked Schultz to remain behind while the other two drifted out. In a few minutes they were alone.

"It's really eating at you, isn't it?" Schultz said.

"What is?"

"Come on, Doc. You might fool the others, but I know you too well."

She wondered if she'd ever be able to say that about Schultz.

"I've got a real problem with loose ends," she said. "I don't like them."

"This case has got more loose ends than a men's prison," Schultz said. He started to laugh, then caught himself.

PJ knew he was thinking about his son Rick, serving time for selling drugs. He had confided to her that he was worried about Rick contracting HIV in prison. She reached down, opened the bottom drawer of her desk, and pulled out a bag of doughnuts.

"Here," she said, tearing the bag open so they could help themselves. "There's just enough for the two of us. I got you some sugared jellies."

"Christ," Schultz said, and she looked up at the roughness in his voice. His eyes were bright and moist. "Christ. Loose ends." He got up and busied himself pouring a fresh cup of coffee. When he returned to the desk, his face and voice were under control. He picked up the biggest doughnut and took a bite, nodding his head appreciatively.

"Now what's going on with Charles Horner?" PJ said. "You have anything on him?"

"What makes you think there's something going on?" he said. A blob of raspberry jelly at the corner of his mouth failed to make him look innocent.

"Your stone face isn't always as good as you think."

"Remind me never to invite you to a poker game." He finished off his first doughnut and reached for another. "Aren't you going to have any of these?"

Using two fingers, PJ dragged a doughnut over to a napkin that she had spread out in front of her. "These are so messy. I don't know why they're your favorites."

"Neither do I. Couldn't stand them when I was a kid." Schultz licked his fingers. "Horner's not clean. I'm sure of it. The twerp's got something going. I just haven't pinned it down yet."

"You think he murdered his mother-in-law? Then tried to throw the investigation off by having another patient targeted?"

Schultz nodded. "You've got potential, Doc. A couple more decades and maybe you'd make a good investigator."

PJ ignored the provocation. "I can't picture it."

"Most likely he hired someone. I have an informant checking that out."

"And?" PJ prodded.

"My informant thinks Horner's dirty, too." It was an evasive answer, and they both knew it.

"Who is this informant?"

"If you were regular law enforcement, you'd know better than to ask that."

There it was, that not-so-gentle castigation of the outsider. PJ covered her annoyance by concentrating on licking the inside of her jelly doughnut clean with her tongue.

"Christ, Doc, watching that fancy tongue work's enough to get a guy hot."

PJ laughed. "Lucky for you I'm not wearing my sexual harassment coat of armor today. That sounded pretty suggestive to me."

"I do believe you're blushing. What's the matter, Doc? Never had a guy come on to you at work?"

An unpleasant memory swept through PJ's mind like a

hot desert wind: a situation out of control early in her private practice, pinned against the wall of her office, a man breathing his lust into her face, breaking away, fleeing the office, professional composure trailing after her in shreds . . .

"As a matter of fact, I have," she said, in a tone of voice that indicated that further exploration was unwelcome. "Now about this informant: is he credible?"

"The best. He's a strange guy. Sort of a business vigilante."

PJ knew better than to press for more. She stood up, signaling that the meeting was over, but Schultz remained seated. He watched her as she packed a few folders and disks in her briefcase to take home.

"Something else, Detective?"

"I've been thinking about what you said about Helen."

PJ sat back down. She had been expecting Schultz to talk about this again. She was tired, emotionally down, her throat was scratchy, and nothing seemed appealing except the dual prospects of a hot soak and an early bedtime. But there he was, in one of those rare moments when the mask was off. He seemed so exposed she half expected him to cover his groin with his hands.

"As far as I know," PJ said, "she hasn't changed her mind. She doesn't want to get involved with you."

"Yeah, I figured that. I mean, what does she know about me anyway? Some lunkhead cop who's got more belly than brains." Schultz sucked in his stomach with considerable effort. "Not that I couldn't have a decent body again if I worked at it. I used to be really muscular. Women always coming up and patting my biceps, that kind of thing." He looked at PJ as though for confirmation, so she nodded as if she was about to spring up and try it herself.

"I think it's more than that, Leo," she said. "Helen's been hurt in every sense of the word. I don't think she's willing to take a risk with another relationship."

"That's just it," Schultz said, leaning forward in his chair, which protested with a loud squeak. "I want to make her forget that asshole husband of hers, what's his name again?"

"Jack."

"I'd like to get old Jack alone for a few minutes. He wouldn't be a bother to any woman ever again, I can tell you that."

"I think Helen can take care of herself now. She's made a new life."

"All she has to do is divorce Jack and give me a chance."

"You're arguing with the wrong woman. Tell her that. In person."

"Won't work. She'd say no, automatically. Like Pavel's dogs drooling when the light flashes."

"That's Pavlov's dogs. And it was a bell, not a flashing light."

The phone rang. Grateful for the interruption and very sure her conversation with Schultz was heading where she didn't want to tag along, she picked up on the first ring.

"Who the fuck is calling so late?" Schultz grumbled, loud enough that she couldn't hear the voice on the phone. He was obviously irritated to have his conversation cut off. "Doesn't anybody go home around here?"

"Shh, Leo, I'll be with you in a minute. Yes, Lieutenant . . ."

PJ wrote a few lines on a pad on her desk. She was silent for a full minute on the phone, her eyes engaged with Schultz's, which were pressing for information. "We'll be there as soon as we can." Then she hung up.

"That was Wall. He's with Bert Manning. There's been another suspicious death at Wood Memorial."

"Let me guess," Schultz said with a scowl. "Another patient of Dr. Graham's."

"An eighty-year-old cancer patient. Terminal. Apparently his death was accelerated with an overdose of morphine. He died about three in the morning."

"Shit. Rich?"

"Yes. Very."

"Shit. I thought you had some trap to catch anybody who messed with the computer records."

"I do. This wasn't done with computer tampering. It was done the old-fashioned way."

Schultz stood up, hitching up his pants and running a hand down the front of his shirt as though checking to see that all the buttons were fastened. Or still there.

"About Helen. Leo . . ." PJ began, not certain what she was going to say. Looking at Schultz, she could see that he was all business again. The mask was back in place.

"What?" he practically barked.

"Nothing. Let's go."

CHAPTER
14

Schultz was sweating lightly by the time they got to Wood Memorial, even though the evening was cool, almost cold enough for a coat. His arthritic knees were bothering him today, especially his left one; it had been locking up, sending a jolt of pain up to his hip that drew an involuntary gasp. Medication could only help so much, the doctor had told him. What he really needed was to get some of the excess weight off his joints, but he enjoyed the kind of food he usually ate, and there were few enough enjoyments in his life already. He stopped at a drinking fountain to swallow his second Voltaren of the day. They were supposed to be taken with food, but this was one of the many nights when dinner wouldn't be on time, or maybe happen at all. The doughnuts he had eaten in PJ's office would probably have to do until breakfast.

He and PJ headed for Bert Manning's office. The receptionist had gone home, so they knocked and let themselves in. Schultz's nostrils flared in anticipation of the alcohol smell, but as soon as he got a glimpse into the room, he sniffed deeply and noisily, savoring the greasy aroma of pepperoni pizza. Lieutenant Howard Wall sat in one of Manning's plastic guest chairs with a large, dripping slice of pizza in one hand and a napkin in the other. On the otherwise immaculate metal desk there were two open delivery boxes of pizza and a couple of two-liter bottles of Coke.

As Wall took a big bite, Schultz looked at the man behind the desk. Manning had a look of disgust on his face which he didn't bother to conceal. It was appalling to him that anyone would actually eat in his office. Open mouths. Chewing. Stained napkins that had touched people's lips. Crumbs, and other not-so-innocent detritus of eating, on the desk. Schultz thought it would probably take him days to feel comfortable in his own office again, and then only after he went over every surface with alcohol wipes. The stress of it would keep the guy off balance, though, so perhaps he would be more forthcoming than he had been before. His opinion of Lieutenant Wall went up a notch.

Wall heard them enter. "There you are. I figured nobody would have eaten dinner yet. Hope pepperoni's OK. It was a coupon special."

"My only question," Schultz said, eyeing the two boxes, "is what are the rest of you going to eat?"

Wall laughed. "Pull up a chair, Schultz. If you want some brownie points, pull up one for your boss, too." He poured Coke into small plastic cups and handed them out. Schultz looked at his cup critically.

"Are these specimen cups?" Schultz asked.

"Come to think of it, they probably are. I got them from a shelf in a bathroom."

"Good thing you got Coke instead of Mountain Dew," PJ said. "Otherwise this would look highly unappetizing. Speaking from the viewpoint of a consumer market researcher, that is."

Wall had already taken a mouthful, and he managed to

snort some up into his nose when he laughed. He spent the next minute or so coughing.

"Could we just get on with whatever's necessary here, Lieutenant?" Manning said. "I hardly think this is a time for joking. Another patient has been murdered, and I don't think your attitude is appropriate."

"Mr. Manning," he said, "to you, death is just a column on a report. You don't see it, touch it, smell it. Those of us who do are free to use whatever 'attitude' gets us through the day, and especially gets us through the nights. You have a problem with that?"

Silently cheering, already on his second slice of pizza, Schultz watched as Manning reddened until he looked like a cherry Popsicle. The man straightened his tie and tapped his fingers nervously on the desk.

"Yes, well, you have a point," he said. "Perhaps I should wait elsewhere while you and your fellow investigators eat dinner."

"Nah. That's not necessary. We law enforcement types can eat and talk at the same time. We screen for that on the job application. Right, Schultz?"

Schultz nodded enthusiastically. "Yeah. They teach us in the academy not to let too much food fall out. Bad public relations."

He noticed that PJ was scarfing down pizza almost as fast as he was, but somehow doing it neatly, a pristine napkin draped across her lap. How did women do that, anyway? It must be one of those secret skills they taught on Girl Scout camping trips. On Boy Scout camping trips, Schultz had learned how to belch on cue, spit really far, and write messages in the sand with piss.

After a minute or so, Schultz realized that Wall wasn't going to do the questioning. It would be proper to wait for PJ, but what the hell. He wanted to catch Manning while there was still a trace of redness in his cheeks.

"Let's start at the beginning. Mr. Manning, what can you tell us about the victim?"

"Maximillian Winters was dying of cancer. He had been in and out of Wood Memorial half a dozen times, but it was clear to everyone, including himself, that this was his last visit. His nurses tell me he was comfortable with that fact, as comfortable as anyone could be."

"So he wouldn't voluntarily have taken a morphine overdose?"

"It's impossible to say now, of course, but those who were his daily caregivers say no. He had a large family, and he seemed to be enjoying visiting with relatives he hadn't seen in years. In fact, two are on their way from Germany, and supposed to see him tomorrow. I guess they'll stay for the funeral."

"No sense making two trips," Schultz said, his face carefully straight.

"That would be a waste, wouldn't it?" Manning said, obviously missing the barb. "Mr. Winters was subject to a great deal of discomfort, but the morphine controlled it as much as possible. He showed no sign of unbearable pain."

"Did he have a lot of visitors?"

"Yes, but only family members. Again, I'm reporting this secondhand. It would be better if you'd talk directly to the nursing staff."

"Oh, we will. Has the hospital had any other deaths like this recently?"

"You mean deliberate drug overdoses? There was one last year. A family member brought in drugs from outside the hospital. There could be others that we don't know about. After all, not every patient who dies here is given a postmortem examination. We're just keeping close track of Dr. Graham's patients. Luckily, Mr. Winters's family gave consent."

"I understand that no computer tampering was involved this time," PJ said. "Do you suspect a relative?"

"Suspects are your job, Dr. Gray. I will say that Mr. Winters was a very nice man. He used his money wisely and generously. He was a major donor in our Imaging Pavilion program. One never knows about these things, but he seemed to have a happy family life."

"What about his visitors?"

"Mr. Winters was a very private man. He was in our VIP wing. Visitors have to sign in, and the receptionist checks the guest list that the patient has authorized. Only those on the list are admitted. Unauthorized visitors are highly unlikely."

"That leaves the staff itself," PJ said.

Manning bristled, then sighed. "I know. I know. It's hard to believe, but that's the same conclusion I've come to. I'd like to clear this up as quickly and quietly as possible." He tapped his fingertips again on the desk, and his eyes strayed down to the desk drawer where Schultz knew he kept his alcohol wipes. To rattle the guy a little more, Schultz chewed noisily, with his mouth open, and then took a big slurp of Coke.

"Do you think Dr. Graham was responsible?" Schultz asked.

"As I've said, that's in your realm. But if I had to answer, I'd say no. Dr. Graham works with the elderly all the time, although she's not formally a gerontologist. She even runs that nice long-term care facility, which has mainly elderly residents. When you deal with the elderly frequently, you become accustomed to the idea that a higher percentage of your patients die than, say, a pediatrician would expect. The fact that Mr. Winters was dying, and doing so in a calm, relatively pain-free way, surrounded by loved ones, would seem appropriate to her. Sometimes, tragically, patients die without a shred of dignity to pull around themselves. Not that she would give up trying to save his life. I just can't see her hurrying his demise."

Schultz was surprised that Manning spoke so compassionately. Apparently he wasn't all numbers, costs, and bottom lines. He wondered what other surprises the man might have up his meticulously de-linted sleeve. Schultz looked at the photo on the desk of Manning and his wife with the Grand Canyon in the background. At least, he assumed it was his wife. Like some long-married couples, they had come to look alike. He found that charming, and marveled at the tolerance the woman must possess. Manning's obsession with germs would have driven him out of the house. The fact that they were still together loomed larger in his mind than the Grand Canyon in the photo. Their love, their marriage, had survived. His had not. He looked away, but his eyes remained dry.

PJ moved smoothly into the lull in the conversation. "I'd like to look at this from a different angle. Where did the morphine come from that killed Mr. Winters?"

"Most likely from right here in the hospital," Manning said. "Morphine is in a class of drugs that is tightly controlled, of course. There's a locked cabinet at every nursing station just for such drugs. The pharmacy department has excellent physical security, and all doses are tracked by computer all the way from inventory through ordering, dispensing, and administration."

"But nurses have keys to those cabinets, and legitimate reasons to open them," PJ said.

"Yes, and we've had cases of outright theft. A very small number. Every hospital does." Although Manning had been cooperative so far, Schultz picked up the defensiveness about drug theft. Drastic measures were called for. He knocked over his cup with his elbow, sending Coke across the desk. Manning shoved his chair backward hard, making sure that he avoided the contaminants flowing toward him. Schultz apologized as he wiped up the spill with a couple of used napkins. Manning's eyes bulged out while Schultz smeared tomato sauce and grease from the napkins onto the surface of the desk. It was the first time his interrogation technique had employed messiness to turn the screws.

Damn, he was bad.

It worked. Manning continued, fairly bubbling to give them the information they wanted.

"Normally, such things are caught immediately. Discrepancies show up in the computer records. It always turns out to be someone under financial stress, and that shows up in job performance. Making too many phone calls. Coming in late, leaving early. Depression. Mistakes."

"I thought you said suspects were our business," Wall interjected.

"I'm curious about what happens when a patient refuses a dose, or the nurse drops a pill and steps on it," PJ said.

"Yes, I see what you're getting at," Manning said. "They're called wasted doses. The nurse marks the dose in the computer as wasted, and requests a replacement. The safeguard is that a supervisor's or physician's approval is necessary."

"And that supervisor approves by doing what?"

"Entering his or her password in addition to the nurse's."

Schultz, PJ, and Wall looked at each other. "So if it wasn't actually wasted . . ." Schultz said.

"I'll be in Information Systems," PJ said. "I'll let you know if anything turns up."

An hour later, PJ was flipping through pharmacy administration reports when Schultz came in to tell her that he and Wall were calling it an evening.

"Shouldn't you be heading home, too? How's Thomas holding up?" Schultz said.

"I called home a little while ago. He was going to finish up some homework and then watch a movie."

"I hope you won't be much longer. That's no way for a kid to live, all alone in that house."

"Thanks for the guilt trip. Maybe we can travel together again some time. Besides, Dave went by the house earlier and took him a box of microwave popcorn and a six-pack. I don't think he's suffering all that much."

"A six-pack?"

"Of root beer, Detective."

"Just checking. You never know with Dave."

PJ rubbed her eyes. She could feel the tension in her shoulders and neck. Rolling her head in big circles didn't help much.

"I don't suppose you're good at massage?"

"Say again?"

"I'm really wound up," PJ said. "I never considered how taking this job would affect Thomas. I guess I didn't really grasp how demanding it would be, starting a new career and jumping into single parenthood at the same time. How did you cope with your family's needs, especially when your son was young?"

"I didn't," Schultz said. "This fucking job can put your family life into the toilet. Don't let that happen to you." He turned on his heel and left before PJ could answer.

PJ pinched the bridge of her nose, trying to persuade herself she really didn't have a headache. Hours ago, it seemed, she had been looking forward to getting home. Instead, she focused on the reports in front of her. It would have been handy if there had been a separate report that dealt only with wasted doses, but the hospital's system didn't provide one. She could probably extract that data herself with a special program, but there was no telling how long that would take. So she was bullying her way through, marking wasted doses with yellow highlighter.

By 10 P.M., her eyes were so blurry she could barely read

the small print. She called Thomas again to make sure he
wasn't scared or worried. He was very self-reliant, but these
were unusual times. She hated to miss his bedtime, and
she was sure he didn't like it either. He sounded a little
mopey but brave on the phone. She knew the nuances in
his voice, and they triggered a strong guilt reflex.

It would be so much easier if she still had Steven to rely
upon; that is, if he was still reliable instead of being the
greatest slimeball of all time. She wondered how single
parents did this for years, day in and day out; how they
faced the pressures of the responsibility, the compromises
between the needs of their jobs and those of their children.
It's easy to say "My child comes first," but it's a lot harder
to put that into action. It wasn't a one-time decision, either;
each day the question had to be faced again. She decided
that lately she hadn't been there enough for Thomas, and
she resolved to do something about it. Not only did she
need to spend more time with him on a regular basis, but
the two of them needed a major chunk of time to escape
their respective pressured lives. She didn't doubt for an
instant that there were serious pressures in his life, too.
People who thought twelve-year-olds led idyllic, stress-free
lives were fooling themselves. A long vacation was in order.
A long, cheap vacation.

She forced her attention back to the reports, and almost
at once the pattern jumped out at her. She hadn't seen it
earlier because the wasted doses were spread over a number of nursing stations. But there were nine instances, all
involving morphine, all tagged with one nurse's ID. She
phoned Human Resources and talked to the evening
worker, who was there primarily to answer questions about
sick leave or maternity benefits for second-shift staff. The
woman didn't want to give any information over the phone,
so PJ got directions to the office. Ten minutes later, after
PJ had shown her police department identification, she
got a look at the personnel file on Patricia Mulligan, a

nurse who worked in the float pool. That meant she filled in wherever needed, and had taken recent shifts in all the nursing stations PJ had marked on the report. PJ made note of the woman's address and phone number. Then she asked about Mulligan's current assignment, and found out that she was on duty tonight.

PJ went to the visitor's dining room and got herself a cup of coffee. At this time of the night, there were only a few other people in the room. There were two couples engaged in quiet, serious conversation, and one person at a table by himself, looking as though his world had fallen in. PJ tried to decide whether to confront Mulligan herself, or to call Schultz. This was her lead, her suspect, but she was dead tired and wanted to get home to Thomas, and to bed. She crumpled her coffee cup, tossed it into the trash can, and headed for a pay phone.

Glory would have to wait for better circumstances.

When Schultz got to Wood Memorial, it was nearly the end of the second shift. He contacted Patricia Mulligan's supervisor and asked her to set up a meeting between him and Mulligan when she went off duty. The supervisor suggested the nurses' break room on the fifth floor. He went there to wait for her.

The nurses on the fifth floor at Wood Memorial walked down or up a flight of stairs to use a break room elsewhere. This one was being remodeled, which translated into ladders, noise, suspended ceilings gaping open, and a couple of guys from facilities working at a pace which would have embarrassed a sloth. Maybe the day shift was better supervised and accomplished more. He was reminded of some nursery tale where gremlins came out at night and undid all the work people did during the daytime. He couldn't quite place the story.

Most of the tables were shoved to one side, and blue

tarps covered the beverage vending machines. The only advantage was that a layer of dust blanketed the noise when the workers drilled, pounded, or scraped, which was infrequently. As far as Schultz could tell, they spent most of their time looking for the right-size wrench and discussing the extramarital affairs of Elroy's wife, who apparently was a nymphomaniac. He wasn't able to discern whether either of the two men present was Elroy, but he thought he might enjoy meeting Elroy's wife.

He let his thoughts roam, remembering the look on PJ's face when he had asked her about men coming on to her at work. He wondered what particular kind of shrink crisis she had relived. An image of his former partner lying dead at the feet of a drug dealer bolted through Schultz's mind. He was momentarily enveloped in the memory, and his finger twitched as he mentally squeezed the trigger—once, twice—that sent the dealer sprawling on top of his partner.

It was a common denominator for them—cop, psychologist—that they dealt with human suffering, and they had developed their own defenses, their own compromises.

He had been in the room about fifteen minutes when Patricia Mulligan entered. She took a seat at the table, glancing at the workmen to make sure they weren't eavesdropping. If they'd had any thoughts of doing so, the thoughts evaporated under Schultz's gaze.

"Good evening, Detective Schultz," she said, with a curt nod in his direction. She took a seat at the table across from him. Then her eyes wandered around the room, pointedly avoiding him. She seemed fascinated with the tarps over the vending machines.

It was hot and stuffy. For some reason, the central heating system seemed to be dumping a whole floor's worth of heat into the break room. Schultz wiped his forehead with the back of his hand, then wondered what to do with his wet hand. He wiped it on his pants. Mulligan wasn't looking at him anyway. He might as well stand up and give his ass a good scratching while he was at it.

He studied her, letting the silence stretch out to the point that most people experienced an irresistible tension, like the urge to pop a bubble. She was perhaps twenty-seven, with a face and figure that would have interested Schultz in other circumstances. She was tall, with brown hair and pale blue eyes that could be warm and trusting, but were brittle with apprehension and moving nervously around the room. He noticed that the two workmen had left, apparently heading for their own break area.

"Miss Mulligan, I'm Detective Leo Schultz, Homicide. I'd like to ask you a few questions about Maximillian Winters."

Instead of answering, she opened the purse she had placed on the desk and withdrew a tape recorder.

Alarms clanged in Schultz's mind. Either she was about to make a confession or she was going to be one of those sticklers about harassment. All right, he could handle either of those. He was going to do this formally.

Schultz nodded and pressed the record button. He gave his name, paused while the nurse—"Patricia Jane Mulligan"—spoke her name, and then he added the date, time, and location. Then he pulled a dog-eared card from his pocket and read the nurse her rights.

"You understand everything you've been told, and that you are about to be questioned concerning the death of Maximillian Winters."

Patricia Mulligan nodded.

"Speak your answer so the tape recorder can pick it up," Schultz said.

"Oh. Yes."

"And do you wish to have a lawyer present before we proceed? You understand that you may stop at any time during the questioning and request a lawyer?"

"No, I don't want a lawyer at this time. Yes, I understand I can stop."

Too cool. Schultz thought. *What gives?*

"Would you like to make a statement of any kind?" Schultz asked.

"Yes." She sat forward, leaning toward the recorder. Schultz found himself doing the same, as though the tape recorder was about to reveal an elusive truth.

"I want to say I had nothing to do with Rowena Clark's death or Jerry's insulin OD." She stopped, and began to twist the end of her shoulder-length hair around her right forefinger. "I did give Mr. Winters an overdose of morphine. But the main thing is that I was forced into it."

Schultz simply said, "Please continue."

"See, I did this once before," Patricia continued. "Back in April, there was this woman who was in terrible pain. She was dying, and she had no one. No family. No visitors. I guess she reminded me of my mother, who died when I was sixteen. I used to sit with her, sometimes after my shift was over if I was too busy on shift. She asked me to help her die, to put an end to the pain."

She sighed, and Schultz could imagine her gradually taking on responsibility for the dying woman, coming to feel almost like family.

"It took me over a week to accumulate the drug. I did it by marking doses as wasted in the computer, so that the pharmacy would send a replacement. But actually, the original dose had been given. I didn't want to have too many all at once, so I spread them out over a few days. You have to understand it was like my mother was asking me for something. I couldn't ignore it."

Schultz wanted to dig into the episode she was describing, but figured there was plenty of time for that later.

"About ten days ago—I think it was on a Wednesday— I got an e-mail message on my computer at home. It said that he knew all about what I had done, and that it was illegal. If I didn't go along with his plan, he would report me to the police."

"He?" interjected Schultz.

"I didn't know that at the time, but I talked to him on the phone later. It was definitely a man's voice."

"What happened next?" Schultz said, trying to keep an I-don't-bite look on his face.

"I thought he was bluffing. I ignored it. A couple of days later I got a message with a complete list of all the wasted doses with my ID on them."

"Did you save the e-mails?" Schultz asked.

"No."

"Well, I'll have to find out if there's a chance we could retrieve them. Go on."

"His next message said that he would protect me if I'd do something for him. I was supposed to call him on the phone."

"Why didn't you go to the police then?" Schultz asked.

"I . . . I guess I was afraid. I thought maybe this man could erase everything that pointed to me. Destroy the computer records. Then I'd be OK. I wouldn't do it ever again, no matter how much the patient begged." She was silent for a moment.

"Destroy the computer records?" Schultz said. He got the message loud and clear: this nurse had been in contact with the hacker they were searching for. PJ was going to love this.

"I didn't know what to do. I called him. When I found out what he wanted, I nearly panicked. Maybe I did panic. Over the next few days, I guess I talked myself into it. I mean, Mr. Winters was terminal, and had to be in pain, although he didn't show it a lot. It wasn't like I was doing something horrible. I would get this over, and that would be an end to it. But then, afterward, I felt sick. I mean really sick. I threw up and couldn't come to work. It wasn't the same. I . . . I killed him. I wish I could undo it . . ."

She took a couple of minutes to pull herself together, dabbing at her eyes with a tissue that she had produced from somewhere in the vicinity of her left uniform sleeve. He couldn't decide if it was actual remorse or if she was faking it.

"This afternoon, I was in the bathroom crying, and I couldn't stop. I decided to do the right thing and tell someone. I was working up my nerve to call the police, and well, here you are." Patricia sniffled, then her face took on a harder look that made Schultz think the whole teary bit was just an act.

"The main thing, as I said at the beginning," she said, "is that I was forced into this. Blackmailed. Doesn't that make a difference? I guess I'll lose my job. But going to jail . . . I have proof. I have the blackmailer's voice on tape."

She slipped a hand into her uniform pocket, withdrew an audiotape, and placed it on the table. Schultz and Mulligan started talking at the same time. Schultz reached for the tape, and found his hand closing on air. She had snatched the tape away.

"I think I'd like to have that lawyer now," Patricia said.

CHAPTER

15

When PJ finally dragged herself into the house, she was relieved that the day was over. The first thing she did was go to the medicine cabinet and paw through it for cold medicine. She found a bottle of Nyquil, but it was almost gone. There wasn't even a full dose left. She took the lid off and tossed back the dregs, then ran a little bit of water into the bottle and shook it, holding her thumb over the opening. She drank the water, sucking out every drop. It would have to do.

Megabite came out from wherever she had been sleeping, blinking her eyes accusingly at PJ. Even her cat was trying to provoke guilt over not spending enough time at home, and succeeding at it. PJ sat down at the kitchen table, beckoning the cat with her fingers. Megabite jumped up into her lap, put her white-tipped paws on PJ's chest, and bumped PJ under the chin with her head.

"I know, Purrface," PJ said. "It's been rough, especially with Thomas back in school. Nobody around to treat you in the manner you deserve." The cat jumped down and walked over to her food bowl. It was such an obvious ploy that PJ had to laugh. She rummaged in the refrigerator, settling on a leftover hamburger wrapped in aluminum foil. She had no idea where it had come from. She unwrapped it and smelled it. Her nose was stuffy from her cold, but she thought it was OK. At least it wasn't green yet. She threw the bun in the trash and crumbled the hamburger into Megabite's bowl. The cat, trying to fill its mouth and purr at the same time, sounded like a sewing machine running underwater. PJ gave her a final pat and climbed the stairs.

She ran a hot bath, stripped her clothes off, and left them where they fell on the floor. The soak was delicious. Her muscles, which felt like twanging rubber bands, began to relax. The steamy room did wonderful things for her clogged sinuses, or perhaps that was the Nyquil kicking in. Her headache faded. When the water began to cool, she soaped herself and washed her hair. Then she opened the drain to let the water out and scooted forward in the tub, folding her legs pretzel-style. The faucet was tall and curved, rising high above the rolled rim of the tub in a graceful arc. Thomas said it reminded him of a silver candy cane. Warm water cascaded from it, rinsing her skin and hair.

Flannel pajamas. Thick white terry cloth bathrobe. It didn't get any better than that.

She went into Thomas's room to check that he was underneath the blankets. The house was cool tonight, just the way they both liked it for sleeping. His room was dark except for a night-light, so she waited inside the doorway until her eyes adjusted. Then she went over and bent down to give him a kiss on the forehead. He stirred.

"Mmm . . . That you, Mom?"

"Who else would it be in your bedroom at night?"

"Smarty pants," he said, waking up more fully. "I'm glad you're home. I kind of missed you."

In the dim light, she could see his eyes, and the tip of his nose gleaming, the harbinger of teenage oily skin. She thought it was the dearest sight in the world.

"You smell good," he said.

"Save the flattery for your future wife."

"Mom, can we talk a little? I know it's late, but . . ."

"We can talk all you want. Do you want to go to the kitchen?"

He sat up and swung his legs over the edge of the bed. "Here's fine."

She turned on his desk lamp and dragged over the chair from his desk. They sat close, knees almost touching. He looked worried. PJ waited for him to begin, wondering if he had made any decision about going to visit his father when the baby was born. The time was approaching—she fervently hoped that Carla was bloated and had hemorrhoids that dragged the ground—and Thomas hadn't said anything about it recently.

She noticed that his legs were as long as hers. *That must have happened just today*, she thought.

"I've been thinking a lot about Dad inviting me out to Denver. I sort of decided something, and I'm afraid neither of you are going to like it."

"Lay it on me, dude, I'm a strong chick."

She was rewarded with a smile, but it didn't last long.

"I don't want to go," Thomas said.

"All right."

He rushed on, ignoring her agreement. "I know Dad's going to be really disappointed. He's made such a big deal about it. And I know you want me to keep seeing Dad, trying to stay close to him."

"Honey, I said it's OK. We'll deal with his disappointment together. I don't mean to pressure you to see him if you don't want to. I just didn't want him to slip out of your life while the two of us weren't paying attention."

"You mean it's all right with you?"

She reached forward and placed both of her hands on his knees. "You're calling the shots here. I fully support your decision."

All of a sudden, a hundred pounds of boy shot into her arms, nearly bowling her over in the chair. She stood up, wrapping her arms around him. He buried his head against her shoulder. A minute later, he sniffled and pulled back and sat down on the edge of the bed again. From man to boy and back again, in 120 seconds flat.

"It's just that I don't want to be around him and Carla," Thomas said. "They act so lovey-dovey, and all I can think about is what he did to our family."

"T-man, it's important to know that in most divorces, there's blame on both sides of the fence. From his point of view, I'm sure I was responsible for the breakup."

"I don't buy that, Mom. He's still my dad, but that doesn't mean I have to love him. Or forgive him. That's between him and me."

"I just hope you won't totally shut him out of your life. There's no telling how you'll feel a year from now."

"A year from now I'll have a little brother. A half brother, isn't that what he'll be? Because you're not his mom."

PJ nodded, feeling a pang of emptiness. She had always wanted Thomas to have a brother or sister.

"Maybe I'll get to know him. Maybe that's how I'll keep Dad in my life."

"That's a nice thought, T-man. You'd make a good big brother."

He yawned, and she could see that he was wound down and ready to sleep again. A burden had been lifted. He didn't resist as she tucked him in.

"Good night, Mom," he said sleepily. "And thanks. Thanks for understanding."

"Good night," she said, backing out of the room. "Don't let the bedbugs bite," she said, but he was already breathing in his sleep rhythm, and she didn't think he heard.

* * *

The phone rang just as her head hit the pillow. She grabbed it hurriedly, hoping it didn't wake Thomas.

"What?" she said, with sleep-deprived annoyance.

"Did I wake you?" Schultz asked.

"Technically, no."

"Good. Don't like to be a bother. I've got some news, though. Hot stuff. Speaking of hot stuff, got your baby doll pajamas on?"

"None of your business," she said, with all the iciness she could muster in her half-asleep state.

"OK, no fooling around. You were right on the money. Mulligan offed the old man with extra doses of morphine she saved up. She actually confessed. Chalk one up for you, Doc."

"I'm not keeping score," she said, wondering if, in fact, she was. "Couldn't this have waited until morning?"

"She wasn't acting alone. She was being blackmailed."

"You mean by our hacker?"

"Yeah. Has to be. And here's the best part. She's got his voice on tape."

PJ was excited, although she could practically feel the pillow reaching out and tugging her down. "Is that good? What can we do with a taped voice?"

"I'll forgive that little remark since I woke you up. You don't have your head on straight, Doc. Voiceprints aren't infallible. They don't even hold up very well in court. But they're good during an investigation. They can be matched with a suspect's voice."

"Once you have a suspect."

"Yeah, there is that. Well, shit, you gotta start somewhere."

PJ lowered her head to the pillow and reached to replace the receiver. She could still hear Schultz's voice: "Doc, you there? Doc?'' Then she clicked the receiver down, and the next thing she knew it was morning.

It wasn't until four o'clock the next afternoon that PJ heard the tape. She waited in a room crammed with audio-visual equipment, most of which she didn't recognize. Louie, the A/V tech, had acknowledged her entrance into the room, then gone back to his work. He had some hapless gadget pinned on a board and laid open like a frog being dissected. When Schultz and Wall arrived, Louie rolled his wheelchair over to a console with a lot of slides, buttons, and dials.

"Poor quality," Louie said. PJ imagined him turning up his nose. "Noisy recording made on a unit with dirty heads, handheld a few inches away from the phone handset. Variable volume. She kept moving the unit, probably trying to shift back and forth between ear and mouth. I had to clean it up a lot."

"Crank it up, Louie," Wall said. It seemed to be the only thing he ever said to the man. It was probably the only thing anyone ever said to Louie. PJ tried to picture someone whispering sweet nothings into his ear, but failed. One ear permanently sprouted a device which didn't look like a hearing aid. It fit snugly into his ear canal, but it had an antenna about an inch long. The other ear sprouted hair. She resolved to treat him as much like a human being as possible and less like an overgrown radio. Louie punched a button, then wheeled over to the battered green table the others were clustered around.

"Hello," said a woman's voice. Her greeting was immediately followed by a loud thunk.

"Dropped the unit," Louie said. It was apparent what he thought of people who abused audio equipment, however low-end.

". . . call. Have you thought about our little joint venture, Pitty-Pat?"

"Yes, I've thought about it. What is it you want me to do?"

"I want you to do what you've already done."

"What? I don't understand."

"It was illegal, you know. I could turn everything over to the police."

"Exactly what is it you want me to do?"

"Help someone die. That's the way you think of it, isn't it? Helping?"

"I don't . . . Who are you talking about?"

"His name is Winters. He's almost dead already. It wouldn't take much, would it, Pitty-Pat?"

"I know Winters. He's DNR, but that doesn't mean he wants any active help."

"Active. Yes, that's the word. I want you to be active with Mr. Winters. Do it the same way you did before."

"Why should I? Then there would be two cases hanging over me . . ."

"No one will know. I'll fix everything. From both cases. It will all be gone."

"What do you mean, gone?"

"The computer records. I can change them, erase everything. Remember, if I found the pattern, others could, too. It's only a matter of time."

"Let me think about it."

"I need your answer now. Or I'll send the same list of wasted meds to the police as I sent to you."

There was a long pause.

"All right, I'll do it. Only because Mr. Winters is terminal."

"Excellent. Just one more thing."

"Nothing else. I won't do anything else!"

"Sure you will. You don't want to go to jail, do you? I

want you to make it look like Dr. Eleanor Graham did the dirty deed.''

"Dr. Graham? Why?"

"You don't need to know that," the voice said harshly. Then, cajoling, "It will be easy. Just use her ID for verification when you report the meds wasted.''

"Doctors don't usually make that kind of entry. Besides, I don't know her ID.''

"But it's not unheard of, is it? Doctors have done that before, after rounds. I know. I've checked.''

"I guess it's possible.''

"Her ID is RCTE9054. She's been changing it once a week, on Mondays. I'll get you the new one next Monday.''

Louie slapped his hand down on his console, and the recording stopped. Schultz, Wall, and PJ rose, without saying anything, and headed for the door. Yesterday she had felt like she was on the ragged edge of a cold, and today had confirmed it. Her head ached, her nose was stuffy, and her throat hurt. She was glad to be leaving. On the way out the door, PJ remembered her resolution, and turned around.

"Thanks, Louie. You've been a big help.''

The man angled his chair toward her and gave her a grin that could melt an iceberg.

"You're welcome, Dr. Gray.''

"Call me PJ.''

"Sure. Anytime you need something, maybe a movie copied, something like that, you just give me a call.''

"I'll remember that.''

"See you later, PJ,'' he said.

CHAPTER
16

Cracker broke his dial-up connection to the police department network. He had just finished checking the active arrest records and was not terribly surprised at what he had found there.

He was disappointed in his last effort. He had made sure no trace remained of the e-mail messages, and there was no longer any record of the local phone call the Mulligan woman had made to Hardee's. The computerized record of the wasted drugs still existed in the hospital's system, as he meant it to. There was nothing to connect him to the whole ugly thing. She might blab—probably would, to save her skin—but the police would have only her word for it. The identity of her mystery blackmailer would remain a secret. Most likely the police wouldn't believe her story, which did sound a little outlandish. He chuckled, trying to put a mechanical sound to it. Mulligan was supposed to have claimed that Dr. Graham helped her obtain the drugs. Fat chance of that working out. The little wimp had caved in at the first difficulty, even before there were any difficulties. It had all gone smoothly, and poof—she let it tumble down around her.

Looking back on it, he should have known the woman was inadequate for the purpose. After all, her idea of concealing her trail had been to go to a different computer from the one at her usual post to enter the dispensing requests, as if merely using another input device could fool someone. She was a fine sample of the raw material he had to work with, to try to bend to his will. No wonder he kept missing the target.

Wanting to get back at Mulligan for being such a weak lump of flesh, he took a few minutes to ruin her credit rating, report all of her credit cards stolen, give her a criminal record for prostitution, and order a hundred magazine subscriptions and ThighMasters in her name. He hadn't messed with that kind of petty stuff since he was a kid, but it made him feel better.

Then he went out to the kitchen and peeled a banana while considering what to do next. It was time for Plan C, and it had to be one with no loopholes.

Cracker opened his mind, let in the thought that was circling like an airplane in a holding pattern. Picked at it, rolled it around, examined the thought from as many different directions as he could. Let it settle in, put its feet up, and ask for a beer.

When the thought of killing Mom Elly was good and comfortable in his mind, he walked back to the spare room. He took a tablet of stationery, the kind that comes from drugstores, from a desk drawer. He wrote a short note, then searched through the desk until he found the ink pad he kept for just one purpose. Pressing his right thumb onto the black spongy surface and then onto the note, he signed with a thumbprint. It took him a couple of minutes to find a small envelope. It had a torn corner, but he used it anyway. Longer still to find a stamp. The address he didn't have to look up, couldn't anyway, because it wasn't recorded anywhere in his office. Cracker made a quick trip to the post office.

Driving there, he pretended that he and the car were one.

CHAPTER

17

When PJ got home that evening, she dropped into a chair at the kitchen table without even turning on the light, folded her arms, and put her head down. She stayed in that position only a minute or two, because if she stayed longer, she knew she would fall asleep right at the table. She had been fighting off a cold all day, and now she felt like surrendering to it. She wished she had someone there to wait on her and comfort her. She felt the gentle brush of a cat's whiskers on her cheek and, moments later, a scratchy tongue grooming the hairs of her forearm. She sat up and encircled Megabite with her arms. The young cat flopped over on her side and presented her tummy for stroking. PJ did as the cat expected, and was rewarded with a sweet purr. Running her fingers through the fur, PJ felt that the incision from the spaying was almost completely healed. There was a small bump of scar tissue underneath, as the vet had said to expect. The purring got louder when PJ tickled the scar and the short fur around it. It probably itched. She remembered, with renewed chagrin, the time Stephen had talked her into shaving her pubic hair. It had itched when it was growing out. For days she had gone around furtively scratching, hoping no one noticed, afraid that others would think she had lice.

She could smile about it now.

Her whole week was shot, and the only thing there was to show for it was the arrest of Patricia Mulligan. So far this case had turned up one killer, but not the right one. PJ believed Patricia Mulligan when she said she had nothing to do with the earlier murder and attempted murder at the hospital. She began to run through the facts, playing them back like a VR scenario in her mind. She felt as though something was just beyond her reach, something that could be crucial. If she could just determine the killer's motive, everything would fall into place.

Just as her head was beginning to sag back down toward the table, Thomas came into the kitchen and flipped the light switch. She blinked and looked at him. For a moment, her wearied senses fed her false information. She glimpsed Thomas as a grown man, taller, muscular, and confident, and felt his physical presence not as a gangly preteen but as the dynamic man he would become. Her pride in her son swelled in her throat and a soft gasp loosed itself from her lips. She blinked again, slowly, and when she opened her eyes, there stood her undeniably twelve-year-old boy, with his face painted in red-and-white stripes and red handprints on his undeveloped bare chest.

"Hi, Mom. Winston's here, and we're watching *Pocahontas*. I'm supposed to be an Indian brave. What do you think?" He puffed out his chest and put a grim look on his face. "These are bear paw prints," he said, pointing to his chest.

"Aren't you a little old for *Pocahontas*?"

"It's a neat movie. Besides, it's only Winston. It's not like it's anybody who matters or a girl or something."

PJ knew that Winston did matter to her son. He was the

one Thomas had turned to when they first arrived in St. Louis. PJ had worried at first that Thomas was using the boy as a temporary convenience and would drop him later when he became more confident in the new social environment. Winston was an unpopular boy, not gifted with the appearance or personal skills which would make him part of the rapidly changing cliques at the school. Thomas, on the other hand, was handsome and outgoing, and could navigate the treacherous waters of the seventh-grade social milieu with ease. But he had chosen to deepen his friendship with Winston, and now the two were inseparable. With Winston, Thomas didn't have to worry about appearing cool. He could be himself, with maturity and childishness flipping as fast as alternating current.

Winston's dad, Bill Lakeland, was a nice guy in a tough situation. When they had first met a few months ago, his wife was in a treatment center, trying to overcome multiple addictions. Now she was living in a group home, under close supervision. His story seemed to parallel Mike Wolf's—a wife struggling with addiction—but PJ hoped there would be a happier ending in Bill's case. Bill had taken on the role of single parent with determination and goodwill, without dwelling on what could have been. She resolved to invite Bill and his son over for dinner sometime. Maybe she could have some semblance of a normal social life herself, have some enjoyable company in a nonthreatening way. The thought of the four of them sitting around her kitchen table warmed her.

"Since you're in the kitchen anyway, how about some snacks?"

Ordinarily, Thomas was self-reliant enough to fix his own snacks, but she could see that he was eager to get back to the movie. She bowed her head melodramatically.

"Yes, Master. Anything you say, Master," she said. "Will that be popcorn or grapes, Master?"

"Actually I was thinking of cookies and milk."

"Yes, Master. Your humble servant will suspend nutritional guidelines for this special occasion. But Master will eat a good breakfast in return."

"Cool, Mom," Thomas replied. He was halfway out the door. "Don't bother with plates. Just bring the whole package."

"Nice try, Master."

PJ fixed a tray with two huge glasses of milk and a plate of Oreos. She snitched a couple off the plate and slipped them into her pocket before delivering the tray.

She spooned some decaf into the Mr. Coffee and filled the water reservoir, then went upstairs to change into a T-shirt and sweatpants. In the bathroom, she splashed cold water on her face. Refreshed, she followed her nose back to the coffee and poured a big mug, which she took into the study. She closed the door behind her, which toned down the video noise to an indistinct babble, and made her way over to the chair, admiring the screen saver Thomas had left running. It was from a program called Triazzle, a fascinating puzzle which featured rainforest creatures such as brightly colored frogs, beetles, and butterflies. They moved across a blackened screen, emitting soft chirps and squeaks. She sat down and ran through a few puzzles, delighted as always when the creatures came to life as the puzzle was correctly assembled. The discipline of puzzle solving calmed her mind and energized her. She sipped her coffee, which felt great on her sore throat, and made plans for the coming day. The first thing she wanted to do was play the tape with the hacker's voice for Dr. Graham, and see if the woman showed any reaction to it. It might be someone she knew.

Since she was wide awake, she decided to work until the movie was over and Winston needed a ride home. It was a school night, so the boys weren't allowed to stay up too late. All day she had felt something tickling the back of her mind about the case, something she could pick up on if she was just in the right frame of mind.

She had an abbreviated version of her VR software on her home computer. It wasn't nearly as powerful as the version that ran on her Silicon Graphics workstation in the office, but it could limp through a simulation. The renditions of three-dimensional objects weren't very good; they simply looked like flat objects with oddly shaped shadows. The motion was jerky, and there was no artificial intelligence routine which allowed the computer to extrapolate and present its own solutions. There were just enough functions to make it useful. Cranking up the simulation of Rowena Clark's last few hours of life, she tried to clear her mind of preconceptions and watch as if it was the first time she had been through it.

When the figure that represented Dr. Graham entered Rowena's room, the screen flickered, and then PJ was startled to see a new character in the playback. There was a shadowy figure standing near the door, half again as tall as the others. She halted the simulation, ran it back fifteen seconds, and played it again. *Flicker.* Then the tall figure near the door. The blinds were closed on the window in Rowena's computerized room, as they had been in reality that morning. The doorway to the room was partially hidden by a closet that jutted out near the bathroom, so that area was poorly lighted on the screen. PJ paused the playback, walked over to the door, and called for Thomas.

"T-man, have you been messing around with my work files on the computer?"

"No."

"We have a deal about that, remember."

"I said no. Now can I go back and watch the movie?"

She held her son's gaze for a moment, then, certain he was telling the truth, sent him back into the living room. She started up the simulation again. The dark figure moved into a better-lighted area of the room. She saw at once that it was intended to represent the Grim Reaper: hooded robe, face hidden, a long-handled scythe concealed partially in the folds of the robe. Although her playback had sound capability, the Grim Reaper advanced across the screen in total silence. He seemed to float rather than walk, a much smoother motion than when he first appeared. As he approached the hospital bed, Dr. Graham turned to face it. A stylized look of fear formed on her face. The Reaper raised one hand to his hood, and tugged it back so that his face was revealed.

A moment later, he whirled the scythe, slicing Dr. Graham in half. Both halves toppled over and gushed fountains of blood. In the hospital bed, Rowena's eyes opened wide and then closed as her head sagged to the side, apparently in a faint. The whole floor filled with blood, vastly more than could have been contained in Dr. Graham's body, and the level was rising, sloshing onto the Reaper's robe. The Reaper turned to face PJ and pulled the hood more completely away from his face.

He was a gleaming robot. Multifaceted clear eyes shone, like diamonds lighted from behind. The planes of his face were sharp, as though plates of shiny metal had been glued onto a human skull. There was no discernible mouth, but PJ knew that the Grim Reaper was beyond all those things a mouth would be used for: speaking, eating, kissing. He bowed stiffly and walked, through the rising blood, back to the shadows near the door. The severed halves of Dr. Graham's body continued to spout blood, and soon the whole screen was filled with it. *Flicker.* He was gone.

The simulation stopped. A few silent seconds later, PJ's emotions caught up with her, and she began to shake. She fumbled at the keyboard, quitting the program, then made a backup copy of the simulation on a Zip cartridge. By the time she finished those mechanical tasks, her breathing was back to normal, and she trusted herself to make a phone call to Schultz.

She waited for him at the back door. It took him twenty minutes to get to her house, but in that time, she had gotten her composure back and come to some conclusions about the simulation.

Schultz's disheveled hair indicated that he must have been in bed already, even though it was barely 9 P.M. She wondered if perhaps it wasn't sleep from which he had been rousted. It was the first time she had seen him in clothes other than his office outfits. He was wearing Levi's and a T-shirt decorated with realistically drawn baseballs, basketballs, soccer balls, tennis balls, golf balls, and footballs. Underneath was an inscription that said "The way to a man's heart is through his balls."

"Nice shirt," she said, as he brushed past her.

"I'll bet you wish you had one," he replied.

"I thought two was the customary number."

His face blanked for a second, then he shook his head. "Let me give you a piece of heartfelt advice, Doc. Don't tangle with a man on ball jokes. You'll just get your ass whipped."

She closed the door to the study; the movie was still going on. Schultz watched impassively as the altered simulation played itself out on the screen.

"Looks like some of those video games for kids. One step up from splatter flicks. I wouldn't let my kids see that kind of shit."

PJ didn't want to bring up the fact that he had only one child, fully grown, and a drug pusher serving time at that. It was a little late to worry about what kind of video games he played.

Schultz nodded at the screen. "I guess you were right about the motive being revenge. Whoever made that up doesn't have warm, cozy feelings for the lady doc. How did this change get here?"

"I've been thinking about that. Either the hacker—we

are considering him the killer, aren't we?—broke into my house and sat right here in this chair and put in the changes, or he used a back door."

"You saying he broke in the back door and used this computer?" Schultz started to lever himself out of the desk chair he had claimed. PJ realized he was going back to examine the kitchen door.

"No, no," she said. "I mean either he was here physically or he hacked in while I was dialed up to the computer at work, which is connected to the departmental network."

"He can do that?" The look on Schultz's face was priceless. He looked like a little kid finding out that the Mickey Mouse at Disney World was just a person in a costume.

"If he can get into the hospital network, what makes you think your own department is immune? He probably had it easy. I think he's the one who left this computer on my doorstep, and he put in some special code to make it easy for him to bypass any security or passwords I set up. It's called a back door. Programmers do it all the time."

"Do you?"

"Well, now that you mention it . . . I've got systems out there running at client sites I could still get into. But I don't have any bad intentions. Besides, cookies are my favorites."

"You've lost me, Doc," Schultz said.

"Cookies are little goodies for the users. Special features, like maybe a funny graphic, that a user can stumble upon after doing a particular set of actions in a row. They're very popular in game software, with the programmers and gamers alike. But even stuffy old business software can have cookies. It's funny to think about some executive giving a presentation, and he hits the magic combination, and up pops an animated dinosaur that stomps out his charts."

"This is nerd humor, right?"

"I suppose it is."

Schultz shook his head, signaling back to business. "We need to go for the obvious first," he said. "I'll get an ETU over here to look for signs of entry and take fingerprints from the computer." He made a quick phone call.

When the Evidence Technician Unit arrived, the two boys were thrilled. The movie was forgotten, and they crowded into the doorway of the study to watch. One of the techs took their fingerprints in order to exclude them. They had free access to the computer, and certainly their prints could be found there. PJ made sure they promptly washed their hands with the gritty liquid soap offered by the tech so they wouldn't ink her walls. She knew that Thomas's prints were already in the department's database from the break-in last spring, but she didn't want to spoil his fun. He was showing off in front of Winston: *Bet nothing like this ever happens at your house!*

When the techs were done with the outer casing of the computer, she put on gloves and opened the case. She examined the inside carefully, looking for unusual boards or chips or programmable memory that didn't belong there. Satisfied, she reassembled the case. Her next step would be to look for hidden files or application programs that were larger than they should be, meaning that code had been inserted. But she could do that after Schultz left. As she plugged the computer back in, another thought came to her.

"Neptune," she said.

"Pardon?" Schultz looked up from a notebook.

"The note that came with this computer said 'My name is Neptune.' That's either the name of the code that lets him break in, or his back door password. Son of a bitch," she said, sinking into a chair. "The bastard was waving it right in my face. Flaunting it, and I didn't pick it up."

"Christ, Doc, don't take it so hard. Nobody could have figured that out."

"I could have. I should have. If I hadn't been so convinced that Mike Wolf was responsible for the computer . . ."

"Lover boy at the university?"

"That remains to be seen, but yes, that's the guy. I thought he sent this hardware to impress me, or just to be nice."

"So how about him as a suspect?"

"Mike? Oh, no, I don't think so. What could his motive possibly be?"

Schultz shrugged. "I'll put Anita on it. She'll fit right in with those college students. Let her nose around, see if anything smells."

"I really don't think that's necessary."

"Yeah, and maybe you're thinking with your gonads, or whatever it is that women have down there."

She opened her mouth to retort, but bit back her words. He was just doing his job, and she wouldn't have it any other way.

The ETU was packed up and gone. "I still have a lot of work to do, Detective," PJ said. Now that the excitement was over, her cold reasserted itself. Fatigue tugged at her, and she would have liked nothing more than to give in to it, but there were other demands on her time.

"I can take a hint. You don't have to see me to the door."

"Actually, I was wondering if you'd mind driving Winston home."

"Christ, Doc, I'm a cop, not a taxi driver."

"His house is only a couple of blocks from a Dunkin' Donuts. How about a dozen on me?"

"Hey, Winston, get in here," Schultz said, holding out his hand and rubbing his thumb and middle finger together. "Doc says you have to go home now. What kind of a wimpy name is Winston, anyway?"

PJ winced, but at least she knew the boy would be delivered safely home. She dug into her wallet and came out

with a five-dollar bill. "Here," she said, placing it in his
outstretched palm. "Get yourself a cup of coffee, too."

Schultz pocketed the money, then playfully grabbed
Winston by the back of the collar and tugged. "Are you
coming peacefully or do I have to cuff you?" he said. The
boy's eyes went wide.

"Ever see the inside of an official undercover vehicle,
son?" he said, dragging Winston out the door toward his
orange Pacer.

Later, when Thomas was finally asleep, PJ returned to
the study. She used a utility program which checked her
computer's hard disk for hidden files or "fat" software.
When the search came up negative, she initialized the disk,
wiping out the directory and the data, then rebuilt it from
original software installation disks. She didn't put back the
corrupted simulation. By 1 A.M., she was exhausted but
satisfied that her computer was clean. She made a connection with Merlin, her mentor and advisor on all things
computerized. There was something she wanted from him,
a program she had never had use for until now. It was
called a spike, and it was used to trace the deliberately
convoluted paths hackers took to break into networked
systems. Her computer at work was probably the end of a
long chain of way stations, or hubs, across which the hacker
had skillfully probed. A spike, if initiated while the hacker
was logged on, could bounce back along the hubs like a
reflected shaft of light. Unfortunately, that was all part
of the game for hackers. If the spike was detected, the
connection would be broken before it reached the terminus.

As she was downloading the program Merlin had provided, PJ formed an image of the spike gathering speed
and physically bursting from the hacker's computer and
impaling him in the chest, transfixing him like a stake

through a vampire's heart. It wasn't her usual type of imagery, but it felt good.

Finally, she dragged herself up the stairs, took a couple of Tylenol, and dropped into bed.

CHAPTER

18

CHAPTER

18

Cracker strolled past the bear pens once before doubling back and sitting down on a bench. It was Flash's idea to meet at the St. Louis Zoo, but Cracker didn't mind the outing. On his way back, he was planning to visit Aunt Karen.

It was October 26th, a Saturday morning. The sky was filled with pendulous gray clouds waiting for just the right moment to soak the sparse crowd, and the temperature was in the low forties. Determined mothers, red dots of effort and windchill riding each cheek, pushed strollers with babies so bundled up that only their eyes showed, while toddlers in too many layers of clothing tried to keep up. Cracker wore jeans, a long-sleeved shirt, and a sweatshirt, and he was comfortable. He didn't require much in the way of warmth, and actually preferred machine room environs, the year-round air-conditioned rooms which housed mainframe computers. The heat spilled by the equipment was pulled away by air circulation strong enough to create a draft from underneath the raised floors which hid the cabling. More and more computers were being built to minimize the need for a special environment. Personal computers were a triumph in that area, but a lot of progress had been made with minis and even some mainframes. Cracker wasn't sure it was progress, though. He liked the idea of pampering computer equipment instead of treating it like a blender or a can opener.

The sweatshirt he was wearing was black, with large red letters that said "Panic Button." Underneath the words was an arrow running all the way down the front of the sweatshirt, so that it pointed at his groin, and he accentuated the reference by slouching down on the bench, legs extended. That was the outfit Flash was expecting. He had already gotten some amused looks from other zoogoers, with only one mother scrunching her eyebrows together disapprovingly.

Across the walkway, a polar bear was enjoying its pool, splashing around and playing with a large tough rubber ball. The bear would hold the ball down under the water with its paws, then let go, watching the ball shoot way up into the air. The bear did this over and over, as though it were studying the effects of buoyancy.

He had bought a box of popcorn to give his hands something to do. There was a certain amount of tension involved in meeting Flash, and his hands had a tendency to reveal his emotions. If he didn't have butter on his fingers, he would probably have been running them nervously through his hair.

"You Cracker?" said a voice behind him. It was a surprisingly childlike voice, not at all threatening. Cracker kept himself from turning around, in case the man had decided that he didn't want to be seen after all.

"Yes," he said, and tossed a piece of popcorn up in the air and caught it in his mouth, the way Dad had shown him years ago.

The man came around to the front of the bench and

sat down, leaving at least two feet between them. Apparently he wasn't going to hide his identity. Cracker slid his eyes over for a glimpse.

"Why do we have to do this in person?" Cracker said.

"Because it's the way I work. Had a client once, changed his mind after the job was done. Said he didn't really mean it, was going to turn me in for murdering his wife. Cried his eyes out. Good thing I had him on tape planning the whole thing. Exchange of money, criminal conversation, conspiracy to commit murder."

"You go down, so do I," Cracker said.

Flash patted his jacket where his right shirt pocket would be underneath. "Every word on tape. Just so you know."

Cracker shifted a little so he could see the man better. He studied him without saying anything for a couple of minutes. The man he knew only as Flash had a round face with an odd scar on his left cheek, a large reddish area, irregularly shaped, with a kind of puckering at the edges. He was younger than Cracker expected, only a few years older than himself. The eyes were busy, moving constantly, an unremarkable gray. The face rode a neck with a roll of fat at the base of it, although the body below was not noticeably plump. It looked as though the man had lost weight everywhere but his face and neck. His brown hair was caught up indifferently in a rubber band at the nape, although it appeared more an expediency to keep the wind from blowing it in his eyes than a style. He was wearing a leather jacket, cracked from age and weather. His stone-washed jeans looked a size too small and had grass stains on the knees that seemed out of character. Gardener? Handyman? Lover?

As Cracker was trying to determine how old the man was, he noticed that there were no eyebrows on the man's broad, flat face. Short, stubby eyelashes marked the threshold of an enormous expanse of forehead, unbroken by the slash of eyebrows or a hairline. The man had long hair in back, but it was attached to his skull in a U-shape. It came to Cracker that Flash's trademark was written on his face.

The man had encountered fire in the past, and it had seared both his face and his outlook on the world.

Cracker didn't know a lot about Flash, and that made him nervous. He preferred to be in the position of knowing every detail of a person's life. Knowledge was power, and Cracker was accustomed to holding the reins. This man had been recommended to him by a previous client, who told him matter-of-factly that killing was what Flash did best. To Cracker's knowledge, Flash had no dedicated association with organized crime, although occasionally he was given a job. He was in business for himself, and looking at him, Cracker sensed that he was a man who loved his work.

"We looked each other over enough? Or do you need more time?" Flash asked. A smile, or what Flash took to be a smile, turned up the right side of his mouth. The left side of his face, where the puckering was, didn't appear to be too animated.

Cracker transferred the popcorn box to his right hand and used his relatively clean left hand to reach into the left front pocket of his jeans. He pulled out an envelope which had been folded several times and carried an impression of his keys, which had shared the ride in his pocket. It contained thorough documentation on the target, including the fact that Dr. Graham was currently under suspicion by the police in a murder investigation. This was important, because it was possible that Dr. Graham was under surveillance. It wasn't fair to send his man into such a situation without foreknowledge. He handed the envelope to Flash, who took it by one corner as though pocket germs were a serious consideration.

"Let's review the terms. Twenty-five thousand in this account."

Flash extended his hand, offering a business card with numbers on the back. Cracker took the card and slipped it into his pocket without looking.

"When I have it, I'll make plans and get back in touch with you. Then another twenty-five afterward."

Cracker nodded. The amount of money meant little to him. Once he made up his mind to do this, he wasn't about to quibble over the price. His own efforts hadn't done the job. He was increasingly jumpy, anxious to complete something that had been years in the planning.

"Male or female?" Flash asked.

"It makes a difference?"

Flash glared at him. Cracker noticed that Flash's left eye sometimes closed halfway, apparently without its owner's permission, making him look owlish.

"All right, all right. Female."

"How old? I don't do kids."

He marveled that the man had any standards at all. "She's no kid."

"Relationship?"

Cracker nervously stuffed a whole handful of popcorn into his mouth and chewed it slowly while he considered. He hadn't expected all this interviewing. The only other time he had been involved in murder for hire, when he had his friend Diver taken out by a rental truck, there had been no questions, no meeting. It had all been done by phone.

"My mother," Cracker said. "Stepmother, actually."

Flash nodded. "No baby brothers or sisters still suckling at Mama's breasts?"

"I'm a lonely only."

"Soon to be lonelier. Method?"

"What?"

"I think given the context of our conversation, that question should be perfectly clear."

Cracker thought about the tape spinning beneath

Flash's jacket, thought about the belt-driven capstans, his
own voice magnetically encoded, himself as a gleaming
mechanical man, disdainful of clothing and comforts, his
voice perfectly modulated, controlled by subroutines that
handled volume, inflection, and tone.

"I suppose that's up to you," he finally said in his disappointingly human voice. "Whatever seems best."

Flash nodded again. "A few clients have specific
requests. I like it better this way. I like to have a free hand."

Like it better this way . . .

Cracker felt a sudden cold sensation that began at his
feet. He looked down, expecting to see a rush of water,
perhaps from an exuberant splash by the polar bear.
Instead, it seemed as though a fog swirled there, clinging
damply to his clothes. He closed his eyes, felt the chill rise
to his waist. He stood abruptly, spilling his popcorn on the
ground. He bobbed his head weakly at Flash, a gesture of
dismissal that didn't come off as composed as he hoped.
Flash showed no sign that anything was wrong or unusual.
Apparently he was accustomed to weird behavior by clients.
As Cracker hurried away, sparrows were already descend-
ing on the bounty, chirping possessively over the kernels.

That afternoon, Cracker found it difficult to relax, even
with Aunt Karen's gentle ministrations. He was spread-
eagled on the bed, with her lying curled between his legs,
resting her head on his thigh. The drapes were open on
the bedroom windows, which ran almost floor to ceiling.
Sunlight poured in, falling across the bed and warming
his bare skin and the disordered sheets beneath him. The
apartment was chilly, the way he liked it, so the feel of the
sun on his skin was sensual, as though a great warm hand
lay over his body.

Aunt Karen had picked up on his mood, and knew that
he didn't feel like talking today. So she talked, and was

prepared to carry the conversation for hours if necessary, or lapse into silence if it seemed appropriate. She was very good at such things.

He admitted to himself, grudgingly, that he was going to miss her.

Today she was talking about her family, and he was surprised to learn that she had a twin sister who had died while serving as a nurse in Vietnam. Her father had died years before that, and there were no extended family members with whom she felt close. Her mother was eighty-seven years old, having come to motherhood rather late. The woman was still going strong mentally, but physically she required assistance. Obviously, she couldn't live with her only daughter, because of the nature of her daughter's livelihood. The woman lived in a nursing home in Dallas, and Cracker was aware that Aunt Karen had made several short trips there to visit her.

"It's so much nicer for me, living in St. Louis," she said. "I can fly down to Dallas, have a nice visit, and be back the same night."

"Mmm . . ." Cracker said. He knew he was expected to make listening sounds at intervals.

"I just like knowing she's so close. She's all I have left of my family."

Cracker thought he detected a little self-pity creeping in, and decided to head it off before she got around to mentioning that she was disappointed she had never found time to raise a family of her own. It seemed to be the only crack in her professional demeanor.

"Is this place in Dallas costing me an arm and a leg?" he asked. He pictured himself, robotically perfect, detaching his limbs without a care. He followed the small fantasy to see where it would lead him. Experimentally, he raised one arm and twisted it with the other. His flesh failed him, as it did regularly when it craved food, drink, sleep, or sexual release. He sighed and let his arm fall in a dead way, as he imagined it would if the power were cut off.

"Maybe one arm. It is expensive," she said. She ran her fingers lightly over his inner thigh. "It has the best reputation in that area. Good care doesn't come cheap." She laughed lightly. "Am I taking good care of you?"

"Yes." He surprised himself with a straight answer. She was quiet for a moment, apparently thinking about his response. Then she started talking again, as though he had made one of his usual obtuse statements.

"It's called Sunshine Haven. That sounds so much better than an old folks' home or nursing home, doesn't it? It's clean and bright. She can even have her meals delivered to her room if she wants. She never did like eating in a big group. Says some of the others are bad-mannered and sloppy."

Cracker formed an image of a long narrow table with elderly people seated on both sides. They were eating rapaciously, clawing each other with deformed, arthritic fingers, scrabbling for the last dinner roll. Chewing, drooling, some with mouths slack and food slipping out, some unable to chew, mashing their food into mush and spooning it in.

"Let's skip the brownies today," he said.

"What? Oh, sure. You can take some home. I'll wrap them in foil when you're ready to leave." She sounded puzzled. Obviously she hadn't made the same mental leap that he had. He banished the image as a new connection struck him. Did Aunt Karen's mother know the details about the relationship, enough to be a link to Cracker? Almost certainly not, he decided. But the risk was there. He pondered for a moment what effect that had on him and his plans.

No reason to panic. No reason even to be slightly upset. He took several deep breaths and practiced suppressing his emotions. His mind moved swiftly ahead to the next conundrum: did he have to eliminate Aunt Karen's mother when he disappeared? When he was certain his voice wouldn't betray him, he casually asked Aunt Karen an important question.

"Does your mom know about me? I mean, specifically who I am?"

"Of course not, silly. Mom's no dummy. She knows confidentiality is important in my line of work. She just knows I live in St. Louis now. That's all."

"Just wondering. You haven't told anyone else, have you?"

She sat up, moved to the edge of the bed, and sat there silently. It was several minutes before it dawned on him that he had probably upset her. He wasn't good at reading other people's feelings. He often thought others should have status lights in their foreheads. That way he could gauge the results of his words without all this messy guessing.

"Did I hurt your feelings?" he asked. The proper thing to do would be to take her in his arms and apologize, but he was unable to do that.

Aunt Karen's shoulders sagged for a moment, then she turned around. "No. You have a right to ask. After all, ours is a business relationship, and we both know it. I was just a little disappointed that you didn't trust me."

"I trust you."

"Then you'd know that I can keep my mouth shut. I'm a professional. I take my job seriously."

"And you've been doing a wonderful job," he said. It was the closest he could come to an apology.

When he was on his way out of the lobby, he was greeted by the doorman, Gary Rollins. He had finally learned the man's name, after coming to the building for over three years. It occurred to him that Rollins knew about his regular visits to Aunt Karen. Rollins thought Cracker's name was Harold Worth, but the name wasn't important. He was certain that under ordinary circumstances Rollins was very discreet. But being questioned by the police might not qualify as an ordinary circumstance. Rollins would have to go. He was a link to Cracker, and when Cracker reinvented his identity, all those links had to be severed. Anything else was too risky.

19

FIRE CRACKER

CHAPTER

19

Flash sat down on the park bench with a sigh of relief. His feet hurt, and he was glad to reach his destination. He had parked several blocks away in a lot belonging to a furniture store. The parking lot was busy, so he didn't think he was noticed leaving his car and making his way down the sidewalk. He had gritted his teeth and walked normally, ignoring the pain from his feet. Flash frequently had problems: corns, bunions, ingrown toenails, blisters, pain in his heels or in the balls of his feet. Today's particular torment was a stabbing pain in his left heel every time it hit the ground.

Once seated, he began stretching exercises, pointing heel, toe, heel, toe, which eased the pain. After a minute or two, he opened the sack lunch he had brought and ate his peanut butter and jelly sandwich in leisurely fashion. He brushed the crumbs off his lap, pulled an apple from the bag, and took a big bite. It was delicious, crisp and juicy. When he finished the apple, he pulled his legs up onto the bench, folded them pretzel-style, and opened the book he had brought. Just another citizen, taking a break, enjoying lunch and a good book. The sky was now deep blue and cloudless, although the morning had been gray and dreary at the zoo with his client. The sun was warm on his back and the top of his head. He was sitting in a small neighborhood park, called a greenspace or pocket park. It was about half an acre in size, almost all wooded except for a small clearing with a few benches and a fountain with a statue of a dolphin. The fountain had been turned off for the winter, and the dry basin around it was collecting leaves. A couple of oaks at the edge of the clearing still clutched their russet leaves, but most of the tree branches were bare. The ground was thickly covered with yellow and orange leaves, which stirred and rustled as his feet moved through them. In a week they would be brown and brittle.

Flash appreciated the beauty of his surroundings. He had grown up in rural Vermont, and fall was his favorite season. He remembered rolling hills blanketed in colors, yellow, orange, here and there a touch of brilliant red. Usually there would be the smell of burning leaves drifting from the scattered homesteads to add to the experience.

Seeing the hills in autumn was almost as good as seeing them burn.

Luckily, there was no room for playground equipment in the park. Playgrounds attracted kids, and inevitably, their suspicious mothers. He couldn't spend much time on a bench near a playground without being monitored by moms. Perhaps he drew more attention because of his appearance. He knew from experience that plenty of people found his scarred face unattractive to the point of repulsion. That was something he liked about his current client. Cracker stared, sure. They all did. But Flash had detected only curiosity in the gaze that had moved over his face like a searchlight.

Across the street from the park, some of the elderly

residents were sitting out in lawn chairs, enjoying the sunshine. They reminded him of a row of pumpkins left in the field to rot, frost gripping them at night, sun heating up their innards during the day, until they began to sink in on themselves, crisscrossed with lines that deepened into fissures, finally withering into flat pancakes of leathery skin.

He couldn't make out the faces well because nearly all of them had scarves wrapped around their necks and pulled up high, to guard against the wind. But he knew what the faces would look like: seamed, genderless unless whiskers sprouted, eyes rheumy, shapeless mouths slightly open, revealing toothless gums and dark recesses which were only good for collecting spit. He knew what was under the scarves because he had grown up with it, with old people around constantly.

His foster mother had run an old folks' home, the old-fashioned kind with no nursing care, where discarded people waited out their time. They were his foster mother's primary source of income—she was widowed, and had no skills to get an outside job. She cared for them perfunctorily, provided adequate food, and kept them and the house clean enough in case the county inspector came, which he never did. In her own quarters in the basement, she provided a home for a succession of foster children, at least three at a time, because the county paid a stipend. The children received the same sort of indifferent care, and in return for a roof over their heads were expected to help care for the old folks. It was a good system, and she guarded it well.

Flash came to live with her when he was eleven, with a psyche already ruined by his violent, unpredictable parents and a series of foster-home placements. His thick folder, which detailed the sorry circumstances of his life, had a red sticker on the front. That meant "At Risk," by which the social workers meant unable to bond in a normal relationship, prone to violence, and difficult to control. His foster mother didn't care about the labels. She saw in him a strong, healthy boy who could carry overflowing laundry baskets, help lift some of the ones who couldn't sit up without help, change urine-soaked bedding, and bring in the heavy grocery bags. From the moment she brought him home, he was put to work. He found that he didn't mind, because when he wasn't working or going to school or sleeping, she left him alone. His other foster parents had put him to work doing chores, too, but had then expected him to participate in social activities. He hated that, and after a few months, when he knew what would really upset them, he did whatever he needed to do to get his placement disrupted. With Mrs. Randolph— no pretense about calling her Mom—he didn't have to put up with phony activities. So he worked hard, didn't sass her, and lived there until he was legally free of the county's benevolent care.

During his childhood, there was one consistency. He loved fire. Flash was his secret name for himself. To Mrs. Randolph, and the others who came before her, he was just Larry, or even "hey, you" to those who didn't bother to learn his name. Almost every home in rural Vermont had a wood stove or fireplace, and that was his first exposure to the captivating flames. As a toddler, he had to be pulled back repeatedly from trying to grab the yellow-and-red flickers. When he was forced into school, where his work was below par, the thing he missed most was sitting and watching the fireplace. It drew him as nothing else did, and it was a glorious sensory experience: flames curling around the logs, the smell, the sounds, the heat on his face and body. As he grew older, he began to appreciate the contained power of fire, and to wonder what would happen if the fury was turned loose.

Still later, long after he was secretly experimenting with fires, another dimension was added to his enjoyment. A neighbor's home caught fire during a lightning storm. Flash saw the glow above the trees and sneaked out of his house. It was late at night; Mrs. Randolph was asleep. He ran to the fire, then watched breathlessly from the shadows as the volunteer firefighters struggled to save the house and the family trapped inside. Watching the fiery spectacle, with flames shooting high and the red glow reflecting from the clouds, he experienced sexual arousal. He unsnapped the boxer shorts he slept in, but didn't rub frantically as he did the times when he woke up in the morning with an erection. He watched, feeling the power of the fire, letting it flow through him until his blood felt as though it were boiling. He spurted into the bushes, wave after wave of pleasure spreading through his body, as the flames licked out the windows and taunted those who would contain it. He sagged to the ground, his legs weak, and remained unseen as the fire burned itself out, out of fuel but still triumphant.

The firefighters solemnly removed three bodies from the skeleton of a house, one large and two pitifully small, and quickly covered them with gray blankets. Seeing the charred bodies as they were brought out transformed Flash's idea of death. He had seen the old people in Mrs. Randolph's home after they died. They were not impressive. They were like dry husks, with no drama, no excitement. But the burned ones he saw in the dull glow of the house and the white glare of the firefighters' lanterns—there was something wonderful about them. They were purified by the flames. They had achieved something Flash had not been able to accomplish—joining with the fire, becoming one with it and sharing its power.

He envied them.

He had tried to become part of the flames. When he was twelve, he started a small fire behind the barn and put his right hand into it. He kept it there, willing himself to ignore the shocking level of pain, a level he wasn't at all prepared for. His body pulled the hand back, without the permission of his brain, and he found himself shrieking in pain. He stamped out the fire and ran to the house. Mrs. Randolph ran cold water over his hand and took him in her battered pickup truck to the county hospital's emergency room. He had to be admitted so that the burned skin of his hand could be cleansed away and a new, shiny pink layer could form underneath. He screamed in pain as the nurse unwrapped and dipped his hand, until finally the pain became bearable and then dull and then just a memory. He had failed. He was too weak to be joined with the flames. But when he saw the burned bodies, he knew that those people—and two were kids younger than he—had triumphed over their pain.

When he turned eighteen and was free to leave, he burned Mrs. Randolph's home. He started the fire late at night, when everyone was asleep. His foster mother, two foster kids living there at the time, and eight residents died. One foster child, Joey, aged ten, escaped because he was behind the barn puffing cigarettes. Flash climbed a tree nearby and watched the beautiful flames, while his body responded with a string of orgasms that he felt certain must have shaken the tree to its roots. He wondered what kind of sticker the social workers would put on his file if they knew. By nine the next morning, thanks to an obliging truck driver who stopped when Flash stuck out his thumb, he was eating breakfast at a truck stop across the state line in Massachusetts. He didn't plan to stop there. He had money he had saved, and some that he had stolen, and he was going west to live his own life. And fire, glorious fire, was going to be a big part of it.

It didn't take long for Flash to find out what he was good at. He bought a gun, practiced at a firing range, and hung out his shingle as a hired killer. He did that by insinuating himself into the festering wound right below the skin of Los Angeles. It took him six months to get his first job, six months of scrimping by on the money he had saved. And then he nearly botched it, nearly got caught at the first scene, while he gawked at the mess he had created where moments before there had been a living person. But he didn't get caught, and he did get paid. He built up confidence and clients quickly. After a while, he was secure enough to set his own terms and to turn down cases that didn't interest him.

Across the street, nurses in white uniforms began moving the residents back inside. *Probably time for basket-making class,* he thought. Flash watched until they were all inside, then stood up for the slow walk back to his car. During the time he spent on the bench, he had decided on a method for the current target. Cracker had given him free rein. The parallel to Mrs. Randolph's home was irresistible. He was going to duplicate his first really successful fire-starting. He was going to burn GeriCare to the ground, along with everyone inside it.

Lucky them.

On the way back to his hotel, driving a rental Escort, Flash made a phone call from his cellular phone. He got Cracker's voice mail.

"Call me at six sharp. You know the number. I'm ready to get to work."

At six that evening, Flash was standing at a pay phone a couple of blocks from his downtown St. Louis hotel. Cracker was prompt.

"Yo," Flash said.

"Flash?"

"No, it's Santa Claus. What do you want for Christmas, little boy?"

"Flash." This time it was a statement.

"I want to thank you for a sweet assignment. I've had a whole string of boring ones lately." He took Cracker's silence for "you're welcome," marveling that the nerd could carry on a phone conversation at all. "The deal was, I get half, then I check out the situation. Then the other half when I'm done."

On a couple of occasions, Flash had declined the job after receiving the initial payment, after finding out that the client had misrepresented the circumstances. In that case, he kept a 15 percent kill fee. He loved that phrase, which was the term for the compensation a writer received when an editor rejected an assignment already under contract. It seemed so much more appropriate to his line of work.

"Yes, you've said all this before," Cracker said.

That irritated Flash, but he was so pleased with the assignment that he ignored it. He already knew the guy was a social misfit.

"It's going to be great. You know that place Dr. Graham has on Lemay Ferry? The old folks' home?"

"Yes." Cracker was puzzled.

"Picture this: the target goes into her office. Boom! Flames all around. She's trapped. No windows. She rushes to the door. It's blocked, somehow, she can't get out. Her hair catches fire. She screams and runs to the hallway door. Son of a gun, it's blocked too. The room is engulfed in flames. First her clothes catch, then the rest of her. Ever seen a burned corpse?"

There was no response, so Flash continued.

"The skin splits right off sometimes. The muscles in the arms and legs contract, so the body ends up with bent arms, clenched fists, and drawn-up legs. Here's a neat part I'll bet you never knew. Really hot fires make the brain swell up and burst through the skull from the inside."

"Oh God," said the voice on the other end, very softly, just loud enough to be heard.

"Of course, the rest of the place will go up like a fireworks warehouse. I'll make sure of that. Some of the old guys might make it out, but most of them will fry right there in their beds. Crispy critters.'' Flash was feeling good just talking about it. He started to form the images in his head, but decided that was too much of a distraction. This was business, after all.

"I have a problem with this," Cracker said. His voice was controlled, almost back to normal.

"Yeah? What, exactly?"

"The whole plan. I hired you to kill Dr. Graham. I assumed that meant you would shoot her or something."

"Well, the 'something' was a lot more interesting."

"I'm not paying for interesting. I'm paying for a simple, quick killing. Anything more is inefficient and risky. And since I'm the one paying, I choose how."

Flash slipped the tape recorder from his pocket, pressed the PLAY button, and held it up to the mouthpiece of the phone. Cracker was treated to his own voice saying *I suppose that's up to you. Whatever you think best . . .*

"I didn't mean mass murder, for God's sake," Cracker responded, his voice edging up in volume. "This is between me and my stepmother. Those old people have nothing to do with this. Killing them is unnecessary. Don't drag me into your twisted idea of a good time."

"We had a deal. Clients don't back out."

"This client is doing just that. You can keep the money. Just go back to whatever rock you crawled out from under."

That did it. Flash had a short temper, and this guy had crossed the line. Besides, his feet were hurting, and that put an edge on everything.

"Listen, motherfucker, we had a deal. You hear me? I do the bitch, and I do it however I want. I got my reasons, and they're none of your fuckin' business. And if I don't get my second payment after the job's done, you won't be sleeping too well at night. You get what I mean?"

No answer.

"Say it."

"Yeah."

"Say it."

"Yeah, I get it. You're a fucking looney, man," Cracker said.

"You're right, I am. What does that make you? You hired me. And because you're such a prick, I won't tell you about the freebie you're gonna get." Flash, his anger gone as quickly as it came, hung up.

Flash walked back to his hotel room, stopping on the way to pick up his favorite meal, a couple of flame-broiled Whoppers.

CHAPTER

20

By ten o'clock Monday morning, PJ had been waiting in Dr. Eleanor Graham's stuffy office for about thirty minutes, and she was almost ready to slap a nasty note on the woman's desk and leave. Having been a psychologist whose daily work was governed by the clock—fifty minutes each session, ten minutes for phone calls and breaks—she never did understand why medical doctors felt it was their right to keep others waiting. The problem was in the scheduling of appointments. Some physicians set up routine appointments every fifteen minutes to keep the money rolling in. All that was needed was one patient who ran over the time limit: a routine case that turned out not to be routine, a talkative hypochondriac, or an elderly patient from whom facts had to be gleaned from among reminiscences. Two or three such instances could really snowball, and the physician would end up an hour late, or more, by the end of the day. Then there were phone calls to return and prescription refills to OK. Maybe they counted on no-shows to make up the time. Obstetricians had a legitimate excuse for tardiness, but Dr. Graham's work didn't fall in that category. Appointments every forty-five minutes or even on the hour seemed reasonable to PJ, but she figured doctors (or more likely the HMO they belonged to) wouldn't want the cut in earnings.

Dr. Graham had three offices, and this was the second one PJ had visited. It was part of her private practice, a suite of rooms in a medical building a few blocks from Wood Memorial Hospital. She also had a cubbyhole in the hospital itself, plus her office at GeriCare. This office was large, but the space was not well used. Furniture was placed almost haphazardly, requiring visitors to walk through a maze just to get to a chair. The desktop was probably impressive, judging by the beautiful oak grain on the sides, but it was so cluttered not an inch of the surface showed. Instead of having a desk with a return, a credenza was placed at right angles to the desk. It held a computer, but the work surface was so narrow that the keyboard had to be perched on top of the monitor when not in use. Dr. Graham would have to hold the keyboard on her lap to use the machine. The usual assortment of framed certificates was on the wall behind the desk. There were some bookcases against the wall in one corner. One shelf of reference books was obviously heavily used. The books were worn and left partially sticking out of the shelf. Books on the other shelves were perfectly aligned and dusty. Across from the bookshelves was a water dispenser, the kind with the big glass bottle on top. PJ had already availed herself of it twice, filling the little paper cones with delicious chilled water and gulping them down. During her cold, PJ hadn't gotten enough to drink, and her body was making its needs known. If Dr. Graham didn't come in soon, PJ knew she'd be ready to give a urine specimen.

When Dr. Graham finally breezed into the room, she brought coffee as a peace offering. PJ accepted it without comment, sipping while Dr. Graham bustled about, put-

ting the stacks of files she had brought with her into different piles around the room. PJ opened her notebook on
the desk in front of her, pushing aside a stack of papers
to do so. Finally the woman settled into the chair behind
her desk. It was an oversized leather chair, sized for a
large man, complete with quilted back and huge padded
armrests. It made her look childish. A smile crept onto
PJ's face in spite of her bad mood.

"What?" Dr. Graham said.

"I didn't mean to stare. It's just that the chair . . . doesn't
reflect your style."

"Oh, that. Mine broke last week. I ordered a new one,
but in the meantime I borrowed this one from a conference
room on the second floor. Tacky, isn't it?"

"It looks like you could hold an entire board meeting
in it."

Dr. Graham smiled, then tapped her pen on the desk,
signaling that the small talk was over.

"I presume you're already aware of the circumstances
of Maximillian Winters's death," PJ said.

"Yes. I heard from Bert and also from the lieutenant."

PJ knew she meant Detective Schultz, but didn't bother
to correct her. "The nurse was contacted by phone. I have
with me a tape recording of the voice of the person who
coerced her. It may very well be the person who is responsible for the earlier incidents too. I'd like you to listen to
the conversation."

Dr. Graham's eyes narrowed. "You think I will recognize
the voice? That I know this person?"

"That's a strong possibility. It has become very clear that
this whole case is a personal vendetta against you. At least,"
she said, thinking of Schultz's view of things, "I feel that
way."

"I'm glad you do. I wish I could say the same for Lieutenant Schultz. He always looks at me as if I was already wearing
a prison uniform."

"It's just his way," PJ said. She switched on the player, which contained a copy of the original tape. Dr. Graham straightened in her chair and listened attentively. The slight lines on her forehead grew deeper as the tape played. There was tentative recognition in her eyes, along with genuine puzzlement. When the tape finished, she folded her hands and leaned forward on the desk.

"Well," she said.

"And that means?" PJ prompted.

"I don't really know what to say. This is going to sound dumb, I'm afraid. The blackmailer's voice sounds a little like my stepson Will. It's hard to be certain, since the last time I heard him was years ago, and he was young then. But that's impossible. He's dead."

PJ flipped the pages of her notebook. "That would be Will Carpenter, the suicide in California."

"Yes, but as I said, he's dead. We had a funeral service here for him."

"The body was never found. Presumed lost in the ocean." This time it was PJ's turn to tap her pen. She made an intuitive leap. "Have you had any communication from Will Carpenter?"

"No," Dr. Graham answered, a little too quickly. "What makes you think that?"

The woman was nervous. PJ knew she was on to something, and she was going to stick to it like a barnacle to a hull.

"Early in the investigation, I was talking with you in your office at the hospital. You got a message on your computer screen. Remember?"

Dr. Graham nodded.

"You cleared it right away and said it was some kind of staff prank. What exactly did that message say?"

"I don't remember. Something embarrassing."

PJ took a moment to digest that. It didn't ring true. If PJ had gotten an embarrassing message in front of someone else, it would be burned into her mind. Fat chance she'd forget it.

"So just out of the blue, you recognize your stepson's voice on this tape," PJ said. "It's been years since you've talked with him—years during which his voice would have changed to an adult's—and you pull his name out of the hat after hearing a few sentences."

"I told you it was going to sound crazy. I shouldn't even have mentioned it."

Dr. Graham was getting defensive. She would clam up any minute.

"All right, then let's skip to the big question. Why would your stepson make you a target? This isn't some kid being naughty. We're talking about murder."

The woman seemed to have regained her composure, and was undoubtedly regretting her first comments after hearing the tape.

"I'm sure I have no idea. Anyway, I'm probably mistaken. It must be someone else who just sounds like Will. Same rhythm and word choice, maybe. I told you, he drowned years ago."

"Why did he leave home at age . . ." PJ paused while searching through her notes. "Fourteen?"

"Who knows why teenagers do anything? Will probably got mad because I made him stick to a reasonable bedtime on school nights, or something. Ran away in a snit and was too embarrassed to come back."

"Being on your own at that age would be frightening. It's not like a camping trip in the backyard with a flashlight and ghost stories. If it was something innocuous, I'm sure he would have come back."

They both knew the primary reason young people ran away from home: physical, sexual, or emotional abuse. PJ found it hard to picture the diminutive Dr. Graham as a child abuser, but she had been fooled before. Appearances didn't count.

"He wasn't abused, if that's what you're getting at," Dr. Graham said testily. "He must have been depressed, and depressed people have their own logic. He took his own life a year later."

"Did you enjoy becoming a mother, Dr. Graham? I mean, marrying a man and suddenly acquiring a family?"

Dr. Graham looked thoughtful. The question had taken her off in a new direction.

"Truthfully, I don't think I was a very good mother. I'm not cut out to be nurturing. Strange thing for a doctor to say, isn't it? I do OK with my patients. I manage to project enough warmth to keep them satisfied. But I never planned on having kids of my own. I loved Harvey very much, and he accepted me the way I am. I guess I wanted Harvey enough to take the package deal."

"Did you resent being stuck with the kid after your husband died?"

"You don't beat around the bush, do you?" Dr. Graham sighed. "Yes, I suppose to be brutally honest, I did resent it. It probably showed. I always thought Will blamed me for the fights, and even for his father's death, as illogical as that may seem. At one point, I even insisted that he get counseling. It didn't take."

"Fights?"

"Oh, it was nothing. Harvey was a physician, too, and we used to have arguments over professional practices. We were both strong-willed, and we clashed a lot. After an argument, Will would give me the cold treatment for days, even though he wasn't directly involved. And Harvey's death . . . Well, that was a shock to both of us."

"When was the last time you heard from Will?"

Dr. Graham hesitated before answering. "It was the suicide note he sent me. According to the eyewitnesses, he was dead already by the time I got it in the mail."

PJ searched the woman's face. She would stake her reputation both as a psychologist and as a fledgling investigator that Dr. Graham was hiding something. Maybe Schultz was right after all to suspect this woman. But it was inconceivable that she was trying to ruin herself after working so hard to build a career in the medical field.

"Is there anything specific in the tape recording which made you think of Will when you heard it?"

Dr. Graham lowered her eyes and kept silent. She drummed her fingers on the table nervously.

"Talk to me, Dr. Graham. It's the only way I can help you." A few more moments of silence followed, then Dr. Graham nodded her head slightly.

"Two things," she said. "First there was the use of the nickname Pitty-Pat with someone he obviously didn't know well. Will used to make up names like that for everyone. With some people it would be endearing, but with Will it wasn't. It was sarcastic, a way of bringing people down to a level well beneath him. It used to get on my nerves. He even had a name for his computer."

My name is Neptune.

"And the second reason?"

"The pattern of seeming to be reasonable followed by threats. It was the way he got what he wanted, and it usually worked. But that could apply to a lot of people I know." Dr. Graham glanced at the wall clock. "I don't mean to push you out, Dr. Gray, but I've got another appointment in a few minutes."

"One last thing, then. Do you have a tape recording of Will Carpenter's voice?"

"I don't think . . . Yes, I do, only it's a video clip, not a tape recording. When he graduated from the eighth grade, I gave him a video camera. He used it all summer, hiding behind it, most likely. I think I have some of the videos he made. I think he was thirteen then."

"That sounds perfect. When can I get hold of the tapes?"

"I'll look for them tonight."

"I'll have one of my team members stop by your house tomorrow to pick them up. When would be a good time?"

"Between five and five-thirty. I get an early start."

It was after five by the time PJ got back to her own office. Schultz was nowhere to be seen. She left a message for him on the office voice mail, and another on his answering machine at home. She described her interview with Dr. Graham, and asked him to get Dave or Anita to pick up the videotapes in the morning.

She and Thomas had pizza delivered. Megabite's nose registered cooked prey, and they took turns feeding her sausage from the pizza. PJ was subdued, and Thomas respected her mood. After dinner, he parked himself in front of the computer, leaving her to take out the trash from the pizza dinner. She cleared their places at the table, but left the dishes in the sink. She had forgotten to buy more Nyquil, and a search of the medicine cabinet turned up nothing helpful. Checking her nightstand for reading material, she found she had a choice between a psychology journal and a new Patricia Cornwell book. She was only a quarter of the way through the Cornwell book, but her eyes were getting heavy when Thomas came in to say good night. Disappointed that Schultz hadn't called, she turned out her lamp after Thomas left, deliberately leaving the alarm off. She was hoping that a good long night's sleep would shake off the remnants of the cold.

Monday evening, Schultz was back in Hattie's Saloon on Laclede's Landing, drinking Cokes. He had been there for over an hour and was beginning to think he'd been stood up. He left his barstool to go take a leak, and when he returned, Edward Jennings was sitting on the next stool. There was a slim briefcase on the bar between their two

stools. Edward already had a Chivas in hand, and he raise
it in greeting as Schultz rearranged his posterior on th
wooden barstool for minimal damage.

The briefcase looked like it probably cost more than
week of Schultz's salary. Edward was, as he had been ever
time Schultz had seen him, impeccably dressed. Clothe
fit him well, especially the expensive tailored variety tha
he favored. He was wearing a dark gray wool suit with a
Oxford-style shirt, white with tiny plum stripes. The whol
package looked as though he had just put it on, fresh fror
the cleaners, yet it was almost 8 P.M., and Schultz knew
Edward had probably worked a twelve-hour day. Did th
guy keep fresh clothes in his car or something? Schult
flashed on Edward stripping down in the backseat of hi
car and pulling on a clean suit. The image added a littl
punch to his smile when he said hello.

The first few minutes of their conversation had to de
with the two women seated at a corner table who kep
glancing in their direction. The blonde wore a red shim
mery dress which did not look like business attire, unles
her business had nothing to do with the financial district
She had an attractive, friendly face, with lips that looke
kissable and delicate ears that invited nibbling. Her hai
was piled on top of her head in a complicated way, ane
Schultz indulged himself in imagining unpinning it ane
letting her hair fall heavily into his hands. But it was th
other woman who grabbed him by the cock and held on
She was Hispanic, with skin the color of toast and long
hair as black as a raven's wing, which swung freely wheneve
she moved. She wore a sleeveless sheath of cream silk tha
skimmed her body, accentuating the gently rounded parts
The dress was cut low in front, and there was plenty to
admire, starting from her collarbones and moving up or
down. There was a single strand of pearls around her neck
and she had brown eyes that looked like melted chocolate
in the light of the candle in the center of the table. The

eyes danced across his face, and he turned away, flushing lightly.

"The brunette's not wearing a bra," Edward said. "I've got such a fucking hard-on I can't even go over there and introduce myself. How about it, Schultz? Go ask the ladies if we can join them at their table."

"Christ, Edward, I'm a married man."

"I notice you didn't say a happily married man. That leaves room for hanky-panky."

"Could we get a little business done here? I'd like to get this over with."

"Relax," Edward said. "The work'll get done when it gets done."

This from a man who regularly worked seventy hours a week and loved every minute of it.

And now he was going to collect a thousand dollars. He was willing to use his insider knowledge in the financial community to bring down the cheaters, but he got paid for wild-goose chases. Schultz had been sure that Charles Horner was involved somehow in Clark's murder. But with the latest revelations, including the hacker's voice on tape, it looked as if his hunch had been dead wrong. He sighed, pulled a folded stack of hundreds from his pocket, and placed them on Edward's briefcase. He looked at the man's face, expecting to see him gloating. Instead, Edward was uncharacteristically serious. In that moment, as he locked eyes with Edward, Schultz detected a faint perfume, wafted toward him from the women at the table. It was a musky scent, natural, clean, and enticing. He flared his nostrils and inhaled deeply as he tried to gather in more. He knew it came from the dark-haired woman, and that if he turned around to look at her, she would reward him with a toss of her sleek mane. She was coming on to him, but he couldn't figure out why. He was at least twenty-five years her senior, and his face bore the years and the emotional and physical battering that had come with them. He was acutely aware of his ass hanging over the stool and his paunch hanging over his belt. He could only imagine that the woman had a father fixation, and that her father had been one ugly son of a bitch.

Somehow Edward picked up on Schultz's discomfort and, uncannily, on its source.

"I'm not the only one with a hard-on, am I, Schultz? Look, I think she's making kissy-eyes at you."

"Prick."

Edward smiled, then abruptly pushed the stack of bills back toward Schultz.

"You can keep your money."

It took a few seconds for the realization to dawn on Schultz. "No shit. You mean Charlie had something going after all?"

Edward shook his head. "He's clean as far as the murder is concerned. It's his other activities that are going to get Charlie Boy in deep shit. In fact, he's already there, he just doesn't know it yet."

Disappointment about the lack of involvement in the murder was quickly followed by elation, which traveled through Schultz, tingling his fingers and tightening his scalp so that he was sure his hair was standing on end. He reached up and palmed the few strands down.

"Christ. Tell."

"First thing I did was check the guy's bank accounts. I've got a good source at his bank, and it only cost me a couple of drinks. He's got about two hundred thousand in assets that aren't jointly owned with his wife. Smart woman. She's only given him access to one small shared account, like household money. It floats around half a mil. The rest is in her name only."

"Well, at least someone had some sense."

"I think that was what Mama insisted upon. Anyway, of Charlie's two hundred thou, only about thirty is liquid. The rest is in long-term municipal bonds. Poorly rated ones, at that. This guy's such small potatoes, he'd be rejected for Tater Tots.''

Edward stopped to suck at his drink and raise his eyebrows at the blonde in the red dress. Schultz considered his own financial portfolio, consisting of about six thousand in a money market account and twelve thousand in an IRA. He still owed about sixty thousand on the house, and his personal car, a Vega that had been in a serious crash and not exactly repaired to factory specs, was a pile of crap he only drove in emergencies. At least it was a wholly owned pile of crap. He wondered what Edward would think of him, then decided he was probably better off not knowing.

"OK, so we know the guy's only high society because of his wife. This is news?" Schultz asked.

"What's news is that the account balance for his basic thirty thousand in cash swings wildly. Very large deposits in, very large withdrawals out. A couple of weeks ago, the balance shot up to six hundred thousand. It stayed that way for three days, then dropped to thirty grand after a wire transfer. That suggest anything to you, oh Great Detective?"

"The little shit's laundering money. I could have dug all this stuff up myself."

"Let me tell the story, will you? I don't like to be rushed."

"Sorry."

"Yeah, like hell you are. Anyway, I tracked that wire transfer through three more U.S. banks before it flew the coop to Switzerland. That's where I lost it."

"So there are limits to your abilities," Schultz said. "That's good to know. Next time, maybe there won't be a whole thousand bucks riding on the outcome. I gotta get value for the money."

Edward chuckled softly. "You're priceless, Schultz. I should do this for free, just to enjoy our little get-togethers."

"Shit, Edward, I've been called a lot of things, but never priceless. Maybe I could get you to tell that to my boss."

"No way. I don't even like being seen with you, not to mention with a decent cop."

"She's no cop. She's a lot of things, but a cop's not one of them."

"She, eh? You have my sympathies."

They raised their glasses and drank to the bewildering reality of female bosses.

"I checked further back in Charlie's account history," Edward said. "Same pattern, every two or three weeks. I haven't figured out how he's getting paid for his services, though. There must be a hell of a lot of cash underneath his mattress. The worst thing is, Charlie's so dumb he probably doesn't know that he's on the sucker end of the transactions."

"Explain."

"When the money leaves his account, it goes into a multimillion-dollar brokerage transfer account, where large sums of money rest temporarily between stock purchases. If you toss six hundred thousand into a pot that has thirty million in it already, and large amounts are transferring in and out practically hourly, then it blends in. The FTC supposedly monitors those brokerage accounts, so there's some risk. But you'd probably have to do something obviously nasty to get the FTC swarming all over you. If you keep your nose clean otherwise, the risk is minimal. All of the subsequent transfers are like that. The further down the chain you are, the safer you are."

"You speaking from personal experience?"

Edward looked offended. "Drug money isn't my thing. Drug dealers are slime," he said vehemently.

"Take it easy, OK? So Charlie's got his balls on the line. How do we cut 'em off?"

"I thought you'd never ask. It so happens that one of the local organized crime bosses and I are on friendly terms. Gangsters in these times are businessmen, Schultz, and so am I."

Schultz leaned forward like a jockey with the finish line in view. "I'm not hearing this, you know."

"Do you think I'd tell you if your hearing wasn't so bad? The boss and I have a common interest, that's all. Nothing sinister. I play chess with him a couple times a week. Used to be he'd whip my ass every time, without even breathing hard. Now I give him a little exercise first. You play?"

"Nope. I'm more the poker type."

"You'd be surprised how many good poker players also make good chess players. You should give it a try."

"Get on with it, Edward."

"Yes. The last time we got together, I asked a few discreet questions about money laundering."

Schultz tried to imagine what sort of questions would be considered discreet. He couldn't come up with any.

"At first, he thought I was trying to set up something myself. Finally we got that cleared up, and had a good laugh about it," Edward said.

"Just you and the Godfather, yucking it up."

"Something like that. Anyway, he confided in me about a problem he's having. He deals with white-collar stuff. Another guy in town does drugs and prostitution. That guy's been giving him some trouble."

"Trouble like how?"

"The guy's starting to do deals outside his territory. Did a little real-estate speculating, although you can hardly call it speculating when you've got inside information. Turned a nice profit, a quick two mil."

"So your man is getting his toes stepped on a little."

"That, plus the guy gave my man's daughter a cheap birthday present."

"You're kidding."

Edward shrugged. "It's the truth. So my man would like to give this bum a little slap and see if he shapes up."

"I take it Charlie works for the bum."

"Not directly. People like him don't mix with the low-lifes. But I got the name of Charlie's contact, plus enough info to go to the feds. That's where you come in. How'd you like to hand over Charlie to the DEA?"

"The thought is enough to make me cream my pants. I wanted that jerk the first time I laid eyes on him." Schultz closed his eyes. Mentally, he reached for the thread, the connection between himself and the killer. Psychic? Schultz was not willing to define it, to pin a word on it. If he ever did, he might stop believing in it himself. No one else knew about it, and no one else ever would. He tugged the thread. It was firmly anchored at the other end, which he now knew was the hacker whose voice he had on tape. He sighed. Charlie certainly wasn't numbered among the saints of the world, but he didn't kill his mother-in-law.

"I need to stay out of this, Schultz. It's going to have to look like you uncovered the money laundering while you were checking Charlie out as a murder suspect."

"Yeah, I can do that."

"The main question is, will your people believe you were that smart?"

Schultz raised his eyebrows. He studied Edward's face. The man was perfectly serious. "I think I can do a credible job," he said, letting a little sarcasm slip in. "After all, I was a cop when you were in diapers." Schultz sipped at his Coke. "I'll bet this boosts your standing with the boss."

Edward grinned. "Certainly doesn't hurt. Maybe he'll let me win a game of chess every now and then."

Schultz laughed, a loud hearty bellow. The release felt good.

Some days, he thought, *this job is worth it all.*

CHAPTER
21

Billy steps out of the patch of moonlight in the hallway. For a moment, the chill continues to crawl up his body like a thousand inchworms. He puts his arms around himself and hugs tightly. What's happening? He has walked down this hallway many times before, but now it seems different. Frightening. The other times, there has been a night-light plugged into the wall in the long hallway. Then he would study his shadow as he walked down the dimly lighted hallway, because his shadow always does interesting things. First it's very big and fuzzy around the edges, then it grows small and sharp as a knife blade—ouch—as he passes the plug-in place, then big and fuzzy again when he gets to the far end of the hall. He likes that, especially the big, fuzzy times, because he can pretend to be Hunny Bear from his good-night book.

Tonight there is no light, no Hunny Bear, just Billy, who feels too small and powerless to save his father from Mom Elly. Something terrible is happening in the room at the end of the hallway. He knows it with all of the certainty his four-year-old imagination can muster. His father is groaning behind that door. Billy hears the groans a little better now that he is closer. Mom Elly is killing him, pulling off his skin or turning his insides out. Dad will be like one of those sad animals on the road, the ones whose lives leak out or whose heads are mashed or who have great tears in their bodies that show the slick wetness. Grown-ups pretend not to notice them—the sad animals—but Billy does. Billy not only sees them, he feels the small agony of each of their deaths.

He dreamed once, a waking dream, of being able to reach down from the sky with a hand that glowed and had fingers all colors of the rainbow, of reaching down and scooping the animals up before they became sad, and taking them to a place where no cars could squish them.

Unable to move himself forward, Billy takes a step backward into the distorted rectangle of light on the floor. He turns and looks out the bathroom window, where Mr. Moon is shining down on him. Only this time, Mr. Moon does not smile. He is not friendly. Mr. Moon has a hideous half-grin on his half-face, a face that now appears to have been whacked in half by some awful hand. Billy thinks he hears Mr. Moon screaming inside his head. He presses his hands to his ears, but that doesn't help. He squeezes his eyes shut. He knows he has to get out of the moonlight to stop the screaming. Run! His legs pump, and he moves fast. The screaming stops, and Billy opens his eyes. He huddles down into the darkness at the end of the hallway, away from the patch of moonlight and its soundless terror.

But he's at the wrong end of the hall.

Instead of going back to the tentative safety of his bed and his covers, his legs have propelled him farther toward the evil magic. He knows now that was what it is: evil magic, the worst thing his mind can conjure up, a dreadful force that sneers at little boys who try to be good in clean, dry pajamas. His thoughts run in terrorized circles, then slow down enough for him to catch hold of them.

When he's able to think, he realizes it: of course he had gone in the direction of danger. It is all up to him to save Dad. Hiding under his blankets isn't going to help Dad. Billy waits in the darkness for his breathing to slow down and his heart to stop making so much noise. As soon as he is able to hear outside noises over the inside ones, he hears the groaning again. Louder, and more urgent. There are no words he can make out, but he knows his father's voice, even though there's something odd about it, a kind of low, thick rumbling that Billy hasn't heard before. But he hasn't heard his father getting killed before, so the oddness is understandable.

Dad says there are no monsters, and Dad always knows.

Doubt springs up in Billy's mind. Maybe Dad's talking about real monsters. What about magic monsters? Does Dad even know about them? Has Dad ever looked up at old Mr. Moon, and seen the twisted face sneering and leering down at him, and screamed at the unexpected horror?

Billy feels the evil magic whirling around him in the dark hallway, and he wants to run back down the hall to his bedroom. Instead, he does the bravest thing he has ever done. He puts out his hand, turns the knob, and opens the door. It swings inward, carrying him along with it as though his hand has become part of the metal knob. His eyes, fully adjusted to the dark, roam around the edges of the room, looking for telltale signs of monsters, like claw marks on the walls. Nothing. A long dresser, a tall chest of drawers, a chair with a pair of shoes on it. Clothes scattered on the floor, not neatly put into the hamper, but he has seen that before. His eyes are riveted by a small shape on the floor which shouldn't have been there. He stares at it for some time before realizing that it's a picture frame, the one from Mom Elly's dresser which holds the picture of Mom Elly and Dad getting married.

He doesn't like that picture. He isn't in it.

As he stares at the picture frame, he becomes aware of small shiny pieces glinting on the dark carpet. Broken glass, like the time he had broken Mom Elly's bowl. Where is the light coming from? How can he see the pieces, which shimmer in pale light?

Moonlight.

He raises his eyes from the floor, following the light. The curtains on the windows in Mom Elly's and Dad's room are usually pulled tight, but tonight they are separated like the jaws of a hungry beast panting after a chase. Caught in the jaws is Mr. Moon. Billy's eyes skip across the room to the mirror above Mom Elly's dresser. There's another Mr. Moon, an overwhelming double dose of evil magic that fills Billy with dread. He jerks his eyes back to the center of the room. Trapped between the two moons, his father lies pinned to the bed.

CHAPTER

22

Tuesday morning PJ woke at her usual 6:30 A.M., even though she had stubbornly left the alarm off. Her cold seemed to have vanished. She dressed quickly, then went downstairs to start some coffee and toss together a sack lunch for Thomas in return for not fixing him breakfast. Upstairs, she went into his room. He was asleep, arms and legs akimbo, Megabite curled up on the pillow where his head should have been. Instead, his head was halfway over the side of the bed. Thomas had always been a restless sleeper. She momentarily felt sorry for the woman he would marry.

PJ bent and kissed him on the forehead.

"Wake up, sleepy. School this morning."

His eyes popped open. He had an instant-awake ability she envied. She didn't care to think about what she looked like during her first few minutes of wakefulness. Thomas sat up and pulled Megabite onto his lap.

"Hey, Bite, you stole my pillow," he chastised the cat. Megabite didn't take it too hard. His hands were busy finding all the spots on her lithe body which hadn't been petted for at least eight hours.

"I'm leaving a little early this morning, T-man. I made your lunch. Think you can get yourself off to school?"

"What if I said no?" Thomas asked.

"I would stay here and coddle you and call you Cuddle Bunny in front of your friends." Thomas walked to school with a couple of other boys who lived down the block.

"Just checking. I'll be OK. Go ahead and go. Please."

"I haven't fed Megabite yet. And I think she should have something besides Cheerios and milk. Give her some Tender Vittles or open a can of cat food."

"What's wrong with Cheerios and milk? I've had that every morning for years."

"You're not a carnivore the way she is. She needs protein."

"She gets protein. She caught a spider yesterday."

"Gross. I certainly hope we don't have enough of them in the house to meet her protein requirement."

"Yeah, big, hairy ones with legs about this long." He held his hands about a foot apart. "And huge round bodies and fifty bulging eyes. I think I saw one in your room last night."

She ruffled his jet-black hair. "Get dressed. Or if you need a bath, the tub's all yours."

"No kidding, Mom, it was running across the floor really fast on great big legs. I think it went under your bed."

"I love you, too," she said on her way out of his room.

She went out to the car, which was parked in the roughly circular gravel parking area behind her house. There had been a light frost overnight, which she hadn't noticed from inside the house. For the first time, she wished her rental house had a garage. She got into the VW, started the engine, and turned on the defroster. After a couple of minutes, she still couldn't see clearly out the window. She needed to scrape the window free of frost. An ice scraper was on her mental list of home and auto necessities, but hadn't made it to the forefront of her attention. Somehow, the wintry weather sneaked up on her, as it seemed to every year. She opened her purse and got a credit card out of her wallet. Getting out of the car, she scraped the windshield with her credit card. Standing outside with ice on her fingers made her realize that she was underdressed for the weather. She had put on a heavy cardigan sweater, but now she wanted a jacket instead, and some gloves. She left the car running while she went into the house, thinking that at least the car would be warm inside by the time she got back.

She got out a gray wool car coat and pulled off the dry cleaner's plastic bag.

"T-man," she called up the stairs, "it's chilly outside. You'll probably need that jacket with the flannel lining."

"Geez, Mom, I can pick out my own stuff."

"Bye again," she said, feeling appropriately motherly. She opened the back door, trying to button the jacket with one hand. To her chagrin, it was a snug fit. Twenty extra pounds took its toll.

A fireball engulfed her VW like a miniature sun that had fallen into her backyard. Almost instantaneously, the heat and pressure of the blast slammed into her. Reflexively, she pulled back into the kitchen and shut the door. Glass tinkled at her feet. She closed her eyes, and the red burst replayed itself as a residual image. When she opened her eyes, she found herself looking out the shattered window set into the back door.

"Mom? Mom, are you all right?"

She turned. Thomas was in the doorway to the kitchen. His face was pale, and his eyes were wide and dark. He had certainly felt and heard the explosion.

"I'm OK," she said. She took a quick inventory, and saw a shard of glass embedded in the leather of her shoe. She bent over and gingerly removed it, expecting a gush of blood, severed toes, the works. There was a neat slice in the leather, but nothing more. "I didn't like these shoes anyway."

"A couple of windows are broken upstairs," he said, his voice wavering a little. Relief that she wasn't hurt shone on his face, and she reflected back his concern, looking him over thoroughly. "I put Megabite in the bathroom so she wouldn't hurt herself or try to get out," he said.

"Good thinking," PJ said, amazed at how calm she sounded. Then she looked out into the backyard again, and realized that she was numb rather than calm. She heard sirens coming closer. One of the neighbors had obviously called the fire department. It seemed that only seconds passed, and then a firefighter in a bright yellow protective suit rounded the rear corner of her house. He looked briefly at the burning car, then disappeared, only to be replaced by a team of firefighters lugging a hose into her backyard. Another yellow shape with a black helmet and clear face shield appeared suddenly in her view, right on the back steps. The face shield was pushed up to reveal a young male face, blue-eyed, red-cheeked, and full of concern. In the background, water gushed noisily and urgently toward the Rabbit, which by now was burned down to the metal framework.

"Please come with me, ma'am," the firefighter said politely. "My name's Ted. Anyone else in the house?"

PJ stepped out onto the porch, with Thomas at her elbow. "A cat, upstairs in the bathroom," she said.

As Ted lead PJ and Thomas to the front of the house where the fire-department vehicles were parked, one of the firefighters near the car gave him a thumbs-up sign.

"It looks as though the fire's contained, ma'am, and the house isn't in any danger," Ted said. "But we'll be sending a couple of people in to make sure no flying pieces of debris have started a fire elsewhere."

A paramedic looked PJ and Thomas over quickly. She

spotted the cut in PJ's shoe, and removed the shoe to check for injury. "I guess these panty hose are shot," she said. "Probably an expensive pair, too. I can take you to the hospital if you want, but it looks like it'd be an unnecessary trip."

"No, thanks," PJ said. Just then Dave pulled up to the curb in his red Honda Civic. He got out, waved to PJ, and went around back to look at the cause of all the excitement. PJ noticed then that a few of her neighbors had gathered across the street, and she knew that the grapevine was already buzzing with the morning's event, which was a lot more exciting and immediate than anything they could see on TV. Dave came back out front.

"Well, it looks like a bomb," he said.

"I already knew that," PJ said sharply. Her numbness was wearing off, and underneath it was fear and anger. Dave was a convenient target. "I want to know who did it."

"Whoa, take it easy, Boss," Dave said. "We'll get the right folks working on that immediately. Now tell me what happened."

PJ related the sequence of events.

Dave whistled. "Damn, you were lucky. Sounds to me like the bomber used a heat-sensitive detonation device. Popped as soon as the car's engine heated up. If you hadn't gone back in to get a coat, you would have been toast. Little pieces of very burnt toast."

"Thanks, Dave. I needed that. Perhaps you can be even more graphic in front of my son."

Dave reddened. "Oh. Sorry. Tell you what, I'll give your insurance company a call."

PJ gritted her teeth. "I only had liability coverage on that car." For some reason, that realization was the final straw for PJ. She pressed her lips together, but they quivered anyway, and tears overflowed onto her cheeks. She hugged Thomas fiercely, drawing a squeal of pain from him as she squeezed him tightly to her. It was followed by a muffled sob. Dave seemed to be at a loss, and he put his hands in his pockets and looked down at the ground. Just then Anita appeared, bounding out of a blue-and-white before it came to a full stop at the curb. She put her arm around PJ and Thomas, and walked them over to the front porch.

By the time she sat down on the steps of the front porch, PJ's composure was coming back. Thomas leaned against her, not saying anything, but drawing strength from her ability to handle the situation.

"Sorry," she said to Anita. "I'm OK now."

"No need to apologize, Boss. It isn't every day you get your car blown up."

"Who could have done this? The killer? I can't think of any reason why he'd be after me. It's not like I'm breathing down his neck on this case."

"No way to know right now if it's connected. Maybe it was your ex-husband. I've heard of things like that."

PJ almost burst out laughing. The thought of Steven blowing up anything other than a balloon was ludicrous. She felt Thomas shaking against her and pushed him away to look at his face, thinking he was crying. He wasn't. He was giggling.

"I think that's one suspect we can cross off the list," PJ said. Her thinking was clearing up. "Say, T-man, aren't you going to be late for school if you don't get a move on?"

Thomas blinked a couple of times and got to his feet. "Wait 'til I tell everybody. Nobody can top this!" He started walking down the street, then turned around. "I don't need a jacket, Mom, I'm not cold."

"Wait!" She hollered after him. "You forgot your backpack!" He kept going. She suspected that he heard her, but with news like this bursting to be told, he didn't want to worry about mundane things like books and lunch. She and Anita looked at each other and shrugged.

"I'll stay around with Dave for a bit. You can get a ride with the blue-and-white. Sometime today you'll need to make a statement, but there's no big hurry."

When PJ approached the patrol car, a young officer hopped out and ran around to open the door for her.

"Could you drop me at Millie's Diner, please?" she said.

"Glad to, ma'am."

On the way, she thought about the firefighter and the officer both calling her "ma'am." She reached up and patted the hair over her right temple, where she was certain there was more gray than anywhere else. When did she become "ma'am," anyway? In her own mind, she was still a young married woman with a promising career and a beautiful baby boy. She wasn't married anymore, the baby boy was teetering on the edge of manhood, and the promising career . . . Well, she would hardly call her current work promising. Challenging, maybe, or rewarding. And as for being young, the assessment of those around her indicated that she no longer qualified.

Mike Wolf's face floated into her mind.

Perhaps I shouldn't worry about romantic love, she thought. *That's for the young. I should be looking for companionship. Dependability.*

The thought saddened her. She looked out the window as the patrol car moved through the neighborhood. She noticed a car parked along the curb, with an older couple, probably in their sixties, in the front seat. They were kissing passionately, obviously lovers, whether married or not she didn't know. It was comforting to see them.

We old geezers can get it on, too.

PJ opened the door of Millie's Diner and looked around for Schultz. He was there, at his favorite stool at the

counter. She crossed the black-and-white-checkered linoleum and took her usual seat, leaving one stool between
them, the one that wobbled. She put her jacket on the
empty stool. The diner wrapped itself around her like a
comfortable old robe: the smells of eggs, pancakes, sausage; the sounds of low conversation and the muted tin-
kling of dishes and utensils; the many visual treats, like the
wide polished chrome band that ran the length of the
counter, cinching it like a belt. Millie appeared with a cup
of coffee. PJ held the cup in both hands, enjoying the
warmth, letting it steady her. It certainly wasn't the best
coffee she had ever tasted, but it was the right color, and
on this particular morning that was good enough.

"You sure you want to sit so close, dearie?" Millie said,
tilting her head in Schultz's direction. "I gotta . . ."

"Wipe the stool with disinfectant after he leaves. The
floor, too," PJ said.

"What'll it be this morning, dearie?"

"How about a big bowl of fruit?" From where she was
sitting, she could see into the kitchen. There were shelves
along the back holding huge cans which said things like hot
sauce and vegetable combo and fruit cocktail. "Whatever
you've got that's fresh," PJ added.

"I have just the thing. Got some cantaloupe and grape-
fruit at Soulard Market this morning. You gotta get there
real early. All the best stuff's gone by six." She bustled
away.

"Fruit bowl?" Schultz said. "Watching your weight,
Doc?"

PJ was well aware of the extra twenty pounds that went
everywhere with her since the divorce. Somehow she never
got around to trying to lose them.

"I just happen to feel like having some fruit. And good
morning to you, too." She looked pointedly at his plate,
which contained a mound of eggs, a couple of biscuits,

and four links of sausage. "Detective, there are other food groups besides fat."

Schultz shrugged. "I left off the hash browns, OK?"

"You brought it up."

They sat waiting for Millie to return. PJ thought Schultz looked smug about something. Apparently he hadn't heard her news yet. She was bursting to tell, and she wanted to ask him if he had gotten her voice mail message. She was eager to get his impressions about her interview with Dr. Graham. She thought it might represent a big breakthrough in the case, and she was proud of her contribution.

He looked awfully smug.

Her fruit bowl arrived. It was a generous serving, topped with a cherry. Stuck into the cherry was one of Millie's flags on a toothpick. Schultz had probably gotten one stuck in a biscuit. Millie waited while PJ speared a chunk of cantaloupe, tasted it, and pronounced it delicious.

"See there, you old coot," Millie said to Schultz. "Somebody appreciates the finer things in life. Somebody's got class."

"And it certainly isn't you," Schultz countered. "Now scoot, babe. That is, if you want a tip today. We have police business to discuss."

Millie moved off, muttering something under her breath. Neither of them had any doubt it had something to do with Schultz's twenty-five-cent tip.

"Did you ever consider that Millie might not like being called babe?"

"She loves it. You can tell by the way she makes eyes at me."

"Down to business," PJ said, wielding her fork. She told him about her car exploding. As she was relating the story, she thought again of how close she had come to death. The smallest thing, ice on her fingers, had spared her life. If the weather had been ten degrees warmer, she would indeed be toast. Her philosophy about turning points in a person's life creating new paths to the future was certainly bearing itself out. She was on a different path now than she had been when she woke up that morning.

Schultz was appropriately shocked and worried, and fussed over her for a long time. When she first told him, he sloshed coffee from his mug onto the counter, awkwardly mopped it up with napkins, then tried to cover up his messy reaction with gruff questions. She assured him that everything was being handled by Dave and Anita.

"Did you get my message about Dr. Graham?" PJ was eager to move the conversation along to other revelations.

"Yup. I sent Anita over at the crack of dawn to pick up the videos. She's got more tact than Dave, especially at that time of the morning. By now, whatever she picked up should be on Louie's worktable."

"So what do you think?" PJ asked.

"Of what?"

Again, the smugness. She allowed herself a quick fantasy of punching him in the nose.

"Of what Dr. Graham said. That the voice of the person who blackmailed the nurse sounded like her supposedly dead stepson."

"Let's give Louie a crack at it before we start clanging all the bells. I think it's farfetched that she could recognize his voice after seven, eight years. Especially since a boy's voice changes a whole lot during those particular eight years."

"It wasn't just voice recognition. There were other things. Speech habits, like making up nicknames for strangers. Will Carpenter used to do that."

"So she says."

"For heaven's sake, Schultz! What do you want of this woman? Isn't there any way you could see her as a victim?"

"Yeah," he replied, raising his voice enough to make Millie glare at him. "Yeah, I could. When she's in a box six feet under."

"There's just no reasoning with you."

"I stick by what I said. I don't think the lady's been honest with us, right from the start."

PJ stared into her fruit bowl, looking for solace where there was none. Then she nodded.

"You're right," she said grudgingly. "When we talked, I had the strong feeling she was hiding something. When I asked her when she had last heard from Will, she said years ago, when she got his suicide note. I don't think that's true. If he's alive—and I believe he is—she's heard from him recently. I'd bet on it. I can't help thinking of that incident when she got a message on her computer and erased it right away."

"If she heard from him and didn't tell us about it days ago, then there's only one reason. Billy-boy's got something on her."

As soon as he said it, PJ knew it was true. Her mind took the next step. "And if we find him first, we find out what she's hiding. She doesn't want that to happen."

"It's either something very damaging personally or something illegal, or both. Hmmm . . ."

"Isn't that my line?" PJ said.

"What? Oh . . . Don't worry, I won't be hanging out my shingle as a shrink anytime soon."

"Heaven forbid. Although I can think of a couple of patients who might have benefited from your . . . no-nonsense approach."

"I was thinking that maybe she's trying to find him. Actively, I mean. Maybe hired a private investigator. And she's got a jump on us, too, if she knew who the killer was right away. If she's hired someone, I can probably find out."

"I thought private investigators didn't tell who their clients were."

"Usually, they don't." He didn't offer more, and she didn't ask. There were some things about Schultz she didn't want to know. They both concentrated on eating for a couple of minutes.

"So tell me already," PJ said. "If you wait any longer, you're going to pee on the floor, and Millie will be mad at me for causing a mess."

"Thought you'd never ask," Schultz said. He wiped his mouth and fingers on a napkin, making her wait a little longer. "Remember Charles the Snake?"

PJ listened carefully as he told his news about uncovering the money laundering. He was practically beaming by the time he finished.

"Well done, Detective. I'm impressed, and I'm sure Lieutenant Wall will be," she said. "Your news is a lot better than mine because it's something concrete. All mine does is raise more questions."

"That just shows you're making progress with the investigation," he said magnanimously. "When no questions are being stirred up, that's when you've got trouble. That's when the case is stagnant."

She thought he was actually puffing up his chest a little. Well, why not—his accomplishment was secure. The things she had turned up were starting to sound vague.

"One murderer and one crooked son-in-law caught already, and we still haven't hit the mark," PJ said. "Maybe I can get Lieutenant Wall to hire Helen Boxwood. She suspected Charles Horner from day one."

As soon as the words were out, PJ regretted mentioning Helen. Schultz smiled but made no comment. He pushed his plate away and eyed the bowl in front of PJ.

"You going to finish that fruit?" he said.

CHAPTER

23

When PJ got to her office after breakfast with Schultz, she decided to dial up her Power Mac at home to retrieve some files. The car bomb still bothered her, especially when she allowed herself to think that she might have driven Thomas to school, as she had occasionally done. Puzzling over the whys and wherefores of it hadn't gotten her anywhere, so she decided to bury her anxiety in a blizzard of paperwork. She was working on justification memos for a couple of expenditures she hoped to get approved. The first was for her own HMD—head-mounted display—and data gloves, which were necessary to immerse in her virtual reality simulations. The equipment she was using was on loan from Mike Wolf, and sooner or later, he was going to need it back for his research at Wash U. His project, which was placing two surgeons in different physical locations into the same virtual operating room, was fascinating. She could see tremendous potential for training purposes in medical schools—especially since the "patient" could be used over and over again without complaining—and also for ongoing education. If the simulation was refined enough, a surgeon who developed a new technique could teach it to others around the world.

The second memo made a convincing, she thought, case for a CHIP conference room, complete with computers networked to the one on her desk. Her team was spread out in the building, and the only place they could get together for brainstorming sessions was her office—so tiny as to be barely sufficient for her own needs. Every time she needed to get into the file cabinet, she had to roll the laser printer stand out of the way. At least that was an improvement. Up until a month ago, she had to pick the printer up off the floor.

She knew both projects were going to be tough sells, and the sooner she got the memos in to Wall, the sooner they could start arguing about them. She had intended to copy them to disk and bring them in with her, but had forgotten to do it this morning. A few taps on the keyboard, and her office computer dialed to make the connection. To her surprise, the phone line was busy. Assuming someone was leaving a voice message for her, she waited a few minutes, sorting through the stack of paperwork from her IN box in the meantime. Then she tried again.

Still busy.

There was a two-minute limit for her voice messages. It had to be the hacker.

She had left her computer turned on at home for this specific reason. She felt electrified with the thought that the killer was so close. At this very moment, she knew what he was doing. Heart racing, hoping that the spike she had installed would nail the hacker's location, she quickly picked up the phone and punched the numbers for Schultz's desk. He answered on the first ring.

"Someone's breaking into my computer again," PJ said without preamble. "The one at home. Is there any way to trace the call from here?"

"What do you think this is, Doc, *Science Fiction Theater*?"

"Damn it, Schultz," she said, "you're never any help." She hung up with his protestations issuing from the receiver.

On the third try, the connection went through. Eagerly she examined the log kept by the spike program. There were five entries. She went through them one by one, starting with the one immediately prior to the connection, then backing up toward the source of the call. Paris, France. Boise, Idaho. Sidney, Australia. Lima, Peru.

The last entry read "Naughty, naughty." The hacker had detected the spike and disabled it.

"Fuck!" PJ said, just as Schultz came in her office door.

"Is that an order, Boss?" he said, settling into a folding chair.

She cradled her head in her hands for a moment, ignoring his remark.

"I know the prospect leaves you speechless," Schultz continued, unperturbed. "I've had that effect on women before. With the lights out and a little mouthwash, everything will seem much better."

PJ still didn't raise her head.

"That lights and mouthwash business, those are for my benefit, not yours." He leaned heavily on the desk, as though testing its strength. "Seems sturdy enough. Going to take quite a beating, though. Hope you don't get any splinters in your ass."

PJ couldn't hold it in any longer. She snorted, trying one last time for decorum, and then gave way to laughter. She reached for a tissue and wiped her eyes.

"I had him," she said. "He was right on the end of a phone line, and he got away."

"I know exactly how you feel," Schultz said, soberly. A minute went by while PJ marshaled her feelings.

"So. What'd the creep do this time?"

"Do? Oh, I haven't checked yet."

The first thing she looked at was the simulation which had already been altered once, when the Grim Reaper made his appearance. The file was exactly the same size as before, so she doubted that any changes had been made. She would make a more thorough check later, but her eyes were fastened on a new file named CALL 911.

Before examining the new program, she checked the cabling behind the computer. She had unplugged her connection to the department network, and she wanted to make sure it was still disconnected. That way, any possible damage would be confined to her computer at home and the isolated one in her office. She had up-to-date backups of each one's hard drive. Finally, she copied the new file to her office computer.

"Here goes," she said. She angled the monitor so that he would have a good view. Schultz, who had been twiddling his thumbs impatiently, leaned forward.

It was a crude simulation, done with the software she had developed, but not refined. PJ ran it in real time. A boxy vehicle pulled up to the curb in front of a two-story building. A Genfem got out and walked jerkily around to the back and into the building. A moment later, a digitized voice said "BOOM," and the windows blew out of the rooms on the lower floor. Flames showed at the windows, and smoke rose from the building. The flames looked like comical yellow tongues. A window opened upstairs, and a series of Genfems and Genmen appeared, threw up their arms in fright, and then leaped from the window to the sidewalk below. Some got up and limped away, and others lay in crumpled heaps. The simulation ended abruptly. The whole thing ran about two minutes.

PJ looked up at Schultz and saw dark clouds in his eyes.

"Where's Thomas?" he asked.

"At school." PJ was puzzled. "Why?"

"Are you certain he's not at home?"

"He left before I did."

"Call the school and make sure he's there. I'm sending the bomb and arson squad over to your house."

"What . . ." PJ cleared her throat and tried again. "What makes you think . . ."

"Just call the school. We'll talk after we know that Thomas is safe."

While PJ made the call, Schultz left the room. The school secretary thought her request odd, but complied. She returned a few minutes later, saying that she personally had seen Thomas in gym class. By the time PJ thanked her and got off the phone, Schultz was back.

"The squad's on its way," he said. "They're good people. I asked them to remove your cat until the house is checked out. If they can catch it, that is."

At the mention of Megabite, PJ started to rise from her chair.

"Take it easy, Doc. Let the pros do their job."

"You're taking that simulation as a direct threat to me. A bomb in my house."

"Duh. You got it." The fact of the earlier bomb in her car lay between them, and couldn't be ignored.

"Then you think that's supposed to be me, pulling up in front of the house. When I go in, the bomb goes off. That means the house is rigged. Isn't the bomb going to go off as soon as the bomb squad tries to enter the house?"

Schultz scowled at her, and PJ realized she was not thinking straight. Of course the bomb squad wasn't that stupid. Otherwise, they'd have a mighty high turnover rate.

"All right," she said. Her heart rate was almost back to normal. "Let me see if I can make any sense of this." She sat and thought about Schultz's interpretation. "Something's not right here. In fact, several things. If this is a revenge situation, which was our working hypothesis, why would the killer be after me? Why bother to send me a warning if he seriously intends to kill me? He didn't warn anyone else. And who are all the people jumping out of my house?"

"Who knows how this creep's going to act?" Schultz said. "Maybe he thinks you're getting too close. Most likely there's no bomb. You want to take that chance?"

PJ shook her head. "What about all the extra people, Schultz? That's an important part of the simulation, and it doesn't seem to have anything to do with my house."

"So we'll consider other angles. But I wanted your house checked out."

"Let's start by watching the simulation again," PJ said. Schultz grunted his agreement, and the two of them watched the monitor.

Halfway through, another interpretation burst into PJ's awareness. "Oh my God, Schultz," she said. "It's not my house. It's the hospital. The bomb's in the hospital."

"Then that's Dr. Graham getting out of the car, and all those people jumping out . . ."

"Are the patients. It fits. What do we do?"

"Call Wall," Schultz said. "Explain what's going on, and ask him to get in touch with what's his name, that guy with the germs."

"Bert Manning."

"Yeah, him. Let old Bert decide if he wants to evacuate the hospital."

PJ was already reaching for the phone.

"I'm going to take a run out to your house," Schultz said. "Talk to the guys, see how things are going."

PJ waved him out impatiently. Her worry about her own house had been eclipsed by a bigger one: a hospital with five hundred beds going up in flames. After she contacted Wall, he came to her office to look at the simulation. He got there so fast he must have run the entire way. When he left, he looked grim.

PJ, alone in her office, felt as though things were spiraling toward disaster. CHIP's case had now spread well beyond her realm. She wondered if Wall blamed her for not making more progress, for letting things get to this point. Examining her own feelings, she found some guilt lurking. If anyone else got hurt at the hospital, it would come down right on her shoulders, even if she was the only one who felt that way. She felt a strong urge to get up and do something.

Take charge, find the killer, and wrestle him to the ground. And all before lunch time.

Instead, she decided to put her own skills to work. A question was nagging at her. How had the hacker gotten into her home computer? She thought she had taken safeguards, and never really expected the spike program to be triggered.

It was time to bring in the big guns.

She dialed a private bulletin board, and a couple of minutes later settled into a comfortable conversation.

Merlin here. What's the buzz, Keypunch?

He stopped the spike, PJ typed. No small talk this time.

Sigh. Well, it was a long shot. After all, it wouldn't have worked against humble little me. I should have given him more credit.

Merlin, tell me straight out that it isn't Mike Wolf we're trying to catch. Because if it is, I think I'll go crawl in a corner.

Nothing in this life is certain, but I'm as certain as I can be that Mike isn't a killer. Think now: would I be able to answer the same question about you?

PJ pondered a moment. He was asking how deep their friendship—no, their trust—went.

Yes. I hope so. Yes.

There are others I trust as I do you. Mike is one of them.

So where do I go from here? At this moment, Schultz thinks my house is about to be bombed, and I think the hospital is at risk.

How exactly did the hacker get in?

I haven't had a moment to think about it. Let me tell you what I've already done.

PJ went through the steps she had taken. As an afterthought, she quickly told him about her car being blown up. When she was finished, there was no response from

Merlin for a couple of minutes. Just when she thought the connection had been broken, he was back.

What about the bad blocks on your hard disk?

As soon as she read Merlin's response, she knew how the hacker had gotten in. After the first tampering, she had initialized the hard drive, wiping out all the programs and data there. Every hard disk has the possibility of bad blocks, which are unreadable because of manufacturing defects. The initialization program attempts to read every block, which is a small chunk of storage. Those that are unreadable are marked as bad, and none of her files could utilize that space. When the formatting utility erased the hard disk, it skipped the bad blocks. That's where the hacker's code was, his back door that enabled him to bypass her security precautions. He had spread his code out, a little piece here, a little nugget there, and then tricked the utility into marking those blocks as defective. Once marked, the blocks are virtually invisible.

Groan, PJ typed.

There, there. We all get the chance to feel like fools, some of us more often than others.

Thanks. I needed that.

Glad to oblige. What did he do this time?

PJ described the simulation the killer had left for her to discover.

It certainly does sound serious. I wish I could help.

You already have, just by listening.

Thank you. I'm always here for you. One thing: don't limit your thinking. Look beneath the surface. And now, the list. Thought you were going to get away without one, didn't you? At least it's mercifully short.

1. *Get to know the wonderful folks at your nearest fire station. It may come in handy. Perhaps you could send them a fruit basket. A big one.*

2. When you trash that corrupted disk drive, do it with a baseball bat. It's highly therapeutic.

3. There is such a thing as too much bran. I know this from experience.

4. The word for the day is void: a depressing noun but a potentially satisfying verb. Take care, Keypunch.

CHAPTER

24

PJ waited nervously in her office after talking with Merlin. She got up and paced, then forced herself to sit back down. She suddenly had an image of herself as a maladjusted animal in a zoo, with a pace path worn down, muscles anticipating the distance so that the head turned just before hitting the wall. Sniffing at the scent post marked with its own scent, walking, sniffing again. *Nope. Nobody's been here but me.*

She called Lieutenant Wall for an update. Miraculously, he was at his desk and picked up on the first ring.

"Oh, it's you," he said. Obviously he was anticipating a call from someone else. She was determined to keep her fingers in the pie, though.

"Heard anything yet?" PJ asked. She was tapping her pen rapidly on the desk, noticed it, and set the pen down in case Wall could hear the tapping.

"Nothing at your house. The squad'll be pulling out of there any minute. There was a note for you, where is it . . ." PJ heard papers shuffling, then Wall came back on, reading from the note. "Marion said to tell you he and your cat got along very well, and he wonders if the claw-footed bathtub is original. If so, he'd be interested in buying it. Call him at . . . What the fuck, we're not running an antique sale here. This is a police department."

PJ could hear the tension in Wall's voice, and couldn't tell if his indignation was fake or not. She decided the best course was to say nothing. After a moment, there was the distinct sound of paper being crumpled into a ball. Mentally, she followed the arc into the wastebasket in the corner of his room. It was an excellent coping mechanism, one that Wall used at all levels of frustration: wad up your troubles and toss them out of your life.

"The dogs are out at Wood Memorial," he said. "We're playing it low-key, alerting the staff but not panicking the patients. Unless the dogs find something. Then I guess we'll get everybody out pronto."

"Is there a formal evacuation plan?"

"You bet. They even practice it, on a small scale. But this time, it wouldn't be a drill."

They were both silent for a moment, trying to picture the exodus of the injured and ill.

"Another thing," Wall said. "Your house is under surveillance. The bomber might try to come back. I'm going to have an officer pick up Thomas at school and drive him home. When you're ready to leave, let Dispatch know. They'll take care of getting you home. Same routine tomorrow."

"Thanks. I especially appreciate someone keeping an eye on Thomas."

"You bet. Well, if there's nothing else, I'm expecting another call," he said.

"Yes. Right. I'll let you know if I come up with anything from here."

After hanging up, PJ wondered if the case was still hers.

She hadn't gotten around to asking. On top of that, her closing comment sounded pretty lame in her own ears.

Something Merlin had said was still bouncing around in her mind. She closed her eyes and tried to concentrate, to block out the unproductive thought that things were slipping away from her.

Don't limit your thinking. Look beneath the surface.

Of course. What she needed to do right now was examine the two simulations the killer had sent to her, not just by watching them play out on the monitor, but by getting inside them, by looking underneath the surface.

Eagerly, she retrieved the HMD and gloves from a table in the corner and plugged them into the I/O ports on the Silicon Graphics workstation. She closed the door to her office because she didn't want to wander out into the hall during the simulation. She knew from experience that she tended to move around physically as well as virtually. The cables probably weren't long enough, but no sense taking chances. There was also the fact that if she left the door open, a small audience would gather to watch the eerie ballet. It had happened before.

She called up the first simulation and changed the program settings to allow herself to play the role of an observer, not the victim or the killer. She brought the simulation to the point where the extra character had been inserted and paused it, so that it would continue with a single keystroke. Then she pulled on the gloves. They looked and felt like fine steel mesh, but they were very flexible. She could move her fingers freely. She tucked her hair behind her ears, then hefted the awkward-looking headset onto her head and buckled the chin strap to keep it from slipping. It wasn't a sleek commercial type. Schultz had kidded her about it, but she had to admit it did look like an upside-down spaghetti strainer. She opened her eyes to the neutral blue screen displayed directly in front of her. The HMD blocked her outside vision and permitted her to see only what the tiny dual monitors showed.

She reached out and felt around for the keyboard, found the return key, but hesitated before pressing it.

This was unknown territory.

There was no way to know what it would be like in the killer's playground. Other times when she had immersed in her own simulations of homicides, she had found the experience so unpleasant that she had jumped out. It was deeply disturbing to see everything through the victim's eyes; even more so, through the killer's. She urgently felt the need to make more sense of things, though, so before she could give it too much thought, her thumb found and pressed the return key. The scene popped into view on the dual monitors.

PJ was in the corner of Rowena Clark's room.

She looked down the front of her body first, and found that the computer had put her in a nurse's uniform. Then she turned her head to look around the room. Details sprang into view wherever she looked, things that didn't show up when the room was only four and a half inches high on the monitor: the smoothness of the walls, the textures of the upholstered furniture, the folds in the sheets, the rich shadows and dark corners, like the one in which she stood. There was a lamp turned on next to the bed. The blinds were closed, and the room had a cool, efficient look to it, just the sort of place that people went to recuperate. A life-sized Rowena was in bed, blankets pulled up to her neck, with the head of the bed slightly elevated. Her head rested on two stacked, plump pillows, and she was dozing lightly. The room was quiet except for the soft *whoosh-whump* of the respirator. The lamplight fell gently on Rowena's face, flattering her so that in sleep she looked like a woman in her sixties.

Dr. Graham was also in the room, standing at the foot of Rowena's bed, about to wake her patient. Since PJ had placed herself into the scene as an observer, Dr. Graham's figure did not give any indication that she was aware of PJ's presence.

PJ watched a rectangle of light move across the floor, not exactly rectangular on closer inspection, but broader at the end closer to her. It took her a moment to associate it with a door opening, letting in light from the hallway. She turned in that direction, and suddenly her knees were shaky. She put out a hand to support herself, connected only with air, and stumbled slightly.

A tall figure clothed in black stood in the doorway. His long, deeply folded robe seemed to gather in light from a wide area, and air, too, as PJ was having trouble breathing. A capacious hood, pulled forward and draped, concealed the face. The figure bent stiffly at the knees to avoid hitting his head on the doorframe as he entered the room. Then he glided over toward Rowena's bed, intent on Dr. Graham. As he moved, the hood shifted, and PJ caught a glimpse of his eerily glowing diamond eyes. Something else . . . An imperfection near the chin, as though the metal planes of his face which intersected there hid something underneath. Another face? Wanting to get a better look, PJ took a deep breath and moved out of the corner with the idea of pulling back the hood so she could study his face. She moved herself directly in the path of the figure, then gasped as he did not stop but passed directly through her simulated body. She was an observer, and the computer was confining her to the role. There was nothing she could do to affect the course of the simulation.

The figure was past her now, relentlessly advancing on Dr. Graham. There was no sound with his passage, but somehow Dr. Graham became aware of his presence. She turned to face him, and her mouth contorted. PJ thought she saw recognition on Dr. Graham's face before fear took over, a detail lost when the figures were three inches high but apparent at life size. Rowena woke up, looked sleepily at the events in her room, but made no effort to rise from her bed.

The figure—and there was no avoiding thinking of him as the Grim Reaper—withdrew a scythe from the folds of his robe. Although PJ was prepared for it, the sight and size of the weapon the figure held made her shiver. He spun it smoothly and held it horizontally, waist-high, still advancing on Dr. Graham, who was frozen to the spot. Moments before the Grim Reaper reached her, Dr. Graham's expression changed from fear to resignation, almost a welcoming acceptance. Dr. Graham lowered her guilty eyes as the curved blade swung toward her, but made no move to flinch away from it. It caught her above the widest point of her hips and swept across her lower abdomen. PJ clamped her lips shut tightly and felt bile rising in her throat. The experience was far different during immersion. Dr. Graham's body flew apart in two segments, which then settled to the floor, each spouting blood and spilling organs. The light of the lamp glistened on the slick surfaces.

PJ wanted out, and fast. The floor of the room was covered with blood, and the level of it was rising. Looking down, she saw that her ankles had disappeared into a red pool. She flailed her arms about, trying to find the keyboard to shut off the simulation, but she had moved away from the computer and couldn't find it. Gulping air and near panic, she looked down again and saw that the blood had cut her off at the knees. She started to fumble with the chin strap that held the helmet in place.

Then she felt a heavy hand on her arm, steadying her.

"What should I do, Doc?"

"Press F10. I want out of here!" Her voice rose, although she was trying to keep it under control. A moment later, the reassuring blue screens filled her vision. She felt hands under her chin, and then the helmet lifted off. She blinked and tried to catch her breath. Schultz took her under the arm and guided her back to the chair behind her desk. She sat down, propped her elbows on the table, and cradled her head in her hands, which were still encased in the data gloves. Months ago, when she first met Schultz, she would have been mortified to show weakness of any kind in front of him. Their first private conversation had turned into a pissing match over who had the more challenging job, a cop or a psychologist. She hadn't forgotten, and she doubted that Schultz had.

A cup of coffee appeared at the edge of her vision. She took a hot gulp, then another.

"You OK?"

She looked up to meet Schultz's eyes. His gaze was intense, as though he were trying to bore through her and exorcise her fear. If he responded so strongly to her fear where there was no actual danger, how could he bear to replay in his own mind the last minutes of a murder victim's life, as he has done many times? Schultz was willing to cling to the edge of the abyss of madness by his fingertips if that's what it took to bring a murderer to justice. He had told her once that he felt he owed that to murder victims, that he had touched on their lives too late to do anything but provide the cold solace of justice. She had never considered the price he paid to do it: controlling and channeling an empathy strong enough to feel the knife himself.

She took a deep breath. "Actually, I feel a little silly now."

Schultz waved a hand in dismissal. "You really revved up my curiosity, Doc. What's going on?"

Just like that, he put aside the whole topic of being tough enough for the job.

"I was going over the Grim Reaper scenario," she said, pleased to find her voice steady. "It looks a lot different when it's right in your face."

"Said the whore as the john dropped his pants. Different how?"

"The Reaper's face. I think he's wearing a mask, with something else underneath. It might be important."

"A clue, Sherlock?"

PJ felt exasperation starting to build, then realized that was exactly what Schultz was trying to do, to relieve the tension of a few minutes earlier. She forced her hands to become still on the desktop.

"Yes. Maybe. It's worth checking out."

"Set it up. I'll do it."

Tempting. But it was her clue, if there was anything there.

"I'm going back in," she said. "But this time I'll leave the meter running." She took a couple of minutes to set up a run which was bracketed by two events: the Grim Reaper's entry into the room, and the instant before he swung the scythe. And this time, she couldn't be an observer, if she wanted to have an effect within the simulation.

She was going in as Dr. Graham.

PJ stood in the center of the room and put the headset back on. Blue screens. Schultz pressed the return key. She blinked and found herself looking at Rowena sleeping lightly in her hospital bed. She looked down at herself and saw Dr. Graham's white lab coat and her name tag. She spun toward the door, not willing to wait until the Reaper approached. He was there, filling the frame. She moved toward him, aware of the weapon concealed in his robe. He began gliding to her, and they met in the center of the room. The bedside lamp was the only light in the room, and it was behind PJ. She couldn't make out his face clearly, since it was hidden in the folds of the hood. She could see only the icy glow of his eyes. She reached for the hood, and found herself, in the persona of Dr. Graham, too short to draw it back. The Reaper was at least seven feet tall.

Then she remembered that at this point in the simulation, he pulled the hood back himself. Sure enough, a moment later he did so. She was now blocking his way, and since she was a "solid" character this time, he could go no farther. She reached for his chin, which was low enough for her to touch, at the point where the plates that formed his metallic face came together imperfectly.

Hooking her fingers under the gap left by the plates, she tugged. The robotic face lifted off smoothly, all in one piece, as though it were a shell. Underneath was a man's face, a young man with unkempt brown hair, large ears, and a weak chin, all atop a neck that didn't look strong enough to hold up his head. It was a face she knew, although years had passed and the boy had grown to a man, from Dr. Graham's home videos: Will Carpenter. On his cheek was a detailed tattoo. She moved in for a closer look until she was chest to chest with him, or rather her chest to his waist, and peered up at his face. It was a creature she recognized from mythology, a harpy. This one had an eagle's body with exaggerated talons and a woman's head and breasts. PJ couldn't make out the woman's face—the light was poor, the angle of her vision was bad, and it was crudely done.

PJ was about to back away from the Reaper when she noticed that his human face was itself a mask. There was a line that ran down the side of the Reaper's head, and only the front portion was flesh-colored. She reached up again, curling her fingers under the skin at the line. The face peeled off like a rubber Halloween mask. Below it was a metallic skull that revealed circuitry and tiny pulsing lights: the inner workings of the robot.

Keeping her reactions in check for later examination, PJ backed away from the Reaper and waited. In a short time, she saw his arm move, and the scythe was pulled from the folds of his robe. The lamplight glittered on the long curved blade. Involuntarily she took a step back. Then she remembered that she had set the simulation to terminate at this point. As the blade began to swing, PJ stuck out her tongue at the Reaper in defiance, safe in the knowledge that she would be gone before the blade struck.

As the monitors abruptly went blue, she heard Schultz laugh. It was a nice human sound, not like his usual rumble, which reminded her of a garbage disposal.

"I guess I didn't have to worry about you this time," Schultz said.

PJ calmly removed her headset and stripped off her gloves. "Not when I know the cavalry's coming," she said, "so to speak." She filled him in on what had occurred.

"That cinches it," Schultz said. "The stepson's our killer." He looked as though he was confirming, for her benefit, something he already knew.

"Unless you want to get really devious and suggest that someone's trying to frame a dead man," PJ said. "I heard from Louie right before you came in. He says the voice on Mulligan's blackmail tape and the voice on Dr. Graham's home video are the same. In his humble opinion, at least."

Schultz didn't respond. He thoughtfully stroked his chin. "So all we have to do is find a runaway kid who fooled everyone into thinking he drowned, but actually set up a new identity for himself, and who has been leading us around by the balls so far."

"So far."

"Got any ideas on how we're going to do that?" Schultz asked.

"Through Dr. Graham. She's the target, but he seems to be able to act only indirectly. She's got to know more than she's told us. For instance, what's the motive?"

"Maybe he's just a looney with some imagined grudge," Schultz said.

"Pretty focused for a looney. But I've known some people who have blown up an incident in their minds until they can't think of anything else. And usually what set them off was trivial, or something that was misinterpreted."

"To change the subject," Schultz said, "there wasn't anything amiss at your house. I checked with Wall when I got back here, and nothing's turned up at the hospital either."

"I can't believe that simulation was meaningless. We just haven't got the answer yet," PJ said. "Maybe the danger isn't immediate. We've been given a peep through the keyhole into the future."

"Very poetic. We both know what the next step is, don't we?"

PJ nodded.

"OK," Schultz said. "Press the right buttons, Doc. I'm going into that burning building." He reached for the headset and gloves on PJ's table.

"Wait," PJ said, putting her hand on his arm to stop him. "That's my job. The message was meant for me."

Schultz sat and looked at her. She knew he was taking her measure, and factoring in her state of mind when he found her in the grip of the Reaper simulation.

"OK, so I got a little carried away earlier. I'm over it now. I won't get rattled again. Since this message was for me, there might be something in there you'd miss. I . . . we can't take that chance."

"Good point." Schultz let his hands drop back into his lap, away from the headset. She tapped the keyboard, bringing up the second simulation she'd received. As she fastened the chin strap and drew on the gloves, he patted her arm.

"Don't forget I'm right here," he said. "And don't look in the closet."

PJ didn't want to be a passive observer, so she had chosen the role of the Genfem who arrived in the car and walked into the building. When the blue screens changed to images that filled her vision, she was disoriented at first.

The images were moving by swiftly. She was in a moving car, and the scenery outside was blurry, a hallmark of quick-and-dirty simulations. The car stopped, and she opened the door and got out in front of the brick building. There was no identifying sign, so she walked around the back. A door pulled open easily and she was inside. She was in a short hallway which led to a lobby area. To her right was an open door. It was a small office, and there was a nameplate on the desk: Eleanor Graham, M.D. The office was very similar to the one Dr. Graham had at Wood Memorial, reinforcing PJ's belief that the brick building was the hospital. The office occupied a corner position, and in addition to the door where she stood, there was another door diagonally across from her.

PJ looked around the office. There were tempting file cabinets and an even more tempting computer on the desk. There were no windows, so the room felt even smaller than it probably was. She knew that she had little time; the whole elapsed time of the simulation was a couple of minutes. She walked over to the desk. On the monitor there was a picture of a young boy waving, apparently at the camera which took the picture. Underneath it said "Hi, Mom Elly. I'm back from the dead, like a lot of your patients."

PJ was trying to make sense of this when the monitor screen suddenly exploded, with sharp fragments of glass flying directly at her. She heard a voice say "BOOM," and the building visibly trembled around her. Her mind went blank for a moment, and then she saw the flames. The desk was on fire. The flames looked artificial, like the perfect ones in gas fireplaces, and there was no sound accompanying them. But it was frightening. She hurried to the door she had entered, which was very close to the building's rear exit, but it was blocked somehow. It wouldn't open. She whirled and headed for the other door, the one that led to the interior of the building. It was blocked, too. The room was fully ablaze now, and to her horror, at the edge of her vision she could see her own hair burning. There was no pain and no heat, but she threw up her arms in dismay and tried to put the flames out.

Two minutes, she told herself. *I'm safe in a room with Schultz. There is no fire. A few seconds and it will all go away.*

A scream bubbled up in her throat as her clothing caught fire, but she wouldn't let it out. Then she couldn't see anything but the flames, totally engulfing her.

A moment later it was over. Trembling, she removed the headset and fell into her chair. She took a moment to collect herself, knowing that Schultz was watching her closely.

"Well," PJ said at last, "I don't think that one's quite ready for the kiddy market."

"Tell," Schultz said tensely. She went over what she had seen, including the picture and the quote on the monitor.

"'Back from the dead, like a lot of your patients,'" Schultz said. "What's that supposed to mean? The first part's clear enough. There was actually a funeral of sorts for Will Carpenter years ago. But that part about the patients doesn't make sense. As far as we know, Rowena Clark is still dead. And you say the office was Dr. Graham's from the hospital?"

"I think so. There were a few differences, though. For instance, there were two doors, not that they helped much." PJ put both hands up to her head and pressed her fingertips to her temples. She glanced at the clock. It was almost 1 P.M., and she hadn't had lunch yet. "I've got a terrible headache. Think we can leave this until after lunch? It's all a blur now anyway. I might think a little better with some Chinese under my belt."

* * *

"You go ahead," Schultz said. "I've got some paperwork I need to catch up on. That stuff gives me the farts anyway."

He walked out of the office with her. At the first hallway intersection, he made a left turn, ostensibly heading for his desk, and she turned right on her way out of the building. As soon as she was out of sight, he doubled back to her office. He felt a little sneaky.

It felt good. He vowed to do it more often, like in the old days.

He closed the door, although he was unlikely to be disturbed. PJ's office wasn't exactly Grand Central; most converted utility rooms weren't. He knew about her proposal for a workroom for CHIP, a place where the team could gather and bounce ideas around. It sounded good to him, but he thought its chance of succeeding was about the same as his chance of being swept away by a princess on a white horse. Or of getting Helen Boxwood to give him the time of day.

He hadn't wanted PJ around, in case the memories proved too intense.

Schultz came from a small farm in Missouri. When he was nine years old, a late-afternoon storm came up suddenly, born of summer heat and farmers' prayers. Lightning struck a grand old oak tree next to the farmhouse. A burning branch fell on the roof and minutes later, the old house was a torch that smeared red on the underside of the heavy gray clouds. Leo and his little brother George saw the smoke and flames from their tree-house hideaway. The two boys rushed across the pasture as the storm hit. The brief downpour wasn't enough to quench the fire. Schultz tackled his brother and pinned him, screaming, to the ground to keep the six-year-old from rushing into the house, which was now hopelessly ablaze, the flames gleefully spurting from the windows, the heat at twenty-five yards enough to redden his face and curl the flyaway hair around his face.

His parents and two sisters died that day. Leo and George went to St. Louis to live with their aunt. The farm boys adjusted to city life with the special resiliency of children who have been loved.

Pulling the keyboard toward him, he repeated the sequence of commands PJ had entered. He had been watching closely. When presented with the choice of which role to play, he picked one of the patients at random. Donning the gear, he found himself in a small room with a narrow window, a hospital bed with a rollaway table next to it, an inadequate-looking dresser, and a metal chair. It had a sterile look to it, even though there were some framed pictures on the dresser. Nothing on the walls. A door stood partly open, beyond which he could see a toilet and the edge of a sink. Something was wrong with his perspective, though. He was seeing everything from a sitting height, not from a standing one. Finally he looked down, and the answer was obvious. He was in a wheelchair.

He was curious about what he looked like. There was probably a mirror in the bathroom, but he didn't know if he could maneuver the wheelchair there. The door looked wide enough, but there was a sharp turn to reach the sink, and the mirror would be above the sink. Instead he rolled over to the low window, which happened to be directly in front of him and required moving the wheelchair only in a straight line. The rolling sensation was very strange. He wasn't actually moving, but objects in the room glided by and left his field of vision. When he got to the window, he focused on the pane of glass rather than looking through it. It worked well enough, and he could see a reflection.

Looking back at him was a woman's face that he recognized as a standard Genfem, or generic female. It was a shock at first, but he realized he had picked a patient without regard to sex.

"BOOM." The voice was loud enough to startle him. The glass in the window swayed outward, then burst away from him. The expected rush of air didn't come, but around him he could see the furniture vibrating against the floor. Time was rushing by in the simulation, and he hadn't learned anything of value yet. After a couple of false starts, he was able to turn himself around and wheel toward the door which presumably led to a hallway. He had no practice maneuvering the chair, and so he rolled right up to the door, only to be presented with the problem of opening it with his chair in the way. He heard screams coming from the hallway and from rooms on either side of his. Backing up and moving to the side, he finally managed to open the door and wheel himself out into the hall.

Around him was chaos. Flames were shooting from rooms at both ends of the hallway. Fire doors had failed to close, so that fire was curling in from the stairwells. Genfems in nurse uniforms were moving rapidly this way and that, yelling to patients and trying to explain that the stairs couldn't be used. A few wheelchairs were clustered around an elevator in the middle of the corridor, but the doors wouldn't open even though one patient was pounding frantically on the DOWN button. The only way out for the trapped patients was through the small windows in each of the rooms. Thick smoke hung at the ceiling level, and the layer was dropping fast. Soon it reached those who were standing, and they were overcome. Schultz felt his heart thudding and his breath coming fast, courtesy of the flight response. To his relief, his feelings weren't overpowering. He firmly pushed thoughts of his parents and sisters into the little compartment in his mind where a nine-year-old's grief still ruled. Mentally, he slammed the door before the grief could bubble out around the edges, like air finding the tiniest passages out of an inflated inner tube pushed and held under the water.

Unable to do any exploring out in the hallway, Schultz wrenched his wheelchair around, intending to go back into his room. The photos on the dresser might be worthwhile to examine. On the wall outside his room there was a bulletin board, which he was now facing. It was hung low on the wall, so that wheelchair occupants wouldn't have to strain to look up at the notices. One of the papers posted there caught his attention because it was flapping loosely, a response to the virtual gusts of air moving in the hallway, the fire breathing in and out with its own hellish rhythm, a parody of life. He reached out and held the corner of the paper down so he could read it. Then he was ready to leave, so he simply waited in his wheelchair for the simulation to end.

Black smoke descended around him, flames licked ineffectually at his feet, and images of his family burned brightly in his mind.

CHAPTER
25

When PJ came back from lunch, she found Schultz waiting in her office. He had taken his usual spot, the sturdier of her two folding guest chairs. She wasn't surprised to see him there. She had brought him back a fortune cookie, and insisted that he open it before they talked. He snapped it open and pulled out the strip of paper.

"Your love life will improve," he read.

Chuckling, he balled the paper and tossed it, missing her wastebasket by several feet.

"Hey! You should keep that," PJ said. "Besides, how do I know that's what it actually said?"

"Nosy Rosy." Schultz tipped his chair back. She knew his love life wasn't much to talk about now. "How's Thomas doing?"

PJ was used to the abrupt changes in direction in a typical Schultz conversation, and she didn't miss a beat. "Fine, I think. He's amazingly resilient. He was eager to get to school today so he could brag about being the only family on the block with an exploding car. But I feel guilty about leaving him to cope with it on his own."

Schultz nodded and smiled. "That sounds normal enough, for both of you."

"He likes school," PJ said. "He and his friend Winston have a lot of classes together. They're even in the same homeroom." She went on to tell him about getting roped into making Halloween cupcakes.

"You do realize that's this Thursday?" he said.

"Oh, my goodness! No, I didn't realize it was coming up so soon," PJ said. "I don't even have muffin tins."

"I do."

She raised her eyebrows. "Leo Schultz, president of the Secret League of Macho Detectives, has muffin tins?"

"Real men are prepared for anything," he said. "Besides, Julia bought them. I doubt they'll be a contested item in the divorce settlement, though."

"I'm surprised you know your way around the kitchen enough to find them."

"Then you'll also be surprised to hear that I've actually made cupcakes before. Decorated them, too."

"You should publish one of those thought-for-the-day calendars," PJ said. "You could put some little-known fact about Leo Schultz on each day."

"Tell you what, Doc. How about I come over with my pans on Wednesday? I'll even bring cupcake liners. You get the other stuff together."

"Cupcake liners? You'll have to drop the technical jargon, Schultz, if you want to work in the kitchen with me."

"I take it that's a yes."

"It's an irresistible offer," she said, a smile brightening her face. "It's a date."

"Who's going on a date?" Anita asked. She was standing in the doorway of PJ's office.

"It's more of a culinary adventure, not that it's any of your business," Schultz answered. He waved her in. "You too, Dave. I know you're out there. I can smell you from here."

"Pastrami with extra onions," Dave admitted. Anita was already seated in the other guest chair. Dave was rolling his own chair in front of him. He closed the door after he wedged his chair inside. PJ wrinkled her nose ever so slightly as Dave's lunch made itself known in her tiny office. She lifted herself out of her chair so she could reach across her desk to the small fan in the corner. She turned the dial, upping the speed from low to medium, hesitated, and then turned it to high.

PJ turned her attention to Anita and Dave. "Schultz and I have just been doing a little exploring with the simulations that the killer inserted into my computer," she said. "You do know about the second one?"

Anita nodded. "Yup. Schultz called from his car radio and told us about it. He was on the way back from your house."

PJ showed them both simulations. "First, about the Grim Reaper," she said. "He's clearly a stand-in for the killer, and that's a crucial thing with him, the stand-in part. He goes to great lengths to get other people to do the nasty stuff for him. When I got inside the simulation, I found that the Reaper's metallic face is a mask. Below it is Will Carpenter's face. And, interestingly, underneath his human face is a robotic one."

"He thinks of himself as a machine man?" Dave asked.

PJ frowned. "It could be a reference to his close association with computers."

"Or wishful thinking," Schultz said.

"Yes, that fits," she said thoughtfully. "Mechanical men don't have to cope with feelings. There are some other parts of the simulation I haven't given much thought to yet, but they do seem important. For instance, Dr. Graham has a distinctly guilty look on her face. When the Reaper approaches her, she lowers her eyes in acceptance of what's to come. What does Will Carpenter think she's guilty of?''

"Being a bad stepmother?" Dave said. "Like in all the fairy tales. 'Hansel and Gretel.' 'Cinderella.' 'Snow White.' "

"Fairy tales," PJ said. "On his cheek—the one on his human face—there was a tattoo. It was a harpy, a mythological creature. I think it had Dr. Graham's face, although I can't be positive."

"I saw one of those in a movie," Schultz said. "*Jason and the Astronauts*, I think."

PJ opened her mouth to make the correction, but Anita beat her to it.

"That's *Argonauts.*"

Schultz glared at Anita. "Don't you start in on me, too. I may not be able to bust the doc's ass, but I sure as hell can bust yours." He looked around, noticed that his little speech didn't seem to be going over well with the ladies. Dave was impassive. "What, we can't talk about busting asses these days, just because they're women's asses? Would you prefer I said tushies? How are we going to talk about the harpy, then? Harpies have got tits. Not breasts like chickens."

Schultz was red-faced by the time he finished. PJ and Anita looked at each other and shrugged. "Are you done, Detective?" PJ asked. She knew something was bothering him, so she was willing to ignore his outburst if Anita was. Maybe he would let her know later on what the real problem was.

Schultz nodded in answer to her question, then pointedly turned away and found something interesting to look at on the wall above Dave's head.

"So why would he think of his stepmother as a harpy? Is Dr. Graham the type to nag a lot?" Anita said.

"Probably not," PJ said. "But I think the imagery is more vivid than nagging implies. Harpies were supposed to be dreadful things. Vicious, foul-smelling, and prone to ripping people open and eating their smoking entrails.''

"Yuck," Dave said. Of the four of them, PJ thought he probably had the weakest stomach.

"The second simulation, the burning building, is still a puzzle," PJ said. "Inside it there's an office, clearly intended to be Dr. Graham's. It's detailed down to a computer on her desk." She told them about the message displayed on the computer.

"Back from the dead. That reminds me of something," Anita said. "Damn! I just can't get hold of it right now."

Everyone paused for a moment, as if making a group effort to pry information from Anita's memory. The fan, churning away at high speed, lifted the long hairs at the front of Schultz's head, the ones he combed across his bald spot in the hopes that no one would notice. It was like putting a doily on the radiator. Although Schultz was facing away from her, she could still feel his eyes drilling into her, questioning . . . What? Competence? Courage? Foolhardiness?

"I've got something on the burning building," Schultz said into the conversational hole. PJ looked at him quizzically, wondering how he could have read more into her visit than she did. "It's no longer a continuum."

"That's conundrum," PJ said. It was out of her mouth before she could stop it. She flinched, waiting for Schultz's response.

"Yeah. Anyway, I went in while you were at lunch," he said.

"Did you search Dr. Graham's office?" PJ was thinking of the file cabinets and desk drawers she didn't get to examine.

"No. I was upstairs in the building," Schultz said. He clearly didn't want to be pinned down, so she let him continue without asking the many questions she had. It occurred to her that there must have been some reason why he waited until she left the room to enter the simulation. She could only think of two reasons: he either wanted to show her up, or he didn't want her to see his reaction. One long look at his face told her which alternative was correct, and what probably accounted for his earlier diatribe. He had met something disturbing in the burning building, something that stirred the ashes of his past.

"There was a notice pinned to a bulletin board. It was a recreation schedule."

"You mean recreational therapy at the hospital?" Dave said. "My cousin's a therapist there."

Schultz glared at Dave until he slouched down in his chair. "Nope," Schultz said. "It was for an old folks' home. GeriCare."

PJ slapped herself on the forehead with the palm of her hand. "Geez, why didn't I think of that? He's still trying to get at her in a roundabout way. Of course he would know about GeriCare."

Anita mumbled something, causing everyone to look at her. " 'Back from the dead,' " she said. "That's it!"

The group waited expectantly as Anita put her thoughts together. "The killer said he was back from the dead, like most of Dr. Graham's patients. I remember reading about insurance scams using nursing homes. Claims submitted for services that weren't performed, or even long after the patients had died." Anita was practically bouncing in her chair. "Don't you get it, guys?"

Schultz snorted. "We get it. So what? Our killer is an insurance vigilante?"

Anita's cheeks colored. "It's not so farfetched. Maybe Dr. Graham's padding the claims, and he's morally outraged."

"Christ. I'm surrounded by members of the religious right. Morally outraged. Gimme a break."

PJ stepped in quickly. Schultz might be hurting from

some memory jabbing at him, but his comments were getting out of hand. "Anita can follow up on her theory," she said, "and in the meantime, shouldn't we be doing something about the killer's arson threat at GeriCare?" Heads nodded. "Dave, Anita, go talk to Lieutenant Wall. It's his call, but I'd recommend getting the arson team out there."

There was a scuffling of feet and chairs, and the two junior members of CHIP left the office. PJ pursed her lips and gave Schultz the silent treatment. It beaded up and rolled off him like raindrops off a freshly-waxed car.

"OK, what's the problem?" she asked. His "Who, me?" look didn't deter her. "You were downright rude to Anita. And before that, to all of us. What's this business about tits?"

His eyes dropped insolently to her chest.

"For God's sake, Leo." She spun her chair around so that she was facing away from him. She was trying to recall the arguments she had used with Lieutenant Wall months ago when he wanted to yank Schultz from her team. She needed to give herself a little internal pep talk on the wisdom of her decision to fight for him.

His hand landed heavily on her shoulder. The noise of the fan had covered Schultz's approach, so his touch seemed to come out of nowhere. Startled, she looked up and found herself looking at the front of his shirt. It didn't fit well across his stomach, and gapped open a little between the stalwart buttons.

"Sorry. I was out of line," he said. "I'll talk to Anita. To Dave, too." She sensed that he was about to say something more, maybe tell her the reason the burning house simulation bothered him, but that he didn't want to tell her. So she cut him off, just as he had dismissed her earlier fears with a wave of his hand.

"Apology accepted."

The haunted look on his face lingered only a moment,

then the curtains were drawn across his feelings again. He eased his rear end onto the corner of her desk. "I've been thinking about this GeriCare shit," he said. "I have an idea."

CHAPTER

26

At 11:45 A.M. Tuesday morning, Flash slipped coins into the pay phone and dialed Wood Memorial Hospital. He asked to be connected with Dr. Eleanor Graham's office. After a delay and, thankfully, no Muzak, she picked up the phone. As soon as she identified herself, he said, "Sorry, wrong number," and hung up. He had been studying her schedule only a few days now, but he thought he had everything down. Didn't hurt to check, though.

He got into his rented white utility van and drove the four blocks to GeriCare. He had gotten a magnetic sign made which said "Lightning Phone Systems—Service in a Flash." With the sign on the side panel, the van looked official. He parked in the rear of the building, near the delivery door. He got out, opened the rear doors of the van, and pulled out a couple of orange traffic cones, which he set on the pavement about five feet behind the van. He was particularly pleased with the traffic cone idea. They actually came from a sporting goods store and were sold to mark the boundaries of soccer fields for kids. Little touches like the wording on the magnetic sign and the use of the cones gave him satisfaction.

He was wearing a blue jumpsuit with an embroidered name: Harold. Above the name, he had sewn a patch with a lightning bolt on it that he had gotten at a fabric store. Another nice touch. His voluminous attaché case was plain brown leather, but worn and scuffed as though it had seen hard use. Actually, it had, but not in the service of Lightning Phone Systems.

He walked around to the front door of GeriCare, went inside, and went straight to the information desk in the small lobby. The lobby was sparsely furnished, as if no one really expected it to be used as a reception area. There were probably not a lot of visitors. Behind the desk was a middle-aged woman with red hair that didn't match her olive complexion. It was a jarring sight. She was working at a computer, rapidly pressing keys. As he approached, he noticed the earphone and the tiny cord leading from it to a dictaphone machine resting in an open drawer. Apparently, GeriCare didn't need a full-time receptionist, so she transcribed letters to fill the hours. The nameplate on the desk said Gloria Edwards.

"I'd like to speak with Dr. Eleanor Graham," he said confidently. "She contacted our company for an evaluation for a complete new phone system." He looked down his nose at the simple two-line phone on Gloria's desk.

"Dr. Graham's not here at the moment. I'll ring Mrs. Ruhling, our day supervisor. I'm sure she can help you."

Flash looked at his wristwatch. "Oh, she's probably at lunch, or getting ready to go," he said. "I'll do my walk-through first to check out the basic requirements, then meet with Mrs. Ruhling. That way I'll have some preliminary suggestions for the new system."

"All right," Gloria said. "When you're done, check back here at the desk, and I'll find her for you." The earphone went back into place.

Flash pulled a notepad from his briefcase. He studied the phone on her desk, then picked up the receiver and pressed the buttons for LINE ONE, LINE TWO, and HOLD. Shaking his head slightly, he scribbled on his notepad. Then he ambled down the hall to the right, pausing at the first open door. Inside, an elderly woman was propped up in bed with pillows. She was watching cartoons on TV, totally absorbed. The room was clean and smelled faintly of pine-scented disinfectant. He could see a phone on her nightstand. He made another note, then moved on down the hall until he was certain he was out of view of the receptionist. Picking up his pace, he headed for the stairwell at the end of the hall.

The door to the basement was at the foot of the stairs, and it wasn't locked. He pulled it shut behind him and groped on the wall for the light switch. A string of bare bulbs set in utilitarian sockets illuminated the center of the basement, but the edges were in shadow. He found the delivery door easily. The building had a walk-out basement, but there were no windows, just the one door to the rear parking lot. He would be able to bring in the things he needed without going past the receptionist again.

It didn't take long to locate the controls for the sprinkler system. All of the sprinklers in the building were plumbed separately from the rest of the water delivery systems, with a supply pipe that branched away right near the point where the city water line entered the basement. A valve with a bright red handle allowed the water to the sprinklers to be shut off. The fire department had to have a way to shut off the sprinklers, either after a fire had been contained or, more likely, in the event of a malfunction.

After hauling in a heavy toolbox from the van, Flash set to work. His first job was to disable the two components of the fire-alarm system, the one that set up a terrible clanging in the building and the one that automatically notified the fire department. Then he shut off the water to the sprinklers and moved down the pipe to a point where it ran behind some other pipes. He wanted a less obvious location, far from the shutoff valve and control panel. He cut out a six-inch section of the pipe, slipping a length of hose over the end to channel the standing water into the floor drain. He worked carefully, not wanting to leave a wet floor which wouldn't dry quickly in the cool, damp basement. He took a chunk of Styrofoam from his toolbox and fashioned a cylindrical plug about an inch long. He worked at it until the plug would just barely fit into the pipe and slide, in close contact with the inner wall. He coated it heavily with Vaseline and shoved it into the pipe. An image of pushing a suppository into a willing asshole made him chuckle.

God, he loved his work!

He repaired the copper pipe with straight fittings and a short length of new pipe from his toolbox. When he was done, he rubbed lemon juice on the new section, dulling it so that it didn't stand out as shiny and new. He dried it with a towel and used a syringe, the kind found in drug-stores for cleaning earwax, to puff dust over it. The dust was actually ashes from a fireplace, but it looked convincing. Stepping back a few feet, he appraised his work. It was barely noticeable, and if anyone glanced at it, it would look like the repair had been done a long time ago.

He made another trip out to the van to bring in two five-gallon gasoline cans and the special pump he had designed. His hair was damp, stuck to his forehead, from the effort and, he had to admit, from the danger.

If he was discovered now, there was no possible excuse for what he was doing in the basement of a nursing home with ten gallons of highly flammable liquid.

Moving still farther down the supply line, Flash screwed a small water tap into the pipe. It was the same kind used to install automatic ice makers for refrigerators. The device clamped around the pipe, then a few turns of the T-shaped handle punctured the pipe, simultaneously sealing it with the screw. A fitting on the side of the tap permitted the attachment of a small hose or light tubing. Once he had securely attached a flexible copper tube to the fitting, he turned the T-handle again, backing out the screw from the hole. There was now an open passage into the pipe. The flex tube went to the outlet of the pump, and a hose ran from the pump's inlet to the first can of gasoline. He plugged in the pump—there was an extension cord in his toolbox, but he didn't need it—and after considerable sputtering, gasoline began to flow into the sprinkler supply pipe. He pumped in both cans. It was a two-story building, so the pipe ran a considerable length. There was no way to bleed the air out of the far end of the pipe, as it branched and branched again to reach each sprinkler in the building, so he couldn't fill it completely anyway.

He shut off the pump and tightened the T-handle again. He could feel sweat trickling down his back. From his toolbox, he took a plastic bag filled with sand, plopped it on the floor, and opened it up. As he disconnected the hose and flex tube from the pump, he directed them into the sand, which soaked up the gasoline. No spills. He capped the fitting where he had removed the flex tube, and opened the T-handle again.

He heard the gasoline trickling back down the pipe, with gravity drawing it to the lowest point it could reach. It would back up until it reached the Styrofoam plug. While the plug didn't seal the pipe totally, it would only permit a small amount of leakage. He hurried back to the main shutoff valve and spun the red handle, turning the water supply back on. He pictured the effect: the pressurized water sped down the pipe and slammed into the back of the plug. The plug slid, as it was meant to do, with the force of the water behind it, shoving the gasoline ahead. The plug caught at the first right-angle bend—there—but its job was done. There would be some minor mixing of gas and water around the edges of the plug, but that was OK.

When a sprinkler was triggered, it would first sputter air trapped in the pipe, then spurt gasoline, then perhaps a trickle of water would come out—whatever could leak past the plug.

Flash went back to the T-handled tap. He had to leave it in place. If he unclamped it, gasoline would leak out. He gave it the lemon juice and dust treatment, then carried the gas cans, pump, bag of sand, and hose back out to the van.

Only one thing left to do in the basement. The sprinkler system had to be triggered, which meant he needed a fire source. He carried in a medium-sized cardboard box. There was an ideal setup point, a stack of boxes containing supplies, a few yards away from where he had worked on the pipe. He took a heavy-duty appliance timer from the box and plugged it into a wall socket about fifteen inches from the floor. Into the timer he plugged an iron, and he set the iron on its highest heat setting. He set the timer for 10:30 A.M. The next day was Wednesday, and that was the day that Dr. Graham spent most of the morning at GeriCare. He set the iron into the cardboard box, on top of a fluffy layer of wood shavings. The shavings were fatwood, heavily impregnated with resin that flamed easily and burned hot. Fatwood was made from pine scraps left over after milling. The trimmings were compressed into small sticks as starters for fireplaces. He closed the lid of the box and shoved it up against the wall. There was a cutout shaped for the timer, so he could get the box close to the wall. He put a couple of other boxes on top of it, so that it blended into the stack. Perfect.

He knew that after the fire, arson investigators would detect his handiwork. It didn't matter. What mattered was the anticipation, then the glorious time of the fire. And collecting his money from the client when the job was done. Nothing tied him to the job. The receptionist, if anyone bothered to ask her about unusual events the day before, would remember that he wore a blue jumpsuit and said he was from the phone company, or something like that. If she was still alive. He expected the fire to spread fast and to be very intense. It had been his experience that practically no one made it out. Not that it would be impossible. But people panicked, or they just didn't act fast enough because they didn't realize the tremendous speed of the flames.

They didn't respect the flames, as he did. Or love them, as he did.

Flash checked the basement to make sure he hadn't left any tools lying around. He closed and locked the delivery door and went back upstairs, carrying his attaché case. On the first-floor landing, he stopped, pulled out his notepad, and studied it while checking out the hallway. He heard sounds of occupancy—TVs, radios, soft conversations— but no one was in the hall at the moment. He approached the door to the hallway, which was, as he expected, a fire door. It would close automatically when fire was detected, confining the flames to the basement. That would only be temporary, because the fire would be hot enough to burn right up thorough the floor. But the fire doors would give people an extra couple of minutes to react, and that didn't fit his plan. He pulled a tube of SuperGlue from his pocket, checked again to make sure he was unobserved, and squeezed some into each hinge on the fire door. It effectively froze the hinges and immobilized the door. Slipping the tube back into this pocket, he walked casually down the hall to the lobby, nodded to Gloria, who didn't look up from her keyboard, and went to the far end of the hall.

There were four fire doors in the building, and he hit them all.

The fire would be free to surge up the stairwells. Whenever he could, he removed barriers ahead of time for the fire, so that it could move unhampered. He pictured the flames hungrily climbing the stairs toward the helpless old people on the first floor, and felt such a rush of excitement that he had to stop and close his eyes to savor it.

Just as he closed the door of the van and inserted the keys in the ignition, a city vehicle rounded the corner of the building and came to a stop in the rear parking lot. It was the bomb and arson squad. His pupils grew into dark marbles, and he held his breath, wondering what could possibly have tipped off Gloria. Through his open window he heard the members of the team grousing about having had two wild-goose chases in one day, and now probably a third. But they swung open the rear doors of their van, and began unloading equipment. Flash forced his fingers to turn the key. He pulled his van away, trying not to look too much in a hurry. In the narrow driveway at the side of the building, he met an oncoming second squad vehicle, this one carrying the dogs that sniffed out explosives. He had to back up to let the other van through, and the driver waved pleasantly at him.

Flash finally got out of the parking lot and out onto Lemay Ferry. Checking his mirror, he saw that no one was following him. Now that his terror was sliding away, he realized that it almost certainly wasn't Gloria who had called the arson squad.

It was his client, the son of a bitch wimp. And to think he had tried to do the guy a favor by tossing in a car bomb for free. Flash thought that had been a really nice touch, like an appetizer before a meal. He had studied the background information his client provided, including the bit about possible police surveillance, then decided to kill one of the investigators. It would be a distraction and give him some breathing space. When he had a choice, he always chose the woman to kill. He almost changed his mind when he found out she had a twelve-year-old son, but then he decided that was old enough for the kid to be on his own.

He would have to do something about that motherfucking client of his. Soon.

First things first.

CHAPTER

27

Cracker sat back in his chair and picked up the apple he had brought in from the kitchen a couple of hours ago. He remembered how optimistic he had felt when he fetched the apple, an optimism that had since slipped away, leaving him with an empty feeling he interpreted as hunger. He had been trying to dip into Flash's background, get a feel for the man, find his weaknesses, but had run into dead ends everywhere. The guy just didn't exist. He was as much of a cybermystery as Cracker himself. He bit into the apple and wondered how in the hell he was going to stop Flash, or if he should bother.

He would never have selected him for the job if he'd known about his obsession with fire. That small but very important piece of information had not been passed on to him by his former client with organized crime connections. It was difficult enough dealing with his own peculiarities—and Cracker knew he wasn't like other people. Some days he felt as though his entire personality was nothing but a door slammed against unspeakable horrors, which from time to time oozed out around the edges. But taking on the burden of Flash's pyromania was too much. Events were spiraling out of his control.

First, there was the principle of the thing. If he paid for a bagel, he expected to get a bagel, not a blueberry muffin. If he paid for a straightforward murder of his stepmother, that's what he expected to get. He didn't want the hired help to show initiative. It set a bad precedent.

Second, there was the annoyance of the tape recording that Flash had made. Cracker didn't like that in the first place, and especially didn't like having it thrown back in his face. When he got off the phone, Cracker had decided he had to have that tape. He hired a private investigator to break into Flash's hotel room, find the tape, and replace it with a blank one. He didn't have much hope for success, because he didn't think Flash would leave the tape any-place as accessible as a hotel room. He had assumed it would be in a locker somewhere, or sent to a mail drop.

To his surprise, the PI had returned triumphant. The tape had still been in the recorder, and the recorder was in plain sight on a dresser top. While glad to have the tape in his possession, the issue raised even more doubts about Flash. The guy meticulously concealed his past, yet left vital, and incriminating, information lying around in his hotel room. A maid could have flicked on the recorder, thinking it contained a music tape. Flash was unpredictable and inconsistent, and that made him a loose cannon.

Third, there was the problem that a whole lot of other people were going out with Mom Elly. Was that really a problem? Would there be any regrets? He suspected—knew—that in his pre-Karen days, he wouldn't have been sitting here struggling with the morality of it. He had sent a warning to the police about GeriCare. It was an oblique one, but if Dr. Gray wasn't smart enough to figure it out, well, that was hardly his fault. He should wash his hands of it.

He had been up most of the night, sitting in his work-room surrounded by the many small status lights on his computer equipment. He had left the desk lamp off, so that the red and yellow-green dots and rectangles seemed suspended in the blackness of the room. He knew each piece of equipment by its characteristic lights, and even though he had known fear in the darkness before, he was comfortable, as if surrounded by friends. He admired the machines around him, admired their objectivity, precision, and logic. No harpy nightmares. No treacherous feelings, no risk taking. Risk was dangerous; risk opened doors and let in the insistent wind that stirred memories. He had set up a life in which he was always in control, except for brief terrifying moments of sexual release.

A series of failures had sent risk cascading into his life, and now he had played a wild card—Flash. The man was abhorrent and volatile, totally ruled by desires Cracker could never understand.

He wondered if Flash thought the same of him.

Cracker shook his head in the dark. The status lights left faint trails in his perception as his head moved, tiny streaks of light all around him. He imagined his eyes as cameras taking pictures at night, long exposures of city traffic where headlights and taillights snaked across the frame not as discrete points but vibrant ropes of white and red. He toyed with the image, expanding it: his entire self as one of those lights, leaving behind a luminous trail as he moved through life. His trail should have been like a shooting star, the hotly incandescent life of a child born to parents who loved him, a boy full of promise. It was instead a tangled, wormlike thing, blood red and tormented.

Cracker pulled himself away from the images before he could drown in them. If he permitted self-pity to claim him, he wouldn't stay focused on the rage that churned his stomach and the bitterness that froze his emotions and drove his desire to be machinelike. Fear was there too, although he rarely acknowledged it, terror sealed in the black heart of him, where four-year-old Billy dwelled. While Mom Elly lived, he could never be at peace, or anything even approaching peace. It was she, with her treachery and murder of his father, who had spun the wheel crazily and sent his life careening toward insanity.

He had anchored himself with hatred. It would have been easier to slide back into numbness, the way he did right after his father was killed. His father, all he had left after the bad thing happened to his mother, his father looming like a benevolent giant in a small child's world—gone, hideously murdered in front of his eyes, eyes in a helpless, four-year-old body. He closed his eyes, letting the memory wash over him in a cold wave. His father, groaning in the heartless moonlight, pleading with Mom Elly to end it as she bent over him, indulging her savage appetite, gorging herself on his vitals, her face slick and ferocious. The vision burst on him unfiltered by the knowledge gained in the intervening years, powerfully invoking the same childish terrors over again. His body shuddered with the force of it, every detail as sharp as a razor and just as untouchable, and locked into a four-year-old's mind. A mind that believed in monsters in the closet, in sharks in the bathtub, in the Big Bad Wolf.

He wasn't helpless anymore.

He thought about the lives he had already taken in his quest for revenge, starting with his friend Diver years ago. Was he really so different from Flash? He forced himself to think logically, pictured the electrical and chemical impulses in his brain moving in an orderly fashion yet whirling in grand patterns others could never fathom. Whirling, then coalescing into certainty. The deaths were unfortunate, but necessary. They were part of the plan, steps on the way to reclaiming a life for himself, a life free of Mom Elly.

She should have received the letter he sent to her today. It contained a printout of some patient records he had downloaded from the computer in her office at GeriCare, which she had thoughtfully provided with dial-up access. He surmised that she worked from home sometimes. He put a note inside which said *Still at it, I see.* He liked the idea of taunting her, keeping her off-balance.

Cracker finished the apple and tossed the core in the direction of the wastebasket. It bounced off the rim, joining other litter which had accumulated in the past couple of days. Since he was leaving soon, very soon, he couldn't work up any interest in keeping the place clean. After he was out of the country, the house would be liquidated as quickly as possible. He figured it should bring about $110,000, all of which was going to his attorney for services rendered. In his dealings with the attorney, he had used a false name, the same one he had used to purchase the house, and had only spoken to the woman over the phone. He felt comfortable that she would not be a link to him.

The attorney was handling not only the sale of the house, but certain other duties, such as the delivery of three sealed envelopes which would pass through the hands of several intermediaries before reaching their final destination, a trusted client in South America.

The envelopes contained directions for clearing up the loose ends Cracker couldn't leave behind if his new identity was to take root and flower. Loose ends such as Flash, the doorman Gary Rollins, and Aunt Karen. The client was a drug lord for whom Cracker had obtained information about DEA agents. The man, whom Cracker knew only as Lonzo, had paid generously, then indicated that Cracker could call upon him one time in the future for a favor, and if it was within his power, he would do it, no questions asked and no payment required. Apparently, that was Lonzo's goodwill program.

Cracker was certain that the taking of three lives fell

within the scope of that favor. He had considered using Lonzo's resources against Mom Elly, but he wanted to have more personal involvement. For him, personal involvement didn't mean getting a gun and hunting her down. It meant directing from the sidelines, first her professional ruination and then her death. In retrospect, he admitted to himself, it would have been better to use the favor. So far he was batting zero, from the effect of his computer tampering to hiring Flash. He doubted that Lonzo would have gotten himself into this ridiculous situation. It wasn't at all like Cracker to mess up in such spectacular fashion. But then he hadn't gone after Mom Elly before, with all the tremendous emotional ramifications. Whenever he dealt with emotion, he feared loss of control, and fear made him inefficient.

In his bedroom, there was a small suitcase packed and ready to go. It was all he was taking with him from this house, this identity. Paper and computerized records had already been destroyed. He had compressed the computerized records he felt he needed and hidden them, highly encrypted, in the voluminous storage of a large chemical manufacturer. Later he would retrieve them, and the manufacturer would never know Cracker's data had briefly nestled in their data repository. All of the computers and storage devices in his home would be abandoned where they sat. With the exception of the one on which he still worked, they had all been lobotomized. Their hard drives had been erased, then removed and thoroughly cleansed with an industrial-strength magnet he kept in his bedroom closet for that very eventuality. He had loaded plain-Jane operating systems back onto the drives, so that the computers around him were superficially functional. He would have been uncomfortable doing anything less for them. They had, after all, been faithful.

Aunt Karen had been faithful.

He went through the whole process with the last compu-

ter, the one he had been using to try to pry the lid off
Flash's tightly contained life. When it, too, stared dumbly
back at him with none of its former intelligence, he left
his workroom and closed the door. That was that.

There was one other thing he planned to do this evening.
He was going to visit Aunt Karen for the last time. It was
perhaps a morbid thing to do, but he was drawn to it like
a vulture circling over the not-yet-dead. It would be strange
to sit across from her, knowing that she would be dead in
a few days. He would take a glass of milk from her, and
their fingers would touch on the glass. He would ejaculate
more than once with her, in her mouth and elsewhere.
And then he would walk out, and file the Aunt Karen
experience away in its entirety, to be accessed whenever
he wished.

Whenever I get lonely.

He terminated that thought immediately, like coming
to the END statement in a program.

CHAPTER

28

PJ climbed up the ladder, grateful that she had worn comfortable walking shoes and slacks today rather than a skirt. She was holding one end of a ten-foot banner that said "Open House" in gigantic red letters. Dave was on the other end of the banner, also on a ladder. The two of them were hanging it above the front door of GeriCare. The banner had been hastily borrowed from the Chamber of Commerce. There were bolts stuck into the mortar between the bricks, and the grommets on the banner were supposed to fasten over them. She found hers, slipped the grommet on, and twisted on a nut to hold the banner in place. Unfortunately, the banner was too large for the spacing of the bolts, and it sagged quite a bit in the middle. At least it was clearly visible from the street.

There wasn't really an open house scheduled tonight, but the banner was part of Schultz's plan. He had discussed it with PJ, then they brought Wall in. By midafternoon, approval had been obtained and tasks were assigned. PJ had been a hard sell, but once she was won over, she threw herself into the preparation.

Schultz had proposed using GeriCare as flypaper to snare the arsonist. The place would be watched closely, and when the arsonist broke in, he would be caught. It was possible that the arsonist and the hacker were the same person. If so, the murderer would be in hand. If not, Schultz was confident he could wring the hacker's name out of the arsonist.

There were a lot of problems with his plan, which PJ hadn't hesitated to throw up in his face. It wasn't right to put the residents of GeriCare at risk. There was no indication of the time of the fire in the simulation which PJ had received as a warning. It could be hours or days away. The building had been checked out by the bomb and arson squad and declared clean, so they were reasonably confident they were ahead of the timetable. Something which still nagged at PJ was the question of why the hacker had sent the warning in the first place. Cold feet? Contrition? Then why not simply cancel the arson attempt? She didn't understand the dynamics of what was going on. It was almost as though the hacker was slipping, losing control of his own plan. The only way it made sense at all was when she tossed another person into the equation. Like a double star system, the hacker and arsonist could be orbiting each other, each vying for ascendance. If the balance between them was upset, they could tear each other apart. And if that happened, she didn't want the residents of GeriCare in the middle.

Schultz was adamant. He seemed to be guided by some internal certainty: do this, and the case will be resolved. The end result was a compromise. She suggested that the residents be transferred out to other local facilities, a few here, a few there. There were only forty of them to worry about. How difficult could it be to find short-term care for a day or two? At least, that's what PJ had thought when she started making phone calls. Other care facilities were full. There were waiting lists. Some of the patients were confined to bed, and couldn't simply be shuffled off for a couple of nights' visits with relatives. In most cases, relatives weren't local.

The plan had been in shreds during the afternoon. Then the mayor, still pissed off because murder had invaded his social circle, interceded and found space in a most unlikely place: the St. Louis State Hospital on Arsenal Street, a psychiatric facility. A section of rooms had been emptied for remodeling, but then state funds were slow in coming, so the rooms were currently unoccupied. If PJ had tried to make the arrangements, she would have been hopelessly entrapped in bureaucratic red tape. A few phone calls from the mayor smoothed the way. PJ had expected Dr. Graham to balk at the cost of transferring the residents, but she seemed cooperative. Dr. Graham had been informed that her missing-and-presumed-dead stepson was alive, and that because of the voice match, he was the primary suspect. Now the woman seemed unnaturally eager to find him, which made PJ think that he had sent Dr. Graham a message of some kind, in the way that he had sent the computer simulations to PJ. What kind of message? What was it that was hidden between those two?

The plan was in place now. GeriCare was under surveillance to make sure the arsonist didn't have a chance to do his work before the residents were evacuated. Tonight, with the open house as the excuse, there would be traffic going in and out of the parking lot. Residents who were ambulatory were going to be transferred in private cars. Those who needed stretcher-type transport were going to be moved in vans with no windows. Anyone watching would simply think the open house was well attended.

A crucial part of the deception was the help Schultz had obtained from a group of retired police officers. They had agreed to make themselves visible in and around the building, passing as the residents. Tonight, curtains open in a window and a lamp on in the room would reveal an old man watching TV. Down the hall, another window would feature an old woman sitting in a chair, knitting with phantom needles. In the morning, "nurses"—young officers on active duty—would push the oldsters around in wheelchairs out on the grounds of the building, so that everything would look normal. PJ marveled at the dedication and courage of the retired officers, who were willing to serve as decoys. It certainly wasn't her idea of a fun way to spend her retirement years.

Dr. Graham had confirmed that Wednesday mornings were Doctor Days at GeriCare, when she normally spent the morning in the building seeing patients. The arsonist was likely to be familiar with her schedule. Schultz was counting on a strike tomorrow morning. He wasn't sure what form it would take, but seemed certain of the timing. Another of his hunches.

On her way down the ladder, PJ missed the last step and landed awkwardly. For a moment, she thought she had sprained her ankle, but then the pain receded and she was able to walk normally. It was 5:00 P.M., and she was hungry, not just for dinner, but for contact with her son. He was home from school now, escorted by a uniformed officer, and probably doing his homework at the small desk in his room. There would be a cop on the front porch and one on the back, a very visible—and, she assumed, effective—deterrent to the arsonist. But no twelve-year-old should be coping with that situation alone.

She thought about the boarded-up windows on the rear of the house. The blast had broken several. One of them was in Thomas's bedroom, directly above his desk, a reminder of tragedy narrowly missed. If she hadn't gone back to get her jacket this morning, she'd be dead.

PJ had been anxious ever since school let out at three o'clock. Her work was done for the day, since she wasn't going to be involved in transporting patients. She requested a ride home, and Dave obliged. Getting around without a car was a nuisance. The events of the day had been so dramatic, there just hadn't been time to think about the practical aspect. Money was certainly a problem. Her salary didn't come close to what she used to make in Denver, and of course Steven wasn't contributing to the household fund. The car had been old and not worth much, and she had no replacement insurance. In the next few days, she would have to go car-shopping. She wondered if she should apply for a department vehicle. Schultz had gotten one months ago, and seemed to have claimed it permanently.

She used Dave's cellular phone to order a pizza for takeout, and Dave went a few blocks out of his way to swing past the restaurant. By the time she got there, the pizza was just being taken out of the oven. The smell filled Dave's Civic and made her mouth water. Thomas accepted a big hug, and the two of them devoured the pizza at the kitchen table. She got the full story of how Thomas had played up the bomb at school, apparently making himself a hero. It didn't matter. It was wonderful to be home, even if home was temporarily a prison with cops on the front and back porches.

At ten o'clock, the phone rang. PJ, who was reading in bed, reached over and picked it up.

"Yo, Mama, how they hangin'?"

"Leo, isn't there a gender problem in that question?"

"Now that you mention it, I guess so. Just calling to see how you and the kid are doing."

"We're fine. It's nice of you to be concerned."

"I also called to tell you the transfers are finished. We're all set for tomorrow morning. Dr. Graham's going to show up there at her usual time."

"Is it just me, or have you noticed that Dr. Graham is being awfully helpful lately?"

"Yeah, I've noticed. Remember we talked about Will Carpenter having something on her, something that's making her nervous?"

"You suggested that she might be looking for Will on her own, maybe by hiring a private investigator."

"Exactly. I poked around a little, asked a few questions, and bam! She did hire an investigator, just last week. Guy named Terrence Eubanks. Former cop. When he got back to his office this afternoon, I was waiting for him. Place is a dump."

"So that's where you went. I almost sprained my ankle thanks to your disappearing act."

"Terry and I go way back, but now that he's gone private, his mouth is shut tighter than his asshole when it comes to information about clients. I already knew he's been showing Will's picture around, so he didn't bother to deny he was looking for the boy. That's what he called him, the boy. Like he was still fourteen and a runaway."

"Does he have any leads?"

"If he does, he didn't tell me. Seems the good doctor approached him, offered him five thousand bucks to find her beloved stepson, and told him she had good reason to think he's in St. Louis. He found out about the suicide, checked it out, and thinks it's bona fide shit. He was going to see Dr. Graham again tomorrow and pump her for some more expense money. I put him off. I told him the whole thing might be wrapped up tomorrow."

"So he thinks Will's dead, but he was going to try to squeeze more money out of her anyway? What kind of old friends do you have?"

"Ones who know a good situation when they see it."

"Good night, Schultz."

" 'Night, Doc."

CHAPTER

29

Billy, standing in the doorway of his parents' bedroom, knows it's his father on the bed because he recognizes the feet. Dad has huge, lumpy feet. He thinks about how Dad gets down on the floor and plays horsy. When Dad gets tired, which is really quick, they always end up stretched out on the carpet, bare feet to bare feet. To Billy, being a grown-up means having big feet. Sometimes he examines Dad's feet, looking at the fuzz between the toes, the toenails, the little hairs growing on the back of the foot. He knows exactly where the best tickle spot is. There's an interesting place, a hard bump Dad calls a corn. Billy can't figure out why it's called that, because corn is yellow stuff to be eaten.

Billy is so distracted by Dad's feet that he almost forgets what he's doing there. Then he hears the groans again, and this time there are bad words mixed in, words he knows are bad because Mom Elly tells Dad not to say those words in front of Billy. He knows then that Dad is desperate to be saved, so desperate that he will say anything, even bad words.

Billy has to help. He forces his reluctant legs forward a few steps. He looks at the moon through the parted curtains on the bedroom window, and then at the moon in the mirror above the dresser. His father is trapped between the two monstrous faces, and now Billy is too. He shivers, waiting for the evil magic to take him, to draw him into the dark place and lock him in. He is far enough into the room now to see beyond Dad's feet. His naked legs are like tree trunks, but softer, the flesh pale in the moonlight, and trembling, just like Billy is. At his hips, there is a dark shape, like a bumpy, furry blanket thrown over him. It's moving, thrashing around on the sheets.

A bear. A wolf. Maybe a monster that lifts itself off the pages of a book, peels itself up and then pops into life. Wile E. Coyote does that all the time.

Dad's hands move suddenly, grappling with the beast. Billy knows that if he doesn't do something now—NOW— he won't get another chance. He's still too far from the bed to reach out, and his paralyzed limbs won't heed the order anyway. He opens his mouth, tries to scream, tries again, and out comes something that sounds more like a squawk.

The effect is dramatic, even more than Billy hopes for, certainly more than he expects. Any creature that overpowers big, strong Dad won't consider little Billy much of a threat. The creature sits back on its haunches. Dad turns his head in Billy's direction, a grimace on his face unlike any expression Billy has seen there before. There's a strange smell in the room, too. It isn't overpowering, just a trace, really, but it's not within his experience, and it is disturbing on a deep level.

"Billy?" his father says in a low voice, like thunder rumbling far away. Billy knows thunder; that's God smacking the clouds to make them cry rain. His father's voice smacks into him now, making him sway on his feet. He is unsure. Then he feels other eyes on him, their gaze crawling over his skin. Evil eyes. The beast is looking at him.

In the pale moonlight that comes in through the parted curtain, Billy barely makes out the shape. It isn't fur-covered, as he thinks at first. It is naked, with skin like his own, and a wild tangle of hair making its head look far larger than it is. Its face is in the shadows, but he can still feel the eyes, like a cold wind blowing on him. The body is rounded in front, the way he knows that women are, that Mom Elly is. He has seen her as she stepped out of the shower, before she wraps herself up in a towel. Breasts, and they are moving with the creature's breathing, and it's breathing fast. He hears it breathing, the hot breath going in and out. He hears it above his pounding heart. The face turns away from him, just enough to catch the light. He gasps.

It is Mom Elly. Her mouth is slightly open, and her teeth gleam within like ghosts in the darkest corner of the basement. Her lips are moist, and her chin glistens. In an instant of terrible knowledge, he knows that the wetness on her face comes from Dad's heaving belly. She has torn open his belly, and is feeding on the slippery insides.

He remembers seeing a big black bird crouched over a smudge of brown fur and smear of red at the edge of the road. It was a sad rabbit, with its mysterious ropelike intestines glistening wetly on the pavement, outside when they should have remained inside. As the car approached, he saw the bird's head dip down into the open belly.

Mom Elly is like that bird. Billy knows that what he was seeing is bad, very bad, that Dad can't get up and walk around with his insides hanging out, that Dad can't get up ever again.

He is too late.

"Billy, get out!" his father says, thundering louder. Billy realizes his father is trying to save him from harm, telling him to run away while he still can. Conflict seethes inside his small body, and he trembles. Then the urge to act burns in his limbs, and he turns and flees from the room, arms and legs jackknifing, flying down the hallway.

He huddles miserably underneath his blankets. He closes his eyes and tries to shut everything out, but he can't stop his racing thoughts. Dad's gone, Dad is beyond help, and it's his fault. No, he tried to help. It's Mom Elly's fault. She isn't just a witch, she's a man-eating monster.

He is trapped in the house with her. When she finishes with Dad, maybe she will come after him. He hugs his stomach hard, so that nothing that belongs inside can get out, but she will come, and pry his hands away . . .

He doesn't know how long he stays there in the dark. He wets himself again, but it doesn't matter. There is no chance of escape, so why bother trying to be a perfect, dry boy?

He becomes aware of flashing red lights reflecting from his ceiling. For a while he stays motionless, then he creeps over to the window to look out. There's a police car in front of his house, and a bigger car that reminds him of Jeffy's mom's minivan. The bigger car has red lights on the top, too. There are a couple of men standing next to the cars, and someone else: Mom Elly, in a bathrobe, her hair still wild around her head. The red lights glow on her face, and he sees tracks of wetness on her cheeks.

Tears? No. What would a monster have to cry about?

Blood, then.

He hears noises downstairs, and crawls on his hands and knees, pee-wet clothes clinging to his thighs, over to the door to his room. He had slammed it shut after his flight down the hall.

There's a line of light at the bottom of the door. The hallway light is turned on. Feeling a little bolder because of the light, he cracks open the door and peers out. The light's on in Dad's room, too, and the door is standing open. He sees another couple of strangers inside, a man and a woman. They're standing next to a rolling table, and as he watches, they maneuver it around the foot of the bed and out into the hall. On top is a still form covered with a white cloth.

Dad.

They are taking him away, now that he's dead. His body is hollow now, and covered with a cloth so that the ripped edges of his belly won't show. When the rolling table gets to the stairs, it folds up on itself somehow, and the man and woman lift it and carry it down the steps. They grunt a little.

Back to the window. The red flashing lights are turned off now, and one of the men is leaning against the police car, smoking a cigarette. Bad. Dad says smoking is bad for your body. Mom Elly is standing alone, her arms wrapped tightly around herself, holding the robe closed, holding in the horrible contents of her stomach. Billy gags at the picture in his mind, and throws up his bedtime snack on the carpet.

Not a perfect boy, never will be. Only robots, like Jeffy's, can be perfect.

The man and woman put what's left of Dad into the back of the van. Then it and the police car drive away. Mom Elly watches them until they make the turn at the corner. Then she comes back inside, walking slowly. Billy dives for his bed. He's afraid she will come up the stairs and do to him what she did to Dad: rip him open. If Dad couldn't stop her, there's no way he could. He shivers with fear.

Minutes go by, and he doesn't hear her in the hallway. He has left the door to his room open wide enough for his arm to slip through, and a slice of light comes in, cutting across the floor and climbing up the side of his bed. He yanks his feet away from the light, pulls his knees up, and makes himself as small as possible. His toe still hurts, and he remembers that he stubbed it on his wooden toy chest. That seems so long ago now. It was back when Dad was still alive.

Maybe she isn't hungry after eating Dad. No footsteps on the stairs, but he hears her down in the kitchen. She makes strange noises, like soft whining, but it stops after a while.

His eyelids sink, and he sleeps.

In the morning, he wakes to find her in his room, cleaning up the throw-up. Without the unfriendly light of Mr. Moon on her face, she looks like Mom Elly has always looked, only sadder.

She tells him that his father died suddenly last night. Something inside his body called an artery had a weak spot in it, like a balloon blown up too much. It broke open, and spilled blood inside his body. She called for help, but he was dead by the time the police and ambulance arrived. She cries a little while she's talking to him, then a lot more when she finishes. She tries to grab him and pull him to her, but he's quick, and able to get away.

Billy knows the truth about his father's death. He knows what happened before the strangers came. He saw it with his own eyes, and his certainty is unshakable. She's a monster, and his own life is in danger every moment that he spends with her.

He stays out of her way as much as possible the next few days. She doesn't take him to Kiddy Care, so he stays in his room. She serves him meals at the kitchen table, but leaves him alone to eat. At night he closes his door and piles toys in front of it, so that if she tries to come in, she'll trip on the toys and he will hear her.

Then his father's body is put into a box and buried in the ground. As the dirt thumps onto the box, a change comes over Billy, climbing up his legs all the way to his head, like the cold, ghostly fingers of air in the rectangle of moonlight in the hallway. He can't keep up his constant state of fear and anger. His body seeks protection, and he becomes numb, as if his feelings are frozen. He comes to believe that, like Pinocchio, he isn't a real boy. The nightmare starts then, the night Dad's body goes into the ground, the harpy nightmare.

By the time Billy is sent back to Kiddy Care, he is as machinelike as Jeffy's robot with the flashing eyes.

CHAPTER
30

PJ woke up at sunrise Wednesday morning. Daylight savings time was still in effect, so the darkness wasn't as pronounced as it would be by the same time next week. Outside her window the sky had lightened from black to deep gray, with heavy, roiling clouds, and the tree branches were moving in a strong wind. There was frost on the ground. As she sat on the edge of her bed, thinking how nice it would be to snuggle back under the covers, the heat came on in the house. The metal ductwork popped and zinged as the nearly new gas furnace churned out hot air.

By six-fifteen, she was dressed and ready to go. She went into Thomas's room to give him a good-bye kiss. He murmured, smacked his lips a couple of times, and turned over with his back to her. His alarm clock gave him another hour to sleep. She called Dispatch from the phone in her bedroom and asked if she could get a ride. She left a note for Thomas on the kitchen table, mentioning that she had already fed Megabite. That was futile, she knew, since the walking stomach wrapped in fur would surely charm another breakfast from Thomas. PJ wondered how the cat managed to keep her trim shape in spite of the quantity of food she ate. She pictured Megabite doing vigorous feline aerobics after everyone left the house.

She chatted quietly on the front porch with the young officer on duty. The woman was pleasant enough, but it grated on PJ that protection was needed. If the situation didn't get resolved soon, she would have to move out, or at least move Thomas out.

Her driver stopped briefly at Millie's Diner. The diner had already been open for nearly an hour and a half, and was packed with an early-morning crowd that held no familiar faces for PJ. A red-faced Millie barely had time to toss a "Good morning, dearie," at her as she whooshed by with four plates, one in each hand and one balanced on each forearm. PJ had planned to get an entire takeout breakfast but settled for a large cup of coffee. She was let out of the patrol car a couple of blocks away from GeriCare, and made her way through alleys, feeling suitably like a law enforcement professional, until she got to the rear entrance. It was then she realized she didn't have a key. Her law enforcement image sinking like a punctured balloon, she raised her free hand to knock on the door to the main level, wondering if anyone was awake inside, or even if anyone was inside at all. If no one came, she would have to try the basement door.

Before her knuckles made contact with the door, it opened, and she found herself looking at Schultz's grinning face.

"Burgmeister radioed in that you were on your way. Spotted you in the alley. C'mon in, Doc." He held the door open for her, then led her across the small lobby and down the hall to the residents' dining room. The hallway was lined with patients' rooms, all with the doors closed.

"What's in here?" PJ asked, stopping in front of one of

the doors. "The residents are all gone, right?" She opened one of the doors without knocking.

Inside, a man rose swiftly from an upholstered chair. He was old, perhaps seventy, but wiry and quick. And he was pointing a gun at her.

"Easy, Larry," Schultz said, blocking PJ's entrance into the room with his arm. "Dr. Gray, meet Lieutenant Larry Hennepin, Vice, retired."

The gun vanished behind Larry's back, presumably into a holster. He shook hands with PJ. "There are six of us on the first floor," he said. "The second floor's empty. Too hard to get out in case anything happens. We'll be keeping to the regular schedule for this place, which means that in a couple of hours we'll go sit out front and act old. I'll be the one in the wheelchair with the red plaid blanket."

"Thanks for your help on this, Larry. You and the other guys."

"No sweat. Hope you get your man." He went back to the chair, sat down, and picked up the book he had been reading before he heard PJ turning the doorknob. She hoped that she would be that fast on her feet in another thirty years.

The dining room was large, doubling as a recreation area in between meals. Schultz had closed all the blinds on the windows. The only light in the room was a lamp at the table where he had obviously been sitting. PJ seated herself across from him at the long table, feeling like she was back in her high school cafeteria. Under the guise of removing the lid of her coffee, blowing away the steam, and taking a few sips, she studied his setup. Spread out in front of her were a portable police radio, a cellular telephone, an ancient green metal desk lamp trailing a long extension cord, a gigantic thermos, a paper cup stained with coffee and with the rim chewed a little, a dog-eared deck of cards, yesterday afternoon's *Post*, a partially eaten package of oatmeal raisin cookies, and a slim paper-back, open and facedown on the desk, titled *Wet and Wild*. Judging by the picture on the front, the book wasn't about planning an island vacation. She raised her eyebrows, and he followed her gaze.

"Makes good bathroom reading," he said. She wouldn't have thought it possible, but Schultz actually sounded embarrassed. The bald spot that occupied most of the top of his head took on a distinctly pink tone, or perhaps she imagined it in the lamplight. He closed the book and slid it onto the chair next to him.

"It looks like you've set up camp," she said. "How long have you been here?"

"Just a couple of hours. Couldn't sleep. I guess you couldn't either," he said. "Here, have a cookie. They're the kind that are good for you."

"Strange. They look like ordinary chunks of fat to me."

"Raisins, Doc. They've got raisins." He glanced at his watch and pushed his chair back from the table. "It's time for me to make another quick check around the building. Care to go for a walk?"

"No, I think I'll stay here and eat some health food."

"Suit yourself. I'll be back in about ten minutes." He picked up the radio, and she assumed he'd be in contact with the officers watching the outside of the building.

By the time he got back, she had eaten half a dozen cookies and successfully resisted the temptation to go and peek out of the blinds.

He sat down heavily across from her and looked at her appraisingly.

"What?" she said, automatically brushing her shirt for cookie crumbs.

"You're holding up pretty well for a lady on her first undercover operation, Doc. Not to mention what's going on at home."

"Oh, so this is an undercover operation? That'll look good on my résumé."

"Of course, it was all my idea."

"Aren't we jumping the gun here? We haven't caught anybody yet."

"He'll be here," Schultz said confidently. "Dr. Graham's always here on Wednesday mornings. We found that out, so the killer knows it, too. Nothing'll happen until after nine-fifteen. That's when she arrives."

The time passed slowly. They played gin rummy and munched cookies, arguing over the last one before breaking it in half. At a few minutes after eight, Schultz was notified by radio that a man matching the description of Will Carpenter had been spotted across the street from GeriCare.

"So he's just sitting there?" Schultz said.

"Yeah," came the answer over the radio. It sounded like Dave. "He came in from the far side of the park, sat on a bench, and watched the front of the building for a few minutes. Now he's got his chin on his chest, like he's asleep."

"Mr. Cool."

"Absolutely. We gonna bust 'im?"

"For what? Taking a nap on a park bench? All we have is the voice analysis, and that's not enough to prosecute. We need something else."

"Gotcha. I'll let you know if he makes a run at the building with a gas can and a book of matches."

"Dave, I can't tell you what a relief that is."

"Here to serve, Boss."

As Schultz put down the radio, PJ spread her cards out on the table. "Gin."

At eight-forty-five, there was a minor commotion in the hallway as all of the retired officers left to take their positions out on the front porch. PJ was restless. She wanted to get up and walk the halls, but if anything did happen—

such as a sudden outbreak of fire—the dining room was the best place to be. At the end of one wing of the building, it was remote from Dr. Graham's centralized, windowless office. The dining room offered large, unobstructed windows through which she could escape easily. She would break a window with one of the dining chairs, climb out, and drop to the grass a few feet below.

Schultz got tired of losing at gin rummy. He folded his hands across his belly and stared at the bland artwork on the wall. After a minute or two, his eyes slipped out of focus, and he had effectively closed her out.

She read the *Post* in great depth and helped herself to hot coffee from his thermos. At nine-fifteen, just as she was beginning to read the obituary section, the radio crackled, and a male voice came on which she didn't recognize.

"Hotshot, this is A3."

Schultz came alert in an instant, his hand on the radio before the man finished speaking. "Go ahead, A3."

"Dr. Graham's car has entered the rear parking lot." There was a short pause. "She's on her way into the building via the rear main level entrance."

"I'll take it from here. Hotshot out."

Schultz stood up. "I'll go meet the good doctor."

"Hotshot?"

"That's what we call the on-site coordinator. It's nothing personal." He headed for the door, but turned back to face her when he was halfway there.

"You know, this would be a good time for you to leave," he said.

PJ stopped herself from snapping out an angry response. She realized that Schultz, in his blunt, inept way, was trying to shield her from harm.

"I'm staying, Leo," she said, her voice steady in spite of the churning in her stomach, which she was certain wasn't due to the coffee and cookies. "I need to see this through."

"You got it, Boss."

He was back in a couple of minutes, with Dr. Graham trailing behind him. She moved quickly into the room, clutching her purse tightly under her left arm, walked around the end of the table, and sat down next to PJ. As soon as the purse and a medical journal she had carried in were out of her hands, she immediately picked up a paper clip lying on the table and began turning it end to end with her fingers. PJ had never seen the woman so agitated.

There was a legitimate reason to be nervous. She was serving as decoy to bring a killer and an arsonist—PJ was convinced there were two people involved—close enough to be apprehended. Thinking back to the time her car exploded, PJ wondered if she would have had the courage to be a decoy herself, knowing that something was going to happen but not knowing when and from what direction. Some part of her said *Yes!*, the part that welcomed the newly found challenge of law enforcement and the satisfaction of bringing criminals to justice. The mother in her said *No way!* She didn't want Thomas dragged into her work, and she wanted to live a good long time, to see Thomas as a grown man, maybe get to spoil grandchildren.

The clock on the dining room wall seemed to be moving in slow motion. Schultz got up for his check of the building's interior twice more, coming and going without a word. PJ retrieved a couple of news magazines, months old, from a table at the side of the room and paged through them, thinking that next time she'd be better prepared. She envied Dr. Graham, who had at least brought professional reading material with her, and was trying to concentrate on it. Finally, the woman gave up and put the journal down. It was ten-thirty. PJ had been in the building almost four hours, and she was thinking that she wasn't cut out for this kind of work—not from the danger, but from the tedium of it. She was actually thinking of asking Schultz if she could borrow *Wet and Wild*.

She glanced sideways at Dr. Graham, who was nervously shredding the edges of the *Post-Dispatch*. It was hard to reconcile the jittery way she was behaving now with her former coolness. Schultz, who had resumed his inspection of the watercolors scattered throughout the dining room, gave no indication that he was disturbed by her behavior. Taking her cue from Schultz's silence, PJ had said nothing about the man sitting across the street on a park bench, the man who was probably her stepson Will Carpenter, now a grown man and a murderer.

What forces could have been at work in that family years ago? What could have led to the need for revenge that Will now felt? As a psychologist, PJ knew that small children sometimes blamed the surviving spouse—or themselves—for the death of a parent, and that feeling, however irrational its basis, could persist into adulthood. If Will thought that Dr. Graham was responsible for his father's death, and no one had intervened to explain otherwise, the idea could have strengthened over time. Hadn't she helped him deal with his grief?

PJ wanted to shake the truth out of her. She had the urge to go over to the window, raise the blinds dramatically, let Dr. Graham see her stepson, and shout "Isn't it about time you faced up to motherhood?"

"Dr. Graham, why did you hire a private investigator to search for Will Carpenter?" Schultz said. PJ came out of her reverie to find him focused on the doctor.

Uncharacteristically, Dr. Graham fidgeted under his gaze. "I just found out that there's a strong possibility that he's alive. If you were his parent, wouldn't you want to find him?"

"I asked you first."

"How did you know about the private investigator?" she asked, sidestepping his question again.

"A big, loud birdie told me. A vulture, in fact. If I were you, I wouldn't pay Terry Eubanks another dime. He doesn't think your stepson's suicide was faked, and he's trying to milk as much as he can out of you before you figure that out."

Dr. Graham's lower jaw dropped. Schultz's revelation had gotten the desired effect: to disorient her even further before he went for the jugular.

Just then, the radio came to life.

"Hotshot, this is S1. Got something interesting."

"Go ahead, S1."

"There's a car parked about a block away from the target, green '90 or '91 Mazda 626, Missouri license DER 746. Pulled up about ten minutes ago, driver didn't get out. Here's the weird thing."

"Suspicious activity? Maybe holding something that looks like a remote control or an electronic timer?" Schultz stood up and moved over to the window, carrying the radio. He parted the blinds slightly with his finger and peered out, but evidently couldn't see the car from his vantage point.

There was a chuckle from the other end of the radio. Schultz narrowed his eyes, and a crease formed down the middle of his forehead.

"Say again, S1."

"Hotshot, he's holding something, but it ain't no remote control. The sucker's jacking off."

Schultz blew out an exasperated, and relieved, breath. "I hear you. Don't break cover. If the pervert's still there after we wind this up, you can take him downtown. Maybe he'd like to perform for the judge."

Before the cop could respond, another message came through.

"Hotshot, this is A3. Suspect from the park bench, possibly Will Carpenter, is up and moving. He's heading for the entrance." A moment later, "He's opening the door. He's in. Repeat, he's in the building."

CHAPTER

31

At 8 A.M. that morning, the cab dropped Cracker on the far side of the small park across from GeriCare. He strolled into the park, doing his best to look casual, which was not his natural state, at least when he was away from his workroom. There had been a heavy frost overnight. The fallen leaves under his feet had faded from their fall colors and now blanketed the grass with brown. Each leaf was thickly outlined with frost crystals, so that the blanket shimmered in the sun. It was early yet, so the sun was still too low in the sky to melt the frost. He bent down and touched the edge of one of the leaves with his finger, keeping it there until the heat of his fingertip did what the sun would do later. Looking back, he saw that his footsteps were doing the same thing on a larger scale. He had left behind a trail of wet leaves. It gave him a heady feeling of his own significance.

Even Mother Nature paid attention when he walked by.

He crossed the park on a bisecting path, passing the leaf-filled basin of the fountain. There was no one else in the park. It was a school morning, so older kids were occupied. Mothers of toddlers would keep their little dears inside, with the temperature around twenty-five degrees and a cold wind prying into loose clothing at ankles, wrists, and necks, drawing heat from carelessly exposed heads. The wind was driving clouds across the sky rapidly, whipping them along, signaling a change in the weather. Perhaps a storm would arrive tomorrow, maybe even the first snow of the winter, although that would be early for St. Louis. For now the slanting sunshine cast long shadows of the bare tree branches, and the wind contented itself with lifting some leaves every now and then, sending them rustling across the path in front of him.

He got to the edge of the park and sat down on a bench with a good view of GeriCare's grounds. He was wearing a light jacket over his T-shirt, a concession to the weather, but it was open in the front. He reached inside the jacket, checking that the computer disk that stretched the pocket of his T-shirt was still there. Then he buried his hands in his pockets and watched the building. The first thing he noticed was a large banner that said "Open House" above the doorway. One side was hung higher than the other, so it made a sloppy effect. There was no date on the sign, so the event must have been last night.

After a few minutes, it occurred to him that he should have brought a book or newspaper, anything to make himself look occupied. As it was, the only thing he could do to avoid looking like he was watching the building was to pretend to take a nap and hope that the police didn't roust him as a street person. He slouched down a little on the bench, crossed his legs at the ankles, tilted his head forward, and partially closed his eyes. A harmless Sleeping Tom.

It was eight-fifteen, and there was no sign of activity at GeriCare. The large front lawn had been raked clean of fallen leaves, and the frosty grass was untouched except by a couple of squirrels. Cracker dozed for a while, his sleeping posture becoming a self-fulfilling prophecy, and when he woke it was a few minutes after nine. The wind had settled down, and the sunshine on his face was a warm contrast to the chill air. GeriCare had come to life. There were half a dozen old folks sitting out in wheelchairs or lawn chairs. They were dressed in layers of clothing, and their laps were draped with blankets. They seemed to be enjoying the antics of the squirrels on the lawn, which had multiplied to five or six. A nurse wearing a white dress partially covered by a jacket sat nearby, with the newspaper raised in front of her eyes. Every few minutes she lowered the paper and checked out her charges.

Everything looked distressingly normal to Cracker. He assumed that Dr. Gray was too dense to have interpreted his warning. He had expected—hoped?—to find the building deserted.

What did she want him to do, anyway? Hire a skywriting plane? He didn't have any obligation, not really, to warn her. He had gone out of his way, and look what it had gotten him. Cracker halted his thoughts, suddenly unsure which "she" he was thinking about, Dr. Gray or Aunt Karen.

All he had to do was get up and walk away. His plans were in place. Flash, the doorman, Aunt Karen—his links to this identity—were to be terminated. His suitcase, a small carry-on, was already at the airport in a locker.

Get up. Walk away.

He was still there on the park bench ten minutes later when Mom Elly's car turned into GeriCare's driveway, heading for the rear parking lot. Although he had sent her several messages via computer, he hadn't seen her in person since he was fourteen years old. She looked small behind the wheel of her black Lexus. That surprised him, because he remembered her as a towering figure.

When Cracker found himself still on the bench an hour

later, he had to admit that he didn't fully understand why. Was he there to see the thing to completion, to watch Mom Elly snatched out of his life, and out of his nightmares? He had planned for years to get to this point, had killed coldly and mechanically, though always through others. Sometimes the others were flawed, but he couldn't help that when humans were involved. It would be so much simpler and cleaner to do everything by computer. Although his plans had zigzagged a bit toward the end, the clock was ticking down toward victory. The goal would be accomplished, even though the heavy-handed approach would result in more deaths than were absolutely necessary. Flash was one bloodthirsty son of a bitch, but he was simply a tool, wasn't he? A disposable one, at that, like a cheap plastic paint bucket used once and thrown away.

Or was he still on that bench for another reason, a reason with thighs that opened easily and hands that stroked and comforted after the terrifying loss of control?

He allowed himself to speculate about the destruction, to picture it. A bomb blast? Perhaps. Flash hadn't been too explicit. Even though Cracker could retrieve the conversation word for word from his memory, there wasn't much to go on.

Boom! Flames all around. She's trapped.

Cracker wondered if he would see the windows explode before he actually heard the sound of the explosion, as he saw lightning before hearing thunder during a storm. No, that was silly. He was too close for the difference in the speeds of light and sound to have any effect. Would the blast kill everyone, or would the fire that followed do that? By smoke inhalation or actual burning?

She rushes to the door. It's blocked, somehow, she can't get out. Her hair catches fire. She screams and runs to the hallway door. Son of a gun, it's blocked, too. The room is engulfed in flames. First her clothes catch, then the rest of her.

He really should have gotten more details from Flash.

After all, he was a paying customer. He was entitled to know the workings of the plan. But he had been upset on the phone. Why? Wasn't this what he wanted?

The skin splits right off sometimes. The muscles in the arms and legs contract, so the body ends up with bent arms, clenched fists, and drawn-up legs. Here's a neat part I'll bet you never knew. Really hot fires make the brain swell up and burst through the skull from the inside.

Cracker stood up from the bench as if it had suddenly gotten searingly hot beneath him. He crossed the street and walked the brick path that led to GeriCare's front entrance, scattering the squirrels on the lawn.

When Schultz got word that Will Carpenter was on his way, he was out of his chair like a jack-in-the-box. His mind registered that he was moving easily today, one of the days when his arthritic knees seemed to function as they did years ago. The medicine he took helped a lot, but there were still bad days. He was glad this wasn't one of them.

"OK, ladies, stay here. I'll answer the door."

PJ opened her mouth to retort, then snapped it shut again. He could have said something about catching flies, but it was one of the big regrets in his life that so many good lines were missed owing to actually having to do police work. Dr. Graham's eyes were wide, and she was hugging her purse to her chest as if it were a life preserver. There was something underneath her fear, something that he had sensed all along. Duplicity. A separate agenda of her own. No time to worry about that now. PJ would have to handle her, if there was anything to handle.

Schultz went out of the dining room into the hallway. Carpenter was in the lobby, his back turned to Schultz, looking down the hallway of the opposite wing of the building. He took a couple of tentative steps down the hall, evidently perplexed that the reception desk was unoccupied. Schultz quietly slipped into the stairwell at his end of the hallway. He had decided to go down to the basement, cross the length of the building, and come up the stairs at the far end of the other wing. If he was lucky, he'd be able to observe what Carpenter was doing. Very aware that all the police had against the guy at the moment was the voiceprint analysis, Schultz wanted to catch him doing something with obvious criminal intent. Coming inside an open building and walking down the hall didn't qualify.

He briefly watched Carpenter going down the hall to make sure he didn't turn around and come back in the direction of the dining room. Then Schultz went down the stairs to the basement. Something nagged at him about Carpenter's appearance. The man wasn't carrying any tools of the arsonist's trade: gas cans, electrical devices, nothing. Had he wired himself? There was no way to tell his frame of mind by looking at his back. Was he so bent on killing Dr. Graham that he had turned himself into the murder weapon? Schultz shuddered at the thought of a living bomb making his way down the hall, wanting to get close to Dr. Graham, hoping to catch just the tiniest glimpse of her horror in the fraction of a second before he was blown away.

The basement was dark, but Schultz found a light switch inside the door. Bare bulbs showed a large area with a central corridor and boxed supplies on either side. There was no commercial laundry facility, which he had expected to find. Evidently GeriCare contracted out for laundry service. There were a lot of cleaning supplies, though, and the place smelled of furniture polish and floor cleaner. Some of the boxes were recently delivered, but many had a layer of dust on them. The place smelled like the basement of his old high school, where he had hidden a time or two to avoid particularly loathsome classes.

When he was about two-thirds of the way across the basement, he picked up smells that weren't cleaning supplies. He stopped and sniffed deeply, and the action set off alarms in his head. There were smells that shouldn't be there: hot metal, and inexplicably, a wood fireplace. As he scanned the basement looking for the source, his thoughts were racing. Carpenter, or someone else, had beaten them to the punch. The fire trap was already set, and it was probably moments from being sprung.

Smoke began to pour from a pile of boxes behind him and to his right, against the wall.

On the wall outside the door where he had entered the basement, he had noticed a fire extinguisher. But he was closer to the other end of the basement, so he ran forward, hoping that there would be a similar installation outside the other door. There was, and he yanked the extinguisher from its mounting. He turned and started back, but got only a few feet inside the door. A layer of smoke hugged the ceiling; it would descend as the fire worsened. Bright flames flickered up from the boxes. Then, with a whoosh, the sprinkler system came on.

Schultz knew the full horrible extent of the trap in an instant. The smell of gasoline came to him, and the hair on the backs of his arms stood up. He dropped the extinguisher and spun toward the stairwell. The fire giddily embraced the added fuel, gathered itself, and sent a ball of flame rushing after Schultz.

CHAPTER

32

PJ put her hand on Dr. Graham's arm. The woman had half risen from her seat, and PJ was worried that she would dash out after Schultz.

"Let Schultz do the skulking around," PJ said. She put a little more pressure on Dr. Graham's arm, and she dropped back into her chair. "In the meantime, weren't we talking about why you hired a PI?"

"I already told you that," Dr. Graham said, her irritation evident even through the fear that radiated from her. "He's part of my family. Wouldn't you try to find your own son if he was missing?"

"Shouldn't you have been more concerned about that eight years ago, when he ran away?"

"Don't get on some pedestal with me. You have no right to question what I did then or now." Dr. Graham's eyes darted around the room, repeatedly returning to the doorway.

"I have every right," PJ said, hoping it was true, "because I think there are a lot of unanswered questions about these crimes, and you're the one with the answers. Is Will Carpenter blackmailing you?"

"Of course not. That's ridiculous. You can't solve the case, so you're grasping at anything." Her voice was edging toward shrillness.

PJ was trying to decide where to go next with the questioning when she heard Dr. Graham gasp. She followed the woman's gaze.

Will Carpenter stood in the doorway.

He was staring at Dr. Graham with revulsion, but there was a repellent fascination in his eyes also. His face had the slack appearance of a person who is alone much of the time, and whose expression has fallen into neutral. If it wasn't for the heat in his eyes, he would have all the animation of a statue.

"Hello, Will," Dr. Graham said. Her voice was shaky but seemed to be gaining confidence. PJ could tell that she was trying to establish control of the situation. "It's good to see you. You've been away a long time."

"Yeah, I'll bet you're real hungry," Carpenter said. His voice was emotionless.

Dr. Graham's eyes narrowed. She didn't know what to make of that statement, and neither did PJ.

"Who's this?" he said, tilting his head in PJ's direction. He seemed unable to take his eyes off Dr. Graham.

"This is Dr. Penelope Gray," she answered. "If you're hungry, there are some vending machines in the staff lounge."

He sneered, turning down the corners of his mouth slightly. "I doubt that vending machines sell the things you like to eat. Liver. Intestines. Maybe kidney-on-a-stick."

"What on earth are you talking about? You're starting to frighten me."

"Frighten? You don't know the first thing about being frightened."

"Why are you doing this to me, Will? I may not have

been the best mother in the world, but I don't deserve to be treated like this.''

He was no longer expressionless. Rage and terror battled for dominance of his features, and rage won.

"You murdered my father, you lying bitch! I couldn't do anything about it then, no, but I can now. You're going to pay!'' Carpenter visibly struggled to regain control of his feelings, and he succeeded, at least partially.

"Pay with your life,'' he said, his voice carrying the burden of his pent-up feelings.

PJ hadn't said a word yet, and she wasn't about to leap into the confrontation then. There was too much to be learned, a lot of history between these two. She studied Dr. Graham. The woman seemed genuinely confused and upset. She got up from the table, nervously kneading her purse, and moved toward one of the windows. PJ stood up also, and positioned herself where she could move between them if necessary.

"I don't know what you're talking about,'' Dr. Graham said. "You must be crazy. I loved your father. I didn't kill him.''

"I was there. I saw you. I saw you rip him open and eat his insides.'' A dark shadow of memory passed over Carpenter's face, momentarily returning its slack expression. "I saw . . . the blood on your face.'' His voice had fallen to a whisper.

"Dr. Gray, tell him it isn't so,'' she said. "Harvey died of natural causes. He had an aortic aneurysm. There was no warning. It burst suddenly and he died before the ambulance arrived.'' She paused for a moment, reliving her own hell. "Harvey was the love of my life. I know what that sounds like, but it's true. I swear to God I didn't kill him. You've got to believe me.''

PJ wasn't sure whether her appeal was directed at her or at Carpenter.

"Liar, liar, pants on fire,'' Carpenter said. His voice was

eerily childlike. His face had taken on a robotlike stillness. The effect was chilling. PJ didn't like the way things were heading, so she finally intervened.

"Will, tell me what happened," PJ said. "I'd like to hear your side of the story."

"There are no sides to this story. There's only the truth."

"The truth then. I'm listening."

"It was late at night. I was in my room, listening to the fighting. Dad and Mom Elly fought a lot. It was always her fault."

"We fought, yes," Dr. Graham said. "We were both strong, stubborn people. He could be infuriating. But we tried to keep it private, when little Billy wasn't around."

"I heard you from my room. I heard the crash when you threw something at him."

"The wedding picture," Dr. Graham said. PJ could see her drifting into her own memories of the night her husband died. "I threw our wedding picture at the wall. The glass broke. I cried. Harvey . . . held me."

"You pinned him to the bed and tore his guts out."

"I did no such . . ." Her voice faded away, and her gaze was unfocused. "You came into the room that night."

"I came in because Dad was groaning. He was being eaten alive. I saw you lift your face."

"Oh, God," she said. "Oh, my God. We thought you were asleep. Harvey told you to get out. I remember . . ." She looked at him, understanding falling into place on her face. "You've got it all wrong, Will. You didn't see a murder back then. Harvey and I made love after the fight."

Her revelation bounced off Carpenter as if it was a ray of light reflecting in a mirror. "I know what I saw."

PJ heard a thump from below, something heavy dropping onto the concrete floor of the basement. She wondered where Schultz was. If he was supposed to be sneaking up on Carpenter, he wasn't doing a very good job, unless he was right outside the door, listening. It was likely that the man was going to get violent, and it would have been nice to have some help. She edged herself a little closer to Dr. Graham.

"I know why you wanted to get rid of him, too," Carpenter continued, dragging her attention back to the scene before her. "The fights were about cheating and something on the computer. I heard you. I didn't know what it meant then, but I do now. He found out about the fraud, and you killed him to keep him from telling anyone you were a crook. I have it all right here." He patted the pocket of his T-shirt, underneath the jacket he was wearing. "You've been cheating the government for a long time. This little setup," he gestured at the surrounding room, "has made you millions. Dad knew it was wrong. Dad always knows."

PJ caught the present tense in Carpenter's last words, and she wondered if he was schizophrenic, living in a world where reality ebbed and flowed, and time along with it.

She noticed that Dr. Graham's face had reddened with anger, but when she spoke, her voice was cool. All of the agitation seemed to have drained away.

"What are you saying, exactly?" Dr. Graham said.

"I don't have to explain it to you," he said contemptuously. "You know the whole story. Padded Medicare claims. Patients living on for years after they were in the ground, getting their wheelchairs and their physical therapy and their sitz baths. I'll bet everyone who attended your open house last night gets a bill submitted to their insurance company for a group therapy session."

"That's nonsense."

"Got it all right here," he said, patting his pocket again. "I've got files going back nearly ten years. I knew about it before I left home."

PJ watched Dr. Graham. The woman seemed to be trying to come to some decision.

"Oh, I know you erased those files. But you were too

late. I copied them before you pressed DELETE." He took a disk from his pocket and put it on the table. "The police should be very interested in this. The feds, too."

PJ glanced away from Dr. Graham only for an instant, to look at Carpenter's disk. Then something strange happened to her, strange but horribly familiar. Time seemed to slow down. It had happened once before: glass shattering, floating slowly to the floor, a man spinning, falling, blood flowing down her back, inching its way to her waist like slugs crawling. But that was in the past.

In the dining room at GeriCare, in her state of heightened awareness, she smelled smoke. She took a deep breath that seemed to take forever to fill her lungs. There were several bursts of gunfire outside, not too close, rapid rat-tat-tats. She saw a reddish glow out in the hallway, and heard the crackling of flames and a distant *whump*. Carpenter's mouth was open and his eyes were unreadable. She turned, slowly, slowly, and Dr. Graham had dropped her purse and was holding a gun, and it was pointed at Carpenter. Dr. Graham's face was frozen in a purposeful grimace. PJ saw her finger begin to tighten on the trigger, and somehow she had already launched herself. She slammed into the woman, her elbow pressing deep into Dr. Graham's midsection, knocking the woman's breath out explosively, and the gun fired close to PJ's head. The noise felt like a crack of thunder inside her head, and then she couldn't hear the flames anymore. PJ landed hard on the floor, crashing into a table leg. The gun was right in front of her face, so she reached for it. In her peripheral vision, another shape appeared, also reaching for the gun. The barrel was toward PJ, but she didn't have time to be choosy. She snatched at the hot barrel with her left hand, then quickly shoved the grip into her right hand. Dr. Graham, who had been knocked to her knees but was reaching toward the gun, backed away and stood up. Then she pressed her forearm against her ribs.

Hope they're broken, PJ thought. *Damn! Where is Leo, anyway?*

PJ got to her feet, carefully keeping the gun aimed at Dr. Graham. Carpenter was in a crouch near the doorway, unhurt. He straightened up, watching her closely. PJ moved to the table and picked up the incriminating disk. Dr. Graham took a step in her direction, but PJ, who could hear only a loud ringing in her ears, waved her back with the gun. Carpenter stood in the doorway, dense smoke coiling over his head and entering the room. The redness in the hallway was intense. There was a cracking noise, and suddenly flames shot up through the floor between PJ and Carpenter. With an unnatural calmness in his eyes, and the corners of his mouth turned up in a slight smile, he saluted her. Then he was gone, ducking low and disappearing out into the hallway.

That wasn't an option for PJ, because flames were filling the space between her and the door. She didn't want to head into the interior of the building, anyway.

"Pick up a chair," she shouted at Dr. Graham, unable to hear her own voice. "Throw it through the window."

Dr. Graham yanked the cord of the blinds on the nearest window, raising them out of the way. Then she did as PJ had instructed, even though the effort clearly hurt her injured ribs. The pane burst outward. PJ heard it, in a muffled fashion. She was still deaf in her right ear, but the left, which had been turned away from the gun when it went off, was beginning to recover. Dr. Graham used the leg of a chair to quickly sweep away the remaining shards of glass on the lower edge of the window.

"After you," PJ said, but Dr. Graham had already seated herself on the window, and then swung her legs over and out. She hesitated for a moment. PJ moved up behind her, thinking she might have to push. The heat in the room was growing unbelievably fast, and the smoke had dropped to face level. Then Dr. Graham was gone from the window. It was her turn, and not a moment too soon.

She was on the first floor, but the foundation was tall. It was about a ten- or eleven-foot drop. She could see Dr. Graham lying on the grass below, holding her side. Two people rushed up to her, both of them with guns drawn. PJ recognized the retired lieutenant Schultz had introduced her to, Larry Hennepin. He turned his craggy face up and spotted her.

"C'mon down, little lady," he said, loudly enough for PJ's left ear. "We've got this one covered for you."

As PJ let herself drop from the window, she felt a flash of irritation at being called "little lady," then annoyance at herself for letting it bother her. Given the circumstances, she could cut the guy some slack. *Just let him try it later on, though.*

Her landing wasn't nearly as graceful as she would have liked it to be, especially considering she was still holding a loaded gun. Her legs buckled and she rolled, ending up inelegantly positioned, glad she was wearing slacks and that Schultz wasn't around to see her. She accepted help getting to her feet from the gracious ex-cop, who was a lot stronger than his age and lean frame implied. He also relieved her of the gun, which she was embarrassed to notice she was pointing at his groin.

Clutched tightly in her other hand was Carpenter's disk.

CHAPTER

33

The force of the fireball lifted Schultz and deposited him several feet away, at the base of the stairs. He scrambled about halfway up the stairs, then turned to assess the situation. One glance at the billowing flames told him it was impossible to go back down and close the basement door to confine the fire. He would have to use the fire door at the first floor landing to do that. As he hurried up the rest of the steps, he became aware that the shirt on his back and the seat of his pants were smoking. He stopped, pressed his back hard against the wall, and rubbed back and forth to make sure no flames would erupt. When he moved on, there were shreds of cloth left behind, and his skin felt seared, especially on his buttocks, which apparently had been the last to leave the vicinity of the fireball.

On the first floor, he tried to close the fire door and found that he couldn't move it. The hinges were frozen, another deliberate piece of the trap. There was no shrill fire alarm ringing in the building. He looked down the hallway. The sprinklers on the ceiling should have been spurting water, but only a few drops leaked from each one. There was a light haze everywhere, and a choking odor, but the dense killing smoke was above his head. He knew the layer would be dropping fast. There was very little time to get out of the building. One of the rooms down the hall was engulfed in flames, but he could get by it. He squinted, trying to see through the haze to the other end of the hallway, where PJ and Dr. Graham were. He hadn't forgotten that Carpenter was around somewhere, too.

Just as the thought passed through his head, he saw the man, dimly. He was backing out of the dining room. As Schultz started down the corridor, Carpenter walked rapidly but calmly toward him. If the man didn't duck into one of the residents' rooms, they would be face to face in the lobby. Schultz quickened his pace and drew his gun.

Carpenter did not deviate. They stopped about fifteen feet from each other. Dense black smoke rested on the tops of their heads like a deadly blanket. Schultz coughed and wondered what to do. He couldn't apprehend the guy, cuff him and search him for weapons, in the middle of a fire. He waved the tip of his gun toward the front door. Once safely outside, Carpenter could be captured, if not by himself, then by one of the officers in front of the building.

"Outside," Schultz said forcefully. "Walk slowly, keep your hands in sight, and no tricks."

"Sorry, old man," Carpenter said. "That's not on the schedule. It does not compute." Schultz saw a trace of a smile.

"Are you nuts? Get outside, asshole, or I'll blow a hole in you bigger than Rhode Island."

Carpenter shook his head. "So long, Pop." He turned his back on Schultz and walked toward the rear door.

"Shit." Schultz raised his gun, held it with both hands, and took his stance. He didn't want to do it, shoot him in the back, not someone young enough to be his son. He could do it, had done it years ago when his partner was killed by a drug dealer. Schultz had blasted the guy in the back as he stood over the body. Could he let Carpenter walk away?

He thought about Sheriff Al Youngman, who had seen, or convinced himself that he had seen, something worth saving in a young man who later went on to kill and kill again. If he let Carpenter go, would he be the one getting the news decades later that he had failed to prevent further loss of life?

Carpenter kept walking. He disappeared into the thickening haze.

"Shit." Schultz lowered the gun. *Let the cops outside worry about him.*

He turned and started trotting down the hallway toward the dining room. If the two women weren't out already, if Carpenter had left them unconscious or worse, they were in big trouble.

He heard the flames before he saw them, a rushing sound that reminded him of a waterfall. Halfway down the corridor, he met a wall of fire advancing rapidly toward him, licking out hungrily. It was just like in the vivid computer simulation, only this time he could feel the stifling heat. He turned and ran back to the lobby and out the front door, flames at his heels the whole distance.

Cracker walked to the rear door, trying not to think about the man at his back with a gun. He opened the door and looked around, but saw no one. He had thought the building would be surrounded. He darted across the parking lot and into the alley. Certain he would be observed but having no choice, he ran down the alley to the end of the block. There he turned right and headed to Lemay Ferry. He hoped to get across the street and into the park.

There were dense woods there; if he could make it to them, he had a chance of getting away.

He forced himself to a walking pace. He put his hands in his pockets and tried to look like he didn't know the big brick building halfway down the block was on fire. As he rounded the corner onto Lemay Ferry, he stopped and stared before schooling himself to move on. Mechanical men don't stare.

Clustered at the corner were half a dozen blue-and-whites, their red lights flashing. Officers were gathered near a car parked at the curb, but maintained a good distance from it. Inside, he could see a body, head thrown backwards on the seat. As the driver's side came into his view, he saw that the glass was broken out, and the car was dotted with holes, lots of them in several distinct streaks. Bullet holes.

At least he wouldn't have to worry about paying the other half of Flash's fee. He wondered if there was a way to get the first half back, then dismissed the thought. It would be too risky to try.

An officer noticed him, and firmly waved him across the street, not wanting him to linger in the area. "What happened?" Cracker asked as nonchalantly as he could. "Drive-by. Got a man dead in the car. Keep moving." Traffic was stopped by the police cars. Cracker walked past, nodded at the officer, and kept on his way into the park.

At the airport, he retrieved his luggage and boarded the chartered jet he had standing by. A few minutes later, he was airborne and heading for Los Angeles, the first step of a complex journey to a new identity. His thoughts were disorganized and as thick as clotted cream. He had been awake for thirty-four hours, and he had been shaken to his roots.

Was Mom Elly telling the truth? He searched inside himself, looking for doubts, for cracks in what he believed. There were none. He was certain he was right. He hadn't succeeded in killing her, unless she didn't get out of the building in time. But the evidence he had left behind was enough to send her to prison for a long, long time. The rest of her life, he hoped. Perhaps that was better than death, which got over and done with and left nothing to savor as the years went by.

He closed his eyes and willed himself to sleep. He needed the rest. His sleep was fitful, and he woke from a bad dream, not the harpy one, but one he couldn't remember clearly. It left an ache inside him, and he couldn't get back to sleep.

He used the skyphone to contact his attorney. He was put through to her immediately.

"Have all three of the envelopes been delivered?" he asked.

"Yes. According to your instructions."

"Send another one, by the same route. Put a note inside that says 'Disregard envelope number three.' Sign it with the last code number I gave you, the one that was for emergencies."

"I'll take care of it."

"Do it now. It's . . . important to me. Later on, when a claim is made against the trust agreement, honor it."

"Will I be hearing from you again?"

"No. The balance of the fee is yours."

Cracker leaned his head back against the cushy seat. He called up a memory of the smell of brownies, and he slept soundly.

CHAPTER

34

PJ dipped her finger in the bowl of leftover icing and licked the chocolate sweetness from it. Then she dunked the bowl into the hot soapy water in the sink. She was cleaning up after a marathon session of baking Halloween cupcakes. The finished products now stood in neat rows in shallow cardboard boxes which she still needed to load into her rental car for overnight storage. If they were left on the countertop, Megabite damage was inevitable. As it was, the cat was at her feet contentedly cleaning icing from her whiskers.

PJ hadn't actually done any of the preparation. Thomas and Leo had done that, making a gleeful mess in the kitchen, measuring, stirring, baking, and decorating. Ordinarily she would have balked at being relegated to cleanup, alone in the kitchen. But Leo had taken charge from the moment he walked in, and she had been ordered to relax while the men took over the kitchen. Shrugging, she went along with it because Thomas had been looking forward to it. Now she could hear their voices from the study, where Leo was getting trounced in some computer game.

Tomorrow she would take all the cupcakes to school and face the wrath of Mrs. Cartwright, who had requested no ghost, witch, or black cat decorations. Not only were those in evidence, but when she inspected the cupcakes, PJ had spotted bats with blood dripping from their fangs and grimacing vampires with stakes in their hearts. The kids were going to love them.

It was Wednesday night, just one day after the fire at GeriCare. During the day she had examined the information on the disk that Carpenter had given her, and found it to be a fascinating and thorough history of insurance fraud, at the private, state, and federal level. Dr. Graham had been part of a long-standing fraud network that extended over several states. That evidence was out of her hands now, but one thing remained.

There had been a file on the disk meant specifically for her. It had been titled "Lucky Penny," and she immediately thought of Carpenter's idiosyncrasy about making up pet names.

> Lucky Penny,
> By the time you read this, Mom Elly will be dead, and I'll be out of the country. My appearance and my identity will be altered. Don't try to come after me. You're good, but I'm better, and you know it. I have tried to use you as a tool to lessen the loss of lives in my quest for justice. You have nothing to fear from me. Merlin is our link. He is aware of me, but not as I really am.
> Cracker

She had copied the file and erased it from the original disk. It was an odd, very personal connection, and she was still trying to determine how she felt about it.

If Dr. Graham was telling the truth, Carpenter had witnessed an event he didn't understand, one that frightened him terribly, and he had connected it with his father's death shortly afterward. Carpenter's life had been horribly twisted, and his hatred and desire for revenge were all based upon a deeply rooted childhood misunderstanding. He had killed, and he had lived in a tortured fantasy of his own making. His stepmother was not an innocent woman, but hers was a crime of greed, not of dealing death. If Carpenter could examine his experience objectively, with an adult's clarity of vision, he might realize the true nature of it. But his perceptions were locked deep inside, where his four-year-old self had shoved them, slammed the door, and thrown away the key.

Schultz had spent most of the workday behaving badly, and she had let him. For one thing, he seemed physically uncomfortable, far more so than she did. Her left leg was bruised and her ankles both hurt, but time and a little aspirin would take care of that. When she had asked about his injuries, he had mumbled something about a blistered butt and made it clear it was none of her business.

She knew he felt deeply responsible for not bringing Carpenter in himself. The shooting of the man in the parked car at the corner had drawn away almost all of the officers, and in the confusion, Carpenter had apparently walked away from the scene. With the same cunning he had shown when he disabled PJ's spike program, Carpenter had severed the links with his former identity, making it impossible to track him down. PJ suspected that the dead man, who had yet to be identified, was the arsonist. If so, he had come to the fire to revel in the death and destruction, and for the sexual gratification he couldn't get otherwise. He certainly hadn't anticipated being part of Carpenter's clean sweep.

She wiped the last bowl, dried her hands on a towel, and went to enjoy the company of two people who had very different places in her heart.

Turn the page for an
exciting sneak preview of
CHAMELEON
Shirley Kennett's new novel
coming from Kensington Books in
NOVEMBER, 1998

CHAPTER

1

Columbus Wade was on his hands and knees, rummaging in the kitchen cabinet, the one with all the glass bowls in it. He was sure he had seen a gallon jar on his scouting mission the day before. There it was, and now the problem was to get it upstairs without Nanny noticing. He extracted the jar as quietly as he could, his small fingers grasping the screw-on lid because his hands couldn't span the entire jar, but it clinked against the lemonade pitcher.

"Columbus, what are you doing in there?" came Nanny's voice from the living room. She had shut off the volume on the TV. How she heard that tiny clink over the talk, talk, talk of the TV was beyond his understanding. But it was as predictable as Pop having two eggs for breakfast.

"Nothing, Nanny," he answered, keeping the hated quivers from his voice.

"Is that a good nothing or a bad nothing?"

"Just nothing," he said.

He eased the gallon jar back into the cabinet in case she didn't go for it. A long moment passed in silence. He knew Nanny was considering whether it was worthwhile getting up, which meant putting aside her lap table with its diet root beer and magazines with fancy cupcakes on the front, pushing down the foot support of her recliner, and probably getting the shoes she had kicked off her swollen feet caught in the foot support. Then she would sit there getting red-faced, unable to get her feet down, and would finally call Columbus to pull out her stuck shoes. In the meantime she would have missed the last round of her quiz show.

The TV talk started up again, and Columbus thought it was certainly good to be five years old. Last year Nanny would have come in to check on him. Now she gave him just that little edge of independence—after all, he would be in school next fall—and he took full advantage of it. He was better at things, too. He had waited until her favorite show was on to make his trip, and his timing had paid off.

Upstairs, he eagerly carried the gallon jar to the hall bathroom to fill it with water. The jar wouldn't fit upright in the shallow sink, so he could only run the water into it part way. He dried off the outside so it wouldn't be slippery and carried the jug to his room. He had cleared a spot on his dresser for it. He made several trips to the bathroom, bringing a glass of water each time, until the jug was full to the very top.

Columbus walked over to the window. There was a strong glare from the sun shining on the snow outside, but his eyes adjusted as he looked out at the front yard. It snowed yesterday, halfway up to his knees, and Pop grumbled about shoveling the sidewalk one last time. It was almost the end of March, and apparently it wasn't supposed to snow in Nashville in March, at least not this much. Nanny just shook her head and said "In like a lamb, out like a lion," which Columbus didn't understand at all. But she helped him put his boots, coat, hat, and gloves, and watched him through the window of the front parlor as he built a snow-man. Columbus reveled in that creative act, adding a lump of snow here, chopping off a bulge there. He modeled its face after Nanny's, framed in the steamy warmth. When he came in, she stripped off the wet snow clothes and hustled him into the kitchen for hot chocolate. It wasn't just the bite of the wind that reddened his cheeks. For a time he had held sway over the snow, molding it to his will, knocking it down at his whim.

The sun had done its work on the yard. The grass was showing in places, and he could see the crocuses along the front walkway, purple spikes pushing up through the white. Water gurgled in the downspouts, washing out all the itsy bitsy spiders, if there were any in March. His snow-man had gotten smaller, and it was tilted. Soon it would fall on its carrot nose, which was short and thick like Nanny's.

The sun had power. Columbus wanted power too.

In the corner of his room under the window there was an elaborate habitat for his pet mouse Robert. Robert had tunnels and wheels and a hiding place shaped like a cave. Columbus lifted the lid of the habitat and looked for the white mouse, which had retreated to its plastic cave as soon as the lid was raised. He removed the shelter, revealing the mouse, with nowhere to hide, huddled in its bedding. Closing his hand over the mouse, Columbus felt the small heat of its body, and the shaking of its fear.

He didn't know the jar would overflow when he put Robert in, lowering it by its tail. He screwed the lid on tight, and then went to the bathroom for a washcloth to wipe up the spill.

He looked over the railing, down into the living room, to make sure Nanny was still watching TV. She didn't know what he was doing. Probably she wouldn't like it. Maybe she would make him stop. Columbus suspected that he wasn't supposed to play with his pets like that.

It was a good thing Nanny's favorite program was on.

He pulled a stool over to the dresser and sat down to watch as the mouse swam round and round. In a disappointingly short time, the exhausted animal sank below the water.

"Good-bye, Robert," Columbus whispered. There was no sadness in him.

Columbus liked the sense of control, of power. Partly it satisfied his curiosity, and partly it fed something else, something dark for which he had no name.

At any time before Robert sank, Columbus could have taken the lid off, pulled the mouse out, and put it back in its habitat to lick itself dry. He had done that several times already, using a bowl he found underneath the bathroom sink. That had gotten boring. Always there was the need to take things further, to learn more, to experience more, to see if new sensations would trigger the emotions that should have been there and weren't.

Columbus learned that his mouse couldn't live in water, and before that, that his shiny goldfish couldn't live in air. Most importantly, he learned that he had power over their small lives.

He pulled the wet body from the jar and dried it as well as he could with the washcloth he had taken from the bathroom. He put the dead mouse back in the habitat and covered it with the plastic cave so that it was out of sight. No one tended the mouse except him, so no one would notice. Tomorrow he would "discover" the body, dry and curled inside its shelter. No one—Mom, Pop, or Nanny—would question the death. Mice died all the time. That was, after all, part of the mystery that he wanted to understand, and to control.

Even though he felt no grief, he would produce a few tears. It was expected at moments like that, and he was getting better at mimicking the emotional responses of people around him.

Mom and Pop would console him and offer him a new pet.

He slid his latest video into the slot and settled back to watch. Snack time would be coming up soon. As the cartoon images moved across the screen, he replayed in his mind Robert's last fierce struggle to live.

Where would his curiosity take him next?

At the age of twelve, Columbus Wade still spent a lot of time with his bedroom door closed.

On this particular Thursday night during his school's spring break, he was out on his bike, pedaling casually toward the school, hoping that he wouldn't encounter a police patrol car along the few blocks to his destination. Fortunately, the four inches of snow that had fallen a couple of days ago had succumbed to plows and milder temperatures. The streets were clear and dry, but snow was still piled at the curbs.

Strapped onto the luggage rack of his bike was a small cooler. He had lined the inside of it with thick foam padding salvaged from the school's dumpster. The night was chilly and there was a strong March wind, but he had worn a jacket. He hated physical discomfort and always planned ahead to avoid it.

When he rode into the front parking lot of Deaver Junior High, there wasn't a car in sight. The lot was deserted, just as Columbus had anticipated. Just as he was getting off his bike, a car roared down the street, highschoolers whooping through the open windows. It was an unwelcome intrusion, although he was fairly sure they hadn't seen him in the shadows near the front of the building. He pushed his bike behind the bushes near the front entrance. In the rear, soccer goal nets were orange-lit by the building's security lighting, and beyond them he could make out the softball backstops. He walked around to the delivery door, where he had ensured that the security light was not working. He knew that the door didn't fit well in its frame, and that the lock was old and ineffective. If he jostled it just right, he could spring the lock and gain entrance to the building.

Once inside, he waited near the door for a couple of minutes, resting the cooler and his backpack on the floor and taking slow, deep breaths through his nose. He pressed the crown of his Indiglo watch and noted that it was 10:15 P.M. Mom and Pop, or the Cow and the Turd as he now called them, wouldn't be home from their weekly bridge game for another two hours.

Project Brimstone was underway, and the outlook was promising.

He made his way through the darkened halls toward the science lab. EXIT signs glowed with a brilliance not apparent during the day, and there were dim lights at each corner and every twenty feet or so of the hallway.

The hammer and chisel from his backpack took care of the puny padlock on the chemicals locker in the lab. He wasn't worried about leaving his fingerprints; as one of the lab monitors, his prints were all over the locker anyway. The ceiling panel light right over the locker was turned on, so he had enough light to work. He reached for the heavy glass jar of acid, with its label that said H_2SO_4 and had a black skull-and-crossbones. It was toward the back of the locker, since it was used only for demonstrations by the science teacher, and not by the students. The sulfuric acid would provide an added dimension to his experimentation with cockroaches. He had a science paper due in a week, and he had chosen as his subject the ability of the hardy insects to survive environmental stresses. Columbus didn't believe in passive learning. He conducted his own research wherever possible, even if most of it had to be kept to himself.

He had brought duct tape in his backpack to wrap tightly

around the ground glass stopper so it wouldn't work loose in the padded cooler on the way home. He set the jar on a counter next to the hammer and chisel, and dug into his backpack for the tape.

"What are you doing, Columbus?"

The voice lashed at him from the darkened doorway of the lab. He straightened abruptly, backpack forgotten. As he twisted to see who had caught him, his elbow sent the jar of acid flying. It landed with a crash that echoed in the hallways.

A man stepped forward, into the light where Columbus could recognize him. It was Mr. Mitchell, one of the teachers at the school. Thoughts raced through Columbus's mind, colliding with each other and leaving him dumbfounded.

"I'm surprised, Columbus. You know chemicals don't leave this room. You should have talked this over with Mrs. Garfield, and maybe you could have done whatever it is you're trying to do under her supervision."

Mitchell was calm but very stern. In fact, Columbus had never heard him use such a tone of voice. It snapped Columbus back into cunning mode, and he began to get angry.

"I'm sorry, Mr. Mitchell," Columbus said. It was hard to keep his voice sounding humble, because he was seething as he thought of the trouble the man would make for him. Project Brimstone was rapidly heading into the toilet, and he'd have to do his science paper on acorns or something.

"Now we've got quite a mess to clean up," Mitchell said as he approached the lab counter. "Help me get out the kitty litter."

Mitchell bent and reached for the cabinet door near Columbus's legs. Inside was a tub of kitty litter, the first line of defense against spills in the lab, something to keep

the problem from spreading until it could be dealt with
properly.

Somehow the hammer jumped from the counter into
Columbus's right hand, and he swung it at the back of
Mitchell's head as the man was bent over. Mitchell didn't
go down immediately, as Columbus had hoped. Instead,
he grunted and fell heavily to his knees, reaching out for
Columbus's legs. Columbus almost panicked and dropped
the hammer. But he held on, and gave the man a satisfying
whump above the ear. Then it was just a matter of swinging
again and again, until his shoulders hurt.

CHAPTER
2

Penelope Jennifer Gray mentally crossed her fingers and struck the last match. It flared, and she closed the few inches between it and the corner of newspaper she was trying to light. The wind immediately snuffed the tentative flame out. PJ closed her eyes tightly against both the wind and her misfortune, squeezing tears of exasperation from the corners.

It was the last night of PJ's vacation with her son Thomas. They were staying at a rustic cabin in Big Springs State Park in southern Missouri. Part of the National Scenic Riverways, Big Springs certainly lived up to its name: the park contained a stream that gushed millions of gallons of water a day from a modest-looking cleft at the base of a hill.

PJ and Thomas had gone to the site of the park's namesake soon after their arrival. It was only March, so the flow hadn't reached its late spring peak yet, but it was still impressive. Where the water rushed from the hillside, its motion was enough to keep ice from forming. Water vapor rose into the chilly air and condensed on their hair and eyelashes. Ferns on the shaded hillside above the spring were lush and green, even that early in the year. The air was heavy with moisture, so heavy that droplets condensed on anything or anyone that held still more than a moment. Moss covered rocks were washed constantly with the turbulent water of the spring, trapping bubbles of air in the green mats as they were lashed back and forth. Further downstream, a thin layer of ice remained on the surface while the water moved rapidly underneath.

PJ had been energized by the place and could have stayed all day listening to the water tumbling over the rocks. Thomas had reacted very differently. He couldn't seem to stay in the vicinity of the spring, and could offer no explanation beyond not liking the sound, which he described as a roaring that drowned out his thoughts. He stayed as far away from the spring as he could get, preferring to hike the park's wooded hills instead. So they rose early, dressed warmly, and walked on the trails while the ground was still frozen.

The forest was just beginning to waken from winter. Leaf buds were swollen and small green plants nudged aside last fall's leaf drop as they pushed their way up to the sunshine. Squirrels dug and chattered, chickadees called to each other, and woodpeckers rapped out their staccato searches for lunch under the bark of trees. The sky was a deep, brilliant blue and the sun warmed their shoulders through the leafless tree branches.

In the afternoon, when the forty degree warmth thawed the frozen ground and the trails became slippery and unpleasant, they either went back to their cabin to read and relax, or explored the nearby town of Van Buren, where they browsed in small stores with dusty postcard racks and salt and pepper shakers shaped like corn on the cob or a gold prospector and his mule. In the evenings, they ate whole fried catfish in a restaurant overlooking the stream.

At the beginning of the week, PJ felt tension drain from her as though she had gathered it from all parts of her body and set it adrift on a log in the stream. Her job as head of the Computerized Homicide Investigations Project with the St. Louis Police Department had been a challenge from the start. Under the skeptical gaze of Detective Leo Schultz, the experienced detective assigned to CHIP, she had demonstrated that she had the right stuff for the job, surprising not only Schultz but herself as well.

The past week, when Thomas was out of school on spring break, had been their first opportunity to get away since the move to St. Louis from Denver. Thomas had lobbied for a trip to Disney World or the Grand Canyon, but PJ had taken a cut in pay from her previous work in consumer behavioral modeling. Money was tight, as in most single-parent households, and Thomas knew his suggestion was doomed from the start. PJ had gathered information on driving vacations within Missouri, and settled on Big Springs because a picture in the brochure of a cabin with smoke coming out of the chimney reminded her of Rocky Mountain scenery outside of Denver. The cabin had turned out to be delightful, with rough-hewn pine furniture, a huge stone fireplace, open beams in a high ceiling, and a toilet that actually worked, as long as you held the handle down a long time.

Although the weather in the first part of the week had been glorious, it had rained the past couple of days. PJ and Thomas had spent a lot of time in the cabin, and they felt like two cats rubbing up against each other and getting a static electricity shock. Words were said that shouldn't have been, and PJ wanted to end the vacation on a positive note. She decided a cookout was the perfect thing. She dragged Thomas, sullen and sodden, to a grocery store in town, and bought hot dogs and marshmallows. By evening the rain had stopped. There was dry firewood in the cabin's enclosed porch, but PJ had neglected to bring in any kindling earlier in the week.

Undaunted, at dusk PJ scraped the wet ashes from the outdoor cooking grill that stood next to the cabin. Having no kindling, she crumpled newspapers and set a full-size fireplace log on top. Her hopes were beaten down as match after match expired in the brisk wind. Even if she had gotten the newspapers to burn, the likelihood of the log catching fire was slim. She wiped her face and stuck her hands into the pockets of her jacket. It looked as though the two of them would be spending their last evening sniping at each other over cold lunchmeat sandwiches and untoasted marshmallows.

A pickup truck came down the narrow, winding road which served the cabins, and stopped in front of hers. She was familiar with the truck; it belonged to Ellen and Roger Brenner, who managed the cabins. The window on the passenger side rolled down, and in the gathering dark, PJ could barely make out Ellen's rotund face.

"Having trouble with your cooking fire?" Ellen said, with that lilt of hers that took the sting out, so that it didn't sound like the bald statement of PJ's incompetence that it was.

There was no point in trying to cover up her predicament. "I don't have any dry kindling, and I've run out of matches."

"We figured you might have some problems. Muriel down at the store said you bought hot dogs. We thought we'd just check and make sure you got a good hot fire going. Hot dogs don't do a body good when they're cold." Her face disappeared from the window opening as she turned away to speak to her husband.

"Roger'll be right down to get you started."

PJ was aware that Thomas had come out onto the porch of the cabin and was watching the proceedings. Roger got out of the pickup, opened a box in the truck bed, and rummaged around a minute or two. Then he walked over to PJ, carrying a bundle of dry kindling. He nodded to her. She hadn't heard Roger speak in the week they'd been at the cabin. Apparently Ellen wore the voice in the family.

Roger pulled the log out of the grill and re-crinkled the newspaper to his satisfaction. He built a neat pyramid of kindling atop the newspaper, and then pulled a butane fireplace lighter from his pocket. A flick of his thumb produced a flame two inches long that laughed at the wind and eagerly accepted the offering of paper to burn. The dry kindling flared up quickly. Roger went to the porch and poked through the firewood there, rejecting pieces for no reason apparent to PJ. He returned with three small split logs, which he balanced on top of the kindling. He and PJ watched silently as the logs caught fire. Roger put the fireplace lighter on the picnic table and went back to the truck. He was back a minute later with two long metal cooking forks. PJ felt her cheeks redden, and was glad it was almost dark. If she had gotten the fire going, she and Thomas would have had to scrounge in the dark woods around the cabin for pointed sticks to impale the food.

"Just leave the supplies in the cabin when you're done," Ellen said from the passenger's seat. The truck rumbled down the road, presumably to check on the occupants of the only other cabin that was rented that week, which was about a quarter mile down the road. She wondered if they had bought hot dogs too.

Thomas came out and stood next to her. She expected him to gloat about the fire and the cooking forks, but he didn't say a word. He was close enough to touch, so she put her arm around his waist and drew him in. The long bones in his legs and arms were beginning their pubescent growth, leaving the muscular development behind, so that he appeared to be limbs attached to a ribcage. Two months from his thirteenth birthday, he was as tall as she was, and he rested his head lightly on her shoulder. She remembered the way things were when she was thirteen. She and her mother had been at odds over everything from chores to clothes to which movies she could see, and her father just sat there, silently and infuriatingly supporting Mom. Since she was a single parent, she knew she was going to bear the brunt of Thomas's teenage angst.

A phone ringing in the cabin made PJ pull away. She had brought along her cellular phone, but it had been silent all week. As she went to answer it, she found herself hoping that Bill Lakeland would be on the other end. Bill was the father of Thomas's best friend Winston. She and Bill had recently begun having a weekly chat, mostly about the kids. Bill's voice was warm and self-confident, and she felt that he was a man she could trust with her emotions—a safe haven.

She pushed the hair out of her face as she reached for the phone, pushing the long strands behind her ears, and noticed that she had brought the wood fire smell in with her, in her hair and clothing.

"PJ here."

"Hi, Doc. Got some news for you."

"Oh, it's you." It was Schultz, and news he called about was rarely good. Belatedly she realized that he had heard the disappointment in her voice, and would put his own spin on it.

"You really know how to make a guy feel appreciated," Schultz said. "Especially a guy who's been taking care of your cat while you're out playing pioneer woman. Did you know that critter gets right up on the table?"

"Come on, Leo, I thought you liked cats."

"Let's just say that of all the animals commonly kept as pets, I dislike cats the least. So tell, you waiting for Loverboy to call?"

"I wish you'd stop referring to any male friend of mine, yourself excluded, as Lover-boy," PJ snapped.

"Christ. Don't get your ass in an uproar. Don't you even want to know why I called?"

She realized that she had been using her voice like a rolled up wet washcloth, flicking it at him, wanting to hear the "ouch" on the other end. Taking a couple of deep breaths, PJ was silent, waiting him out.

"The news is that somebody killed a teacher at your son's school," Schultz said. "Name of Edward T. Mitchell."

"Ed Mitchell's dead?" PJ had met him at a PTO potluck dinner, and liked Mitchell. He seemed to genuinely care about his charges, and often could be found at after-school activities or volunteering in the one-on-one mentoring program the school had started this year.

"Give the woman a medal. She can talk and hold the phone at the same time."

"Could you be serious for just a moment? How was he killed?"

"Struck with a blunt instrument. ME hasn't said yet, but my guess is man's favorite tool."

"Say again?"

"Christ. Women. A *hammer*. Man's favorite tool. He was hit a lot more times than actually necessary to do the job. The janitor found him this morning in the science lab. It looks as though he interrupted someone trying to steal chemicals."

"How terrible." She closed her eyes for a moment, picturing the scene that the janitor had walked in upon. "Why was Mitchell in the building during spring break?"

"Principal says he was working on some new pilot reading program. He had put in a lot of his own time on it."

"That sounds like the Ed Mitchell I knew. I don't think Thomas was in any of his classes this semester, but all the kids knew Ed. Does CHIP have the case?'' If so, PJ would have to drive back to St. Louis tonight.

"Nope. Barnesworth drew the short straw. He was first at the scene. The chief and Wall think he can handle it. Can you imagine that? Picture Barnesworth interviewing those lady teachers. They'll clam up the first time he says fuck or tries to spit and misses, and ends up with a gob on his shirt."

"Please. I haven't eaten dinner yet," PJ said.

"Anyway, the school's calling in some counselors to help the kids deal with it when they go back to school Monday. I'm sure Thomas will be hearing a lot more about it. Probably know more about the case than Barnesworth by Monday afternoon."

PJ sighed. "Well, keep me informed."

"Sure thing, Doc. So how are you and the kid doing? You had a weenie roast yet? Kids like that outdoorsy shit. Me, I'd rather get a burger at Millie's and rent a couple of shoot 'em ups."

"We're doing fine. We're just about to have a cookout." PJ hoped that he couldn't hear the strain in her voice.

"Burn a marshmallow for me, Doc. See you Monday."

CHAPTER

3

The killing had been clumsy and bloody, like a lion cub taking its first prey.

Columbus hid his clothes and sneakers, and the hammer, in his room until the next day, when his parents were at work. Then he took a long bike ride to a vacant lot where homeless people sometimes built cooking fires. He built a small fire and burned his clothes, mixing the ashes in with those of other recent fires. The sneakers, with bloody soles and a couple of holes burned by splashed acid, went into a trash bin in the back of a grocery store, buried under rotting produce. He didn't think they would burn completely. When it came to getting rid of the hammer, Columbus found that he couldn't part with it. He knew he shouldn't keep it. He'd seen enough cop shows on TV. He took it back home and put it in an old toy chest in his closet, among the stuffed animals and outgrown action figures.

Since it was spring break at the school, he wasn't sure when the body would be discovered. It turned out he had to wait until Sunday evening, when every news station in the city carried the story. Each station implied that their reporters had been first on the scene, and probably had actually been there when the murder was committed, but weren't at liberty to admit it.

It was thrilling to see the news on the set in his room, and then listen to the Cow and the Turd rant about how terrible it was and they hoped the killer would be caught right away. That was when it really sank in. Columbus had taken a life, not a small insignificant life, but a human life, and gotten away with it. There weren't any cops knocking on his door, and there wouldn't be. Who would suspect a twelve-year-old honor student? There was speculation on the TV that the teacher was involved in drug dealing and had stiffed someone important. It didn't matter that anyone who knew Mr. Mitchell wouldn't believe that for a second. The reporters latched onto it, and the story grew from one telling to the next.

Columbus had attained a new level of power. He could play with peoples' lives and no one would stop him. Could stop him.

His parents didn't even catch on that it was Columbus's school that was involved. Columbus wasn't sure they even knew the name of his school.

Since the move to St. Louis two years ago, Norm and Vicky Wade rarely saw their son. The move was tied to a major career step for Norm. They chose a pretentious three-story home in south St. Louis, fully rehabbed with all the amenities. Nanny had been left behind in Nashville, and Columbus was deemed responsible enough to stay by himself after school. When there weren't any bad repercussions from that, he was allowed to stay home during summer vacation. It wasn't the money; the Wades didn't scrimp where their son was concerned. It was simply the path of least involvement.

Columbus lived physically on the third floor of his parents' home on Magnolia Boulevard, which had originally been the maid's quarters, but he spent his time in virtual reality worlds he designed. Specialized programs on his computer, which was a far more powerful model than the first one he had gotten seven years ago, allowed him to set up three-dimensional environments which he could "walk" through by clicking on different parts of the screen.

His first effort at virtual reality was modeled after a Wax Museum he had gone through, eyes wide at the sensational and gory exhibits. His effort wasn't very good, but it did recreate the feel of the place, and he spent many hours visiting its displays even though they were only three inches high on the screen. When he was in a simulation, he didn't have to deal with his parents. He didn't have to deal with emotions, which was good because it required such effort on his part to analyze the situation and pick an appropriate response from his repertoire.

Eventually he set aside the Wax Museum simulation. It seemed rather childish, and Columbus didn't like thinking of himself as a child.

Last September, at the start of the first semester of seventh grade, Columbus had gotten involved in role-playing games. There was a group that met at the house of a kid down the block after school. The group, five boys and one girl, would play Magic or Dungeons and Dragons, taking the parts of fantasy characters and playing out adventures. At first Columbus was intrigued with the colorful playing cards and the pewter game pieces styled as wizards, fanciful beasts, or warriors. After some intensive sessions over Christmas vacation, when the participants barely surfaced long enough to scarf down the snowman cookies provided by the host's mother, Columbus wearied of the games. Too tame. Too much fantasy and not enough reality.

He broke from the group and began playing graphic computer games instead. Cop shootouts, marital arts battles, alien invasions, everything he could get his hands on that had blood and guts. The Cow and the Turd were oblivious to all, simply giving him money for the games, which apparently they envisioned as Pong and Pac Man.

It wasn't long before the violent games lost their appeal, too. One afternoon, while casually ripping the head off a creature he had backed into a blind alley on his computer screen, Columbus imagined that the creature was Mrs. Barry, the principal of his school. She had hassled him that day for being out in the hall after the late bell.

Much better.

Blood gushed from Mrs. Barry's torso as he held her severed head aloft, and satisfaction coursed hotly through Columbus as he gave the ruined body a disdainful kick. He was definitely onto something. Ignoring his science homework, which was usually his favorite, he resurrected the Wax Museum and modified it. A few hours later, he had a passable simulation of Deaver Junior High, complete with classrooms, cafeteria, gym, and playing fields.

By midnight, after he had pretended to go to sleep, he had figured out how he could populate the school with real people. He had gotten a scanner as a Christmas present, a high-profit item suggested by the clerk at the computer store when the Cow went shopping. It was still in the box, buried in his closet under an avalanche of clothes, odds and ends of computer equipment, and used paper plates and plastic forks from the times when he avoided eating dinner with his parents.

The photos came from the school yearbook he checked out of the library the next day. It was last year's, since the new books didn't come out until April. No matter. A few teachers had left, but the majority were there, grinning insipidly at him in black and white. When he got the photos scanned in and pasted over the heads of his standard simulation characters, the results weren't great. The heads looked glued on and weren't responsive to subtle movements. In fact, they sometimes became detached and floated around the classroom like benevolent balloons, smiling down on the students. But the whole effect was good enough, as long as he used his ample imagination.

It had taken him two whole weeks to develop a custom subroutine to handle the blood spatters.

Besides the school, he created other real-life scenarios. The grocery store. The movie theatre. The mall. It became a game to collect photos of people he could put into the mini-worlds. Newspapers were handy, especially neighborhood journals which relied on large, grainy photos to fill the space in their columns.

Once he had a photo, he owned the person.

The VR worlds Columbus created were immensely satisfying to him because he could do whatever he wanted to do with no consequences. He could even kill the simulated people who inhabited his worlds. If a teacher gave him a bad time, or a fellow student criticized him, Columbus would play out the scene again that very night. It would have a different ending, though. He had tied Mr. Gregor, the P.E. teacher, to a soccer goal and bombarded him with soccer balls, then with hockey pucks, then with circular saw blades flipped like Frisbees. Harry Trent, an obnoxious eighth-grader who always called him Brain, got suspended upside-down above a toilet and dunked repeatedly, ruining his great hair, until Columbus got tired of playing with him and just kept his head underwater a little too long. Then there was Patty Remen, rhymes with semen, who had teased him in front of a group of girls when he came out of the john one time with his zipper down. She got the dissection table in the biology lab.

But this Sunday night, Columbus was happier than he had ever been. With the killing of Mr. Mitchell, he had discovered that he had as much power in the real world as he did in his virtual ones.

After hearing the news broadcast, he spent a lot of time in his VR school. He reenacted the experience over and over, breaking in through the delivery door, navigating the hallways, lifting out the heavy bottle, swinging the hammer. He chuckled when he thought that, sooner or later, every kid has a fantasy of wiping out a teacher. But the other kids were satisfied with those wimpy computer programs where someone else, the creator of the program, called the shots. Columbus would never go back to that. The power was his, and it felt good to wield it.

He hadn't actually hated Mitchell. The man just got in the way. On the other hand, there was that science teacher he had last semester, the one who played favorites in class, and he wasn't one of the favorites. He remembered exactly who they were, too.

Columbus needed photos of Winston Lakeland and Thomas Gray.